Keliah's Sweet Angel

Written by
Jeni

Bare Tree Publishing LLC SC

Fall in love with this sweet story!
Jeni

COPYRIGHT

This is a work of fiction. Names, characters, places and incidents are either the product of the author's imagination or are used fictitiously, and any resemblance to actual persons, living or dead, business establishments, events or locales is entirely coincidental.

Kellan's Sweet Angel
Copyright © 2015 by Jeni
Former pen name Jenny Ann
All rights reserved.

Published by Bare Tree Publishing LLC SC

ISBN: 978-0-9970951-5-9

The uploading, scanning, and distribution of this book in any form or by any means- including but not limited to electronic, mechanical, photocopying, recording, or otherwise- without permission of the copyright holder is illegal and punishable by law. Please purchase only authorized editions of this work, and do not participate in or encourage electronic piracy of copyrighted materials. Your support of the author's rights is appreciated.

Cover Design by Deeds Publishing

Second Edition, 2019

Acknowledgements

My cheerleaders: Cheri, Debbie, Leilani,
Thank you for your encouraged words!

Editors: Ann, Amy, Christina, Julie

Jill, thank you for your dedication and the vast amount of time you spent helping me through the grammatical aspects of the book.

Heath, more than words can say…

TYG..

The Angel Series

BOOK ONE

Prologue:

Linda placed the pot roast on the top shelf in the refrigerator. It was for her brother, Kellan. Their mom had cooked it this morning but didn't have time to deliver it so Linda said she would bring it over. The house was quiet; so unlike when she was growing up. At the time there had always been laughter, singing, and playing going on. Happy sounds with a few disagreements scattered in. She smiled at the thoughts of the good memories. She suspected even now when Kellan came home there was some kind of background noise either from the radio or the television. Her house now, with her husband, children and pets was noisy, and she loved it!

She passed by the old fashioned telephone hanging on the kitchen wall. It was white and had a long curly cord. When she was a teenager there were days the telephone receiver was glued to her ear, well one time it literally was. No thanks to Kellan. He had applied adhesive glue on the receiver, and it stuck to her ear. Their grandpa had to cut some of the hair by her ear in order to remove it. It was awful. She could laugh about it now, but not then. The telephone rang loudly into Linda's ear. She yelped at the unexpected but old familiar sound. She placed a hand over her pounding heart answering it by the fourth ring.

"Hello," Linda answered, hearing static through the phone receiver. Rolling her eyes upward, she wished Kellan would call the telephone company to have them come out and fix the line. These days he used his cell phone, but on occasions like this one it would have been nice to hear the person speaking on the other end. She heard the voice ask for Mr. Taylor.

"Mr. Taylor isn't here. Can I take a message for him?" Linda asked.

A shrilling sound pierced through the line when the person spoke. Linda thought the voice was female but wasn't completely sure. "I'm sorry for the bad connection, but where did you say you're calling from?" Linda apologized. "Oh, yes the hiring agency, wonderful!"

A month ago, Kellan had told his family he had contacted a hiring agency to find someone to help with the restoring of their grandmother's old farmhouse. He wanted to enter the house in the town's Historical Homes Tour. A lot of changes needed to be done to the interior, but he was confident it was a tangible deadline. Instead of confident, she thought his deadline was crazy but since she didn't have to help with any of the work it made no difference to her.

"You found someone to help with the house? Fabulous," Linda spoke into the crackling telephone. "Great. Be here by the end of the week….what's that? Yes, let me get pen and paper….Okay go ahead. Spell the name again…great, thanks! What? Yes, we have a one bedroom studio apartment."

"Thank you," Linda heard the voice crackle through the phone.

"You're welcome. See you then." Linda wished the caller good-bye.

After the phone call Linda sent her brother a text.

The hiring agency called. Kyle will be here by the end of the week. Needs a place to stay, I said the studio apartment is available. See you when I get back from vacation. ☺ **Ha-ha, I'm on vacation and you're not!**

Chapter One

    Kellan walked out of the barn and saw his dog frantically barking at a stranger walking up the driveway. The sun was bright on his eyes, and he put his sunglasses on to get a better look at the person. It was a woman. Her blonde hair shining in the sun made her look like an angel. As she approached, he saw thin strapped sandals on her feet. This definitely was not a shoe most women wore around here! They preferred something sturdier such as sneakers or boots. Pursing his lips together he thought, *she's got city girl written all over her! What is she doing way out here in the country?* She was carrying something in her arms. *Is it a child?*

    He admired the way she walked with a determined purpose and held her head high, but he quickly caught the fear in her eyes when his big black dog ran to her. The dog sniffed at the item in her arms then growled. The woman stopped and let out a frightened scream, cuddling the item closer to her body. He understood why she was afraid of the dog's tall height and deep bark, but he still couldn't help the smile tugging on the corner of his mouth. He also didn't think she was carrying a child because his dog loved kids and would have barked excitedly instead of growling.

    Kellan whistled through his teeth commanding his dog with one word. "Come." The dog whined but obeyed by going to his master.

    Kellan took long strides to reach the woman. He stopped in front of her, but not too close. He didn't want to frighten her anymore than she already was. She remained in the same spot and hadn't moved even after he called his dog away from her. His shadowy figure shielded her from the sun. He noticed she was tall, too. Her head came up to his shoulders. It would fit nicely in the curve of his neck when he pulled her against his chest. *Whoa. Where on earth did that thought come from?*

    His eyes grazed over her young face. He guessed her age to be somewhere in her twenties. Her face looked smooth, and he wanted to touch her cheek. Would her skin feel soft or silky beneath his callused fingers? Would she flinch if he touched her? Lost in this thought, he said nothing. Her vibrant blue eyes caught his as if trying to read his mind. Silently, he continued to stare at her, unable to pull his gaze away. He knew he was making her nervous by the way she shifted from one foot to the other giving him a cautious glance. He didn't blame her, but he was lost in her beautiful sky blue eyes.

    "Can I help you?" Kellan asked in a deep voice.

    At first she said nothing as she looked at him. Her lips quivered. He sensed she might be summoning up the courage to speak. His heart went out to her. He could only imagine how intimidating he and his dog were to her. He watched her eyes change from hesitation to determination. When she spoke it was in a rushed anguished voice.

"Mister, I'm sorry to bother you, but I need help. I hit this cat with my car. It's hurt, and I don't know how to help it." She held her arms out to him.

"A cat," Kellan said in surprise, gaping at her, his mouth turned into a frown. This definitely explained his dog's growl, and he should've known by the reaction it was a cat. Why just earlier this morning his dog had chased one out of the yard. Could it be the same cat?

"Yes a cat." The woman nodded her head. "Do you want to see it?" She unfolded the clothing she had it wrapped in.

He peered over her head. Sure enough there was a cat lying lifeless in her arms.

"I think it's still alive," the woman said her voice cracking.

"I can see it breathing," Kellan stated, hearing her breathe a sigh of relief. He felt good, knowing she felt better that the cat was alive. Carefully, he lifted the bundled cat out of her arms.

"Come," Kellan commanded in a low baritone voice, smiling when both the woman and his dog followed. He stepped into the barn to get out of the hot sun beating down on them. He walked over to a work bench setting the cat on it. It wasn't until he began removing the clothing from the animal that he became aware of the silky material on his rough fingers. He held up the article of clothing discovering it was a cream colored nightgown.

Kellan threw her a baffled look. He couldn't help the naughty grin spreading wide across his face, especially when he saw her face turn bright red.

"I didn't have anything else to wrap it in," she said defensively, anger flashing in her angelic eyes, and she didn't appreciate his devilish grin.

Kellan chuckled, "It's too bad the nightgown had to be wasted on a cat."

She opened her mouth to speak, but quickly closed it as the meaning of his words sank in. Again her face flamed hot.

Kellan couldn't help the laughter escaping him. He turned his attention away from her and focused on the cat feeling her cautious eyes on his back. Gently, he poked it with his forefinger but it didn't move. It looked as though it was sleeping. He didn't know a whole lot about cats, other than the females liked to birth their kittens in his hay loft. He also didn't think it would let itself be poked if there wasn't something seriously wrong with it.

Kellan stroked the cat's back then turned it over touching its belly. He pulled his cell phone out from his back jeans pocket and started dialing numbers.

"Hey, man. I've got a cat who was hit by a car. Can you come get it? It's breathing but not awake…no it's not bleeding. Okay, thanks. See you in a few." Kellan ended the phone call. He shoved the cell phone back into the pocket of his jeans turning his head around to face the woman.

"My buddy, Rick, is a veterinarian. He's on his way." Kellan informed her, quietly studying her.

"It was an accident. The cat came out of nowhere, and I didn't have anywhere to go but to drive over it." The woman cringed as she explained in an unsteady voice how she drove over the cat.

"Did it make a big thud sound underneath your car?" Without thinking about her reaction, he asked her in a teasing voice, as though he was talking to one of his friends. He looked back at her with an amused smile, but she had her eyes closed missing it.

"Yes." Her body shuddered at the memory. When she opened her eyes Kellan noticed she was on the verge of tears. Immediately, he was sorry for teasing her.

"Hey, don't worry about it," Kellan said in a softer voice. "No one's going to put you in jail for this," he assured her.

"Are you sure?" the woman asked her face full of uncertainty. Kellan could see that she didn't trust what he was telling her, was the truth.

"For sure," Kellan confirmed giving her a steady eye.

"Do you think it will live?" the woman asked in a sad voice.

Kellan's heart went out to her. She was so worried about this dumb old stray cat it was probably going to cause her nightmares with the awful sound it had made when she ran over it. He hated to think about her having sleepless nights because of it.

"I'm sure it will live." He gave her a roguish grin saying, "This cat looks young. It could be on its third life so six more to go."

He watched her slowly absorb his words. Just as he had hoped, her blue eyes lightened, the worry slid off her face, and a melodious laugh sprang from her lips. He had never heard such an angelic sound before and found himself laughing along with her.

"Nine lives, I get it," she gasped between laughs. "That's funny. Thank you, I needed that."

Kellan answered her with a broad smile. He extended his right hand to her. "By the way, my name's Kellan."

"Kellan, hi, I'm Kylee." She clasped her hand in his, and his hand engulfed hers, but she hardly noticed. What she did notice was the tingling sensation slicing through her when his rough hand slid over hers. Her eyes got caught in the cheerful gaze, he had on her. In this brief moment, she felt an immediate friendly connection with him. It surprised her because usually it took a long time for her to develop this strong of a connection with anyone. What was it about him that made her feel comfortable with his handshake?

"Nice to meet you, Kylee," Kellan greeted her with a deep voice. He kept his eyes steady on her, feeling a rush of heat pulsing through his veins just by their handshake. He didn't want to let go of her hand, but slowly he did. Again, he found himself staring at her. There was something about her eyes that drew him in. When he finally did manage to pull his gaze away from her, he turned his attention back on the cat and began petting its belly.

However, his thoughts were on the woman standing beside him. He liked what he saw. She had a nice slender figure. The pink T-shirt she wore curved nicely over her breasts. He envisioned all that honey blonde hair spilling over him, when her soft pink lips wrapped him up in a luscious kiss. He squirmed in his stance imagining how sweet she would taste. He cleared his throat blaming the heat of the day for getting the best of him with all of the sexy thoughts about her.

Kylee quietly watched him. She had to admit when she first saw him walk out of the barn she had been intimidated by his height, his confident stroll, and his penetrating gaze. When he spoke, his rich baritone voice was full of command, leaving her weak in the knees. Unable to move from the spot she stood in, she was proud of herself for finding the courage to speak to him. She suspected he was a man most people highly respected and not many messed with him. This silent superiority both frightened and intrigued her.

When he had gently taken the cat from her arms, he was genuinely concerned for the poor helpless animal. Speaking with authority he had commanded the word, "come", and for reasons she couldn't explain the deep rich tones of his voice allured her to follow him the same way the dog followed its master. She continued watching Kellan stroke the cat's belly. She was envious of the cat, wishing it was her belly he was rubbing. Despite the callused handshake she had with him, she imagined his touch being luxuriously tender.

Secretly, her gaze roamed freely over his tanned face. He wore a sleeveless shirt exposing his muscular arms and broad shoulders. He didn't have the proverbial farmer's tan. In fact, he had no tan lines at all from what she could see. It made her wonder where on his body he hadn't been touched by the sun. Laugh lines etched around his mouth, enhancing his rugged appearance. Yet the laughing was a contradiction to his rough exterior. His lips looked tantalizing. She imagined his kiss to be firm but gentle. Unconsciously, she wet her lips.

Out of the corner of his eye Kellan watched her do this. The action caught him off guard. Sexual sensations burned through him. He was completely aroused by her tongue running across her lips. Kellan wanted to pull the girl into his arms firmly planting his lips over hers, but he resisted the urge to do so. Thankfully, he heard his dog, Jake, bark as the sound of tires crunched on the gravel driveway. He released a quick sigh of relief.

"I do believe the vet has arrived. C'mon," Kellan announced waving his hand, inviting her to follow him.

Kylee watched him carry the cat out of the barn to meet his friend, the veterinarian.

"Hey, man! Thanks for coming." Kellan greeted Rick.

"K-man!"

Kylee silently watched the other man get out of a hunter green pick up truck that had the word Veterinarian printed on the driver's side door and saunter over to Kellan with a stethoscope looped around his neck. He took the cat from Kellan and cradled it in his arms. After putting the stethoscope nubs in his ears, he placed the chest piece on the cat. It was obvious to Kylee he was listening for a heartbeat.

He whistled and smiled. "He's alive. I'll get him back to the clinic, take a closer look and see what's going on."

Kellan thanked him and introduced the two strangers.

"Rick, this is Kylee. Kylee this is Rick," Kellan said.

Rick held his hand out to her, and she firmly shook it.

"What happened to the cat?" Rick asked her.

"I was driving down the road and all of a sudden the cat was right there in front of my car. I slammed on my brakes, but it was too late and I ended up running over it. I heard it hit underneath my car." Kylee cringed again, remembering the awful sound.

"Is that your car on the side of the road about a mile or so back?" Rick asked.

She nodded. "Yes. I couldn't get it to start again, so I walked."

Kellan raised his eyebrow at her. He was impressed she had walked so far especially in those wimpy sandals. If her feet hurt she certainly wasn't whining about it. Now he wondered how her feet weren't hurting her.

"Alright, K-man, I'll keep you posted about the cat," Rick said.

"Thanks, man." Kellan shook hands with him again.

"See you tonight at Charlie's. Oh, and do you need me to help with the lady's car in the ditch?" Rick offered.

"Nah, I can help her," Kellan said. "Just take care of the damn cat." Kellan waved his hand up at Rick. "See ya tonight."

Rick stuck his hand out the window waving good-bye to them. His truck tires spun in the gravel at the end of the driveway, squealing when they hit the asphalt road. Kellan's dog barked over the screeching tires. Kylee jumped, frightened by the unexpected deep bark.

"Jake's harmless, he won't hurt you unless you are trying to hurt me," Kellan said smiling at her.

"Jake?" Kylee asked him.

"Jake is my dog." Kellan pointed to the big black dog.

"Oh," Kylee replied. She wasn't sure why he felt the need to tell her his dog's name. It's not like she was going to see him again, or maybe she would. Her new job was somewhere in this area. She supposed that in this smaller town, it was possible she could run into him again in the near future. Not likely, but anything was possible. Her dad always did say "It is a small world". She took a deep breath, holding back the tears that threatened to fall every time she thought of her dad.

Kellan turned his attention back to Kylee. Outside in the sunlight he noticed the freckles sprinkled across her small button nose, giving her an even younger look. Her honey blonde hair sparkled in the sun. Her bow shaped mouth, shaded pink, matching the color of her shirt was even more inviting than before. She looked refreshingly delicious. Oh, what he wouldn't give right now to sample a taste of her, but he needed to get back to work and get her back to her car so she could be on her merry way.

"Are you okay?" Kellan asked her after noticing the sad look on her face.

Sky blue eyes stared wide at him. She nodded, as she swallowed the lump of emotion in her throat.

"Are you worried about the cat?" Kellan asked.

Kylee shook her head. "I'm sure the cat is in good hands with your vet friend."

"Rick's the best animal doctor around. He'll do his best." Kellan bragged.

"I'm fine," Kylee said, glancing away from his direct stare. The last thing she needed right now was to let her sad tears fall in front of him.

Then he remembered her sandals. "Are your feet hurting?"

"What?" Kylee swung her eyes back to him, giving him a confused look.

Kellan pointed to her feet. "City Girl, are your feet hurting you?"

Kylee laughed at the way he called her City Girl with his country drawl. She looked up, liking how his sandy brown hair stuck out beneath the dusty green baseball cap he wore. He looked adorable. The eyes that held hers were midnight blue like a moonless night sky. It had her shivering, despite the feeling of the hot sun beating down on them. There was a white scar just above his right eye making her wonder what happened. She wanted to reach out and touch it, but didn't dare to since this man was a stranger to her. However, it was the first time in a long time she didn't feel threatened by a man. He may have intimidated her at first, but now he intrigued her.

"My feet are okay, but I really need to be on my way."

"Okay," Kellan answered slowly. He wanted her to be on her way, and yet there was another part of him that didn't want to see her go.

"Should we go take a look at your car?" Kellan suggested.

"That'd be great." Kylee's smile warmed his blood.

"C'mon." Kellan gestured with his hand to follow him. She followed him around the corner of a red barn where there was a tall green tractor parked. She felt small standing beside the monstrous tire. Kellan looked expectantly at her.

"This is what we are riding in?" she asked him with nervous eyes. How could one piece of machinery scare her so much?

"Yes," Kellan answered grinning at her.

"Don't you have any other vehicles?"

"Nope," Kellan laughed at her perplexed look. He guessed she was thinking he was a poor farmer who spent all of his money on a tractor. Well, a few years ago it would've been the case, but these days he was doing well.

"I do have a truck." Kellan leaned in close, his breath tickling her ear then he smirked when her body shivered.

"It's out in the field. You're lucky that you found me here. I was in the field working and forgot something, so I drove the tractor back here instead of my truck. Here, I'll help you up." He extended his hand to her. Reluctantly, she took his hand, pulling herself up to the first step.

"Just climb up the steps like a ladder," he instructed noticing how her cute ass fit snugly in her jeans. Whistling softly, he happily followed her up the tractor steps.

She climbed up the steps following his instructions without any problems until she reached the top. When she stepped inside the tractor cab, she made the mistake of looking down at the ground. Seeing how high she was and how far below the ground was made her feel a little dizzy. She grabbed hold of the seat to steady herself. The last thing she wanted to do was fall off the tractor. Not only would she get hurt, but it would be embarrassing as well. She looked around the small cab wondering where she was going to sit. This was something she hadn't thought of when she agreed to ride in the tractor. She didn't have time to think about it anymore, because Kellan was behind her.

Suddenly, she felt his hands on her waist easing her down to sit on a tall metal box. She noticed he had closed the door of the cab and moved to sit in the driver's seat next to her. This looked a lot more comfortable than the box she sat on. She wiped the sweat off her nose then folded her hands in her lap. It was stifling hot in here! She didn't know if she was hot from his touch or the heat of the cab.

The tractor engine roared to life and Kellan shouted loudly, "Hold on!"

He expertly shifted the tractor out of park and into drive, but the tractor jumped catching Kylee off guard, even though he had just told her to hold on. She jolted forward then backwards, her hands frantically searching for something to hold onto and found his leg. Her fingers gripped his leg tightly feeling nothing but hard muscle through his jeans. This sudden contact caused a red blush to creep over her face.

Kellan chuckled, "I told you to hold on."

"I am holding on," she said. Her voice and face full of annoyance. "You just forgot to mention what to hold on to."

"Hmm, I thought you'd see this bar here to grab a hold of," Kellan laughed, pointing to a gray handle next to her.

She wondered if he purposely didn't tell her about the handle. She was happy when she felt the coolness of the air conditioner hit her hot face and was glad the tractor cab was enclosed. It was one less worry she had of falling off the darn thing, as they drove slowly down the road.

"What brings a city girl like you out here?" Kellan asked.

"How do you know I'm a city girl?"

Kellan grinned wickedly as he replied, "The way you are gripping my leg says it all."

"Humph," she snubbed and turned her face toward the window. Fields of dirt surrounded her. "There are fields everywhere," she commented.

Kellan snorted out a laugh. "That's why they call it the country out here, Cit-tee Girl." She frowned feeling he was laughing at her.

"Do you own any of the fields around here?" she asked him.

"As far as your city eyes can see," Kellan drawled, giving her a grin.

"That's pretty far," Kylee hedged seeing a lot of land around her.

Kellan nodded but didn't elaborate any further about what he did or didn't own. She came to the conclusion that he was teasing her by exaggerating how much land he owned. That might make a good impression to the women who lived out here, but she could care less. In her opinion it didn't matter how much land or money a man had. It was what he had to offer in his heart.

She saw her car up ahead on the side of the road.

"There it is." Kylee pointed at her car.

"Damn," Kellan muttered as he saw steam coming out from under the hood. "We're gonna need a tow truck."

Kylee sighed, "That bad, huh?"

Kellan nodded and pulled the tractor up behind her car. He got his cell phone out, punched some numbers into it then held it to his ear.

"Hey, Ev, can you bring me my truck? Head to the house and you'll see me before you get there. Thanks." Kellan ended the conversation then turned to Kylee, whose hand was still on his leg.

He glanced down at her hand, winking at her. Kylee blushed as she removed her hand from his leg. Kellan was surprised how much he liked having her hand there. It had been electrifying.

"Let me get out first, then I'll help you down," Kellan said.

Kylee watched him gracefully climb off the tractor. Then it was her turn. Feeling foolish and very much like a "city girl" she held onto everything with a tight grip as she made her way over to the steps.

"Turn around and climb down from the steps like a ladder facing the same way you did when you climbed up," Kellan instructed from below. He saw the hesitation and fear in her eyes. He regretted teasing her about being a city girl. His voice softened, reassuring her, "It'll be okay. You can do this."

Kylee swallowed nervously, but was grateful for his encouragement. He didn't just say the words. He meant what he said, believing she could do it. This struck a strange happy sensation in the pit of her stomach. It gave her the courage she needed. She took a deep breath and followed his instructions. Before she knew it, her feet were planted firmly on the ground and knew he was behind her. She could smell his masculine scent and heard his breath close to her ear.

Standing behind her he was careful not to touch her, but oh, how he wanted to. Inhaling, her sweet scent his heart beat quickened. He was having a hard time not giving into the impulse of pulling her against him.

"See? I knew you could do it," he whispered softly, "besides, if you had fallen, I'da caught you."

Kylee stood still while her insides danced happily over the thought of being in his strong arms. Kellan, too, was daydreaming about her soft body in his embrace. Kylee jumped at the unexpected sound of a horn honking from a passing car as it sped past them on the road. It brought their attention back to reality.

Kellan cleared his throat. Stepping away from her, he asked, "So what brings you out here?"

"A job," Kylee answered taking small steps away from him to put distance between them. She realized how much she liked being near him and that was dangerous. She had a new job to focus on and didn't have time to get tangled up with the affairs of her heart.

"Where?" Kellan asked.

"Ah, ay Mr..," Kylee trailed off not able to remember the name of her new employer. "Let me get the name and address."

Kylee headed back to her car to retrieve the information. Just as she found the information, a guy in a dusty old farm truck pulled up. She had a feeling this was Kellan's friend, Ev.

"Hey, man!" Kellan shouted out casually to the guy in the pick-up truck. Kylee noted that this seemed to be the way Kellan greeted all his friends. She smiled thinking how relaxed he looked when he took the cap off his head wiping the sweat from his brow.

The man in the truck parked in front of her car and jumped out. He whistled through his teeth as he approached her car. He popped the hood open and started tinkering with it. "We're gonna need the tow truck."

Kylee approached the two men.

"That's what I was afraid of," Kellan stated with a frown and glanced at Kylee. He introduced the two. "Kylee, this is Evan. Evan, this is Kylee, owner of the car."

"Howdy." Evan tried to wipe away most of the grease that was on his hand, on to his pant leg before shaking her hand. Evan shook her hand enthusiastically.

Kellan watched Kylee give Evan's greasy hand a firm handshake. He was impressed by how she didn't flinch from the grime, but he did see her regard Evan with cautious eyes. It was the same caution she had given his dog, when he had been barking at her and him when he had first approached her. Kellan noticed Kylee relax a bit; her eyes less cautious and her shoulders less tense, while he and Evan bantered back and forth with their friendly words to one another.

"Kylee, we'll load your things into my truck, and then we'll find out where you need to be," Kellan told her.

"Okay," Kylee said and began taking the suitcases out of her car.

"Here let me help," Evan said taking a big suitcase from her hand.

"Thank you." Kylee beamed at him.

Kellan watched Evan blush and become tongue tied as he stuttered, "Uh-Ur-welcome."

Kellan frowned over the exchange. It irritated him that Evan had a goofy reaction over Kylee's smile. He was acting like a little puppy dog. It was embarrassing.

Kylee giggled finding it flattering that she had this kind of affect on him.

"Get a hold of yourself, man." Kellan scowled at Evan. He sheepishly hid his head under the hood of her car.

"I'll call the tow truck and let you know," Evan mumbled, waving his hand good-bye to them.

Kellan was still scowling as he climbed into the truck. Kylee noticed the hard, rugged look he had given Evan. To defuse the situation she said, "Thank you for your help."

"You're welcome," Kellan said. "Hey, I need to stop at my house for a minute, if you don't mind."

"Yes, of course, that's all right," Kylee agreed. He was being very kind in helping her today. How could she refuse him when he needed to make a quick stop at his house, at least, she hoped it was quick. She was getting anxious to be on her way and excited to meet her new employer. In a matter of minutes, Kellan was turning his truck into his driveway. The ride here in his truck was a lot faster than the ride in the tractor.

"I'll only be a minute, but you're welcome to get out of the truck or stay in here," Kellan offered.

"I'll get out," Kylee said, watching Jake bark excitedly when Kellan opened his door and petted his head. The dog ran around to the other side of the truck to say hi to her just as she opened the door. He jumped up on the door and barked. She screamed, closed the door, and stayed inside the truck. Afraid of the dog she screamed again. Jake continued to lean his paws against the door, his head in the window, and his tongue lolling out of his mouth. Not knowing this enthusiastic bark was his usual friendly greeting, Kylee interpreted his actions as a vicious attack.

Kellan commanded Jake to get down. When Kellan opened the truck door, her arms flew up in front of her face, and she curled her legs up to her chest in a defensive pose. Kellan had mixed feelings of humor and sympathy for her. Humor because if she knew anything about Jake, he was just a big lap dog. Yes, he would defend his master in a heartbeat if he sensed Kellan was in danger. Other than that, Jake just loved people. Kellan's heart went out to Kylee because of the way she was curled up into a ball. He now realized she truly was afraid of his dog.

"I didn't know you were so afraid of dogs," he commented softly.

"Cautious," Kylee answered, peeling herself out of her ball pose. She peered around Kellan to see where his dog had gone. It was way on the other side of the yard.

Kellan rolled his eyes upward thinking cautious was an understatement. "Bad experience with dogs?" Kellan guessed loudly.

"Yes."

Kellan held out his hand to her. She took it, and he helped her out of the truck.

"Thank you," she said smiling.

"Welcome. Did you find the name and address you need me to take you to?"

"Oh, yes." Kylee nodded and reached into the front pocket of her jeans, pulling out a piece of paper. She read out loud, "Mr. Taylor."

"What?" Kellan questioned, as though he was answering his own name.

"A Mr. Taylor," Kylee repeated.

"The one who lives on Main Street?" Kellan's voice questioned her, but his eyebrows scrunched together, and his mouth turned into a peculiar frown. *Why would his parents hire this pretty little thing?*

"No." Kylee frowned and continued to read the information on the paper in her hand. "Mr. Taylor. He lives on County Rd M, house number 15."

"Are you kidding me?" Kellan just looked at her with a blank expression.

"No. Why?" Kylee frowned.

Kellan snickered. "That's me."

"You?" Kylee replied in awe.

"It's me!" Kellan held his arms out wide. "Mr. Kellan Taylor. So what job are you here for?"

Kylee gave him a speechless stare. He didn't know what she was here for? Oh, just great! Was someone playing a joke on her?

He stared back at her, his eyes looking expectantly at her. "Well?"

"You didn't hire a housekeeper?"

"No, not a housekeeper," Kellan frowned. *Did mom hire a housekeeper for me?*

"What?" Kylee gave him a confused look. "You didn't hire someone to help you with the inside of your house?"

"Oh, that. Yeah, I did." Kellan gave a curt nod of his head. "He'll be here in a few days."

"He?" Kylee's eyes questioned him.

"Yes. Kyle," Kellan confirmed, but then he gave her a suspicious look. How did she know about this? "How do you know I hired someone? Do you know this Kyle guy?" he asked his tone accusing.

Kylee gave him a painful look. She had a feeling that the spelling of her name got mixed up again. Many people misspelled her name and like Kellan, people expected a guy named Kyle instead of a woman named Kylee. He gave her another expectant look. She couldn't help the humorous feeling inside her. She tipped her head back giggling.

"What's so funny?" Kellan demanded.

"I'm sorry," she apologized with a shy smile. She extended her right hand out saying, "Hi, I'm Kyle."

"What?" Kellan gave her an absurd look and didn't shake her hand. "What the hell are you talking about it? I thought you said your name was Kylee?"

Unable to help it she giggled again. "Yeah, it is."

"Quit laughing, and tell me what the hell you are talking about!" Kellan shouted angrily. Normally he was the kidder and wasn't used to being kidded. He didn't like it.

"I'm sorry. This happens a lot," Kylee apologized, taking in a deep breath.

"What does?" Kellan asked still angry.

"My name is Kylee spelled K-Y-L-E-E. When the agency called to let you know I was coming, apparently you forgot the last E in my name. So that's why you were expecting a guy named Kyle, and not a girl named Kylee," she explained. "It's okay this happens to me all the time."

Kellan gave her a long look. Confusion floated all over his handsome face. He held up the palm of his hand saying, "Okay. Wait. Give me a minute to process this."

He loudly exhaled a whoosh of air and raised the ball cap off his head with one hand, ran his fingers through his hair with the other hand, before setting his cap back on his head again. He leaned his back up against the truck and folded his arms across his chest. "Yes, ma'am, I was expecting a guy."

His eyes grazed lazily over her from head to toe. Remembering he had pegged her for a city girl in the first few minutes of meeting her, he wasn't quite sure she could handle country living. Surely they wouldn't have sent a girl out for the rough work he needed done to his old farmhouse. However, since the first time she spoke to him he saw a determination in her eyes that has been there the whole time. He could be wrong about her appearances. He had already challenged this city girl's fragility by making her climb up and down on the tall tractor. She had surprised him by succeeding.

Kellan knew if she decided to stay it was going to be a lot of hard work for her slender body. He couldn't afford a dainty female hanging around here who was more of a hinder than help. It made him wonder if she was up to the task, and he wanted to find out. From his quick assessment she looked sturdy enough to handle the hard work, and he was eager to challenge her. He knew better than to tell a woman she was sturdy, even though it was a compliment in his way of thinking. There was something about her that sparked an interest in him, and he wanted to find out more about her. He had a feeling she was strong and would somehow manage. He couldn't exactly say why, but he wanted to be right on this.

Kylee caught his frown and misread it. "Sorry to disappoint you."

Kellan shook his head quickly smiling at her. "Oh, I'm not disappointed. You are a pleasant surprise." He whistled softly.

Then he apologized, "I'm sorry for my surprise. My sister took the message before she left on vacation and wrote down the name Kyle. I didn't talk to anyone at the agency. Again, I'm sorry for the confusion." Kellan wondered if his sister had been playing a joke on him, or did she honestly mess up this girl's name? He wouldn't know anything until his sister returned home.

"Kylee, what's your last name?"

"Kylee Jones," she answered. Kellan thought it had a nice ring to it, but his mind betrayed him as he thought *Kylee Taylor sounded good, too. Whoa!* He shook his head loose of this thought.

"Well, Kylee Jones, are you up for the hard work ahead of you?" Kellan questioned walking over to her.

"Yes." She rolled her eyes up at him. "The job description is the same no matter if a man or woman showed up," she replied sassily, crossing her arms over her chest.

Kellan raised his eyebrow sharply at her. He crossed his own arms across his chest and bent down close to her face matching her sass with a sneer. "Sassiness will get you nowhere."

"And if I leave, your housework will get you nowhere," Kylee retorted, pointing her index finger at him.

"Go ahead, leave." Kellan suddenly threw his arms out wide into the air.

Kylee who was close, but not in harm's way, quickly threw her hands up in front of her face defensively, bending sideways to avoid getting hit. For a split second her memory had taken her away from this innocent gesture and back to a horrible time in her life where she feared any sudden moves from an abusive boyfriend. *Oh,* she cringed in her mind. There were times she thought her abusive past was far behind her, but every now and then, certain movements had her right back there again.

Kellan saw her dart out of the way of his arms but he didn't understand the severity of it. He glanced at her quickly apologizing, "Whoops, sorry. I didn't realize you were so close."

He watched her lower her hands from her face thinking how odd her reaction was but then dismissed it from his mind. He extended one arm towards the road reminding her, "Your car is getting you nowhere."

"You're right, it's not," Kylee simply said. She was relieved he hadn't noticed her crazy moment. She relaxed again. She knew in her heart Kellan was a good man, and she could trust him.

"So, are you keeping me?" Kylee asked holding her breath hoping he'd say yes.

He grabbed her hands examining them. A spark flew through her when he picked up one of her small hands with his big hand. He turned her hand over to look at the palm of it. He squeezed her fingers lightly with his then did the same thing to her other hand and fingers. He liked what he saw. Her hands were average sized, and she had nicely shaped fingers. *A big diamond ring would look nice on her hand.* He was jealous thinking about another man's ring on her hand. He had no right to be jealous of this. Where on earth did these thoughts come from? How in the world was he going to keep his thoughts from straying to this beautiful woman? He was now her employer, and she was his employee. If things got too awkward around them he could always find another place for her to stay; yet he didn't want to see her go.

"Yes, we'll give it a try and see how it goes. How does that sound?" Kellan tossed out. His eyebrow arched upward. He was a little concerned by the way she nonchalantly mentioned how his "housework" wouldn't get done. It's possible she had a misconception about the job she was hired to do. Well, they could muddle through those details later. He really wanted her to stay and hoped she would.

"Sounds good," Kylee agreed. *My how sexy he looks when he arches his brow. Is he aware of how irresistible he is when he does this? He probably is.*

Kellan tossed her a savory smile that made Kylee's stomach do a somersault. This had her wondering if it was a good idea to work for a man who made her insides flutter.

"I was told you have an apartment for me to stay in," Kylee said hoping the information given to her was correct.

"Yes! Let me show you." Kellan pushed himself away from the truck, lifted one of her suitcases from the truck bed, and carried it inside for her. He led her through a screen door that banged loudly behind them into what he called the vestibule.

It was a rectangle shaped room that held an old freezer chest and lots of doors. One door to the right led to the garage. She followed him through the room passing another screen door that went outside to a wooden deck and pool. The last door she saw was the one that led into the house. Outside this door there was a big rug that held several pairs of shoes; some were clean while others were muddy. Beside the rug near the wall sat two chairs.

"You take your shoes off before coming into the house?" Kylee asked.

"Yes. I hate getting mud on the carpets."

Kylee was impressed by this. Most men she knew wouldn't have cared about having mud on the carpet. They stepped through the door stopping on a square area that led in three different directions. Kellan motioned with his hand the five steps to the left went up to the kitchen. His hand swooped downward to the flight of stairs straight ahead. He told her these went down to the basement where the washer and dryer were. To the right of them was another staircase that went up. Kylee followed Kellan up twelve steps and entered the room. Her eyes quickly glanced over it. There was a queen size bed, dresser, and a closet in it. A bathroom was directly off the bedroom. She liked it and couldn't wait to get unpacked.

"I hope the room is okay. I think my sister might have said it was a studio apartment, but it doesn't have a kitchen. I thought since it's so close to the kitchen this would be okay…" Kellan trailed off.

"I like it. This is perfect. Thanks," Kylee replied with a warm smile.

"Okay, good." He gave her an appreciative smile.

"Thanks, Kellan."

"Stay here, rest your feet while I get all of your things," Kellan instructed her. He disappeared before Kylee had a chance to protest. She sat down on the bed liking how soft it was. She cringed when she heard the screen door echo loudly up the stairs when it closed as he went out. The longer she sat, the more her feet started to ache. She removed her sandals and began rubbing the bottoms of them.

When Kellan came back into the bedroom he heard Kylee groaning while she rubbed her feet. He set her suitcases on the floor then knelt down in front of her taking one of her feet in his strong hands. He applied pressure to the balls of her feet with his thumb then rubbed the arch of her foot with his knuckles. He took her other foot and repeated the same steps.

"Oh, thank you."

Kellan nodded. "You're welcome. Do I need to take you shopping tomorrow for better shoes?"

Kylee shook her head no. "I've got tennis shoes packed."

"Why weren't you wearing them?" Kellan scolded her with his eyes.

"I wasn't planning on walking a hundred miles today," was Kylee's cheeky retort. Kellan laughed, liking her spirit.

"I brought in the last of your suitcases from the truck. I'll let you get unpacked and rest these feet of yours. Later on we'll discuss the details of the job." Kellan said.

"Thanks for the feet rub. They feel better already." Kylee flashed him a friendly smile that had him wavering in his steps. Her blue eyes sparkled, lighting up her face. When she smiled he couldn't help smiling back.

"You're welcome." Kellan nodded his head before he disappeared down the steps, his heavy boots thundering loudly with each step he took.

Kylee began unpacking her suitcases and was impressed at how much room there was in the closet and drawers for her clothes. The dresser was an antique with deep drawers certainly designed to be used versus modern day dressers that seemed to be made for decorative purposes and had short drawers. After unpacking, she flopped on the bed enjoying its softness. She rested her head on the pillow listening to the birds singing outside the window. Their song was calming, and Kylee soon drifted off to sleep.

Chapter Two

Kylee opened her eyes and stretched her arms lazily. She glanced out the window noticing the sun was low in the horizon. She quickly sat up. *Oh! For goodness sakes! How long have I been sleeping?* The fact that she had fallen asleep gnawed on her insides. *Kellan...her car...oh crap!* She scrambled off the bed, ran to the bathroom and looked at her sleepy reflection in the mirror. She brushed her long, blonde hair then put it up into a ponytail before heading downstairs.

The kitchen was empty when she walked in. Looking around the room she was impressed with by its modern appearance. Judging by the house's weather worn exterior, she wasn't expecting much for the interior of the house. The outside needed a new coat of paint, and she guessed the inside needed the same TLC. It wasn't fair that she had judged the house by its cover, but she had. However, this kitchen was a pleasant surprise! It had been remodeled with modern appliances and cabinetry. The cabinets were a light cherry wood; something she hadn't ever seen before. Her experience with cherry wood was usually dark and gloomy. This was light and carefree but still had a strong sturdy feeling to it. A lot like its owner, she speculated from what she knew of Kellan in the few hours she had met him.

When she had first seen him he was standing in the driveway with a firm stance: dark sunglasses shading his eyes, muscular arms protruding from his shirt, and the broadest shoulders she had ever seen. He had intimidated her. Her first thought had been to run from the tall, gruff looking man who didn't smile at her. Her second thought was she had nowhere to go. Her third thought had been *Yikes*!

She congratulated herself for finding the courage to speak and ask for his help. He graciously helped her and was so gentle with the cat. Despite his intimidating pose, he ended up being kind. His carefree manner was playful, especially when he gave her a mischievous wink when her hand lingered too long on his knee. Oh, that had been embarrassing. He had teased her about being a city girl. She reflected about how funny she must have looked trying to get off the tractor. Instead of laughing at her, he had been supportive, easily talking her down off the tall tractor as though she was a cat high in a tree. He had stood close behind her when she had reached the ground. She had wanted him to touch her but to her disappointment he hadn't, and she wished he had.

Well, that was before she found out he was her employer. She had to be careful about her feelings for him. She needed this job in so many ways. It couldn't have come at a better time in her life. Kylee hoped this was the right place to make a fresh start for herself. If she did well for

Kellan in whipping his house into shape, she could use him as a work reference on her next job, wherever it might take her.

Her first step was squelching the way he made her insides melt when he raised his eyebrow at her, winked at her, stood close or touched her. She was remembering the electricity that ran through her when her hands had been in his. Okay, distance was her plan. Putting distance between them couldn't be that hard. During the day he'll be working in the fields, and she'd be alone in the house. In the evenings when he came home she could retire to her room. Yes, this would work.

Kylee's eyes continued examining the room around her. The kitchen had two entryways into it, both without doors. One of the entryways was between stove and the refrigerator while the other doorway was where she had entered after ascending five steps. Kylee took four steps closer to the cabinet island in the middle of the floor. To her left, in the corner, in front of a window sat a small round table with four chairs. *Nice! Through the window you can see company coming.* Her eyes swept to the right of the window. There was wall space as big as her arms were wide. The kitchen window was centered in the outer wall with a stainless sink sitting below the window. Upper and lower cabinets lined the wall on both sides of the window and sink; the upper cabinets reaching almost to the ceiling. She walked over to the sink and looked out the window to see the driveway and the homestead barns. She placed her hand on the smooth counter. It was black granite swirled with olive green; all the countertops were the same. Her feet shuffled to the right where she stopped in front of the angled corner where two ovens were housed; a convection oven on top and another convection oven on the bottom with a storage drawer beneath it.

Kylee continued moving clockwise past a smaller cabinet before approaching the counter built in stove that had two deep drawers below it. Her fingertips lightly grazed over the smooth cook top. *It's a five burner induction stove!* She stared in awe over the expense of her employer's new technology for cooking. Excited about being able to cook with newer appliances she let out a delighted squeal. Her eyes glanced upward to the microwave above the stove, and she was thankful for her tall height so she could reach it.

Stepping past the entryway leading into the formal dining room, she stopped in front of the black refrigerator. It faced the doorway and had wide side by side doors with a pull-out freezer drawer on the bottom. On the right side of the fridge was a long stretch of counter with upper and lower cabinets that extended along the inner wall ending at the doorway by the steps where she came in. On top of the counter was a basket of keys and papers, and she guessed this to be Kellan's throw pile. *I love this kitchen!*

Walking back over to the stove she opened the top drawer to see what Kellan kept in it. Several rectangle cookie sheets and round pizza pans were stacked in an organized mess. She pulled opened the bottom drawer looking for pots and pans, but all she found were a few potholders. She began to search for the pots and pans by opening all the cabinets. Finally she found them in an upper cabinet. She thought this was the oddest place to put them. Since they were out of her reach, she looked around the kitchen for a stool or small ladder to use to retrieve them. Seeing nothing of the sort, she slid one of the kitchen table chairs over. It made a loud screeching sound against the ceramic tile floor. She tested her one foot on the chair watching it teeter, but she didn't have any other choice than to use it. She would have asked for Kellan's help, but he was nowhere to be found. The house was quiet, and she assumed he wasn't home.

Carefully, she stepped on the chair with one foot, then her other foot, while holding onto the back of the chair with both hands. She tested the chair again firmly planting her feet on each end of the chair's square seat. She raised one hand up, holding one of the cabinet doors. Slowly, she opened the door as she glanced up at the pans on the shelf above her head. This was a lot like climbing up in the tractor earlier today. Except the tractor was much higher than this shelf, and the ladder on the tractor was a lot steadier than the chair she was now standing on. In the back of her mind she knew standing on this rickety chair wasn't safe. She should probably wait for Kellan, but she was too stubborn to listen to her own self. Besides, she had no idea how long it would be before he came home, and she needed to be working. Organizing his kitchen to her liking just seemed to be the right thing to do this evening.

With one hand on the cabinet door to steady her, she lifted her other hand up retrieving one of the pans on the shelf. Once by one, she brought all the pans down off the high shelf and set them on the counter. The chair and her body teetered with each movement. Kylee was congratulating herself as she grabbed the last pot, but this one was too heavy. It threw her off balance! Holding on tightly to the cabinet door, she tried to regain her balance as the chair wobbled beneath her. She felt the pot slipping from her hands as her body began falling backwards. In one last attempt to save herself, she let go of the pot. It echoed loudly in her ears as it fell hard onto the counter. With her hand free of the pot she wildly reached for the back of the chair but couldn't find it. A piercing scream came out! Her body tensed up in expectation of hitting the floor, but to her surprise she didn't feel the hard floor against her body. Instead she felt strong arms around her rescuing her from the fall and heard a deep grunted curse beside her ear.

"Damn girl, what the hell!"

Kylee sagged into the hard body that held her. She was grateful he had come to her rescue when he did. With her eyes closed, she breathed in his clean refreshing scent. He smelled of soap. While she thought he was still out in the fields, he had been upstairs showering. Next time she wouldn't assume a quiet house meant no one was here. She looked up at Kellan with a sheepish grin. He frowned at her, but she thought she saw concern in those midnight eyes of his. Was she wrong?

She wasn't wrong. Kellan was very glad he had decided to come and see what she was doing the minute he heard the chair feet screeching across the floor. If he hadn't come downstairs when he did, he could have found her lying on the floor. It upset him to think she could have seriously injured herself. He was fully aware that those kitchen chairs were unsteady. He was mad at her for being stupid and risking her safety.

"Just what were you thinking when you got up on that wobbly chair?" Kellan scolded her with disapproving eyes, his arm still holding her against him.

Kylee tried to back away from him, but he wouldn't let her go. "I couldn't find a ladder."

"So you think getting up on an unsteady chair was the right choice?" Kellan asked her. His face held disbelief and anger.

She swallowed nervously. If he meant to intimidate her, it might have worked if he hadn't kept his arms around her for so long. The longer she stayed in his embrace the more she liked it. For the first time in her life Kylee felt safe, even as his midnight eyes gave her a rigid look. She didn't feel threatened by him. Instead, she was beginning to feel aroused. Her heart beat faster, and her breath caught in her throat. Her tummy somersaulted when his husky voice made her promise not to climb up on any wobbly furniture again. Unable to speak, she promised him with a solid nod of her head. But, if it meant she had a chance to be in his arms again, she wasn't quite sure she wouldn't break the promise. The hardness in his eyes began to fade away. His eyes shifted colors from midnight blue to a blue black as he gazed into her wide apologetic eyes. He looked a lot less rugged with the dirt smudges washed away from his face. His hair was wet from the shower water instead of matted with sweat, under his dusty old farm hat. In fact, he looked down right handsome!

Kellan's eyes were intent on her. He ran his thumb lightly on her forehead, down her nose, over her cheek, across the bridge of her nose to her other cheek, then brought his thumb down to her chin, circling her mouth, tracing the outline of her pink lips. She parted her lips slowly, letting out a small whispered breath. She stayed quiet in his arms as if she was in a trance under his touch. He felt her warm breath on his hand. Just when Kylee thought he might dip his head down to kiss her, a car horn echoed in the distance, jarring her out of the trance she was in. She wiggled in his arms. Much to her disappointment, Kellan freed his tight hold on her and pushed her away but kept her at arms' length. His eyes stayed on her and both of them were silent, each of them absorbing the connection they had just made.

Kellan had wanted to kiss her and would have if they hadn't been interrupted by the honking car passing on the road. He was so used to the road noise, but Kylee wasn't. Silently, he cursed the blasted horn that had cut into their moment, but then he realized it probably was a blessing in disguise. He knew he was destined to drink from those beautiful lips, but tonight probably wasn't the right time. He didn't want to scare her away, and he really needed her housekeeping skills if he wanted to make this house look good again. They had a business relationship, and they needed to keep it that way. Nothing more could go on between them even though he was certain he wasn't the only one who felt the heated connection between them.

He groaned as he stepped away from her. "Kylee, what did you need that was so high up?"

"The pots and pans. Who keeps those so high up in a cabinet anyway?" Kylee shook her head.

"I do. It's a good height for me," he explained.

Kylee looked up at him. Growing up she had always been a tall girl. She never thought twice about it but today as she stood next to Kellan she was very thankful for her taller height. She couldn't imagine being any shorter. She thought their heights were perfect for each other for any occasion. A small sigh escaped her while her mind wandered; envisioning the two of them tangled up in the bed sheets, his long legs entwined with hers....

"Kylee," Kellan's said. Lost in her thoughts, she glanced over at him with a dreamy look. His arched eyebrow brought her back to reality making her weak in the knees. She grabbed hold of the counter to help her stay standing. On unsteady legs she walked to the kitchen table and sat down in one of the chairs. She gripped the edge of the table and kept her eyes cast downward, looking at the floor.

Kellan narrowed his eyes, watching her. He saw all the telltale signs of a fantasy. He heard her sigh, watched as a dreamy expression settled over her pretty face. Her face turned red when she saw she had been caught thinking about something she shouldn't have been. He wondered who it was that had her all flustered and sort of hoped it had been about him. Amusement danced in his eyes as he followed her over to the table. He sat down in a chair across from her, hoping for a sign indicating it was him in her dreams.

He noted the guilty look and the way she tried to avoid eye contact with him. A crimson flush sat high on her cheeks where minutes ago he had caressed the pale skin. Heat rushed through him at the memory of her smooth skin under his rough finger. Her eyes caught his and her cheeks stayed a red apple color. Aha! He was right! Her thoughts had been about him! He was pretty sure she, too, had felt the sizzle between them.

Kylee knew her cheeks burned scarlet by the devilish grin on his face. She was an open book, with him reading her impure thoughts. She decided to say nothing and changed the subject.

"You have a wonderful kitchen," Kylee complimented.

"Thanks," Kellan said. Normally he would have teased a girl to no end about having read her sexual thoughts, but something stopped him from doing this with her. He could tell she was different and wouldn't have reacted the same way as the other girls he teased. At this precise moment, Kellan had a different feeling about her than he did with most of the women who flirted with him. Maybe that was it. Kylee wasn't flirting. This definitely set her apart from the others.

The other girls flirted with him, but mostly it was for fun, because they wanted a quick fling with him and nothing more. He could see Kylee was cut of a different cloth. She didn't flaunt sex as a pastime. Sex would mean something to her. He needed to be careful around her since he didn't know how he felt about her. One thing he did know was that he certainly wasn't looking for a permanent relationship. He would need to keep her at arm's length. Surely that could be done. He'd be working in the fields all day and she'd be here. At night it was a big house. She had her room, and he had his room which was a long way from hers.

"Should we discuss the details of the job?"

"Sounds good," Kylee said.

Kellan nodded and glanced at his watch. "Then afterwards I've gotta get going."

He saw a flicker of disappointment run across her face after he mentioned he was leaving. For some odd reason, he too, was disappointed that he was leaving for the night. *Damn. It might've been better if a Kyle had shown up versus Kylee.* Kellan thought dryly.

"Kylee, what job description did the agency give you?" Kellan asked her. "I'm not sure all the details of the job were given correctly."

"Oh?" Kylee said worriedly. She had just unpacked and had started to have a good feeling about this job. She didn't want to leave now. What could they have possibly gotten wrong?

"I was told you needed help with the interior of your house."

Kellan arched his brow in concern. "That's it? That's all they gave as a description?"

"Yes."

"What is your assumption of the job?"

"You need a housekeeper. Someone to cook, dust, vacuum and maybe paint some walls. Is this not what you need?"

"Painting, yes except, it's more than painting walls," Kellan sighed heavily.

"Okay, tell me what it is you need done in this house, Kellan," Kylee said in a cheerful voice. Maybe there was more she could do for him.

The way his name rolled off her tongue made his heart skip a beat.

"I have five rooms in this old farmhouse that need redecorating. The carpet needs to be ripped up. I want the original wood floors exposed. Depending on how bad the wood is, I may need to call in someone to re-strip them. I know my grandmother took great care of the wood floors, but after she moved out there's been several layers of carpet on them. I hope over the years there hasn't been much damage to them."

"What else?"

"The curtains need to be taken down and probably thrown away. I'm sure new ones will need to be bought. The wallpaper needs to be stripped off the wall and then painted."

"Do you have a deadline for all of this to be done?" Kylee asked.

"Yes. By the end of July," Kellan firmly said. "I've entered the house in the town's Historical Homes Tour."

"Cool!" she said with enthusiasm. She was met with an astonished stare by him.

"You're an odd bird, City Girl, if you think this is cool. My family thought I was nuts for wanting to do it."

Kylee smiled shyly. "I guess that makes me a cashew, too."

"What?" Kellan asked. Kylee giggled.

"A cashew, a nut," Kylee explained. "We're both nuts for wanting to redecorate this house."

Kellan threw his head back laughing. It was a natural laugh not a forced one—a low bellowed one that erupted from deep within him. Kylee felt a wide smile spread across her face as she watched him. It made her feel good that she had made him laugh.

"If the house qualifies to be in the Historical Homes Tour, imagine what it has seen." Kylee sighed looking around the kitchen. "If these walls could talk…"

"Oh, I'm glad they can't." Kellan chuckled deeply. "A boy needs his secrets, if you know what I mean." He arched his brows and a playful smile danced across his lips.

Kylee blushed. She had some clue about what he meant. He bellowed out another laugh over her blushing cheeks. He half expected her to leave the table, but she didn't.

She looked him directly in the eye. "I guess I better get started tomorrow then."

"Really," Kellan said in surprise. He thought for sure she'd run away screaming over all the work that had to be done. *Damn, she is pleasantly surprising me.*

"Yes." Kylee nodded. She might be getting in over her head with the deadline, but she had this encouraging feeling to try it. "I'll even dust and vacuum for you, too."

"Awesome!" Kellan beamed. "Hey, did you say you can cook?"

"Yes."

"How about I throw in an extra hundred dollars a week for you to cook us meals, too?"

"Us," Kylee said, but her tone held question. Was Kellan married or did he have a live-in girlfriend? Disappointment washed over her, and she was embarrassed because of the fantasy she had about him.

"Yeah," Kellan said. "You, me, and Evan,"

"Evan lives with you?" she inquired. There still was no mention of a wife.

"No. He has his own house, but he helps me work the fields. It would help us out a lot if you could have dinner ready for us every day."

"One meal only?" Kylee asked. *Was Evan his lover?*

"Yep," Kellan verified. Then he said as though he had read her mind. "I don't swing that way, City Girl. Evan and I have been friends since childhood."

"I never said you did." Kylee said defensively.

"I could see the wheels turning in your head." Kellan said dryly. *Eek! He could see the wheels turning in my head? What other thoughts could he see?*

"So what'dya say about cooking for us?" he asked.

Kylee had a thoughtful look on her face. Of course, she would be able to cook for this farmer too, but she didn't want to sound too eager and give him the wrong impression that she could be taken advantage of. In the end, his dark eyes fixated on her, and she felt lost in them. She couldn't say no. She didn't want to say no. His eyes were full of hope that she'd agree, and she didn't want to disappoint him.

Kellan didn't want to look desperate about needing her help, but the truth is, he was. He needed someone to start the repairs on the house last week. He wasn't quite sure she'd be able to have it all done by the deadline, but he was willing to give her a chance. Worse case scenario, he'd have to wait until next year to show the house.

"Yes," Kylee spoke.

"Yes, we have a deal?"

"Yes, Mr. Taylor, we have a deal." Kylee extended her hand to shake on it. He took her hand in his, shaking it firmly.

"Don't forget to call me Kellan."

"Kellan. Thank you."

"You're welcome, Kylee," Kellan obliged, although he had no idea why she was thanking him.

Kellan gave her a tour of the house. He showed her the five rooms she would be redecorating, four of which were upstairs. At one end of the hallway was a bathroom. It had been redone. The vanity, the shower and tiled floor had been updated. In Kylee's opinion, the bathroom was quaint. It had a stand up shower stall, a sink that sat in the middle of a counter with cabinets beneath it. In the corner behind the shower was the toilet. A window faced the front yard and the road, but it didn't have any shades or curtains on it.

"No shades on the window," Kylee commented.

"Nobody uses this bathroom so there's no need for them," Kellan simply said. "Besides, City Girl, it's not like I have neighbors that can see in."

"They could get binoculars and see in," she mentioned.

He gave her an absurd look saying, "They won't."

On the opposite end of the hallway from the bathroom there was an open door leading to another stairway.

"Where do these steps go?" Kylee asked placing her hand on the door handle. The wooden door was the original and the tarnished copper handle was, too.

"My room," Kellan said gruffly from behind her.

"Oh." She read far more into his gruff than she should have. Nervously, she backed away from the door stepping on his foot. She mumbled, "Sorry."

"There's no need for you to clean in there," he told her, clearing his throat. He didn't mind at all that she stepped on his foot. In fact, she was so light he hardly noticed it. He did, however, notice her quick nervous apology but didn't know why. He also got a whiff of her sweet fragrance.

"Got it," she said in a clipped tone, then regretted her snippy voice and hoped he didn't take offense at it. She stole a glance his way and found him grinning at her. It helped her breathe easier.

It was nightfall by the time Kellan left. He let her know that her car had been towed to local garage in town before handing her a set of keys to one of his trucks. He pointed to a red truck parked beside the barn.

"Feel free to drive it any time."

"Thanks."

"Well, I gotta go," Kellan told her. "Jake will be around outside so he won't bother you."

She just nodded silently and waved her hand good-bye to him. He had reached the door when he turned around and said, "Oh and those feet stay on the ground while I'm away. No climbing up on chairs or counters to reach anything." He warned her pointing his index finger at her making a mental note to get a ladder for her to use around the house.

"Fine, okay," Kylee agreed.

"I mean it," Kellan repeated with a stern look.

"Okay," Kylee answered firmly.

This time it was Kellan's turn to nod silently. He stepped out the door, but after a few seconds he breezed back in. "Oh! Hey, Kylee --"

"What?" She turned to face him.

"Out of all the nuts in the world, why did you pick a cashew?"

Kylee giggled over his random question. "Because they are little smiles,"

Kellan grinned. "Have a good night."

This time he left the house and didn't come back. He felt a little odd about leaving a stranger in his house, or was it the fact he was leaving Kylee alone. If it had been a man alone in his house, he probably wouldn't have felt the way he did. He might have even extended the invitation to the man to join him. But, he hadn't invited her. He tried to remind himself, *she was a big girl and he wasn't here to babysit her. Besides, he had made these plans long before he met her.*

From the living room window, Kylee watched him drive off in a different truck than the one he was giving her to drive. This one was brown and rusty. The truck tires spun in his gravel driveway, squealing when they hit the pavement of the road, the same way Rick's truck had done. When the tires squealed, she heard Jake bark wondering if the high pitch sound hurt the dog's ears and this was why he barked.

Kylee understood that Kellan had a life to live and that these plans had been made before she got there, but she felt lonely in this big old farmhouse. She didn't blame Kellan for leaving her here, although it might have been nice for him to ask her to come along. But on the other side of that, she didn't want to feel like a tag along. What if he had a date with a girl? Oh sure, he probably did. A good looking guy like Kellan more than likely didn't spend many nights alone. The thought of him being with a girl tonight made her envious. Eek! What if he brought a girl back home with him tonight? That would be awkward in the morning, wouldn't it? Or maybe he wouldn't even come home tonight and would spend the night at the girl's place. She gave a sad sigh and didn't want to think about him being intimate with another woman.

Pushing this thought completely out of her mind, she decided to revisit the rooms that needed the most work. Climbing the steep stairs to the second floor of the house, her mind wandered to Kellan. She knew nothing about her employer's habits but had no doubt she would soon learn about them. Hmm, he was her employer and nothing else; couldn't be anything else. In the half day of being here, she liked the area and had a good feeling about this job. She didn't want to ruin this opportunity by crossing any employer/employee lines. Assessing the four rooms on the second floor that needed improving, she quickly made mental notes on which rooms to start with. She shook her head, laughing at herself. Never in a million years did she think her Bachelor's Degree in history would have brought her here, to this small town helping a farmer redecorate his old farmhouse.

She had worked her way through college by cleaning houses for various clients. This led to cleaning for the wealthier women who owned big grand Victorian homes. She cleaned these beautiful houses with great care. The women she worked for appreciated all her hard work and dedication. They admired her for taking care of their houses in the same beloved manner as they did. She loved it and found it fun!

From cleaning houses she had been introduced to renovation. She had worked for a renovating company one summer. She found this to be a lot of hard work and very rewarding, but stripping a house down to the bare wires and building it back to new again just wasn't her forte. After she graduated she worked for an interior designer who gave her an insight into the decorating world for a variety of houses from old to new. Her last job had been to help a couple who had purchased an old lake resort. The renovations required painting cabins, repairs on the outside, decorating the inside, and purchasing furniture for the cabins. She enjoyed working for the couple. They were laid back and easy to work with. Kylee realized this was more along the lines of what she liked to do.

Kellan's job description for this house was similar to the work she had done at the lake resort. There was a lot of hard work to be completed in these rooms, but she was confident she'd be able to get it finished suitable to Kellan's liking. She had some ideas about how to restore some of the house's original charm and keep it comfortable for Kellan.

She stopped in front of Kellan's open door and looked up the stairs leading to his room. Did she dare climb the steps and go in? Not sure if she should because he had been very stern when he told her she didn't need to clean his room. Standing at the base of the stairs she couldn't help thinking his room was forbidden fruit and decided not to climb the steps. She didn't want to do anything to jeopardize his privacy nor anger him that might lead him to firing her. This thought was ridiculous! He wouldn't fire her for going into his room, would he? She felt it in her heart that he wouldn't but didn't want to take a chance. He didn't say she couldn't go in his room just that she didn't need to clean his room.

She scolded herself for being so afraid of a man's anger. Not every man in the world was like Thomas, her last boyfriend, who had physically abused her. She leaned against the door jam sighing wistfully. In her heart she already knew Kellan wasn't an abusive man even though she had ducked earlier when he swung his arm out. She wondered if there wouldn't always be a part of her that would be skittish in certain circumstances.

Kylee found her way back to the kitchen and decided to reorganize the placement of things in the kitchen suited to her needs versus Kellan's. She didn't think he would mind if she rearranged some of the drawers and cupboards since the only items he kept within reach were the pizza pans and cookie sheets for quick and easy meals. She stayed true to her promise to Kellan about keeping her feet on the floor. Since she was fairly handy in the kitchen, agreeing to cook for him and Evan didn't feel like a big chore. Remembering how pleased he looked when she had agreed to cook his noon meal made her feel great. It was a good thing Kellan explained the differences to her about how the meals were served on the farm versus city life. Dinner was served at noon and was the bigger meal of the day. Supper was served in the evening and was the lighter meal. This was opposite of what she was used to. She was happy to know that breakfast was the same here as it was in the city. It could range from large to small consisting of: pancakes, waffles, eggs, to a butter biscuit and cereal. If he hadn't communicated the difference of meals with her, he would've been sorely disappointed with her on the first day.

She made a menu for the first week. Rummaging through Kellan's refrigerator she found many foods she could use to put casseroles together. Some items would need to be bought at the store so she began making her grocery list. By the end of the week she should know what kind of foods

Kellan liked and disliked, and she'd be able to plan more meals around his preferred tastes.

Kylee glanced at her watch. It was close to ten o'clock and Kellan wasn't back. She decided to go to bed. When he did get home she didn't want to be awake giving him the impression that she had been waiting up for him. She left the grocery list on the counter but stuck the meal planner in her front jeans pocket. She walked around the house checking on the windows and the doors. She made sure all the windows were closed and the front door was locked. Halfway up the stairs to her room she realized she forgot to lock the back door. She walked back down the steps but saw that it was a screen door without a lock on it. Now what should she do?

She walked into the vestibule area feeling safer when she saw that all of these doors had locks on them. She locked them all without giving it a second thought. Sleepily, she walked back up the stairs to her room and changed into her pajamas which consisted of a pair of shorts and a camisole. Resting her head on the soft pillow she fell into a hard sleep. She didn't even hear Jake barking later indicating that his master was home.

Kellan noticed the house was dark when he pulled into the driveway. He had mixed feelings about it. He was relieved she hadn't waited up for him, not that he had expected her to. But a part of him wanted to see her before he went to bed. He parked his truck outside in the driveway. One of these days he would need to program the garage door code into his truck so he could park in the garage. Kellan removed the keys from the ignition, opened his truck door, and patted Jake on the head. "Hey, boy,"

Jake barked in response as if to say hi. Kellan walked tiredly to the door thinking about the events of the day. It had been an exciting and the best part was meeting Kylee. He had gone over to Charlie's, a long time friend he had grown up with. The usual gang was there tonight. They sat around drinking beer, played cards and played pool. He had fun hanging out with his friends, but tonight Kylee roamed through his mind a lot. He was concerned about her being here alone and hoped she was okay. He also hoped she kept her promise and that he wouldn't find her injured. He was a little anxious about this thought and admitted to himself this was why he came home earlier than most nights. One thing that had him smiling through the evening was her comment about cashews having smiles. He'd never look at a cashew the same way again.

As Kellan approached the door to the vestibule, he saw the kitchen windows had been closed. It was then he noticed the inner door behind the screen door in the vestibule was closed too. He cursed. Before he tried the door handle, he already knew the door was going to be locked.

Sure enough, the door knob didn't twist in his hand. "Hell," he muttered. Having to tell her not to lock the doors hadn't crossed his mind at all. He was so used to not having to lock a door he forgot not all people had the same thought process as he did. Of course, city people locked their doors all the time. In her defense, she probably thought he had a key, but around here he didn't lock many doors. He walked around to the front door but knew it was a vain attempt. Yep, it was locked, too. Second plan was the windows, but when he walked around the house, all the windows were closed and locked on the inside. He cursed out loud. Tonight would've been a great night to have been able to use the garage.

He walked around to the back of the house to see if he could get in through the back deck door, but it was locked as he knew it would be. Kellan looked up to Kylee's room and wondered if he threw rocks at her window if she'd wake up to unlock the door. He found some small gravel rocks not too big because he didn't want to break the window. He started throwing them at the window, but there was no answer from her. Now he was getting mad. He wished he had her cell phone number so he could call her. He noticed her window was open a crack which irritated him further. She made sure all the other windows were closed except hers! He supposed she felt safer since she was on the second floor. *Ugh, women!*

Kellan yelled her name in hopes to wake her, but still nothing. He did hope she wasn't hurt. Now this thought made him queasy. He had no choice, but to climb up to her window. It was relatively safe since the roof to it housed the pool shed. The shed's roof was flat. From there he could climb up to another part of the roof to reach her window. He had sneaked in and out of this window many times in his youthful days without his parents knowing. He pulled himself up onto the roof and carefully made his way to the window.

Kellan poked his head into the room and saw Kylee sleeping on the bed. He was relieved she was safe but irritated that she was such a deep sleeper. He whispered her name loudly through the screen so he didn't frighten her. He saw her stir in her sleep. He said her name again, but this time he didn't whisper it.

Kylee heard her name being called. She opened her eyes in the dark, propping her body up on her elbow. She heard her name again.

"Kylee," Kellan said much louder this time.

"Kellan?" Kylee asked in the dark, turning on the lamp on the bedside table. The light was dim.

"Yes. I'm at the window," Kellan instructed.

Kylee swung her feet over the side of the bed. She heard the irritation in his voice. At the window she saw Kellan looking tired and handsome. "What are you doing? What time is it?" She yawned.

Kellan took the screen off the window and raised the window higher so he could crawl in. His one long leg was in and he was squeezing the rest of his tall body through the window by the time she got there.

"You locked the damn doors on me!" Kellan declared angrily.

"I thought you had a key!" Kylee raised her voice in defense. "Who doesn't have a key to their own house?"

Kellan gave her an irritated look then asked in an exasperated voice, "Why do you *need* to lock the door?"

Kylee shrugged. She knew this wasn't an argument either one of them was going to win this late at night and watched him replace the screen in the window. Abruptly, he closed the window, slamming it shut. It shook the walls, and she jumped.

Out of the corner of his eye Kellan saw her jump at the unexpected loud noise. It didn't make sense to him that she was so skittish since she came from the city. The city was filled with lots of unpredictable loud noises. In fact, to Kellan's way of thinking, this was the only predictable thing about city life; it was loud.

"You're mad," Kylee observed loudly.

"I'm not mad; just tired and cranky," Kellan growled. He took a step her way and watched her step backwards toward the bed.

"Well, I'm not taking all the blame for this," Kylee hissed.

Kellan's eyebrows scrunched together in confusion. "I never said I blamed you."

Kylee continued speaking as if she hadn't heard him, "You could've let me know that I didn't need to lock the doors."

Kellan stood in silence giving her an odd look. He noticed the defying stance she took. Her feet were firmly planted apart, supporting the weight of her body straight up the middle, not leaning to any side at all, and her arms crossed over her chest.

Then she extended her right arm forward and pointed her index finger up at him. She spat out, "You should be so lucky to live in a world where people are honest and trusting and that you don't have to lock your doors at night."

Despite his crankiness Kellan found her outburst amusing and chuckled deeply.

"Kellan, you have no idea how lucky you are." Kylee's lip quivered. "You take this all for granted, you--." Emotional tears threatened to fall. Oh, the tears, how she hated to cry. She had no idea why she was so upset, other than the fact he was laughing at her. She abruptly turned her back to him so he couldn't see her tears, but he had.

Kellan saw the tears in her eyes before she turned her back on him. He stopped laughing, sighed softly and went to her. He hadn't meant to make her cry, but now that he did, he wanted to comfort her. He stood behind her inhaling her feminine scent, a sweet lavender smell. He rested his chin on top of her head and wrapped his arms around her, pulling her close.

Kylee was shocked at the sudden contact. At first she was wary of it but soon relaxed against his chest, breathing in the perfumed cologne he wore. She remembered the scent from earlier this evening when he rescued her from the fall, but the scent was sensual late in the night. She felt the need to touch Kellan but couldn't. Her arms were at her sides, trapped under his. Instead she reached her hands backwards, touching his thighs. Kellan thought he was going to come unglued when he felt her hands on him. He could feel the electricity shoot between them. He groaned inwardly pulling her tighter to him.

"I didn't mean to make you cry," Kellan whispered apologetically.

"And I didn't mean to cry," Kylee said.

Kellan chuckled softly thinking it was a strange comment to make. She moved her head sideways, her hair tickling his throat. He moved his head where it hovered above her ear. His lips moved softly over her ear as he whispered, "Ah, Sweet Girl,"

Kylee wasn't sure if it was the touch of his lips on her ear, or the words, or both, but it caused a flutter of excitement rippling through her. A wanton sigh escaped her when she felt his lips on the side of her neck. He trailed kisses down to her shoulder.

Kellan heard her sigh and knew she was enjoying his kisses. He nuzzled the back of her neck with his mouth, shedding hungry kisses onto her. He became lost in her sweet scent. The way she responded kindly to him, he could feel her desire. He swept the hair off of her shoulder exposing bare skin. He was hypnotized. He placed hungry kisses on one shoulder to the other shoulder stopping to feast on the back of her neck. Waves of pleasure rippled through her. She whimpered out a groan. He spun her around facing him. He kissed the base of her throat, inhaling her sensual scent. Her skin was tender against his hard mouth. Kellan wanted more of her taste, than he ever wanted from another woman. He looked into her heated eyes. He hesitated before planting his mouth hungrily onto hers.

Kellan knew he couldn't go any further than this. He knew that if he took her by the mouth branding her with his kiss there would be no turning back. He already knew he wouldn't be able to stop with just one kiss, she was too mesmerizing.

Kylee felt his hesitation and wished she didn't want him to kiss her as much as she did. She wanted to feel his fierce hard lips on her mouth, kissing her, the same way he did on her neck. Sensing that the moment was gone Kylee pushed against him. Kellan gripped her shoulders with his hot hands. He looked at her, contemplating his next move. He wanted nothing more than to sink his mouth over hers, sampling her luscious pink lips. Now wasn't the time. She was his employee.

"No. I-we can't," Kellan whispered in a raspy voice. He abruptly let go of her.

The next thing Kylee heard was his brash foot steps on the stairs. Then she heard her bedroom door close loudly on his exit. It was quiet again. She got back into bed her feelings and thoughts confused about what had just happened between Kellan and her. She turned off the bedside lamp, it instantly became dark. She placed a hand over her beating heart and wondered if it would ever beat normal again. She hadn't expected to feel such an intense heat in his arms, nor the sudden fiery passion his touch had ignited burning deep within her. She groaned into the pillow wondering how she was going to face her employer in the morning.

Kylee wasn't the only one shaken up by what happened between them. Kellan was, too. He liked having Kylee in his arms way too much. He frowned at his reflection in the mirror. He had to keep in mind, he was her employer and not to mix the business relationship with any other feelings he might have for her. Maybe he should visit Trina, a girl in town, who was all too eager to have him in her bed whenever possible. Kellan took in a deep sigh, exhaling slowly. He didn't think he'd be satisfied with the visit. He hadn't even tasted Kylee's lips and already he was imagining her kiss to be the sweetest ever. He was restless. He fell into bed wondering how he was going to face his employee in the morning.

"Damn," he muttered. He was frustrated laying in his bed thinking about the blonde haired beauty sleeping under his roof. He hoped she was as miserable as he was. He wondered if his heartbeat would ever return to normal again. Sleep finally found him.

Chapter Three

Kylee woke up to the sound of the screen door banging shut. Sitting straight up in the bed she yawned remembering where she was. Sleep finally managed to find her the night before, but she felt far from rested. Her dreams had been erotic which explained why she was tangled in her sheets.

She got up, remade the bed then headed to the bathroom to shower and throw on a pair of jeans and a shirt. She was thankful she had her own room with a private bathroom. The thought of having to share the upstairs bathroom with Kellan left her blushing. That certainly would have been awkward, especially after last night. However, she pegged Kellan to be a man of integrity who cherished his own space, too. She suspected the person, Kellan originally thought he had hired, would have had this room, too. She fidgeted around the room, tidying up the best she could. She delayed the inevitable for as long as possible and then took a deep breath summoning the courage to finally face him. *He's my employer*, she drummed in her mind.

When she entered the kitchen he was nowhere in sight, but she did notice the filled coffee pot on the counter. The aroma of cinnamon filled the air. Next to the coffee maker sat a clean empty cup. Kylee smiled over Kellan's consideration in leaving it within her reach. After pouring some for herself she took a sip of coffee tasting cinnamon and vanilla. She turned around to see a ladder leaning against the cabinets. His kindness tugged on her heartstrings. First it was the coffee cup and now the ladder. Of course, the ladder was his subtle way of telling her that he didn't want a repeat of yesterday, reminding her of how safety was a concern of his. It was nice having a man care about her safety who didn't want to see her get hurt.

A year ago it hadn't been the case, but she wasn't dwelling on that now. This job had been a godsend and she wasn't going to let anything ruin this opportunity, not even her sad memories. In her heart, Kylee knew she was safe and knew Kellan would be a good employer. She had found this out yesterday when he had kindly helped her and the cat, showing his compassionate side. Her mind wandered to the cat, and she hoped it was okay. She would have to ask Kellan if he'd heard from his veterinarian friend about the cat.

The house was quiet, but this time she sensed Kellan wasn't inside. She looked outside but didn't find the rusty brown truck in the driveway. She had mixed feelings about him being gone. First, she was disappointed that she didn't get to see him. Second, she was relieved that she didn't have to face him. Third, she was irritated that he was no where to be found. She needed directions into town to buy groceries. She looked around for the grocery list she had made last night but couldn't find it. She thought for sure she had left it on the counter. She let out a frustrated sigh but decided not to dwell on it right now. When she saw Kellan she would need to ask him what he wanted her to cook, and she'd make a new list.

Unable to sit and do nothing, she decided to get started on the cleaning. Her first focus was to clean each of the five rooms from top to bottom, corner to corner. She was about to head upstairs to one of the rooms; instead she passed the stairs, walking past the living room and into the fifth room that needed to be re-done. She couldn't explain it, but she was drawn to this room and couldn't wait to get it cleaned. This was going to be the first room she did. She looked out into the backyard. Out one window was the view of the swimming pool, and out the other window she saw apple trees. If she arranged the furniture correctly she could position a couple of chairs near the windows. Turned just right, the person sitting in the chair could view the apple trees. Watching the apple trees throughout the different seasons would be neat to see. They'd be dormant through the winter, but in spring their blossoms would be beautiful. During the summer they would grow until they were ready to be picked in autumn. *My, how relaxing this would be.* She sighed happily. She didn't know what else to call this room, except for the sitting room. With that in mind, this would be her main focus for this room.

Homemade apple pies danced in her head, and her stomach gave a hungry rumble. Despite her hunger she continued her assessment of the room. The east wall faced the pool. She wondered if Kellan ever thought about putting in French doors, and building an adjoining deck connecting with the current one that wrapped around the pool. This way when their kids were swimming in the pool there would be easy access to it from the house. Her eyebrows scrunched together at how her mind said "their kids". For a split second had she pictured their kids swimming? No, no, no. This was a ridiculous thought, but her heart skipped several beats, as she saw herself standing by the window pregnant. *Oh, for crying out loud!* She scolded herself shaking her head to free these thoughts.

"Time to get to work," she said, ignoring the hungry grumbling of her stomach but when she walked through the kitchen she saw a cookie jar on the counter. Opening the lid she saw homemade chocolate chip cookies in it! She grabbed three to satisfy her hunger. In one of the hall closets she found the dusters, vacuum cleaner, disinfectant sprays, polishing cleaners, and old rags.

Kylee ran the vacuum cleaner over the traffic patterns on the main level before pushing it into the other room. At this time she didn't bother moving the furniture away from the walls knowing it would be moved at a later date. Now her main focus was light cleaning. It had been awhile since any of the rooms had been cleaned. She felt better when this was done. She was one step closer to making this house shine again.

Glancing down at her watch she noted this task had taken her a shorter time than she had expected it would. She was eager to start moving furniture in the sitting room. She shoved a heavy dark cherry wood desk into the middle of the room away from the wall. There were two raggedy old bean bags lying on the dusty floor. Who still had bean bags? Did Kellan even know he still had them? Cringing she picked them up, sneezing as a cloud of dust filled the air. She tried not to think about how many dust mites were living inside the bags as she carried them to the garbage cans.

She worked diligently on this room. She swept the hardwood floor. Using the ladder Kellan set out for her, she swept the cobwebs off the ceiling. Then she found some old rags and a pail. She filled the pail with water. Next she got down on her hands and knees and washed away the dirt and dust stuck to the hardwood floor. She grimaced when she thought about all the hard work that lay ahead of her. In the end she knew it was going to sparkle, and that always made her feel proud.

Kylee scrubbed part of the floor before taking a break. She picked up the pail of dirty water and headed to the kitchen. While dumping the water into the sink there was loud noise behind her. Suddenly she heard the squeaking hinges of the back door opening and then banging shut accompanied by heavy footsteps. It sounded like gunfire! It made her whole body jump.

"City Girl, I don't understand why you're so jumpy with loud noises," Kellan gruffly commented after he saw her jump.

Kylee rolled her eyes thinking *if he only knew… If he did know what would he say?* She finished emptying the water pail, filled it again, and then she set it on the counter. Turning around she saw him holding grocery bags.

"You went to the store."

"You think?" Kellan's voice dripped with sarcasm.

"You're being an ass," she said to him.

"Yes." He hadn't planned on being a jerk, but the way she leaped scared to death when he walked in irritated him. Right now being a jerk seemed to be the best way to avoid talking about what happened in her room last night. Taking his cue, she was curt with her words to him. Maybe this was the best way for the two of them to muddle through what happened last night, acting as though nothing happened. That was fine with her. Instead she said, "Thanks for the ladder."

He gave her a short nod. "You're welcome. I'll bring the rest of the bags in."

Kylee took the water back to the sitting room then returned to the kitchen after Kellan brought in more grocery bags. She stood in the doorway while he began putting things away. Sensing that she was behind him he looked her way. He tossed her a head of lettuce saying, "Might as well learn where things go."

"Well, this city girl puts lettuce in the refrigerator; what about you Country Boy? Where do you store your lettuce?" She raised her eyebrow at him, tossing him a saucy grin.

He paused. His dark eyes narrowed. He took one intimidating step towards her as she took one step back. An excited sensation swirled through her as he backed her up against the refrigerator door. Being this close to her he felt a heated rush and inhaling her sweet scent was sending him over the edge.

Not sure what to do with the closeness between them and to steady her own body, she placed one hand on his chest. He felt her hand on him and misread the gesture. He thought she was trying to push him back. He grinned knowing that if he pursued her, she wouldn't have the strength to hold him back, but this wasn't how he wanted her. He wanted her to come willingly to him. When the time was right she wouldn't be pushing him away. She'd be ready to want his kisses and much more. However, this wasn't the time, and she wasn't ready.

In an effort to keep a good distance between them he mocked her, "City Girl." His eyebrows arched. "Country boys keep it in the same place."

As quickly as he had stepped into her comfort zone he stepped out of it. His eyes held warning as he left her standing on unsteady legs. She tightly gripped the refrigerator door handle to keep from falling. Somehow they managed to work together putting away the groceries ridiculing each other on the different places the other one put things. Kellan put cheese slices and sandwich meat on the shelf in the refrigerator, and Kylee put these items in the drawer. Kellan put the bread in the refrigerator while Kylee kept it out of the refrigerator setting it on the counter. The nit picking had been a good way to get rid of the tension between them. After the groceries had been put away Kylee made them sandwiches and asked Kellan if he had heard any updates about the cat.

"Oh, yeah, I forgot about the cat. Let me send Rick a text."

Kellan removed the cell phone from the clip on his belt. His shirt lifted up exposing his bare skin. It caught Kylee's eye, and she stared at his tanned flesh. Her mouth watered thinking how smooth his skin would feel against her lips. She wanted to kiss every inch of him. Kellan was all too aware of her eyes on him, and he was amused by her reaction.

"Like what you see?" Kellan asked with a smug smile on his face.

Kylee cleared her throat nervously feeling herself blushing again. Quickly she pulled her eyes away from his torso. She turned her back on him and continued making the sandwiches.

"If you want to see more of me it can be arranged, you know," Kellan whispered seductively behind her. He saw her inhale a deep breath of air.

"Do you want to touch me, sweet City Girl?" his rich baritone voice had an unusual affect on her. He was weakening her senses. She felt herself melting like butter in his heated atmosphere.

"Not today," Kylee fibbed. The truth was she wanted him to touch her everywhere on her body. She thought about his hands roaming all over her. She wanted to touch him, too. She wanted to feel his powerful muscles beneath her body. She could show this country boy just how good sex could be with a city girl. *Stop! Kellan is your employer*, she reminded herself. *I cannot cross that line. I cannot give in to the sexual cravings I'm having. I just can't!*

Kellan let out a wicked laugh as he stepped away from her. He could feel the heat between them. He had felt her scorching gaze on his skin. She hadn't even touched him, and he had been aroused, but now was not the time.

"Liar, liar," Kellan sang out. His eyes teased her with the beginning of a song from his childhood.

"My pants are on fire," Kylee finished reciting. Her face flamed when she realized how Kellan interpreted the meaning of the words she just sang. Kellan's eyes shot up in surprise, a devilish smile spread across his attractive face. His eyes scanned her body up and down playfully before resting a lingering look on her eyes. She could see his excitement about the fire inside her jeans.

"They are, aren't they sweet City Girl," Kellan teased her in a quiet, low raspy whisper that had her feeling weaker. His voice piqued all of her womanly senses sending her reproductive system sky rocketing to the heavens that lay low in her belly. Kylee gripped the corner of the counter top to keep herself from sinking to the floor.

Kellan stood close behind her as he whispered in her ear, "Mine are."

Kylee made an attempt to move away but her steps faltered. She might have fallen if it hadn't been for Kellan's strong hands gripping her shoulders.

"Whoa. Easy." They both felt the heated rush between them when he touched her. Kylee could feel his rock hard body on her backside. He smelled good and she might have enjoyed being in his arms more if it wasn't for the fact that he was chuckling in her ear. Kylee stepped away from him throwing him an annoyed look. She picked up her plate trying to decide whether she should stay in the kitchen with Kellan or flee from him.

Kellan mimicked her move by picking up his own plate but walked over to the kitchen table hoping she would follow him. He was shaken up, too, by what had just happened. It had surprised him that he had that powerful affect on her. Instead of leaving it alone he teased her about it only to cause himself to be uncomfortable as well. When he had hauled her up against his body, he was sure she had felt his desire for her. He'd never experienced an intense fire for a woman he had barely touched. Nor had he ever had the pleasure of making a woman literally weak in the knees. It felt wonderful having her against him.

"No, don't go," Kellan said when it looked like she was about to leave the room. "Stay. Sit. I'll behave, I promise," he begged. There was something in his voice that had her staying in the kitchen. It was almost as if he couldn't bear to see her leave. She sat down across the table from him taking a bite out of her sandwich.

"I guess it'll be okay as long as I don't invite you to eat me," Kylee teased him. He stopped chewing, swallowing the remainder of his food in a cough.

"What?" He asked his eyes wide in surprise.

Kylee gave him an unruly grin. This time it was her turn to laugh at him. Kellan shook his head with a rueful smile. It pleased him that she teased him back. He was happy he asked her to sit with him instead of letting her flee into the next room.

"Careful," Kellan warned her. "I haven't had dessert yet and you do look good enough to eat."

"I am, but you promised to behave." She threw him a seductive smile. It had him squirming in his seat. A triumphant smile stretched across her pretty face. *Ha! Two can play this game.* For some reason she trusted he would keep his word about behaving and felt safe with the table between them. However, if she could have read his thoughts she wouldn't have been so trusting.

His phone beeped indicating he received a text. Kylee watched him read it. Kellan typed back "thank you" in all caps. Rick had no idea how thankful he was to be distracted from their flirting.

"The cat lives," Kellan announced with a huge smile on his face.

"That is really great." Kylee breathed a sigh of relief. "I was worried how I might have killed it."

"Nah, baby I told you that cat had at least six lives left."

Kylee caught the term of endearment 'baby' roll off his tongue. It made her heart flutter, but Kellan didn't seem to notice what he said. He continued as though calling her baby was the most natural way for him to address her. She acted as natural as she could on the outside, but on the inside she was giddy.

"Rick says the cat had no broken bones or internal bleeding but continues to improve its strength and has started eating."

"That's amazing! Thank you for checking on it." Kylee gave him a radiating smile.

"You're welcome," Kellan said. He was in awe of her beautiful smile, and he was very impressed with her. With the slip of his tongue he affectionately called her baby and yet, she made no ill face. She accepted it as though it was the most natural thing in the world he could have said to her. It caused a heated sensation rippling through him.

After they ate, Kellan left the house and Kylee went back to cleaning the sitting room. They both stayed busy in the afternoon and managed to avoid each other that evening. Kylee ate supper alone in the kitchen then retired early to her bedroom before Kellan came home. This time she didn't lock the back door, but instead locked the door to her bedroom since her room would be chosen first should there be an intruder.

Kellan parked his truck in a field near his house and sat watching each of the lights being turned off throughout the house. He knew it was silly to avoid her this evening, but he didn't know what else to do. The close contact of the night before and earlier today had him feeling weak. He had to keep his distance from her as much as possible. Tomorrow would be better he thought. He'd wake up at dawn and head out to the fields before she woke up. At noon, Evan would be joining them, so they won't be alone. Tomorrow night he might wait again until she went to bed before coming into the house. Then repeat these steps on the next day. He felt better knowing he had a plan to avoid her for awhile. He was fairly confident it was a good plan but couldn't help the nagging feeling telling him it wasn't a good plan.

Chapter Four

Kellan's plan to avoid Kylee worked for a few days but then all of a sudden it didn't. In the beginning, Kellan was up early in the mornings and out the door before he had to see Kylee. At dinner he got to see her but he wasn't alone with her since Evan joined them for the meal. Without Evan's knowledge, Kellan thought of Evan as a good chaperone for him and Kylee. With Evan around the two of them were able to stay out of each other's line of fire. However, they couldn't avoid the silent spark between them when their fingers touched when passing the food or when their hips touched when they walked past each other.

Conversation flowed well between the three of them making the meal time pass quickly, too fast as far as Kellan was concerned. Evan asked Kylee a lot of questions to find out more about her. Where did she grow up, any siblings, college, places she lived, favorite jobs, etc. Kellan noticed she pleasantly answered his questions but carefully sidestepped with her answers when asked about the people she's met along the way and her childhood. Kellan noticed the quick clouds of sadness that covered her face. It left him wondering.

Kylee reciprocated by asking both of them fact finding questions similar to the ones Evan had asked. After a few days of noon conversations Kellan couldn't help noticing Kylee seemed more at ease with Evan than she was with him. This bothered him. The growing friendship between Kylee and Evan was stirring up jealous feelings and he knew he had himself to blame. If he hadn't been so intent on avoiding her she might have started to relax in his company. Kellan admitted that maybe his plan to stay away from Kylee in the evenings hadn't been such a good one after all.

Kellan stepped out of his old dusty farm truck smiling as Jake ran over to him with a happy bark. He patted him on the head. He loved how his dog greeted him every time he came home. Jake was definitely this man's best friend. The dog whined out a greeting as he nuzzled his wet nose in the palm of Kellan's large hand.

"Are you ready to watch some baseball tonight?" He asked. Jake let out a deep bark as if answering yes to the question. The sun hadn't even begun to set in the horizon. There was still enough daylight left to maybe sit on the porch after his shower relax and drink a beer before the ball game started. Oh, how he had been missing his routine. He was glad now that he had decided to come home early today instead of staying away like all the other nights.

Kellan let his mind wander about how it would feel coming home to the waiting arms of a loving woman. He had never thought much about spending his life with a wife. However, recently the thought of having a woman to hold lovingly in his arms, and return his love didn't feel like a noose around his neck. The possibility of having a woman waiting for him to come home to was a new idea. An image of Kylee's pretty face entered his thoughts. *Gosh, I never thought about this kind of future before Kylee came along.* He gave a thoughtful sigh as he lifted the hat off his head and ran his fingers through his sweaty hair.

He stood outside the door trying to gather enough courage to go inside and face the woman who was keeping him away. He chided himself for not being brave enough to conquer his fears of spending time alone with her. He was starting to feel like a stranger in his own house. *It was his house, not hers!* Even though it was Kylee's hard work that was making his house look good again. She was turning it into something worth coming home to…something HE should be coming home to. He was now convinced this house was big enough for the two of them to roam in without having to see each other. With this bit of courage he took off his dirty boots setting them on the rubber mat. Opening the door he stepped inside, colliding with Kylee. Letting out a terrifying scream the papers she had in her hands went flying. Her arms shot up in the air, and her fists came down landing hard on his shoulders. Kylee's eyes were closed when she felt strong hands catching hers, and she let out another ear piercing scream.

"Damn it," Kellan swore. She scared him, too, but evidently not as much as he had her. He hated how he had frightened her as he felt her body tense. At the sound of Kellan's gruff voice Kylee's eyes flew open full of fear. When she recognized Kellan her expression changed to irritation.

"Kellan!" Kylee shrieked. Seeing it was him she relaxed a little but her eyes held venom. "You scared the hell out of me!" Kylee screamed and tried to back away from him, but she couldn't because he still held her arms.

"Let go of me," she hissed through clenched teeth. Kellan didn't want to but reluctantly he did.

"What are you doing here?!" she asked her eyes filled with annoyance. She bent down to pick up the papers that fell to the floor. Kellan helped her. She reached out to grab the pieces of paper he had picked up but he held them up high from her.

"I live here. Remember?" Kellan answered. His own voice held a hint of irritation.

"You're early. Normally you don't get home until after dark," Kylee accused him and started back up the stairs.

Kellan followed her. She had him there, but he had no good excuse that he wanted to give her. He sighed heavily collapsing into the kitchen chair as he said, "I'm tired tonight."

Kylee turned around to look at him. His answer didn't make any sense to her, but she did see the exhaustion on his face. His shoulders slumped wearily. Of course, he was tired from a long day in the hot sun. She wasn't exactly sure what Kellan did all day, but she was confident that he did more than just sit on a tractor since his body was both lean and muscular. The last thing he needed was her screaming at him.

Kylee found herself in an old familiar situation.

"I'm sorry," Kylee apologized in a frantic voice.

"For what," Kellan said absently. He didn't look up from the piece of paper in his hand that he was reading.

"For screaming at you," she explained in a fearful voice. She held her breath waiting for him to yell at her. But he didn't. She took a deep breath waiting for him to hit her. But he didn't. Her heart screamed to her brain how this man wasn't going to hurt her. Unfortunately, it was the memory of Thomas that had her panicking and taking the blame. Everything that had happened was her fault. She should've been paying attention more closely when she heard the dog barking outside.

Kellan swung his head up from the paper he had been reading. He heard the shakiness in her voice. He stared at her in disbelief, her fearful eyes cautiously watching him. *What the hell? Why does she look so scared? And, why on earth is she apologizing to me?*

Kylee swallowed nervously as his blue eyes brooded black and she feared the worst. She had angered him. Now what was she going to do?

"Let me get you some supper," she said timidly opening the refrigerator door. She looked inside for something she could use to defend herself with and found a bottle of hot sauce along with some containers that had food leftover from the other meals. She would get this ready for him right now.

Kellan sat quietly at the table watching her. It was clear to him that she was nervous and it had everything to do with him scaring her when he came in. He watched her as she was careful not to turn her back on him and kept the hot sauce within reach of her at all times. He wanted to get up and help her but he feared that if he got too close she'd use the hot sauce as a weapon on him. He felt he had to tread lightly.

"I don't know what we'd do without a microwave," Kylee said in an attempt to make light conversation with him. When he only nodded in silence he watched her fidget with the hand towel. She fidgeted like a cat on a hot tin roof. It tore at his heart to see her like this. He didn't understand her actions but knew he had to ease her worry...whatever the worry was that covered her beautiful face.

"Kylee, there is no need for you to apologize for screaming when the simple truth is I scared the hell out of you. It was my fault for changing the routine and I'm so sorry for scaring you."

The eyes that looked at her were soft and apologetic. Kylee stopped her fidgeting as she absorbed his kind words. Tears pricked her eyes. He was apologizing to her. In the past it wouldn't have mattered if it was her fault or not she would've been punished. Again she knew in her heart that Kellan was different.

"And, Kylee if you're planning on putting hot sauce on my food please don't," Kellan begged, his eyes softly teasing hers.

Kylee gave him a startled look not realizing that he had noticed her weapon of choice and was making light of the situation. She put it back into the refrigerator, because she knew Kellan wasn't going to hurt her.

"Besides, you're cooking doesn't need any hot sauce. It's great just the way it is." Kellan complimented her and was happy to see her mouth turn upward into a small smile. He saw that she was beginning to relax and this pleased him. He couldn't help feeling that there was a part of Kylee's past that held dark shadows, and this saddened him greatly. He was starting to feel protective of her and wanted to shield her from all harm.

"You really like my cooking?" she asked astonished.

"Yes," Kellan stated simply.

The microwave beeped signaling the food was ready. She looked more at ease when she brought him the plate. He thanked her. Kellan was grateful to eat heated up leftovers versus the frozen dinner he would've had. Much to his pleasant surprise she boldly sat down across from him. This was a huge step compared to three minutes ago when she was armed and ready with hot sauce. He loved that she wanted to sit with him.

"What's this?" Kellan asked her as he slid the paper over to her.

"A menu," Kylee answered hesitantly. "It's easier for me to write out a planned menu for the week. This way I know what I need to buy at the store."

Kellan gave her a warm smile after she explained.

"That's a great idea! It's a smart way to do your shopping," he praised her and noticed the faint blush on her cheeks.

"Kellan,"

He liked the way his name rolled off her lips like a sweet melody of music he was listening to. He wanted to hear her say his name again. When he looked at her expectantly she asked her question.

"Is there anything specific you want me to cook for you and Evan?" Kylee's sky blue eyes met his.

Caught off guard by her question he shrugged. "I don't think so. I know Evan's thrilled with your cooking." A jealous nerve caught a hold of him when she smiled knowing Evan was happy with her cooking.

"Although, Evan doesn't get a say in what you cook, I do," Kellan said harshly. Her smile faded, and he could have kicked himself for making it disappear. He needed to get his feelings in check. So far she hadn't made any indication that she liked Evan, but if she did now was a good time to find out.

"That's true. This is why I'm asking you," Kylee retorted.

It brought a smile to Kellan's face. He loved her spunk and how well she stood her ground with him. Most women would've laughed just to appease him but not Kylee. She was different. He appreciated her sense of humor and genuine laugh.

"You're sure you don't have any special requests?" Kylee asked him.

His eyes swiftly raked over her body with a hungry look and it made her blush.

All he could think about for his special request was her! From her head to her toes he wanted to feast on her. He wanted to see, feel, and taste every inch of her beautiful body. His path of kisses would start with her luscious lips trailing down her neck to her breasts. He would continue on kissing her belly then slide those kisses further down her front side to…In his mind he trailed off feeling a jolt in his groin. He cleared his throat bringing himself out of his fantasy. He tore his hungry gaze off her face and looked down at his plate of food. He was slightly embarrassed by his wandering thoughts.

When he looked up again his face was somber. Kylee was relieved to see he no longer gave her a bon appetite look. For a moment she thought he was thinking she could've been his main course. *Would that have been so bad?*

"Kylee you're a wonderful cook. Everything you've made so far has been great. Both Evan and I feel like kings after we walk out of here with all your good cookin'."

Kylee smiled widely over his compliment and blushed. It amazed Kellan to know that he had made her blush so easily with his high praise when it came to her cooking. He wondered what other ways he could make her blush. Kellan followed Kylee as she took her plate to the sink. He stepped closer to her. He could smell her sweet aroma. She twirled around to face him placing her hands behind her on the counter. He was close enough to touch her. He wanted to, and he could see it in her eyes that she wanted it, too. Kellan reached out his hand to her cheek touching it ever so lightly as his rough knuckles grazed her soft skin. He uncurled his fingers so that his whole palm gently cupped the side of her face. He felt her lean into his warm hand. His eyes gazed intently into hers, and he saw the longing look in her blue eyes. The electricity crackled between them.

"Kylee, pretty much anything you put in front of me I'll eat," Kellan said to her his playful eyes hanging hungrily over her scrumptious body. She knew he wasn't thinking about food anymore. She squirmed beneath his intense gaze that stayed on her making her blush again. Kellan was happy knowing he found another way to color her cheeks pink. He looked her over loving how her jeans wrapped nicely around her slender figure and loved the way her pink shirt curved in perfection over her round breasts. He stiffened below his waist as he thought about his hands on her hips helping guide her down on top of him giving her the ride of her life. Oh, he knew they would be good in bed together!

Kylee caught Kellan's satisfactory smile while he slid his eyes sexually over her body. He gave her a look that told her he thought she was good enough to eat. Frozen in place, she wished he would just kiss her so she could taste and feel his lips. She heard a car horn honking in the distance, but she was far more focused on the magnetic force that was pulling them closer. Kylee could hear Kellan's ragged breath, and she was sure he could hear hers, too. They were inches away when Kylee parted her lips ready for Kellan to take them in his mouth. Suddenly there was a loud commotion of barking, voices, and footsteps coming through the screen door. Kylee jumped back just in time as happy chattering voices entered. She pushed on Kellan's chest, and he reluctantly pulled back. He muttered a curse then heard. "Uncle Kellan!"

Kellan turned in time to see his five year old twin nephews running towards him their arms outstretched ready for a hug. They both reached him at the same time hugging him around the waist. As Kellan wrapped his long arms around them he tried not to interpret the interruption as a sign that he wasn't supposed to be kissing Kylee. Despite his disappointment of not being able to kiss her, he was happy to see his nephews.

"Oh my, gosh, you guys grew an inch since the last time I saw you!" Kellan exclaimed. He looked around the kitchen noticing how Kylee had disappeared. He was disappointed.

"Where's your mom?" Kellan asked the boys.

"Here I am!" Kellan heard his sister's voice coming in through the door.

"Hey, Sis,"

"Hey, Kell," his sister Mary came in with her arms full of dishes.

Kellan whistled through his teeth. "Holy sh—crap!" He changed his word when Mary hissed at him because the kids were around.

"Mom, we know what word Uncle Kellan was going to say," one of the twins said.

"Yeah, we've heard the word before," the other twin piped in proudly.

"Yeah, mom," Kellan chimed in teasing his sister.

"Hush. No more talk about it," his sister replied.

"So what did you guys bring me?" Kellan asked helping change the subject.

"Cookies, cake and a pie," the twins told him at the same time.

Kellan ruffled their sandy brown hair. "Thanks, guys."

"We are headed over to the lake tomorrow for a mini vacation. You're welcome to join us on the weekend," Mary offered.

Kellan rubbed the back of his neck. "Yeah, I don't know. I'll see."

"How's the new housekeeper working out?" his sister asked.

"Good," Kellan replied.

"Good. Glad things are working out. The house looks great," Mary commented stepping into the dining room, then living room, then gasped when she entered the back room overlooking the apple trees. "Oh gosh, Kellan, this room is beautiful!" Mary exclaimed. "I don't think I ever remember this room being so fixed up."

"Me neither. Only in pictures when it was Grandpa and Grandma's house," Kellan commented. He hadn't realized just how much work Kylee had been doing since she got here. This was one of the things he should've been coming home to notice instead of staying away and running himself ragged.

"Oh. How wonderful it would be to sit and have coffee here in the morning watching the sunrise." Mary had a dreamy look on her face as she ran her hands over the back of the chair. She laughed as she said, "Sit and drink coffee. Now where on earth would I find the time to do that?"

"This new housekeeper of yours is really cleaning up the place, isn't he?" Mary said as she made her way back to the kitchen to collect her purse.

"Yeah, doing a good job," Kellan agreed, paying no attention to the fact that his sister referred to the housekeeper as a he. His thoughts were still on Kylee.

"Well, Kell. We gotta get going. I've still got things to pack up, but I wanted to bring these over to you before we left," his sister said to him. She walked over to her brother and hugged him. "If you don't come out to the lake don't work too hard."

Then she turned to the boys and said, "Okay time to go. Last one with their seatbelt on is a rotten egg."

"It won't be me! Bye, Uncle Kellan!" His nephews quickly gave him a hug as they raced out the door.

"Have fun and thanks for the cookies and stuff," Kellan bid them a farewell.

"You're welcome!" she sang out. "I figured with mom and Linda gone you might be getting low on your sweets intake." His sister laughed merrily.

Oh, how little does Mary know about my new sugar high, and it has nothing to do with food.

"Oh, and if you do decide to come out to the lake you're welcome to bring your housekeeper. There will be plenty of single women there for you guys to flirt with."

Her remark about "you guys" staggered his mind as he waved Mary good-bye. Kellan then laughed out loud watching her drive away remembering that his family still was under the impression he had hired a man to help him with the house. Well, when his mom and Linda returned from vacation he'd have to introduce them to "Kyle". He laughed viciously, trying to envision the "Oh-oh" look on Linda, his other sister's face when she met Kylee after mistakenly writing down the name "Kyle".

Kellan grabbed a handful of cookies and went in search of Kylee.

Chapter Five

Kellan was having a hard time concentrating this morning. His mind was preoccupied with the almost kiss he and Kylee had come close to sharing yesterday. Having come so close to feeling her soft lips was driving him crazy. It was consuming his every thought.

After his sister left last night he found Kylee cleaning upstairs. He had offered her one of the chocolate chip cookies Mary had made. She accepted it but kept her distance from him. He made small talk with her about cookies and found they both shared a love for chocolate chip and peanut butter cookies. Kellan made a mental note to ask his mom to make them some when she returned home.

Kellan complimented her on how great the house was looking. His stomach flipped when her face brightened with a big smile letting him know how she appreciated him noticing. He then told her his sister Mary liked the changes, too. She smiled but not as much as when he had praised her. Silently, he stood in the doorway watching her work wishing there could've been more conversation. Sensing that she wanted to keep cleaning he left her alone and headed downstairs to watch the baseball game.

He sprawled out on the couch with Jake lying on the floor by him and thought this was almost perfect. The only way it would have been better is if Kylee was next to him resting her head in the crook of his arm. He thought about how strange it was to feel this way when only a few weeks ago, before he met Kylee, this was the perfect life for him. He must have fallen asleep because he woke up in the middle of the night to an infomercial on TV and a blanket over him. He was touched by her thoughtfulness.

Kellan had missed seeing Kylee this morning. He waited as long as he could in the kitchen for her, but she didn't come in. Reluctantly, he had to leave and now this whole morning she haunted his thoughts. Kellan pulled his tractor up near Evan signaling for him to stop.

"Hey man. I'm heading in with the tractor. I think it needs oil," Kellan told his friend.

Evan nodded knowing full well the tractor didn't need oil. It had just been serviced, but he didn't mention it. "Okay. If you don't mind I'm going to do a few more rows."

Evan watched Kellan drive off slowly in the tractor. He suspected that Kellan heading in early had nothing to do with the tractor needing anything, but everything to do with the new housekeeper he had hired.

"See you in a few." Kellan waved. He was looking forward to having a chance to talk with Kylee before Evan came in. He shifted the tractor into a faster gear. Halfway home he was thinking that maybe he should've driven the truck home leaving Evan to drive the tractor back to the house. Kellan grinned mischievously thinking he would have definitely had a lot more time with Kylee.

He knocked his boots against the tractor tire shaking off the excess dirt. Jake barked out a greeting and ran over to him. Kellan was whistling when he opened the back door leading into the kitchen, bounding up the stairs with his heavy boots. Out of habit he let the back door slam shut behind him and entered the kitchen. With his boots thundering on the stairs and the echo of the slamming door, he saw Kylee's whole body jump in extreme fright. She let out a scream that startled him. His good mood vanished and was replaced with irritation, and he gave her hell for it.

"Damn it, Kylee," he swore out his annoyance then immediately was sorry that he yelled when her face puckered up with fear. With a softer tone he said, "I don't understand why you jump all the time to loud noises."

"I don't understand why you have to let the door bang shut," Kylee retorted with anger both in her voice and eyes.

"It's habit," Kellan said matter-of-factly.

"Maybe you like seeing me scared," Kylee shot back at him. "Some men are like that."

"No. I don't like seeing you scared." He scowled wondering how she could think that he liked scaring her. "In fact, it pisses me off the way you act like a scared skittish cat at every loud noise around here from the screen door to heavy boots walking on the floor to the car horns outside." Kellan glared at her.

His irritation was written all over his hard face enhancing his rugged exterior. It was intimidating and she was thankful for the island between them. He gave a frustrated sigh and lifted the hat off his head with one hand; ruffling his sandy hair with the other. Her eyes were fixated on the long fingers that raked through his hair, and in this moment the anger and fear she had vanished. It was replaced by an aroused heat flaming through her. She wanted to feel those strong fingers in her hair pulling her face close to his for a kiss. Feeling she was watching him, he slid his eyes in her direction. He saw a yearning in her blue eyes and a desire for her slid through him. They both felt the tension in the air between them rapidly change from great annoyance to a sexual heat. No longer in control, they each gave in to the magnetic force that was pulling them together. Kellan wasn't sure how it happened but all of a sudden he was standing in front of her feeling very tall and hoped he didn't frighten her. This time she didn't move away from him, instead she stepped closer.

He could feel the intense heat of her eyes as she watched his hands touch her arms, then shoulders, tightening his hold on her, hoping she didn't change her mind and try to move away from him. He ran his calloused fingers up her neck slowly taking in the softness of her skin. A pink flush covered her face, and he heard her slow, ragged breath then saw the parting of her lips inviting him to kiss her. He cupped her chin between his hands tipping her face up, tracing his thumb over her lips, teasing him with how delicious her lips would taste.

Kellan lingered his mouth above hers briefly basking in her sweet fragrance before he tenderly touched his lips to hers. He rubbed his lips ever so lovingly over hers as though he was getting acquainted with her mouth. It was driving Kylee insane. She wanted him so much. She didn't realize how much she needed to taste him. Why was he being so gentle with her? She felt cherished but it was driving her crazy!

Her insides quaked and she just wanted to smash her mouth into his so she could taste him and satisfy those dreams that tormented her at night of his ghostly kisses. Just when she thought she couldn't stand having his lips whisper over hers anymore he finally wrapped his mouth over hers. Their first kiss was slow, sweet, and sensuous. Kellan enjoyed soaking in her tantalizing flavor just before he overlapped his mouth on hers again in a deep satiated kiss. Kylee moved her lips with his, welcoming the rich exquisite taste of him.

Their dreams hadn't disappointed them!

Kylee's arms slid around Kellan's neck pulling him closer. She didn't want him to stop kissing her, but the sound of the back door slamming shut along with heavy boots on the steps startled Kylee. She jumped away from Kellan. He felt her whole body tremble catching the fearful look on her face as she backed out of his embrace. Kellan frowned at her. *Was the fear in her eyes reaction to the door or his kiss?* His heart sank thinking it was his kiss.

Kylee saw the frown on Kellan's face and immediately thought that Kellan didn't like kissing her. She was appalled now remembering the way she circled her arms around his neck. Oh my, she was now embarrassed as her face flamed. Taking a deep breath she busied herself with getting the rest of the food on the table careful to avoid looking at Kellan. She couldn't bear to see his disappointment again.

Kellan watched as Kylee avoided eye contact with him but smiled at Evan when she placed the food on the table. Today she had made a beef roast. Not only did it look good but it smelled great. Kellan's stomach rumbled but his heart was heavy. He ate in silence listening to

Evan converse with Kylee. He noticed how Kylee talked and looked at Evan, but didn't dare look at him. Feelings of jealousy slid through him. Here he had enjoyed kissing her wishing they hadn't been interrupted only to find out she didn't like it or him! *I feel like such a damn fool! Was she wishing it was Evan kissing her instead of me?* His eyes narrowed vehemently at the two of them smiling at each other in conversation. *Ugh! I can't sit and watch the two of them anymore!*

Kellan abruptly stood up, his chair scraping noisily across the hard floor. He carried his plate over to the counter setting it down hard making a loud clatter. He turned around quickly and his big boots thundered on the floor as he left the house without a single word to either of them.

By Kellan leaving in a hurry he failed to see Kylee's reaction to his quick and angry movement of standing up abruptly. She flinched and leaned into the arm of the chair for support, tension filling her body. He missed seeing her cringe when his plate echoed loudly on the counter. She had taken a deep breath anticipating a hard physical hit onto her body. He also missed seeing her let out her held breath in awe at not being hurt over his frustration. The tension left her body as quickly as it had entered it once he stormed out of the house.

However, Evan had silently witnessed it and his heart broke for her. Her reaction reminded him of his sister who had suffered an abusive husband. She used to react the same way around loud noises and quick movements. He was sure that Kylee, too, had been in an abusive relationship and obviously a survivor. Evan held Kylee with a high regard and deep respect. He knew from experience with his sister how hard it was to get out from under the grips of an abusive relationship. He wanted to let Kylee know that he knew, but he didn't want to embarrass her. Evan also didn't think Kellan knew anything about her abusive past, otherwise he wouldn't have reacted the way he had.

Evan wondered what on earth was up with Kellan's bad behavior just a few minutes ago. He had sensed an odd tension between the two of them when he had come in, but he didn't know what the cause of it was. Then he noticed that neither of them spoke to each other through the meal, and Kylee was careful not to look at Kellan. Evan really thought that Kellan liked Kylee, but the way the two of them acted he wasn't so sure. Kellan was acting like a jealous man…Oh! That was it! Evan smiled suspecting how Kellan might have been jealous by the way Kylee focused her attention on him and not Kellan while they ate. Well, well, well…unbeknownst to Kylee she had put him right in the middle of a big ol' pile of manure. Evan thanked Kylee for another wonderful meal then headed out the door pondering the best way to handle Kellan. From past experiences it was best to talk to Kellan when he wasn't so riled up. So for now he decided to just let his friend blow off steam.

And blow off steam he did. One of Kellan's friends called him and asked him to fill in for his softball team that night since they were a player short. Kellan agreed thinking by hitting softballs it would be a perfect way to let out his frustration, and he had been right. After knocking a few softballs into the outer field, running around the bases and helping bring victory to the team he felt a lot better! He received several offers to join the team on a permanent basis, but he made no promises. He really didn't want to be tied down to a softball team. *Been there done that.*

"Kellan wait up!" Evan called out. "Good game, but I wish you had been on my team." Evan rubbed his shoulder where one of Kellan's balls had made contact with him.
"Your aim is as good as ever," Evan commented dryly.

Kellan kept walking and said nothing, but guilt consumed him. He hadn't entirely aimed the ball to hit Evan…just whiz by him. "You shouldn't have tried to catch the ball, and you wouldn't have gotten hurt."

"Bullshit! I know you," Evan snapped bitterly.

Kellan stopped walking and turned to face his friend with regretful eyes. Yes, Evan knew him all too well, and Evan was right, he had purposely aimed for him. Kellan was sorry that one of his hits of the softball had collided with Evan's shoulder. At the time it happened he had felt somewhat better. As his jealous feelings slipped away he was feeling a lot more remorse for hurting his friend. "Ev, I'm sorry man. I shouldn't have aimed so close. How is your shoulder? I've got a cooler full of ice and beer in the truck."

"I'll take both." Evan followed Kellan to his truck. Evan reached his big hand into the cooler pulling out a hand full of ice cubes and placed them on his shoulder.

"That was some exit you made at dinner today." Evan mentioned roughly raising an eyebrow at Kellan. Then his voice softened when he told Kellan, "You scared Kylee."

Kellan gave Evan a hard look, his jealousy spiked again over Evan's concern about Kylee being scared.

"She scares easy." Kellan gruffly shrugged his shoulder, but it bothered him that he might have upset her.

Evan saw the jealousy on Kellan's face when he had voiced his concern for Kylee. Oh, man, Evan wondered if Kellan was aware of how much he was falling head over heels for his new housekeeper. Probably not, Evan decided trying not to laugh but didn't have much success.

"Why are you laughing?" Kellan growled at him.

"You," Evan pointed to Kellan's fist clenched at his side. "And the murderous look you have on your face. You look like you're ready to punch me." Evan pointed out again.

Kellan unaware of his body language took his fist and folded it into his arms across his chest, but his face still held anger as he said nothing.

Evan decided to come clean about his feelings for Kylee.

"K-man, I have no interest in Kylee."

"You don't?" Kellan squinted at Evan leery of what he just said. "Or are you just saying that so I don't punch you?"

Evan laughed saying, "No way, man. She's all yours."

"All mine?" Kellan questioned.

Evan gave him an all knowing look. "Yes, all yours, friendship is the only thing I want with her. I promise."

Kellan gave a curt nod saying nothing. Then his lips curved upward in a small smile. His body relaxed knowing that Evan had no interest in Kylee.

"Thanks for letting me know."

"So what do you know about her?" Evan asked him seriously.

"Not as much as I want to," Kellan commented slyly.

"Yeah, I already knew that," Evan laughed heartily.

"I like her spirit, but I also suspect she has demons in her past." Kellan's face turned sad. Evan nodded. After what he witnessed today he suspected this, too.

"Kellan, you need to know how you scared the hell out of her today when you left the way you did." Evan winced remembering her frightened look.

Kellan caught Evan's look. His face clouded with concern of his own. "What do you mean?"

"Her body tensed up and her eyes filled with instant fear as she braced herself against the chair waiting for your hand to drop. It was pitiful," Evan told him shaking his head; his eyes full of sadness.

"Abused you think?" Kellan asked, his memory reflected on the other day when he had caught her off guard by coming home earlier than usual. She was nervous thinking she had angered him. She had pathetically apologized to him, and on the first day when he had swung his arms out wide, she ducked in defense. He had thought it was odd at the time, but now it made perfect sense.

Evan nodded. "I think so. Take it easy with her."

Kellan's face twisted in agony knowing it was his jealous tirade that had caused ill feelings to stir inside Kylee. He felt horrible that he let his jealous emotion take control of him. He let out a heavy sigh as he pulled out two beers from the cooler, twisted the caps off both of them then handed one to Evan.

"Aw, shit. I was an ass today," Kellan said.

"Yes, you were," Evan laughed.

Kellan threw him an annoyed look. There were a few people on earth who were able to tell Kellan when he was being an ass, lucky for Evan he was one of them. "Thanks for telling me."

"I never want to miss the opportunity to tell you when you're being an ass," Evan joked, punching Kellan in the arm.

"Hey." Kellan said rubbing his arm.

"Ha. That punch is nothing. You owe me, brother. I should have you stand out in the outfield and hit a couple of balls straight at you for payback," Evan laughed.

"Yeah, I'm sorry about that, Ev," Kellan apologized, his face fully sincere.

"I might be calling in sick tomorrow." Evan said smiling. "Sore shoulder can't drive the tractor."

"Ya, right! I know you better than that, and this isn't going to stop you from driving a tractor. Remember the time when you had your leg in a cast all the way up to your thigh? You had me, Rick, and Dirk hoisting you up onto the tractor," Kellan laughed at the memory.

Evan laughed along with Kellan. The two of them got absorbed in a trip down memory lane that involved many of their past shenanigans together.

"Hey, there's Francesca. I'm sure she'd love to help make your arm better." Kellan jabbed his elbow into Evan's ribs.

He left Evan in Francesca's care and listened to the girl tenderly fuss over Evan's hurt shoulder. Kellan knew the girl would be rewarded later this evening by Evan's personal attention on her and suspected this is what Francesca was hoping for.

"See ya tomorrow." Evan bid farewell to Kellan with a big grin on his face as he let Francesca lead him to her car. Kellan waved good-bye to Evan as he drove out of the parking lot.

At home Kellan opened the refrigerator door pulling out the filled water jug he kept in there. As he drank thirstily from the jug he noticed a soft glow of light illuminating the living room doorway. When he was done drinking he walked into the living room and saw that the light was coming from a lamp in the back room. He stepped into the room remembering how he had thought about turning it into an office. This never happened and now it was a place to store things he didn't know what to do with.

Yesterday when his sister was here, it had been the first time he had seen the results of Kylee's hard work. The transformation from what the room used to look like to now was spectacular! He owed it all to Kylee! She was fabulous!

Looking around the room this evening he was still amazed by the changes. The hardwood floor was polished, and the walls had been cleaned from dingy white to pearly white. The wood trim around the windows shined, the curtains had been washed, and the furniture was neatly arranged. It felt like the room was inviting him to come in and sit. He was drawn to the north corner where two antique chairs that had belonged to his Grandma sat. Gosh, he had no idea these chairs were even in here. Kylee had done a fabulous job positioning them to face the window overlooking the apple trees and one of the fields he owned. He walked closer to the window. He gasped when he saw Kylee sleeping in one of the chairs with her legs curled up under her. He hated to wake her, but he didn't want her to sleep here all night. He guessed that she might have been sitting here relaxing after her long work day. His chest tightened with pride knowing full well she deserved the relaxation. He could almost feel his grandma's warm smile shining down on her from heaven.

Not having the heart to wake her, he quietly gathered her into his arms and carried her back to her room. He noticed the various cuts and scrapes on the knuckles of her delicate hands, and he worried that she might be working too hard. He could kick himself for being such a jerk to her. Feeling his warmth around her, Kylee whimpered and nuzzled her body into his chest. Subconsciously, she trusted the arms that carried her.

Kellan sensed this trust and he hugged her closer. He liked having her in his arms. Her sweet scent surrounded them causing a sexual sensation to flare through him. He laid her down gently on the bed covering her up with the blankets. She looked like a serene angel. *I wish she was in my bed, but if she was she wouldn't be sleeping*, he thought with a devilish grin.

His eyes were drawn to her soft lips, and he wanted to feel them again as he had earlier today. Her wonderful taste had been a gift to him as she had wrapped her arms around his neck pulling him closer. His groin tightened at the memory. Could he have been wrong thinking she didn't like their kiss? But, she had frowned. He walked passed the screen door, and a thought occurred to him. Her frown might've had nothing to do with the kiss, and everything to do with the screen door slamming shut when Evan came in. Of course, that was it! How could he have been so stupid?!

Kellan scolded himself for his stubbornness. He should've asked right then and there why she reacted the way she did. There was a good chance he just built a mountain out of mole hill. Well, he needed to find out her answer tomorrow. His last thought before he fell asleep was *tomorrow will be a better day.*

Chapter Six

The next day came and went, and Kellan didn't see Kylee at all. In the morning when he came downstairs she wasn't in the kitchen. Before he left for the fields he looked for her but didn't find her anywhere in the house. Disappointed, he left with the hope of talking to her at noon, but when he and Evan came home she had their food sitting on the counter along with a written note that read: *I have a headache and won't be able to join you.* She left the same note for him at supper, too. It both irritated and worried him that she had managed to avoid him today. He sat down in the recliner and turned on the television to watch a baseball game.

He fell asleep and woke up in a panicked sweat because his arms were weighed down. There was a blanket wrapped around him. He stood up and tossed it off and was slightly shaken because he didn't remember having it earlier. Where did it come from? Walking into the kitchen he remembered that Kylee was here. She must have placed it on him as she had done a few nights ago. A part of him was relieved that she was okay, while another part of him was irritated feeling she deliberately waited until he was asleep before approaching him. Yet, his heart was touched by her care, and he hoped he'd see her tomorrow.

Kellan didn't see her the next morning which silently pissed him off. Instead of waiting for her, he left the house giving the screen door an extra hard shove as it closed. The sound echoed through the house.

Kylee was on the second floor working in the room located below his bedroom. She had decided the best place to avoid Kellan was literally right under his nose. She thought this would be the last place he'd ever think to look for her, and so far she was right. She had began peeling wallpaper off the wall and found this to be very therapeutic for her mixed emotions.

The day they shared the kiss had been overwhelming, and his taste had been haunting her since then. Remembering the frown he wore on his rugged face after they kissed left her feeling embarrassed and ashamed at how she had wrapped her arms around his neck wantonly. He must think poorly of her. Then when they were eating he sat there silently and didn't participate in any of the conversation she and Evan had. She got his message that he was mad when he furiously stood up and with an emphatic bang he slammed his plate into the sink before he stormed out of the house.

Kylee remembered all too clearly how she felt when he had made those sudden movements that were triggered by anger. She somehow stepped back in time and couldn't help but feel that it was Thomas standing behind her and not Kellan. For a moment she waited for him to hurt her, but the pain never came. Once she heard him exit the house she remembered where she was and immediately felt embarrassed about how she reacted. There wasn't a doubt in her mind that Kellan hadn't missed it either and that was why he stormed out. She couldn't face him. She was too embarrassed.

Kylee shuddered at the sound of the back door slamming as it vibrated through the house. She looked out the window and watched Kellan walk out to the tractor shed. He held his head high but she could see his rigid stride as he walked across the gravel driveway. She ducked behind the curtain when he spun around quickly scanning the house with a stern look almost as if he felt she was watching him. She heard the sound of the tractor's engine but didn't bother to look out the window again knowing that Kellan was heading off to the fields.

Kylee got involved with peeling more paper off the wall then she became aware of a high pitched sound. She stopped ripping the paper then sat still trying to figure out what made the noise. She knew she wasn't baking anything so it wasn't the oven timer. Slowly she walked out of the bedroom. The noise was louder in the hallway. She stuck her head in the rest of the bedrooms and the bathroom but didn't hear the noise in any of the rooms. One thing for sure, was the noise was best heard in the hallway. When she was close to Kellan's room the sound was even louder. Kylee knew immediately what the high pitched sound was. It was from his alarm clock.

She sighed heavily not wanting to go into his room, but she didn't want to listen to the alarm muffled through the walls all day either. It would drive her crazy! On the first day Kellan had told her that she didn't need to clean his room. So far she had respected his request and still would be if it wasn't for the alarm sounding on his clock. Hesitantly, she walked up the stairs. Once she reached the top of the steps she was in awe of his massive bedroom. Stepping into his room she felt as though she was trespassing. She walked over to the four poster bed and turned off his alarm clock.

She liked the height of his bed as it came up to her hip. Her leg brushed up against the crushed velvet blanket, and she ran her fingers over it. It had a strange soft comforting feel beneath her fingers. How heavenly it would feel to sleep under it.

What fascinated her was how tidy his room was. She had pictured clothes strewn everywhere but this wasn't the case. There was a handmade blanket thrown over the back of a chair, all his clean clothes were hung in the closet and neatly folded into the dresser drawers, and dirty clothes had been placed in a hamper that stood against the closet wall. The tops of the two dressers had a few things neatly arranged on them, and the bathroom was neat, too. There was a hand towel, a glass for water, and a soap dispenser that sat on the edge of the sink.

Kellan was the tidiest guy she had ever come across well, except for her dad. Her dad had always been neatly organized and loved to clean. He had inherited the cleaning bug from his mother and passed it on to her. Kylee loved that they had this in common, but since her dad's death a few years ago cleaning became a good coping mechanism. It also helped her survive. Kylee stared out the window caught up in the memory of her dad. Then she came back to the present and enjoyed the spectacular views with the miles of fields that stretched out as far as she could see. She didn't hear Kellan enter the room.

Kellan bounded up the stairs and nearly fell backwards when he saw Kylee in his bedroom staring out the window. He knew she was in la-la land since he hadn't been quiet when his heavy boots stomped up the steps. She hadn't even turned around to look at him. He wondered what she was doing in here and was about to open his mouth to ask but snapped it shut. Instead, he stood quietly watching her look out the window. An odd sensation surged through him as he thought about how well she fit in his room. It was the most natural thing ever. She was beautiful with her long blonde hair tied back exposing the smooth skin on her neck. He fought the urge to walk over to her and bury kisses into the curve of it.

With this running through his mind all he wanted to do was put the last couple of days behind them, pick her up and lay her down on his bed to make sweet love to her. He wanted to hear her melodious voice scream out his name in the throes of passion. Kellan was hard just thinking about it as he sauntered over to her. He heard her wistful sigh and wanted to know what she was thinking about.

"Beautiful view isn't it?" Kellan whispered gruffly in her ear. Anticipating her to jump his hands clamped down on her arms as he pulled her against him.

Kylee yelped in surprise as her senses alerted her that she was no longer alone. All in a matter of seconds she smelled him, heard his gruff voice then felt his hands on her. She let him pull her to him but didn't allow herself to relax.

"Kylee, it's me, Kellan," his voice rang softly. It was recognizing his voice that allowed her to relax in his arms. His masculine scent washed over her, her body reacted in a way it never had to any man before. Her head was spinning and her knees went weak. She would have slid to the floor if he hadn't been there to hold her up. For the first time in a long time it felt good to have strong powerful arms holding her.

Kellan felt her legs give way as she started to sink to the floor, but he held her firmly against him to keep her from falling. He stood motionless behind her enjoying her sweet scent. He was powerless with the feelings she was stirring in his loins that slowly rose to his heart. He felt her trusting him, and she was learning to relax her body against his. He never knew how heady this feeling was until now with Kylee. Suspecting that there were times in her past when she couldn't relax in another man's arms he had this fierce protective feeling for her consume him. Suddenly he didn't want to let go of this beautiful woman whose body was softly melting into his. He wanted to keep her safe in his arms forever.

In the past the thought of being with one woman would have had him instantly feeling claustrophobic but not with Kylee. Instead his chest swelled with pride. How could one woman mess with his emotions like this?

"Breathtaking view isn't it, Sweet City Girl," Kellan said feeling her nod her head against his chest.

"Yes," Kylee answered breathlessly, except the views out the window weren't the reason for her unsteadiness. She wondered what he would say if she told him about her abusive past, but right now she wasn't brave enough to find out.

"Oh, Sweet Girl," Kellan whispered. "I am surprised to find you in here."

He immediately felt the tension rise in her again and didn't know why. It was an innocent statement said by Kellan, but to Kylee it was more than that as her subconscious pulled her back into the past. She was right back with Thomas where everything had to be perfect, and if it wasn't he would fly off the handle with his temper. His anger always took precedent over anything that could have been handled by a simple conversation. Now when she had the chance to handle it with a simple conversation, she was too lost in the past to see what was in front of her. Her reaction was poor, and she regretted it, but couldn't stop the guilty feelings that filled her along with feeling that she had betrayed Kellan's trust by being in his room without his permission.

"I'm sorry. I'm sorry," Kylee started apologizing out of habit. "I didn't mean to disobey you."

"Disobey?" Kellan spun her around in his arms. He gave her a quizzical look. "What do you mean by disobey?"

"On the first day you told me to stay out of your room, but..." she trailed off trying to push away from him, but he held her tight. He didn't understand why she was apologizing, and it frustrated him. He felt the magical moment of her trusting him slipping away fast, and he didn't know what to do but watch as the aura around them rapidly changed and not for the better.

Kylee felt his frustration as he puffed out a breath of air.

"But what?" Kellan asked in a stern voice. His hands loosened their grip around her, and Kylee broke free of his hold on her.

"Your alarm clock was beeping." Kylee's fierce tone bit into him.

His face registered shock. He was hurt by the way her tone cut into him. It showed briefly in his eyes but he covered it up quickly. His eyes turned black, narrowing in on her.

"So what?" Kellan retorted angrily, then instantly regretted losing his temper when he saw the look of fear in her eyes. She started backing away from him.

"I'm sorry," she began, but he cut her off with a bewildered look.

"Are you apologizing because my alarm clock was beeping?"

"Yes and for…" Kylee trailed off again. She felt confused with her confession about the alarm clock beeping and how it was her fault.

"For what?" Kellan asked exasperated. He couldn't believe what he was hearing. She actually thought she was responsible for his alarm clock? That guy really did a number on her.

"I'm sorry for making you mad," she wailed.

"I'm not mad!" He shouted frustrated with what was happening as she cowered before him. She turned her back to him missing the helpless look on his face. If she had seen it she might have understood that he truly was at a loss about what was going on. She was so wrapped up in her past with Thomas's anger she couldn't see that the man who stood before her would never raise his hand to harm her, but he'd protect her.

"Kylee," Kellan spoke her name quietly touching his hand on her shoulder. "It's not your fault."

She spun around quickly with wild glaring eyes shouting, "It is!" Then she turned her back and started to leave the room.

"Kylee, wait!" Kellan shouted, but the eyes that looked at him were full of fear as she escaped down the stairs. He let out an anguished cry when he saw her fear stricken face. He called out her name again and went after her but, of course, she disappeared somewhere in the house.

The rest of the morning Kellan had a heavy heart knowing he had made a big mess of things with Kylee all because he was too proud and too stubborn to keep his temper at bay. He wouldn't be surprised if he found her bags packed and out by the back door when he came back tonight. He hoped she was tougher than that, but he thought if he was her, he wouldn't want to stay.

With the horrible morning he had, Kellan wasn't even sure if he wanted to head back in for the noon meal. He felt so defeated by what had happened. He kept replaying the look of fear she had of him over and over in his mind. He didn't think Kylee would be joining them today either and the thought of not seeing her was keeping his spirits low. Evan finally convinced him to go back to the house with him by suggesting that maybe he would get a chance to talk to Kylee before things went too far south between them. With this hope in mind Kellan agreed to go.

Kylee glanced at her wristwatch and saw she had some time before the men came home to eat. Giving a disgruntled sigh she picked up the old upright vacuum cleaner. She hated this vacuum! It was too heavy and too bulky, but she was impressed with how well it sucked up the dirt. However, she would happily trade it in for a newer lighter model that would suck the dirt up just as well.

At the top of the stairs on the small landing she leaned her forearms on the vacuum cleaner as she took in a deep breath muttering a string of curses as the long hose twisted like a snake around her ankles. She carefully stepped out of the hose. Kylee glanced over to the doorway leading to Kellan's bedroom. She let out an aggravated sigh as she began vacuuming the first five steps. Then her mind wandered freely while the vacuum cleaner hummed loudly in her ears. Her thoughts kept going back to this morning when Kellan caught her in his room.

Her memory of what happened was not kind to her today. She kept mulling the situation over thinking that she might have over reacted to an innocent statement. Everything had been going well and when it looked like they were on the road to mending fences she freaked out about the guilty feelings she had about being in his room. In the back of her mind she knew there was a simple answer. It wasn't fair to Kellan how she blindly put him into a similar scenario of the times she'd been with her abusive boyfriend. She was so angry at herself for letting the past creep into the present. If she wasn't careful, her past was going to ruin her future with a great guy. Kylee wouldn't blame Kellan if he came back here at noon asking her to pack up her bags and leave.

She wouldn't blame him at all but the thing is she didn't want to leave. Strangely enough she felt at home here even with all the unfamiliar, loud country farm sounds. She liked it here. Tears fell from her eyes blurring her vision. She was convinced that Kellan was going to ask her to go. This thought made her sad.

"I don't want to leave," she sniffed, brushing a tear away from her cheek.

Kylee made her way down the stairs with the vacuum cleaner making clunking sounds on each step. She looked down and saw she was almost done. It was all her fault even though Kellan said it wasn't, she knew better. It was! She was the one who let herself get tangled up with an abusive man. It was the choices she made and no one else. And with those choices she let the man rip away all her self dignity and let her think that every man was just like him. She hated being scared all the time and saw how much it irritated Kellan, too. She just knew in her heart he was going to send her away.

She cursed thinking about it while the tears continued to fall. She was bawling now as she pushed the vacuum cleaner down onto the next step with too much force. The vacuum slid out of her hands and down the steps before she even knew what was happening. It fell on the floor at the bottom of the stairs below her but while the vacuum fell with a loud crashing sound, Kylee was unaware how the hose had wrapped around her ankles again until it was too late. It pulled her feet downward. With one hand she frantically grabbed for the railing on the staircase. She was unable to grab hold of it as she was being projected forward the floor was coming up to meet her body fast. She let out a piercing scream as she hit the bottom hard. The breath was knocked out of her. Her last thought was of Kellan as darkness closed in around her while the vacuum cleaner laid nearby.

As Kellan and Evan drove the truck into the driveway Kellan had an eerie feeling wash over him. A cold shiver shot through him even though the hot sun was beating down. He rolled his shoulders trying to shake the feeling away.

"What's up?" Evan asked him seeing Kellan's rolling shoulders.

"I don't know. I've got this feeling that something is off." Kellan said. Evan gave him a grim look knowing better than to make light of Kellan's cold shivers. Between Dirk and Kellan's cold shivers, Evan knew what they felt was legit since they have saved his ass a time or two in the past. Despite what Kellan was feeling with his cold shivers Evan hoped he would be able to make amends with Kylee soon. He knew it was driving Kellan crazy not being able to see or talk to her.

When they entered the kitchen both men were surprised to hear the oven timer buzzing, but there was no sign of Kylee anywhere.

"Something's wrong. I can feel it." Kellan hissed. He opened the oven door to find that the food was more than ready to come out and a few minutes longer it would've been burned. He tossed a couple of pot holders to Evan instructing him to take the food out and that he was going to find Kylee. He heard the whirring noise of the vacuum coming from the other room, and he followed the sound calling out Kylee's name.

Kellan rounded the corner and his heart leaped into his throat when he saw her sprawled out face down on the floor. Horror struck him as he assessed the scene in front of him noticing that Kylee wasn't moving. Her feet were tangled up in the hose, and the vacuum cleaner lay on the floor still on. He moved quickly turning off the vacuum and threw out an alarming yell to Evan. He knelt beside Kylee's still body.

"No, no, no, no!" Kellan repeated in a frightened voice. He wanted to pick her up but was afraid to. Placing his hands on her back he was relieved to feel her breathing.

"Shit! What happened?" Evan swore from behind.

"Call Chase! Tell him she's breathing but not moving," Kellan instructed and Evan did.

"He's on his way," Evan told Kellan, his own voice filled with worry.

Kellan nodded silently, unwinding the vacuum hose from her foot. He glanced up at the stairs muttering, "Damn it."

"Oh, shit! How far do you think she fell?" Evan voiced the unspoken question in Kellan's mind.

"Kylee, Kylee." Kellan repeated her name as he touched the side of her face with the palm of his hand. It seemed like a lifetime to Kellan before Kylee finally moaned but didn't move.

"Kylee," Kellan breathed her name in relief as he continued stroking the side of her face with his hand. "My sweet girl,"

"Oh, baby," Kellan's hushed whisper floated over Kylee. She became aware of her surroundings and where she was. She was lying on the floor and her body hurt. She groaned trying to roll over onto her side. She winced in pain. Kellan's hand laid flat on her back keeping her still.

"Shhh. Stay where you are. Don't move. You've had quite a fall," Kellan whispered sternly. His voice faltered making Kylee look up at his distraught face. His worry for her touched her heart in a profound way.

"It hurts." Kylee choked out. Her eyes glistened with tears. For the first time in a long time she let the tears fall at the pain she was in. With Thomas the tears would have been seen as a sign of weakness but not with Kellan.

"I know, baby, I know." Kellan brushed away the tears with his fingers. "The doctor is on his way."

"Can I sit up?" Kylee asked.

"I'd rather you didn't until the doctor gets here," Kellan said. "Do you remember anything at all of what happened?"

"I tripped on the vacuum hose when I was cleaning the steps."

"How far did you fall?" Kellan asked his eyes deeply concerned.

"I'm not sure," she answered vaguely.

"Oh, sweet Mother…" Kellan trailed off in anguish thinking that she might have fallen from the top step. She could have internal bleeding somewhere.

"It wasn't from the top." Kylee rushed on as though she had read his mind. "I didn't have that much farther to go."

"Are you sure?" Kellan asked her skeptical of her answer.

Kylee nodded her head slightly then hissed at the pain. "A little less than halfway maybe,"

Hearing this he felt a little relieved, but he still was very worried.

"Oh! The oven is on," Kylee said this as she tried to lift her head and shoulders but cried out in pain sinking back down to the floor.

"No, baby its fine. Evan took it out. Stay still." Kellan rubbed light circles over her back with his hand. It seemed to calm her.

Impatiently, he checked his watch waiting for Chase's arrival. Finally he heard Jake barking outside then heard voices coming through the back door and saw the blond haired, brown eyed doctor appear.

"Kellan," Chase extended his right hand out to Kellan who in return grabbed the doctor's hand giving it a firm handshake.

"Chase. Thanks for coming right away," Kellan said and Chase gave him a silent look that read as though he wouldn't have? Kellan stood giving Chase room to work, but he paced nearby.

Chase knelt down beside Kylee introducing himself as Dr. Chase. Kylee felt him place his hands skillfully on her examining her. Dr. Chase touched her head, shoulders, ribs, hips, legs and feet noting when Kylee cried in pain on the places he touched.

"How's your head feel, Kylee?" Dr. Chase asked her.

"It's pounding," Kylee answered him.

"I'm going to roll you over now," Chase told her easing her onto her back.

She grimaced in pain. Kellan kneeled beside her again and began rubbing her arm lovingly. Chase noticed this, but said nothing. As long as he had known Kellan he never once saw the man so concerned or affectionate to another human being as he was with Kylee. Usually, Kellan had a cool exterior except for the times when he was playing a joke on his sister, Linda, but the sibling relationship was filled with animosity.

"Help me sit her up," Chase instructed Kellan.

Kylee sat up and the room spun around her. She bent her head reaching her arm out calling Kellan's name. She passed out, but Kellan caught her body before she sagged to the floor. He gathered her up in his arms lovingly. "I'm taking her upstairs."

He carried her up to his room effortlessly. Chase followed him firing questions out to Kellan about her fall. How far did she fall? How long had she been unconscious?

Kellan gave him vague answers explaining how he and Evan had been out in the fields when it happened, and they found her lying on the floor when they came in. Worry lines etched on Kellan's hard face as he watched Chase's lips purse together.

"Good it wasn't the top of the stairs." Chase looked pointedly at Kellan who nodded silently. Chase looked Kylee over with great detail again. Halfway through this examination Kylee woke up and was more alert than last time. Chase took this as a good sign.

"There aren't any broken bones, and as far as I can tell there isn't any internal bleeding, but the next 24 hours will be critical for internal bleeding to occur," Chase told both of them.

"How does your head feel now, Kylee?" Chase asked.

Kylee brought her hand up to her head touching it lightly. "It really hurts. I feel like there is a marching band inside my head."

"Okay. Don't try to sit up fully. Stay as you are propped up the way I have you. I'm going to give you some medicine. It will help you sleep and should help relieve the pain in your head," Dr. Chase informed her then continued.

"You will be sore for a few days after and you will need to take it easy." Chase threw a stern look Kellan's way as he said, "Don't let her work too hard."

In return Chase caught the appalled look that Kellan threw him. Chase grinned seeing that he had no worries at all about Kellan working her too hard. With the concern Kellan had written all over his face Chase guessed that Kellan would try his best to make sure Kylee didn't lift a finger at all. Now thinking about it Chase wasn't so sure this lovely lady wouldn't try to overdo it herself.

"I'll be back in a few days to check on you, but if you have any nausea, dizziness, intense pain, vomiting, or pass out for any amount of time, even a minute, you need to be rushed to the ER!" Chase said sternly.

Kylee nodded her head, and Kellan said, "Will do."

"And don't be stubborn about the pain." He pointed a stern finger at her. Kylee nodded her head up and down letting him know she took his warning seriously.

When Chase left the room, Kellan sat down beside her on the bed leaning his back against the headboard, stretching out his long legs. He gazed at her for a long time enjoying the fact that she was alive and wasn't seriously injured from her fall even though the next twenty-four hours were still critical.

"Kellan you look so worried," Kylee said when Dr. Chase left the room.

"Ah, City Girl, you scared the shit out of me," Kellan said in a serious whisper.

"I did?" Kylee looked up at him with a skeptical look.

"Yes. I saw you lying on the floor." He paused to swallow a big lump of emotion caught in his throat. "You weren't moving." Kellan ran his hand over his anguished face. "I feared you…might be dead." The last three words fell into a husky whisper.

He clasped his hand on hers, but he couldn't look her in the eyes. Instead, he stared up towards the ceiling. She felt the raw emotion that had erupted out of him when he admitted his fear of seeing her lying on the floor possibly dead and understood why he avoided eye contact with her. She sensed he was on the verge of tears and knew Kellan was a proud man who didn't cry or show endearing emotions.

She squeezed his hand tightly and said nothing. His fear over her safety put a big lump of tears in her throat and feared she might cry again if she tried to say anything.

"Kylee," Kellan started with a heavy sigh. "You have no idea how lucky you are that we came in from the fields today. I wasn't going to, not after what happened between us this morning. I felt that you probably wouldn't have joined us for lunch and the thought of not being near you depressed me. I had this awful feeling that when I got home you were going to have your bags packed by the back door, and I wasn't ready for you to leave." He shook his head sheepishly. "Evan finally convinced me to come in with the hope of maybe we'd have a chance to talk."

"Oh, baby." Kellan put his hands over his face again. "What if we hadn't come in at all? What if there had been a fire from the oven? What if you hadn't been able to get out of the house after falling? What if…"

Kylee gripped his arm. "Kellan, stop with the 'what ifs'. Shhh."

Kellan stopped his ranting. Silently he stared at her hand on his arm.

"After this morning I convinced myself that you would be coming back to pack my bags for me, and I wasn't ready to leave here," Kylee admitted shyly.

"Baby, what did happen this morning? Why did you get so upset with me and what did I do to upset you so much?"

Kylee took a deep breath then exhaled slowly shaking her head. "I'm…"

Kellan interrupted her by holding up his hand to gently stop her, "Don't start the sentence with 'I'm sorry'."

Kylee snapped her mouth closed nodding her head. "Okay." She gave him a small smile. "On the first day you told me I didn't need to come in here to clean your room. So this morning when I was in here, without your permission I was afraid you might have felt that I had disobeyed you."

He had a thoughtful expression on his face. He believed her but there was more to it simply by the way she reacted. This morning she didn't even answer his question. She just flew off the handle assuming he would be angry with her. His shoulders slumped in defeat because he didn't know how to ask these questions without upsetting her again. Plus Chase would kick his ass for upsetting his patient. For now he had to try a different approach.

"Maybe next time you could try talking to me first," he suggested lightly. "Don't guess how I'm feeling. Just ask me."

"I'll try," she said and for now that's all he could ask for.

Kellan sighed softly as he wrapped one arm around her side. He silently thanked God that she was all right despite the threat of internal bleeding within the next twenty-four hours. Kylee looked up at him with her pretty sky blue eyes with a hint of trust that melted him. It wasn't until this moment where Kellan realized how much he wanted her to trust him. He knew it was the key to winning her heart, and he wanted this more than anything in the world. It took almost losing her today for him to see how much he was beginning to care deeply for this beautiful woman who was capturing his heart.

"Baby," he whispered enticingly and stroked the side of her face with his finger. Her blue eyes were drawn to his dark eloquent eyes. Her heart hammered in her chest because she, too, felt the fired passion between them. Her fingers curled around his arm as a provocative desire pulled them together. He captured her mouth and shared his hunger for her…with her. Under his compelling kiss she tasted his yearning. In a shaky breath his name fell softly from her lips.

Feeling unsteady from their kiss he leaned his forehead against hers, inhaling her marvelous scent. He had never tasted anything as exquisite as her sweet kiss! The kiss had been delightfully delicate sparked with a fierce passionate flame. It burned an unfulfilled feeling through him. There was a good chance he wouldn't ever be fulfilled by her taste. But, by golly, he could die trying; at least, he'd die happy. He lowered his mouth to hers again ready for more wonderful kisses.

Kylee closed her eyes anticipating his rugged flavor on her tongue. She could feel his warm breath whispering across her face, his mouth barely touching hers, tormenting her of his taste. She was anxious to feel his firm lips toying with hers again.

Sensing her agitation he continued teasing her by grazing his tongue along her bottom lip.

She smiled because it tickled and a small satisfied smile showed on his face. He was driving her crazy, and she knew this is what he meant to do. When she couldn't stand his ghostly kisses any longer she hastily gripped his forearms digging her nails into his skin. He wound her body into his arms and blanketed his lips around her soft mouth. It was a slow tender kiss that rapidly changed to an uncontrollable kiss. Inside their mouths, his tongue dove deep and hers darted boldly igniting a passion deep within them, stirring a yearning between them.

Kylee heard his satisfied groan as he put his hand on the back of her head keeping her mouth on his. The urgent need to satisfy their hungry craving for each other had them spiraling downward as they started losing control of their disciplined emotions.

In Kellan's hazy state of mind he was happy they had managed to find his bed, but then he tried to remember how they got there. Then he remembered how as her accident of falling down the stairs flooded in his mind. He was horrified with his actions and now thought he could be hurting her! Kellan gasped and pulled away from her. His focus for now had to be her health and not his desires.

"Sweet Girl, you taste good," Kellan murmured against her lips.

"So do you." Kylee placed her hand on his chest.

"I like kissing you," they said simultaneously then laughed at each other.

"I wanted to kiss you like this again after we kissed in the kitchen," Kylee confessed to Kellan whose jaw dropped slightly.

"I was right. You did enjoy it." Kellan slapped his knee with the palm of his hand.

"Yes, but I thought you didn't."

"What on earth gave you that idea?" Kellan asked her his face frowning.

"It's this face. The one you have now. You're frowning."

Kellan's eyebrows scrunched together. "I am? I did that day, too?"

Kylee nodded her head up and down. "Yes. That's why I thought you didn't like my kiss, and then I was embarrassed because I put my arm around your neck wanting more. Then with the face you made, I just thought you didn't like it." Her face turned red thinking about it.

"Oh, baby, no. I liked your arm around my neck, and I loved kissing you. I frowned because you had a scared look on your face, but I realize now it was because Evan came in."

"Yes! That stupid back door slamming shut scares the shit out of me every time."

"I've noticed," Kellan murmured dryly, but he was smiling wide when he looked at her.

Kylee smiled back at him when she realized he was teasing her. She snaked her hand behind his head pulling his mouth on top of hers for yet again another long hungry kiss that had their tongues wrestling wildly exploring the other's exquisite taste again.

"Oh, Sweet Girl," Kellan gasped when they broke from the kiss. "I'd never have forgiven myself if something awful had happened to you today."

"Well, it wouldn't have been your fault," Kylee told him.

"Why is that?"

"It would've been that damn vacuum cleaner's fault!" she hissed her eyes wild with anger.

"Whoa! Why do you say it like that?" He turned his head sideways looking at her sudden outburst in blaming the vacuum cleaner.

"Like what?"

"With so much hate,"

"I do hate it," Kylee said with pure annoyance all over her face.

"You do?" He turned to look at her with surprise again.

"I do." She nodded her head emphatically.

Kellan looked dumbfounded as she ranted on, "It's so old! It's bulky and heavy and back breaking plus it's hard to get into the corners and under things with it."

He was quiet and Kylee feared she might have over stepped her bounds, but then he spoke, "Well, then let's go get one you do like."

"Really," she looked at him doubtfully.

"Yes. Why not? I already told you it's important to me that you are safe."

"It'll be expensive," she said giving him a hesitant look.

"Ah, don't worry about it." Kellan shook his head brushing the back of his knuckles along the side of her face. "You're worth it."

Kylee leaned into him hiding the new set of tears forming in her eyes. She realized she could easily get used to him caring for her. Kellan wrapped his arms around her, holding her tight, and he realized he could easily get used to having her in his arms.

Chapter Seven

Kellan stayed with Kylee and rubbed her back while the medicine Chase had prescribed her took its affect, and she fell asleep. Kellan joined Evan in the fields, but he only stayed two hours before heading back to the house. He was anxious to see Kylee. The sun was low in the horizon when he walked into the house. He took the stairs two at a time up to his room, but when he reached the top step he saw his bed empty. A worried frown creased his face as he wondered where she could be. His bathroom door was open, and she wasn't in there. He hurried down the steps and saw that the hallway bathroom door was closed. Then he heard the toilet flushing and walked over to the door with a puzzled frown. *Why did she come down to this bathroom instead of using the one in my room?* He was happy she was okay, but he was irritated because she had worried him. Kellan pounded his knuckle hard against the door calling out her name and heard her surprised yelp.

"Geez, Kellan!" Kylee shouted angrily through the door. "You scared the crap out of me!"

He groaned inwardly and wondered if she had jumped at his unexpected knock. "What are you doing in there? I told you to stay in bed," Kellan retorted.

"I had to pee!" she shot back.

Her sass made him chuckle as a big smile appeared on his face. He heard the water running from the faucet before she hastily opened the door. Her blue eyes gave him an icy glare. He was ready to fire back a response but snapped his mouth shut when he caught a glimpse of the bruise on her face. Immediately, his face softened and slowly he extended his hand towards it. In her heart, Kylee knew Kellan wasn't going to hurt her, but she instinctively pulled her head back. Kellan reached out farther and tenderly touched the bruise.

"Sweet Girl, I'm not going to hurt you," he said quietly his eyes pained.

"I know," Kylee said casting her eyes downward.

"Does it hurt?" Kellan asked caressing the bruise with his thumb.

His touch was light and loving. It had been a long time since the touch of a man's hand was so careful on her. Tears glistened in her eyes. Misunderstanding her tears he asked her again if it hurt.

She shook her head. "No the bruise doesn't hurt."

"You took quite a fall, Sweet Girl." Kellan shook his head. He pulled her against his chest and ran his fingers through her silky hair. Being able to touch her relaxed him. Being away from her this afternoon had made him edgy, but now being here with her, he felt a lot better!

Taking in a deep breath of her sweet fragrance he was amazed by how much her scent calmed him.

Kylee wrapped her arms around his back and enjoyed his fingers in her hair. She breathed in his masculine scent. His fragrance was a combination of sweat and cinnamon, and she was surprised by how it comforted her and aroused her. Closing her eyes she relaxed in his embrace and mumbled, "At least the bruise is of my own doing."

Kellan absorbed the words she spoke, but wasn't sure he had heard her correctly, but in his heart he knew he had. "Tell me what you mean by this."

Her body tensed and he hated it. With one arm around her, he gently clasped her chin with his other hand and lifted her eyes to his. Her troubled expression met his concerned eyes. She opened her mouth to speak but no words came out. What could she say? She snapped her mouth shut shaking her head saying, "Never mind. It's nothing."

Kellan took a deep breath. He didn't believe her, but her frightful eyes told him this wasn't the time to push the issue. She pulled away from him and reluctantly he let her go. She was feeling vulnerable in his arms and felt the need to put space between them. Her emotions were flying haphazardly inside of her, and she didn't have the energy to deal with them.

Changing the subject Kellan asked, "Kylee, if you had to use the bathroom why didn't you use the one in my room?"

She shrugged and avoided eye contact with him by looking up at the ceiling.

"Kylee," Kellan spoke with a deep commanding voice trying to grab her attention.

Her eyes held panic as she took a deep breath. "It felt too personal."

His eyes flickered with amusement and all he could manage to say was, "Okay." He didn't fully comprehend her answer but he let it be.

"How are you feeling?" Kellan asked stepping closer. It gave him an excuse to touch her, and he did by placing his hand on top of her head.

"A lot better, thanks." Kylee liked Kellan's warm hand on her head. His concerned eyes filled her heart with joy. Impulsively, she flung her body into him wrapping her arms around his waist and buried her face into his chest.

Surprised by her action and delighted, Kellan wound his arms around her tightly. He felt it was an honor to be holding and comforting her, and he didn't want to let her go. His guess about her past relationship was that she didn't have the luxury of being able to rely on a man's strength; instead she had learned to be frightened by it. When she flinched from the touch of his hand, he was even more convinced of her abuse. Although he'd like to hear it from her, he didn't have the nerve to push the topic. It pierced a hole in his heart thinking about the physical pain she had endured.

She ran her hand up and down his spine unaware of the affect she was having on him. The innocent touch of her hand sent a stimulating shiver through him. He was frozen in place and if he didn't move soon he would be weak against the strong temptation of taking her to bed; they wouldn't be sleeping.

"Baby, I've gotta go shower," Kellan rasped. He let go of her taking one step backwards. "Would you like to sit downstairs for awhile?"

"Yes!" Kylee answered enthusiastically happy that she wasn't going to be cooped upstairs. She squealed when Kellan unexpectedly lifted her up and carried her downstairs.

"Great! I know just the place for you to sit." Kellan hinted giving her a wink.

"Kellan, put me down I can walk," Kylee protested. "I'm too heavy."

He gave her a dejected look. "C'mon! Do I look that wimpy to you?"

Kylee giggled and shook her head no. *Just the opposite.* His body was strong from head to toe. His long arms carried her with ease and his tall legs kept her high off the ground. She wrapped her arms around his neck so she wouldn't fall, but she knew Kellan wouldn't let that happen. He was the kind of man who'd take the fall to avoid seeing her hurt. His protectiveness tugged kindly on her heart.

"The sitting room is my favorite place!" Kylee exclaimed when he set her in the chair that looked out into the backyard.

"I know," Kellan whispered unevenly. Seeing her face light up had strange sensations pounding on his heart. He would do anything to keep this lovely smile on her face, and he felt that he might be falling for this sweet city girl.

Kylee wanted to ask how he knew this was her favorite place but suddenly it didn't matter. What did matter was the fact that he did know. She wanted this man more than anything in the world. He not only sparked her sensual desires, but he also had the ability to open her heart. Subconsciously, she had closed the door on her heart and hadn't realized this until she met Kellan. When this job was done she would be leaving, but before this happened maybe Kellan could teach her how to love again. If he could this would be the greatest gift she could take with her. Loving Kellan for a brief moment in time might just be worth the heartache.

Her hand grazed over his chest and stayed there as he leaned over her. She could feel his tight muscles flexing beneath the white t-shirt. Squeezing the material Kylee wished she could touch his bare chest. Kellan left to go take a shower, and she was left with her dreamy thoughts. The images her mind produced were fascinating. She imagined her hands roaming freely over his muscular body from his arms, hands, broad chest and legs. Then her mind rested on one particular muscle located in the center of his body. This one piqued her interest the most. She envisioned his taut muscle between her legs pushing deep inside her, and her vagina fluttered with a warm tingling feeling. A breathless sigh escaped her as she thought about how great having sex with him would be. She guessed he would be a passionate lover and had no doubt he'd be able to lift her high into the clouds of passion.

Kylee squirmed in her chair uttering another sigh. "Oh, damn."

"Are you hurting?" Kellan's concerned voice broke into her thoughts. He scared her as she gasped in surprise.

"I wish you'd stop sneaking up on me," Kylee declared fiercely.

Kellan said nothing, accepting the fact how she was going to jump or scream at unexpected noises. He was confident that with time she would get over it. He asked his question again, "Are you hurt?"

He sat down in the chair across from her wearing only his blue jeans; no shirt or socks. *Oh, how sexy he is!* She cleared her throat nervously and felt her face blushing. "No. I was just thinking about something."

"Hmm," Kellan grinned. "That good of a thought, huh?"

Watching her avoid eye contact with him made him chuckle. "If you hadn't been so deep in your thoughts, you would have heard me walk in." Kellan leaned forward his dark eyes scrutinizing her. She blushed some more.

"I'd love to know what you had been thinking about," his voice was rich with desire. He carefully touched her knees with his hands clasping them affectionately. When she didn't flinch from his touch, he continued squeezing his hands tenderly over her legs up to her thighs. She found this to be sexually exhilarating. He slid off the chair to stand on his knees in front of her. With his strong hands he gripped her thighs and scooted her away from the chair closer to him. Kneeling between her legs it put him at her eye level.

Kylee deeply inhaled his clean soapy smell. His refreshing scent turned her on. Hesitantly, she put her hands on his bare shoulders, splaying her fingers over his hazel chest. An electrifying sensual feeling weaved through her creating a newfound confidence deep within her. She ran her fingers up the back of his neck into his wet hair massaging his head. He groaned not ever remembering a time when he was enthralled by a woman's touch, the way he was now as Kylee threaded her fingers through his hair. He didn't ever want her to stop. She had provoked an intoxicated sexual sensation inside him. He wanted to touch more of her.

Kylee wasn't aware of how Kellan had snaked his hands further up her body until she felt the warmth of his fingers on her belly under her shirt. She gave a happy sigh loving his feathery touch. His hands climbed higher until they found what he was searching for: her twin treasures. He lifted her bra off then cupped her breasts in his hands. She sighed again enjoying his touch. Kellan gasped in awe holding her soft round breasts in his hands feeling the fullness of them. A perfect fit for his large hands. He ran the palm of his hands over the buds of her breasts finding that they didn't need much caressing. Her nipples pointed quickly. He strummed his thumbs ever so lightly over her nipples. Her legs clenched his thighs, her jaw dropped, and a pleasing cry tumbled out while he continued his crusade on the ends of her breasts. He loved hearing her delighted cries, seeing her eyes wild with excitement, and feeling her body twist in desire knowing it was his touch that pleased her.

"Kellan," she cried out and tilted her head back exposing the delicate skin below her chin. He dipped his head down eager to taste her here. His wild kisses sent shivers down her spine forming pools of ecstasy between her legs. Then his hands left her breasts briefly when she felt her shirt and bra being lifted over her head and arms.

"You're beautiful," Kellan whispered gazing hungrily into her eyes before nuzzling his face on her neck, trailing wet kisses up to her lips. Then he captured her mouth in his for a long hungry kiss. He pushed her mouth open as his tongue plummeted deep inside trying to get his fill of her taste. He couldn't seem to get enough of her. While kissing her, his hands stayed on her breasts twisting her nipples between his fingers. She moaned inside his mouth then broke away from the kiss. She inhaled sharply as an orgasm shivered through her.

Kellan felt her body tremble. Together they looked at each other in surprise. A triumphant smile slowly spread across his face. He was fascinated by how magical his touch was on her causing her to come undone so quickly. From the slight flush on her cheeks he could see that no man had ever had such an effect on her before. He was hard thinking about her wet release, and he wanted to be inside her, feeling her move beneath him. He was confident that he could make her come again. As he was thinking this, he heard a slight rumbling of her stomach.

Kylee was embarrassed over her quick orgasm. No one had ever made her come like this. He touched her with a confidence that ignited a fire inside her.

"Oh, Sweet Girl, you are marvelous," he said gazing deeply into her blue eyes. He set his mouth over hers again and she eagerly parted her lips. When the kiss ended he said, "I think it's time we eat."

Kylee gave him a luscious look trailing her tongue across her lips.

Kellan nipped at her tongue playfully. "I mean food."

"Oh," she said with a disappointed shyness.

Kellan helped put her bra back on before her shirt. He cupped her breasts again in his hands. "Next time I'll taste these."

Kylee raised her eyebrows excited about the possibility of there being a next time between them. However, she wished they didn't have to stop right now because a part of her was hesitant in believing him when he said there would be a next time. With these doubts, subconsciously she ran her tongue over her lips. He wiped her wet lips with his thumb then gently grabbed her chin in a steady hold. Catching the uncertainty in her eyes Kellan hated how she didn't trust his truthful words.

"Yes, Kylee, there will be a next time," he declared and let go of her chin. Giving her a playful wink he murmured, "I've only begun my taste of you, Sweet Girl."

"Why, not now?" Kylee asked.

"Your stomach is rumbling. I can't let you starve," Kellan said standing up. Kylee saw the bulge in his jeans, and her insides danced knowing how she had the same effect on him as he did with her. She made an attempt to get out of the chair, but he gently sat her back down.

"No, you are sitting. Doctor's orders are to relax. I'll bring you something to eat," Kellan said to her. "Is there anything your hungry for?"

"I'm hungry for you, Kellan," Kylee answered truthfully, watching him inhale deeply.

She had no idea how much Kellan wanted to give her what she wanted, but he wasn't sure she had the energy for what he had in mind, especially after her accident today.

"I want you, too," he confessed. "But, we can't. Not after your fall today." He placed his hands on the back of the chair and leaned over her. He was about to remind her of the doctor's orders to rest when suddenly she placed her hands on his thighs. Her fingers clutched the hard muscles on his legs as her hands skimmed their way upwards to the bulge in his blue jeans.

"I was thinking about you earlier when you walked in," she admitted in a seductive hushed whisper.

Looking up at him hesitantly, her eyes turned hungry when she lowered her gaze to his protruding crotch. She lifted her hands to the waist of his jeans and wondered how far he'd let her go. She had unfastened the button and lowered the zipper and he hadn't stopped her. Sliding her hands inside she kissed his erection through the fabric of his underwear, and he still hadn't stopped her. Looking up at him she saw his dark eyes laced with a sexual desire. At this point she didn't think he was going to stop her. She was right.

Kellan felt like prey in a spider's web unable to move; mesmerized by her seduction. He couldn't stop her if he wanted to since he was too far gone by the strong affect she had on him; all he could do was stand there and let her seduce him.

"I was thinking about how good the sex between us would be." Kylee whispered softly. She carefully slid his pants down exposing his erection. She took him in her warm hands, and he inhaled sharply. He moved his hands off the chair and slid them onto her head as he groaned. Never in a million years did he imagine this woman who didn't like loud noises would be touching him so boldly. It was a splendid surprise when she put her mouth on him!

Kylee kissed him lightly playfully licking his shaft, her tongue twisting over his tip. A creamy liquid trickled slowly out of him as she took him fully into her mouth. His hands fisted in her hair. He moaned then grunted his own satisfying cries. He clenched his teeth together hissing with pleasure. The wetness of her warm mouth embraced him. Never before had he ever had such a willing partner. New sensations ripped through him and he was losing control. He moved his hips back and forth, and his erection slid in and out of her mouth. He heard her hungry whimper. She willingly drank from him when his orgasm exploded into her mouth.

Her name rang out across his lips and ended with an "Oh my God" as he sang to the heavens above. Bending down to kiss her, tasting him on her lips, he pulled his clothes back on over his hips, but didn't bother to refasten them. Then he swung her into his arms and gently carried her up to his room. Kellan laid her on the bed quickly undressing both of them. After what had just happened downstairs food was the last thing on his mind. He wanted to pleasure her the same way as she did. Giving in to the hungry craving he had for her was the only thing he was thinking about.

Kellan slid on the bed next to her loving that they both were naked. He looked into her bashful, but eloquent eyes. In an effort to take away her shyness Kellan gave her a slow sensual kiss that had her moaning, and he felt her body relax. He continued with his deep kisses while kneading her breasts between his fingers. He was careful not to let her come too quickly this time. He only wanted her moist.

"I'm hungry, baby," Kellan said as he trailed wet kisses from her mouth, down her neck to her chest, pausing briefly just above her breasts. His tongue danced over her nipple before he pulled it into his mouth sucking on it with a starving passion. Kellan then moved to her other breast. Giving it the same attention as the first one; first teasing her nipple with his tongue before suckling it with the same passion he had for the other one. He moved back to the first breast repeating the process, except this time his teeth grazed over her nipple, and he administered the same pleasure on her other breast. Multiple waves of stimulating energy tumbled through her. Her sexual cries were potent to him. He continued his relentless pursuit of her breasts trying to satisfy his own hunger. Before Kellan knew it he felt her body shudder beneath him as another orgasm ripped through her.

"Damn, baby," Kellan whispered fiercely hovering above her. He gave her a triumphant grin before smashing his lips hard on hers. Kylee thought that Kellan might be dissatisfied and done with her. She frowned because she ached to feel him inside her.

"I'm sorry," she apologized.

"For what?" he asked, but she averted her eyes from his. Kellan caught her chin between his fingers; his eyes searching hers for an answer. "Tell me."

"For releasing too soon," she admitted. "Please don't be disappointed."

"Sweet Girl, don't ever apologize for that." He scowled because she felt the need to apologize then reassured her by saying, "I am not disappointed!"

"So you're not done with me?"

Kellan threw her a wicked smile. "Oh, I'm not done with you. I'm just getting started."

Kellan heard her relieved sigh as he bent his mouth down onto her belly kissing it feverishly. He found his way down to her burning bush of desire. She squirmed when he kissed the outer edge of her cavern causing her insides to quake with an unmistakable desire. She thought she was going to come up off the mattress when his tongue darted inside finding one particular spot that drove her crazy. She gripped the sheets beneath her hands but that didn't help much. Her fingers found his hair pulling on the short strands, but she couldn't get a good grip. Her hands slid down landing on his shoulders. Her fingernails dug into his bare skin as he feasted on her. She repeated his name feeling her inner pool wet with enjoyment. When she was about to come again, he stopped his sweet torment on her to lift her higher onto the bed.

She was weak beneath him. He kissed her on the mouth. She saw Kellan pull out a foil packet from the drawer of his night stand. She watched him put it on thinking there was something sexy about him putting on a condom. When he was done he hovered above her. She pulled him down, his muscular arms wrapping around her back. Kylee's mouth found his, her tongue circling his.

Kellan continued kissing her while he positioned himself over her. He hesitated for a moment before entering. He slid in and out of her slowly repeating this process tenderly each time pushing farther. He wanted her to become acquainted with him versus taking her all at once, but he was having a hard time taking it easy. On the last entry he stayed deep inside her until she began to move comfortably around him. In one long stroke he backed out then pushed hard back into her. She let out a sweet groan that echoed in his ear. He did it again and again each time pushing harder. He felt her lifting and meeting him each time he found his way back to her. The excited cries she emitted gave him the encouragement to set a faster pace and she welcomed it by keeping up with him. He liked her partnership. Her provocative way of calling his name, and begging him not to stop stimulated his senses as he brought them over the edge of the climatic mountain.

Kylee's body trembled with the hot release of her emission. She heard her wild scream escape as stars danced around her. She felt Kellan's flaming release and heard his orgasmic cry. Her body lazily sank into the mattress as he hugged her lovingly.

When he finally had the energy Kellan turned himself away from Kylee to dispose of his used condom. Much to his dismay he found it to be leaking! A horrified look covered his face. "Fuck!"

"Yes, we just did that," Kylee mumbled with a satisfied grin on her face.

"No, the condom broke! Oh, my, gosh! This has never happened before!" Kellan cried in horror.

Kylee knew Kellan was thinking he could've just gotten her pregnant, and with their explosive love making anything was possible but not likely.

"Don't want to be a dad?" Kylee asked him nonchalantly.

Kellan gave her a horrified stare. Stuttering at a loss for words, "Uh-uh, Y-yes, N-no." He clamped his mouth shut noticing how much he sounded like an idiot.

"Well, which one is it? Yes or no?" Kylee couldn't help laughing.

"Both. Yes, kids in the future but not today," Kellan finally answered, but he still had an 'oh shit' expression on his face which for some reason she found adorable.

"How many," Kylee tossed out.

"How many?" He gave her a blank stare. "What?"

"Kids, how many kids do you want?"

Kellan shrugged his shoulders. "I don't know…two or three, depends."

"Depends on what?"

A sly grin appeared across his face and he joined her back on the bed. "How pretty my babies' momma is." He howled with laughter when she punched him lightly on the arm laughing along with him. She squealed when he wound his arms around her rolling her with him. She ended up on top of his chest, facing him. He positioned her legs to straddle his torso.

"Now tell me why you are so calm about the condom breaking. Most women I know would be freaking out by now jumpin' around screaming at the top of their lungs blaming me."

"I'm not most women." Kylee's grin spread wide across her lovely face.

"I agree. You are not most women!" Kellan whooped when she pinched his arm. "Ouch. Watch it."

Kylee giggled at his idle threat. Kellan never saw anything so beautiful as her shining blue eyes. They lit up her whole face. She was relaxed and having fun. He wanted to do whatever he could to keep her smiling and laughing.

"So tell me," Kellan prompted her by rubbing his thumbs along the inside of her thighs.

A slow sultry grin curved her lips. "Well," she began. "It's okay that it broke."

"Why?" Kellan arched his eyebrow, curious about where she was going with this.

"I'm covered," Kylee stated.

Kellan snuck his arms around her waist and flipped her over, and she was lying on her back beneath him. "Yes, I've got you covered. What are *you* talking about?"

Kellan lowered his head placing delicate kisses on her neck.

"I'm on birth control," Kylee informed him.

Kellan whipped his head up in disbelief. "Seriously?"

Kylee nodded her head. "Yes seriously."

"You mean I didn't need the condom?" Kellan asked his eyes narrowed.

Kylee shook her head smiling.

"Damn, baby. I wish I knew this earlier." Kellan gave her wide smile. "All of that worry for nothing, you owe me!"

He cupped her breasts, playing with the nipples turning them hard. He covered his mouth over one breast and then the other switching back and forth, his tongue tangling around her taut nipples. Her delighted sighs let him know how much she enjoyed what he was doing. He positioned himself between her legs, his hard penis laid against her vagina. His dark eyes grazed over her. She ran her tongue over her lips, delighted by the affect it had on him as his erection grew bigger against her leg.

"I can't wait to feel skin on skin," Kellan said kissing between her breasts. What he spoke was true. The minute he entered her he was unprepared for the heavenly warmth she offered him. His elongated thrusts submerged into her saturated cave. He lost control, sliding deeper inside, increasing his pace taking her hard. He was unrelenting in his pursuit to have her. She wrapped her legs around his thighs begging him not to stop. He couldn't stop even if he wanted to, she felt too wonderful. He slid in and out, in and out enjoying the way her feminine abyss absorbed his heavy erection. He called out her name, praising her, making her come. Her sweet liquid pouring over him was his undoing, releasing his own flood into her.

Afterwards, Kellan held her in his arms for a long time while their uneven breathing reduced to normal. He snuggled her closely, draping one arm around her, positioning one of his legs between hers. She was too tired, too comfortable, and too relaxed to protest about being in his bed and besides, she didn't want to move away from the warmth of his body. She said nothing about leaving his bed when he covered them with the blankets. She felt confident that Kellan would carry her back to her own bed when he was ready for her to go. For now, she enjoyed where she was as she closed her eyes and fell asleep.

Chapter Eight

Kylee opened one eye, but she wasn't completely awake. The sun was beginning to rise in the horizon and she saw shades of pink in the sky through the window. She yawned, rolled over and stretched her arms out then flinched when her hand bumped into something. With both eyes wide open she whipped her head around to see Kellan smiling at her.

"Morning," Kellan's voice croaked. His mouth curved into a dazzling playful smile that made her heart skip a beat as he asked, "Sleep well?"

Kylee nodded her head silently, but her mind was screaming. *I can't believe I'm still in his bed! How on earth did I fall asleep here with him? And why did he let me stay here? I've never stayed all night. What do I do?!* Somehow this all felt too personal too soon! *Isn't it or am I overreacting?* Feelings of guilt flooded her, although she wasn't sure why… maybe because he was her employer and she was his employee. *Oh! Shit! I just had sex with my boss! We HAVE definitely crossed a line!*

"What?" Kellan asked wishing he could read her thoughts. He leaned in to give her a good morning kiss, but she turned away as she rolled off the bed.

She reached for her clothes and got dressed. "I'm surprised to find myself still in your bed."

"Where else would you be?" he asked.

"In my bed."

"Is that where you wish you were?" Kellan asked confused by her body language. He wanted a morning kiss from her but had this feeling she was in a hurry to leave. *Surely, I'm mistaken.*

She shot him a frustrated look. "No, but I thought you would have kicked me out of your bed last night after we had sex but no you let me fall asleep here!"

"Why would I kick you out?" Kellan reached for her, but she immediately darted away. After her confusing statement he felt if he could just hold her it would settle her. He quickly moved his body over to where she was catching her arm. Then he wound his limbs around her so she couldn't go anywhere and was forced to stand still. Her face and body sagged in defeat.

"Why are you in a hurry to leave?" Kellan questioned.

"I-I…it…" she stammered. *Ugh, this is so embarrassing!*

"It's what?" his voice requested and his eyes expected her to answer.

"It feels so personal," Kylee rushed on feeling her cheeks redden at having to admit this after the intimate night they just shared.

"Damn right, it's personal. You act like you've never woke up with a man before." Kellan chuckled bringing her in for a hug. He held her tight and felt her body stiffen while her arms stayed awkwardly at her sides. It dawned on him that this innocent statement was accurate and true! *Holy crap! I'm the first guy she's ever stayed the whole night with?! How is this possible?* Delighted by this discovery he rolled her onto the bed with him.

"City Girl, you've never had an all nighter?" he asked in disbelief. Her eyes shied away and he knew her answer was yes.

"Sweet Girl," he spoke tenderly, but he had no idea how extremely embarrassed she was.

Inside his embrace Kylee was overwhelmed by her emotions and felt claustrophobic. She needed air! Pushing hard on his chest, she wiggled her way out of his hold. She sat up inhaling a big breath of air. He touched her shoulder, but she moved away from his caring hand. When she was completely out of Kellan's reach she turned and practically ran down the steps out of his room. By the time she reached her room tears were falling. Crying, she hopped in the shower letting her mixed emotions run along with the hot water.

Last night had been wonderful! The sex between them had been earth shattering. The way Kellan had been with her was amazing, but she was most surprised by the hunger she had for him. Her past sexual encounters had been to satisfy a need. With Kellan, it was different. She wanted to reciprocate the pleasure he had given her. Then this morning waking up with him was a new experience. In the past, someone was always leaving in the middle of the night. She didn't know how to behave the morning after but was too shy and embarrassed to admit it.

It would be easier if she didn't live under the same roof, but that wasn't the case. They did live in the same house, plus she was his employee! How was she going to face him or act around him? Taking a deep sigh, she left her room ready to get rid of the agitation in her tummy. Kylee hoped that Kellan had already left the house but no such luck. He was sitting at the kitchen table drinking coffee when she walked in.

Kellan was baffled by Kylee's hasty getaway this morning. It shocked him that she hadn't ever slept the whole night in a man's bed before. However, it didn't give her the excuse to run like she did. He dressed quickly and decided to confront her before he left for the fields. He was determined not to leave things awkward between them especially after all that had happened. He was sipping his second cup of coffee when she came in. He watched her body language with a careful eye. She was nervous when she softly greeted him. He gave her a curt nod, watching her mess with the dishes in the dishwasher. Quietly, Kellan stood up, went to the cupboard, retrieved a coffee cup and poured coffee into it.

"Come, sit and have coffee," Kellan's deep voice cut through the silence.

Kylee was hesitant when she approached the table. Kellan had strategically placed the coffee cup on the other side of him, forcing her to pass by him. When she neared him, his arm swung out and pulled her hard onto his lap. One arm held her back while the other arm lay across her abdomen. He cradled her in his lap, like a child.

She had been expecting him to grab her so she didn't yell out. Kellan's blue eyes gazed softly into hers. He gave her a triumphant smile.

"You didn't scream this time," Kellan said in surprise.

"No, I was expecting you to try something."

"Were you now?" Kellan said with an amused smile. "How did you know?"

"It's where you put the coffee cup," Kylee told him with a pointed look. Then she asked, "Are you disappointed?"

"Disappointed?" Kellan countered.

"That I didn't scream in fright?" Kylee asked.

"No Sweet Girl. I don't ever want you to be frightened of me." Kellan stroked her cheek tenderly with his fingers.

"Even, when we wake up together," This was spoken in a soft authoritative tone.

He said "when" not "if". This quiet promise made Kylee's insides quiver delightfully.

"Okay?" Kellan asked her softly.

Kylee couldn't tear her eyes away from him. His dark blue eyes demanded her to answer. Unable to speak, Kylee nodded her head, holding his direct gaze. A sly grin crossed his handsome face.

"Besides, I found other ways to make you scream." Kellan gave her a teasing smile. His fingers found their way under her shirt making light circles on her belly.

"You forgot to give me a morning kiss," Kellan stated his deep voice charming her. With one arm around her back, he eased her up, her face close to his. His eyes settled on her soft mouth before tenderly placing his lips onto hers. Their mouths melted together like ice cream on a summer day. The cozy kiss quickly turned intoxicating with tongues twisting together leaving them both wanting more.

"Good morning," Kellan declared with a huge smile.

"Morning," Kylee said laughing, touching his cheek gingerly, running her fingers over his clean shaven face. "I like seeing you smile."

Kellan sat quietly. No one had ever told him this before. Seeing his dumbfounded look over her comment made her giggle.

"I like seeing you laugh," Kellan said to her.

Kylee accepted his compliment with a musical laugh. She twisted around in his arms, and he let her go. She hopped into the chair next to him to drink the coffee he set out for her.

"How is your head?" Kellan asked her in a serious tone watching her shrug her shoulders in a noncommittal way.

"To tell you the truth, I hadn't thought about it until now. So I guess…okay," Kylee answered with another shrug of her shoulders giving him a hopeful smile.

Kellan moved his chair closer and gently placed his hand on top of her head. "Easy now, Evan's coming in."

Just as he finished telling her, she heard the back door slam shut. Since he had warned her, she only flinched a little this time.

"That was better." Kellan smiled warmly. It caused her heart to flutter.

"How's our patient doing?" Evan asked concern written all over his face.

Kylee was touched by his concern. She flashed Evan a warm smile saying, "I'm doing all right."

Kylee caught the hardened jaw line and the jealous frown on Kellan's face when she smiled at Evan. She wondered why he was insecure especially after the amazing night of sex they shared. Did he really think she could be interested in Evan? His tense jaw line indicated that yes was the answer. *Silly man, I'll just have to reassure him.*

Kellan had a pang of jealousy as he watched Evan and Kylee exchange smiles. *After the passion we shared last night, I have no right to feel this way or do I? I hope Kylee wasn't leading me on wishing she was in Evan's arms instead of mine. I know Evan isn't interested in her, but I don't know for sure how she feels about him. Still, her friendly smile worries me. I'm crazy to have these feelings, but I can't help it! After our explosive love making and our rocky start this morning, I have this need to protect her. I'm not ready to let her walk away from me!*

The minute Evan walked into the room he sensed the air between Kylee and Kellan had changed for the better. He liked seeing the gentle touch of Kellan's hand on her head and the way his secret smile made her blush. He disguised his knowledge of seeing their affection with each other by asking Kylee how she was feeling. He was bewildered when he saw Kellan's face cloud over with jealousy after his friendly exchange with Kylee. *Damn! Why is he jealous? I thought I made myself perfectly clear the other night when I said I wasn't interested in Kylee. He has no idea how much he likes her! I just hope that Kylee has the same feelings for Kellan otherwise I'll be picking up the pieces of his fast falling heart.*

In hopes of easing his mind, Kylee moved to sit in his lap putting her arms around his neck. Their eyes connected. Her slender fingers covered his heart, quickening its rate. The brave moves she made on him in front of Evan told him exactly what he needed to know…that she was his! Instantly, the worry fell off his face as an easygoing expression covered it. His arms enclosed her.

"Maybe I should stay here and work around the yard today in case you get hurt again," Kellan suggested.

"Kellan, I'm fine. I'll be okay. Go to work," Kylee reassured him. Appreciating his concern she got up off his lap feeling he was being too overprotective. No one had ever been this protective of her, not even her dad. The sudden thought of her dad had formed tears in her eyes. She quickly blinked them away.

"What if you get hurt again? I can…Why the sad look all of a sudden?" Kellan interrupted his own sentence when he caught her glistening eyes. Waving her hand in the air she didn't acknowledge his question about her sadness. However, she did argue with him about getting hurt again.

"If I'm in the house and you are outside, how will you know if I'm hurt? Do you have X-ray vision that you can see inside this house?" she asked sassily, folding her arms across her chest. Her eyes were daring him to tell her he had super hero powers.

Evan chuckled. *She was a good match for Kellan with all of her piss and vinegar. I'm thankful that I don't have to deal with her but I suspect this is what Kellan likes about her, but not me! I like my women quieter, more reserved. After a long day's work I don't have the energy to come home to a high spirited filly. I want my woman already tamed.*

Kellan groaned. He wasn't sure if he should kiss the sass out of her or let her think she won the argument. He pointed his finger at her, but Kylee tossed him a sly smile. He took one big step in her space, and she didn't back away. She thought he was going to kiss her but instead he gently cupped her cheek with his warm hand. Softly he said in a deep voice that melted her, "Be careful this morning. Don't overdo it, take breaks, and stay off the steps. See you at noon sharp."

He gave her a resounding kiss leaving a smile on both their faces.

In their minds, they both were thinking; *Ha! I'm the winner of this argument!*

While Evan was thinking, *this might be their first agree to disagree argument.*

Listening to Kellan's happy whistled tune there was no way he was going to ruin the good mood they both were in by voicing his thoughts.

"What?" Kellan asked Evan noticing his friend's ear to ear grin.

"She's a good match for you," Evan commented.

"You mean she's sassy," Kellan countered.

"Yes." Evan coughed a laugh. "Like, I said a good match for you." Evan slapped his leg.

Kellan scowled and erected his middle finger towards his friend as he started the tractor engine drowning out Evan's laughter.

Kylee worked in the kitchen most of the morning preparing meals for the rest of the week and by mid-morning she was exhausted. Groaning she muttered, "I guess after everything that happened yesterday with the fall and us having sex my lack of sleep is catching up with me."

She allowed herself to sit but after thirty minutes she didn't feel rested and feared she might have worked too hard. *Oh, Kellan is not going to be happy.* At twelve o'clock sharp, Kellan and Evan came home to delicious smells of meatloaf, baked potatoes, green beans and biscuits. Both men were full of compliments eating heartily as though they hadn't eaten in a week.

Kylee watched them quietly while her body ached the longer she sat in the chair. She wanted to get up from the table but then Kellan would see the pain she was in, and she wanted to hide this from him for as long as she could. When Kellan came home she saw a relieved smile dance across his charming face. She guessed he was glad to see her unharmed versus yesterday's incident. He gave her a fierce hug and a happy kiss that made her feel important. She returned his affection by slipping her arms around his waist leaning into his strength. Kylee wanted to tell him how tired she was, but she held back because this is what she was used to doing. For the first time in a long time she had a man to trust, but she didn't know how to. She had to try and hide her pain from Kellan because this is what Thomas taught her to do. Thomas saw pain as a weakness…a mistake she made only one time. She hated that man for making her feel this way. Nervously, she shifted in the chair under Kellan's careful eyes.

Kellan glanced over at Kylee and saw how exhausted she was. When he arrived home he gave her a delighted hug and had felt her exhaustion. He should've insisted that she sit, but she gave him a cheerful smile insisting she was good. He knew it was important for Kylee as an employee to please her boss but seeing her tired or in pain didn't please him at all. A pleasant smile tugged on the corner of his mouth as he thought, *Ah, but I also know how she strives to satisfy me in bed. I too, am to blame for her being worn out. Oh, boy! Our work relationship has crossed some lines.* He wasn't quite sure where their relationship was going but was confident they would figure it out as they went along.

With her hand she covered a yawn and winced in pain from the movement of her arm, and he saw this. His concern heightened and without a doubt he knew she had overworked herself. *No doubt it was the preparation of this meal.* Yes, it was wonderful but it wasn't worth jeopardizing her health just to make it. Prior to her arrival, he and Evan had survived on less before she showed up and started spoiling them with her great cooking skills. She worked her fingers to the bone, so to speak, with all the hard work she had agreed to do when he hired her. He was very happy with the results, but he didn't want her to overdo it where she was at wits ends. Today he feared she might have done just that.

"Kylee, honey, you're in pain," Kellan commented softly putting his hand over hers, but she hastily withdrew it and set it in her lap.

"No," she shook her head. "I'm all right. I'll be fine." she answered quickly trying to turn her face away but it was impossible since they sat in a triangle. Guilt washed over her for lying to Kellan. His face was stern, and she suspected that he didn't believe her. Their magical morning, his carefree attitude, and her happy mood were slipping away. All of it disappearing into thin air and it was all her fault! She became stressed and worried under Kellan's scrutiny stare.

"Kylee," Kellan's voice was firm; almost demanding.

Even Evan looked up from his plate assessing the scene in front of him. *She is tired. Why doesn't she just admit this to him?*

"Tell me how you are really feeling," Kellan said.

"I told you I'm fine," she snipped, and her defensive guard rose up fast.

"Kylee, I don't think you're fine," Kellan speculated. "You look exhausted."

"Now you're the doctor?" she sneered.

His steel eyes narrowed while her eyes blazed wildly matching his hard glare. "You didn't take any breaks this morning," he questioned with suspicious eyes.

"Are you asking me or accusing me!" she snarled viciously.

Kellan gave her a compelling look as he let out a frustrated sigh. His hand slapped the table, but when it did something inside Kylee snapped since it was a familiar sound. In her mind, she was back in the past with Thomas and his hand was striking her.

"Don't!" Kylee shrieked and raised her hands up to cover her face. It was clearly a defensive move as if someone was going to slap her.

Kellan and Evan stared at her. They were speechless; unsure of what to do.

It was, at this precise moment, that Kellan began to understand why she jumped like a jack rabbit every time she heard a loud or unexpected noise and why she lied to him just now about being in pain. He suspected the man who had abused her had taught her to hide the pain. It was all starting to make sense now. He remembered on the first day they met how she had ducked her head from his swinging arm. *Oh! I feel awful for how I teased and scolded her for being frightened all the time. I'm such an idiot!* His heart broke thinking about all the pain and suffering she endured. Hatred for the man who had hurt her consumed him, and he couldn't stop the anger flashing in his eyes, but Kylee saw it and feared it.

"I am hurting! There are you happy now?" Kylee seethed.

It pained Kellan that she compared him with her abuser, asking if he was happy to see her hurt, but his heart went out to her all the same. He knew it was hard for her to lean on anyone for strength but suddenly this is exactly what he wanted…for her to lean on him.

Kylee took a deep fearful breath thinking she pushed him too far, by her sudden outburst. Keeping her head bent down she waited for the blow of his hand to come down on her but it never came. She raised her head and saw the astonished looks on both of the men. *It's Kellan and Evan. What? Where? OH NO! What have I done?!*

It was then that she comprehended how her abused past was affecting her present. She was embarrassed by her lack of control. It wasn't fair to put Kellan in the same category as Thomas. *I know he is nothing like Thomas!* Seeing their concerned looks was overwhelming her but it was the hurt look in Kellan's eyes that had her feeling ashamed. The walls started closing in around her. "I'm sorry. I'm sorry."

Kylee stood up abruptly attempting to leave the table, but she stumbled forward. Kellan's arm shot out, and he grabbed her to keep her from falling. He saw the tears sliding down her face. Without thinking twice, he picked her up swiftly into his arms and carried her out of the room. All the while Kylee repeated her apologies. She was crying hysterically by the time he reached the sitting room. He sat down in the chair cradling her in his lap, allowing her to cry, hoping this is what she needed to let go of her emotional past. His Grandpa used to say, *"A person needed to hurt before they could heal."*

Kellan wanted Kylee to lean on his strength, to let him help her through the pain and trust him. He needed her to see that he was here to help her and not hurt her. It devastated him how she kept apologizing with fearful eyes expecting to be physically harmed. He didn't know how to take the fear away so he just held her tight. He should've insisted she stay off her feet today and then maybe the work stress wouldn't have caused her emotional breakdown. Then he remembered it was his hand slapping the table that had made her come unglued. He felt guilty about it but then maybe she needed to know that not all men are like that. If they were going to have any kind of future together she needed to let go of her past.

He frowned over his own thoughts about a future with her. When just this morning he wasn't sure where they were going. Holding and comforting her was stirring up all kinds of funky feelings inside him. His mind had already started forming a new plan for the future and it all revolved around the beautiful woman crying in his arms. He knew what he wanted in his life and it was a woman to hold, to love, to come home to. She was exactly what he wanted! *Whoa! I can't believe how this beautiful city girl has worked her way into my heart.*

"Shhh, Sweet Girl," Kellan's voice soothed her while he smoothed the hair off of her tear stained face.

Kylee came out of her crying reverie to find herself in Kellan's warm embrace. His hand tenderly stroked her head. She felt his whispered breath on her ear and heard the agony in his voice. When she finally allowed herself to look at him she saw his pained expression.

"Hey, there's my sweet city girl," Kellan said in a hushed tone when she stopped crying and gave him a silent stare. She was in awe over his tenderness.

"I'm sorry, Kellan." Her apology didn't settle very well with him, but he didn't show his irritation fearful she would start crying again.

Her heart skipped a beat when she saw his anguished eyes penetrating hers. Gosh, he really did care for her and she had reacted poorly. She sighed softly, and her eyes got misty again. *Will I ever be able to move forward?*

"Kylee," Kellan whispered. "Why do you keep apologizing?"

"I'm sorry for making you mad," she apologized again.

"So why was I mad?" he asked.

"Because I yelled at you," she whispered back. "I shouldn't have yelled."

Kellan shook his head in disgust. "Baby, I don't care about that. I don't think you actually were yelling *at* me. I think you were just yelling because you needed to. Hell, if you feel the need to yell then by all means do it. Let it out! This house can take it. Believe me it has heard its fair share of yelling throughout the years."

He gave her a lopsided grin. "Yell all you want. I'm tough I can take it. Kylee, I don't ever want you to hold back what you're feeling with me. I want to know all your feelings, Sweet Girl. If you're happy, sad, afraid, confused, and yes even if you're hurting. Understand?"

She nodded then asked, "So why did you scowl at the table?"

Kellan's eyes squinted trying to remember when he had scowled. His eyes got big when he remembered when it happened and he frowned.

"That's the look," Kylee told him but this time she wasn't scared of it. His eyes misted with tears knowing it was his strong emotion of hatred for the man who had terrified her.

"Oh, baby," he spoke in a hushed whisper full of raw emotion. "I hate the man who abused you."

Kylee gasped hearing the truth of her past fall out of his mouth.

"It all makes perfect sense to me of why unexpected loud noises make you jump. I'm the one who should be sorry for teasing you about it instead of changing my habits."

"That's why you were mad? Because of Thomas's abuse," Kylee asked gaping at him.

Kellan gave a curt nod. "Thomas is his name?" His jaw tensed. She, in return, gave her own curt nod of her head.

"That. And you asked me if I was happy because you were hurt. Hell no! I wasn't happy about you being in pain!" Kellan's voice rose.

He continued, "Kylee, I don't ever want you to think I enjoy seeing you in pain. You're safety means a great deal to me." He ran his finger down the side of her face his eyes tormented. "I'm not him. I won't hurt you."

"I know. I knew on the first day we met you were a kind man," Kylee spoke in an undertone but it was her believing eyes that caught his breath. His heart warmed seeing how she already knew he was nothing like this Thomas guy. He wrapped her up in a spontaneous hug. Kylee laughed.

"I love hearing you laugh," Kellan said. This made her giggle more bringing a jovial smile to Kellan's face, relaxing it.

"I should've been more insistent you stay off your feet today," Kellan said.

She shook her head. "It wouldn't have helped. I'm stubborn."

"You said it, not me." Kellan laughed pointing his finger at her.

"You probably would've had to tie me down to get me to stay in one spot." Kylee tossed him a warm smile.

Kellan's eyebrows shot up. A playful smile crept onto his face. He was thinking about tying her down with his body as he made endearing love to her. He wanted to hear his name escape from her sweet lips and hear her satisfying cries float over him. He was becoming uncomfortable in his jeans. "I have ways of making that happen."

Kellan trailed his finger lightly up her arm, up her neck and up to her mouth delicately touching her velvety lips reminding him of a rose petal. His touch was driving her crazy. She didn't want his finger on her lips she wanted his mouth.

When he looked into her beautiful eyes he saw them burning with a fire that ignited a flame inside him. She touched the side of his face massaging it slowly with her fingers. His unshaven facial hair was bristly at first but became softer. She was mesmerized by the way it felt, stirring a heat in her. A hunger for his taste rumbled inside her. Leaning forward she brushed her lips over his and kissed him passionately. Slipping her tongue inside his mouth she enjoyed his exquisite taste while their tongues tangled together.

Kellan united them again, by drawing her mouth into his for a deep fulfilling kiss leaving them breathless. He was selfish in his hunger for her. He didn't give her much time for a breath of air before he was lowering his mouth over hers again. Welcoming him, she opened her mouth. Their lips crushed, their tongues played, and their yearning hunger grew with an intensity that was hard for them to stay satisfied for very long before they were kissing again.

Kellan gave a low growl. He was trying to satisfy his need for her intoxicating flavor, but it was a losing battle. He wouldn't ever be satisfied until he conquered her whole body. Reluctantly, he pulled away from her. He rested his forehead against hers breathing heavy.

"Baby," was all he could manage to say as he placed his hand lovingly on her head.

"Kellan," his name came off her lips in a hungry whisper making his insides ache.

"I want to take you upstairs right now and satisfy my hunger for you," he declared, but she saw the hesitation in his eyes.

"But you can't," she countered.

"I can't," Kellan said, squeezing her arm affectionately. "Sweet Girl, you are exhausted and this worries me. Your health comes first before anything else."

Her eyes misted when she saw his distraught look over her weakness. Except for her dad, she hadn't ever felt the tender touch of a man's heart as she did with Kellan. *Oh, I might be falling in love with this man.*

"Baby, tell me why your face clouds with sadness every so often like it just did." Kellan pointed out.

Kylee's face frowned. "It did?"

"For a brief moment, yes, and you've done it before."

"I have?" Kylee was completely unaware of it.

"Yes," Kellan said quietly. Then he spoke in his low rich voice that made her melt. "So what were you just thinking about?"

Kylee pursed her lips together and the sad look came again as she quietly answered, "My dad."

Kellan squeezed her hand taking in the sadness pouring out of her. "Baby,"

"He died a few years ago from cancer," she told him.

"Oh, Sweet Girl, I'm sorry," Kellan said sympathetically. The only comparison he had of losing a loved one was when his grandparents died. He couldn't relate to the loss of a parent but knew it had to be hard. He was happy she had shared this with him feeling she had taken one step in the right direction to trusting him. Rubbing her arm soothingly, he comforted her by holding her close while she talked about her dad, his death, her feelings, and her abused relationship.

"Kellan, I was lost after he died. I didn't know where to go. He loved me so much! When he died I had no one left in my life, and I was desperate to find someone to love me, but I didn't know where to look. When I met Thomas I was really messed up. I thought he was my savior who was going to help get me out of my grief. He only added to it. In the beginning I didn't know what to think. I thought, like a million other women, that he'd change his ways but somewhere in the middle of it all, I became aware that I was just another statistic. All of a sudden I didn't want to be a statistic. I wanted to get out!" She inhaled a deep breath.

"There's nothing quite like the feeling of desolation, of waking up one day and finding yourself in a country song. I didn't want my story to end up the way it did in the song, and that's how I knew I had to leave." Kylee rolled her eyes with a small shake of her head.

"I came to the conclusion that no man can be or was going to be my hero to the grief I was living in. The only person who could help me was me. I had to be strong and be my own savior. I had to take charge of my life, my body, and my heart. I realized the heartache of losing my dad had been my excuse to be weak and give up on life. This wasn't how my dad raised me. He raised me to be strong willed and independent! By letting Thomas take that away from me, I wasn't honoring my dad at all. I made the decision to get out of my rut of a horrible life and with the help of a friend, I got out."

"Somehow, I found me again by learning to forgive myself and the mistakes I made. I had to learn to trust myself by making good decisions, and I had to learn to love myself again. It's been one hell of a journey for me to get where I am now. I hate it when my past creeps into my present only to jeopardize my future."

"Only if you let it, baby," He watched her mull this statement over in her mind.

Kylee felt something soft on her back, it was her bed. She hadn't even noticed how Kellan carried her to the bedroom. She gave him a look of surprise.

"Sweet Girl, you're so tired you didn't even notice me carrying you. You need sleep." In answer to him a yawn escaped her lips, and she nodded sleepily.

"You'll stay in this bed until I come back for you, understand? I'm going out to check on Evan. Here's the cordless phone if you need me. My cell phone number is already programmed into the phone. Just hit the number 3 and it will call me directly. Stay in bed."

She rolled her eyes at his orders then turned on her side and found a comfortable position. He stood by the bed watching his angel peacefully fall asleep. He was proud of the steps she had taken to trust him by telling him about her abused past. He was proud of her for leaving the man that could have destroyed her. He hoped she would realize that he was here to love her and not hurt her. Over time he hoped to be the man to save her by opening the door to her heart.

Chapter Nine

Kellan was surprised to find Kylee sleeping when he came in for the night. He had expected her to be sitting up in bed with a bored expression on her face. He was disappointed she wasn't awake, but he did feel better knowing she was finally getting the rest she needed. He left her bedside to go shower and eat supper then checked on her again before he went to bed. He laid in his bed thinking about how he liked having her in his bed last night. *I'm missing her. I wonder if she is still sleeping or has she awakened? Is she cold? What if she needs something in the middle of the night? What if she needs me?* His mind and body tossed and turned trying to find a comfortable spot, but it was no use. He gave a frustrated grunt as his body betrayed him because after one night of sleeping with Kylee in his arms, he no longer could sleep alone. Kellan left his room to go check on her.

In her room, he sat on the bed watching her sleep peacefully. He placed his hand on her forehead making sure she didn't have a fever. She didn't. *Poor thing, she did push herself too far! She looks so serene and fragile sleeping here, but she is far from fragile! She's tough, tougher than she gives herself credit for. I'm so glad she got out from under that man's harmful grasp! I'm so proud of her!*

His heart expanded filling it up with so much love for her he thought it was going to burst through his chest. He had this overwhelming need to hold her. Without a second thought he crawled into her bed cuddling Kylee's back to his chest. She let out a small contented sigh. Kellan smiled joyfully as her subconscious spoke for her.

Kellan woke up early with Kylee snuggling close to him. *Ah, she smells good.*

Her scent aroused him. He was amazed how one woman could stir his sexual desires the way she did. He wanted her but decided it was too soon for her to have any strenuous physical activities. She still needed to rest. While he was in the bathroom he heard Kylee mumbling. He stepped into the doorway watching her arm reach for him calling out his name in confusion.

"I'm here, baby." Kellan came over to the bed. Her eyes were wide awake and alert.

"Where are you going?"

"Downstairs."

"I'm in my bed?" Kylee asked confused.

Kellan chuckled and smoothed her hair back. "Where else would you be?"

"In your bed. Did you sleep with me last night?"

"Yes." Kellan braced himself for an argument. To his relief she gave him a warm smile and scooted her body closer to him, hugging him.

"I'm glad."

Kellan's heart filled with happiness hearing her say these words to him. He wrapped his long arms around her and liked the way she snuggled against him tenderly. He had to distance himself or risk giving in to his sexual desires.

"It's early. Why don't you lie back down and I'll bring you a cup of coffee," Kellan said.

Kylee groaned in frustration but did as he said. She fell asleep and woke up when she heard the echo of the back door closing and guessed Kellan was heading out to the fields. She was a little hurt that he didn't say good-bye.

Rolling over she gasped in surprise that it was eight o'clock in the morning. Sitting up, swinging her legs over the side of the bed she suddenly felt wide awake.

Slowly she stood up annoyed by how weak her body felt. The reason had to be because she had slept for one whole day. This wasn't anything she had ever allowed herself to do in the past. There was always too much work to do. As there was here, but Kellan was too much of a force to be reckoned with when it came to her well being.

Kylee held onto the railing while she carefully took each step down the stairs. She was slightly out of breath by the time she got to the bottom. Stubbornly, she went forward into the kitchen. She felt faint and rested against the kitchen wall. She wondered how she was going to be able to cook today. She forced her way over to the refrigerator. There she stood out of breath clutching the door handles. Feeling faint again she rested her forehead on the doors. She took deep breaths in then exhaled slowly, trying to get her breath. *I hate how tired I am!*

"Kylee!" Kellan's concerned voice yelled behind her. She was so exhausted her body didn't even jump at his abrupt voice.

"What are you doing?" he asked the question but didn't wait for her to answer. "I told you to stay in bed," he scolded.

She nodded feebly. "You were right."

Hearing her admit he was right had him striding quickly over to her. She swayed to the side, and he caught her just in time. She fell trustingly into his arms.

"Stubborn girl," Kellan muttered.

"Yes," Kylee said. Her head tipped back, and her body went limp in his arms.

"I'm putting you back to bed," Kellan said firmly. Again he expected her to argue with him, but she didn't. All she said was, "Okay."

For reasons unknown to him Kellan just smiled. He loved her spirit. He loved that she was stubborn, and he loved the way she trusted him just now to take care of her. He loved her.

"If I don't cook what will you and Evan eat today?" Kylee asked him as he covered her up with the blanket.

Kellan shook his head. "Silly girl, we've eaten far less before you started spoiling us." He grinned winking at her.

"But what…"

"Shhh, there are tons of leftovers for us to heat up." Kellan soothed her with his words and patted her head gently with his wide hand.

"It's time to take care of you, Kylee. Let me help you."

Kylee curled her hand over his and whispered his name.

"Go to sleep, my sweet girl," Kellan soothed.

Kylee slept the day away and the night. If it was any other girl, Kellan would have been heavily worried about how her body chose to heal by all this sleeping. He decided not to call Chase because he knew about her and her last relationship now; maybe her subconscious finally felt safe. Kellan climbed into bed with her again that night. She immediately rolled up next to him with a sleepy greeting of hello. He kissed her on the shoulder and he pulled her close. If he didn't see any signs of improvement in her tomorrow he would call Chase. For now he was more than ecstatic to fall asleep with her in his arms.

Kellan had nothing to worry about because Kylee woke up feeling a lot better. He noticed she practically hopped out of bed. She had a bounce in her step as she crossed the room going into the bathroom. When she came out she looked energized and her face wore a bright happy smile. "Kylee, how are you feeling?"

"Fantastic! I feel like I have slept for days," Kylee shouted laughing.

Kellan got out of bed walked over to her giving her a big hug. "You just about have, silly girl. It's good to see you up and laughing." He bent down kissing her soundly on the mouth. "Oh, I haven't tasted those lips in awhile." His mouth lay on hers. He neatly dipped his tongue inside her mouth tasting the minty toothpaste fresh on her breath. Kellan's breathing was ragged when the kiss ended.

On a joyful sigh, Kylee nuzzled her lips into the crook of his neck placing delicate kisses on his unshaven skin. "It feels good to kiss you," she said.

"You too, baby. I have missed your kisses," Kellan agreed. To prove his point he gave her a long sensual kiss. The kiss sent shivers down her spine to her toes then burned a fire deep in her belly. Kylee moaned. She loved his masculine taste and smell. Even though her body was meshed against his, she still wasn't close enough and tried to twist her body closer to him. His arms tightened around her. "I've got you, Sweet Girl."

"Kellan, I think I'm going to take it easy today," Kylee said with her arms around his neck.

"I think that's a great idea. To tell you the truth I'll worry less," Kellan confessed with his arms folded comfortably behind her back.

Kylee frowned slightly. "I hate how I have worried you so much."

He shrugged one shoulder. "What can I say, I like you."
What he wanted to say was that he loved her, but he felt it was too soon for her to hear him say these words. Instead he kissed her forehead then the tip of her nose. His kiss ended on her soft, sensual lips.

"I like you too, Kellan." She hugged him laying her head on his chest. "Have a good morning. I'll see you around noon."

"See you later." Kellan sighed. He found it hard to walk away from her. This time when he walked out the back door he didn't let it slam shut. Instead, he held the door with his hand until the door met the doorframe, closing it quietly.

Kylee stayed true to her word. She laughed at herself for hardly doing any work at all. She sat drinking a few cups of coffee in her favorite wing back chair looking out into the back yard. In her mind she remodeled this room again the same way she did on her first days here. By knocking out part of the East wall and have an atrium door installed they could walk out to the expanded wooden deck. It would be so nice to have the two decks merged into one next to the pool. It also would be a wonderful enhancement to the house. She really needed to mention this to Kellan.

Kylee walked into the kitchen deciding to let the oven do all the work for this afternoon's meal. It was still hard for her to call lunch dinner. She liked the way Kellan teased her by calling her City Girl, and he especially did it when she called his dinner lunch. She laughed. Gazing out the window her thoughts wandered to his loving care. Her heart filled with love knowing how he didn't want to see her hurt. Not only did she see this, but she was beginning to feel it. Kellan wasn't here to hurt her but possibly love her. Earlier, he had said he liked her, but his caring actions suggested it might be more than "like". *Is he in love with me? If he is, what am I going to do about it? Could I love him? Do I love him? Yes, I could definitely love him, but do I? I can't be falling in love with him. It's too soon for us to be in love. Right?*

After some light dusting Kylee grabbed a water bottle then with a tired sigh she sat in a chair beside the kitchen table. She had been amazed by how many dust bunnies had accumulated in the short absent days of her last cleaning. *What is wrong with me? Why am I so tired after this little bit of work?*

In the past she would have pushed herself through the pain because this is what was expected of her, but Kellan didn't expect this. Was that the difference? Finally she was able to tend to her hurting body without anyone being upset about it or looking at her like she was weak. Some of her past employers would have been upset especially if they had guests coming.

*Employer...*Kylee tossed this word around in her head. *I had sex with my employer.* She sighed happily remembering the wonderful night. *Then I woke up in his bed the next morning! Ugh, that was awkward, and I didn't handle it very well.* She chuckled wryly remembering. *But Kellan made me feel better about it. My next crazy moment was when the truth of my past came spilling out of me. He didn't run away, instead, he held me dearly. He also crawled into bed with me during the days I slept.*

A tear trickled down her cheek, but as she wiped it away emotional tears surfaced and clouded her eyes. *What has gotten into me? I am a rollercoaster of emotions this past week. This is so unlike me.* More tears fell down her face. *I am a mess! Kellan must think I'm crazy. Yet he's by my side making me feel better. Maybe he's the one who is crazy.* She laughed mulling over this thought. Again she thought about Kellan being her employer and wasn't so sure he still was. *It's definitely something we'll need to talk about.*

Kylee looked out the window when she heard Jake barking. She saw a dark haired older woman getting out of a shiny black car. She watched the woman open the trunk of the car then lift items from the trunk. She made her way to the house. Kylee quickly wiped away the tears and hoped her face didn't look red from crying. Kylee met the woman at the back door, startling her.

"Thanks. I didn't know anyone was here. I saw Kellan out in the fields when I drove past," the woman said with a puzzled frown. "Mmm, it smells wonderful in here."

"Thank you," Kylee said. She watched the woman set the items down on the counter, and she removed the towels revealing a big tin foil pan. Then she put the pan into the refrigerator. "What's in there?"

The woman paused in mid step turning around to glance at Kylee. "Roast beef. I'm sorry. I'm Kellan's mom, Sara." She extended her right hand to Kylee.

Kylee clasped her hand saying, "Hi, Sara, I'm Kylee."

Sara gave her a big smile. "Hi, Kylee, it's nice to meet you. I'm back from vacation so I thought I'd fix a beef roast and bring it over. Normally this will last him a week."

"Oh. Do you cook for him often?" Kylee asked her. Kellan hadn't said anything about his mom cooking, too.

"Yes, I try to bring him a roast once a week, but sometimes I get busy at work or am on vacation. Kellan's dad and I got back from the beach just yesterday. I got up early this morning to cook this roast for him and wanted to bring it over while it was fresh."

Kylee was slightly annoyed that Kellan hadn't mentioned his mom making beef roast all the time for him. If she had known, she wouldn't have put it on her menu. Gosh, if it was her, she'd be so tired of beef roast. However, he did scarf it up the day she made it and both he and Evan gave her high praise. She silently questioned the sincerity of their kind compliments.

"Normally this much food will last him a week, but I know he hired a man to help with the housekeeping. So it's possible with two men eating the roast this might not last a week. Oh, wait, I forgot about Evan. Make it three men," Sara rattled on. She glanced over at Kylee. First, she had been surprised to see an attractive woman in her son's kitchen. Her next surprise had been when she smelled something wonderful coming from the oven. Sara was curious if her son had hired a cooking maid, too. Lordy, a lot had changed while she had been on vacation. Since Sara knew everyone in town, she wondered where her son found Kylee because this girl certainly wasn't from around here.

"Have you met the male housekeeper?" Sara inquired wanting answers but demanding them wasn't the way to go about it. She felt that if she came on too strong the skinny girl would fall right over.

"Male housekeeper?" Kylee stated with confusion written all over her face.

"Yeah," Sara said. "Have you met Kyle?" *Maybe, she was his wife?*

Kylee's blank stare annoyed Sara.

"Kyle, right." Kylee nodded her head slowly. A smile formed on her lips. His mom had no idea about the mix up on the incorrect spelling of her name.

"Yes, dear," Sara spoke irritably. "Kyle, the man, my son hired for housekeeping duties. Have you met him or are you his wife?"

Kylee gave her a bewildered gaze. Great, now his mom thought she was the male housekeeper's wife. She held back the uproarious laugh inside of her. Laughing at Kellan's mom wasn't the first impression she wanted the woman to have of her.

"Actually, there was a misunderstanding in regard to a man coming to work for Kellan," Kylee began.

"Oh?" Sara asked in an interested tone.

"Yes. Kyle isn't the name of the housekeeper. It's Kylee," Kylee informed her. She watched Sara's face change from the anticipation of a good story to the realization that the girl standing before her is the housekeeper. His mom's eyes narrowed suspiciously. Kylee immediately knew where Kellan inherited his scowl. It was from this lady standing in front of her.

Sara's mouth formed a silent "O" then she said in an astonished tone, "You?"

Sara didn't think Kylee looked sturdy enough to handle the hard work this house needed. The girl's eyes were red, maybe from a lack of sleep or she'd been crying due to the strenuous work.

Kylee nodded her head. "Yes. I'm Kyle, only with an extra "E" at the end making it Kylee."

Sara nodded her head unsure of what to say. She was bewildered over this unexpected news. "So Kellan hired you to do the cooking instead of what he had hired the man to do?"

"I agreed to do the cooking, but I'm also redecorating the rooms Kellan needs done," Kylee stated firmly.

"That's a lot of hard work," Sara countered.

"Yes, but also very rewarding," Kylee pointed out.

"Yes, I suppose it could be," Sara stated. The girl may look thin, but she had a spirited spunk. She had respect for her. Only time would tell if Kylee's beauty would end up distracting Kellan, however, Sara thought her son could use a little distraction. He worked too hard and kept to himself too much in this big old house. Yes, Kylee might be exactly what her son needed. Keeping a poker face to her happy thoughts she asked, "What are you making?"

"Meatloaf," Kylee fibbed. The truth was she had a beef roast in the oven but didn't have the heart to tell his mom this.

His mom smiled. "It smells wonderful."

"Thank you."

"Well, it's time for me to go. I wish you the best of luck, Kylee. Lord knows this house could use all the help it can get in fixing it up."

"Thank you." Kylee gave Sara a warm smile and received one in return.

"Don't let my son work you too hard," Sara warned her then added in a lighter tone, "Get outside and enjoy the pool."

"I'll have to do that," Kylee said with a thoughtful look. She hadn't even thought about going for a swim in the pool. *Too busy,* she thought.

Sara thought Kylee already looked worn out. Kellan was working her too hard, she thought bitterly.

"Thanks for stopping by. I'll let Kellan know you brought him the roast," Kylee told her.

"It's for you too, Sweetie. This way it'll be one less meal for you to cook," Sara said giving her a genuine smile. She liked Kylee and wished her well with the redecorating of the old farmhouse.

Kylee waved good-bye. She liked Kellan's mom. She was genuine with her smile, strong and gentle and now she knew where Kellan inherited his facial expressions.

Kellan gave a jovial laugh when he saw the familiar black car barreling down the dirt path with a dust cloud following it. It stopped near him in the field. He put the tractor in park, turned off the engine, and climbed down to greet his mom. She was smiling and laughing when she got out of the car as she grabbed him in a big bear hug.

"Welcome back! When did you guys get home?"

"Yesterday," his mom announced. "I was just by the house dropping off a pot roast."

"Aw, Mom, you didn't need to cook for me on your first day back," Kellan scolded her with a smile.

"Well, I found the reason why I didn't need to cook anything for you." Sara winked.

Kellan met her wink with a steady expression. "You met Kylee."

"Yes. Nice girl. I like her," Sara said. "Although, you can imagine my surprise to find a woman in your kitchen instead of the man we all were expecting."

"Imagine my surprise when she showed up on my door step?" Kellan laughed.

Sara laughed, too as she pictured Kellan's surprised look the day he met Kylee. She was pretty sure it was the same one she had.

"She's pretty," Sara said, but Kellan just gave her a curt nod not revealing any emotion. Sara pursed her lips together. She was getting nothing from him indicating his thoughts of his pretty housekeeper.

"How is she doing with the redecorating?" Sara asked.

"Really well," Kellan said. "Did she show you the sitting room?"

Sara shook her head no. "I didn't get past the kitchen. She's making meatloaf and it smells wonderful."

Kellan nodded with a smile. "She's a good cook."

"You're working her too hard," Sara mentioned casually but was happy to finally see a small flicker of care cross her son's face. His heart wasn't made of steel after all.

"Why do you say that?" Kellan asked her carefully. He knew his mom all too well. Her questions weren't as innocent as she claimed them to be. She was fishing for information in regards to the female he just hired. He knew his mom wanted more grandchildren. With his sisters happily married they had provided her with several grandchildren, but he was her last hope for more grandkids. He often teased that he didn't have to be married to give her grandkids. A bitter look was always her response.

"She's exhausted. I can see it on her face," Sara said.

"It's not because of what you think," Kellan said. He clearly saw where his mom's thoughts had taken her by the amused expression on her face.

"Ooh-la-la," she sang.

Kellan scowled. Yes, his mom was right, but there was no way he was about to admit this to her. "She fell on the stairs the other day."

"Oh! My, gosh! Is she okay?" Sara gasped placing her hand over her heart.

"Yes. I had the doctor come out and examine her."

"Thank heavens for that! Which doctor?" Sara did the sign of the cross thanking God that the girl wasn't severely hurt.

"Chase."

Kellan watched his mom shrug her shoulders saying, "People around town seem to like him well enough."

Kellan rolled his eyes. He knew she was referring to the part about Chase being an outsider, but she wouldn't say the actual words. She didn't want to sound judgmental. Kellan didn't care that Chase wasn't born and raised in this little town. But his mom, on the other hand, was apprehensive about the new doctor. Since she didn't know his parents, she couldn't say for sure if he was a good man or not. She could only rely on what she's heard through the gossip vine. So far the gossip about Dr. Chase has been positive.

It's not that she was a prejudice person, but she liked the small town living and was defensive, at first, to newcomers. Kellan suspected this is how his mom felt about Kylee, and her next comment confirmed his suspicions.

"She could sue you for falling, you know. Work man's comp. Did you take out insurance for her to be working in your home?"

"Mom, she's not going to sue me," Kellan told her firmly.

Sara gave him an absurd look. The confidence he had knowing that Kylee wasn't going to sue him was ridiculous to her. "How do you know? You know nothing about this girl. Plus when I walked in she had just been crying. Maybe she's in more pain than she's letting on."

"I know she's not going to sue me," Kellan tried to reassure his mom, but she wasn't in the mood to be reassured.

"You sound so sure of yourself, but like I said you have no background of this girl. She could be one of those women who like to sue people just to get their money. How do you know for sure that she really did fall and wasn't pretending? Did you see it happen?"

Kellan let out an exasperated sigh. "Because when we came in from the fields she was unconscious." He hoped this answer would satisfy her; he should've known better.

"Kellan," Sara began, but Kellan cut her off.

"Mom, I gotta get back to work. I've got lots of work to do today, but thanks for bringing the roast." He placed his hand on her back firmly escorting her to the car. He hated how quickly their conversation took on a sour note. He knew his mom meant well with her concern about him being sued. He also knew she could be too nosy at times. He knew Kylee wasn't going to sue him, but to explain how he knew this to his mom would have opened up another whole can of worms. His private life was just that, private. Even after all these years his mom still had a hard time with it.

"When your sister gets back from vacation I'm going to have everyone over at the house," Sara warned him knowing how he liked to squirm his way out of the family functions, much to her annoyance. The excuse of a field having to be plowed, planted, or harvested had run its course with her. She no longer accepted this answer as to why her children couldn't attend a family gathering. Sara had enough gracious excuses from her husband, the father of their three children, of having to be home every morning and night to take care of the cows. They had to be fed and milked daily, twice a day. That certainly had been a chore. Once the decision had been made, for the two of them to move into town, Sara had been thrilled. She dragged her husband on vacations all over the country. As Sara drove her car away from Kellan her mind wandered. She was envious of the future Mrs. Kellan Taylor. Who ever it may be the girl didn't know how blessed she was that Kellan was only tied to his fields and didn't have any animals to take care of. It meant their lives would be more flexible to having days off.

Of course, it would still take the right kind of woman to love Kellan and accept his farm life. Sara pondered. *Hmm, I wonder if Kylee is that right woman. My son certainly isn't interested in any of the girls in town. Is there a chance this outsider could turn his head? Could it be I just met my future grandbabies' momma? Only time will tell.*

Kellan climbed up into the tractor with Kylee on his mind. His mom had mentioned she had looked tired and had been crying. An urgent need to see her consumed him. He should check on her to make sure she was okay even if it was only to put his mind at ease. Kellan steered his tractor over by Evan.

"What's up?" Evan called out over the tractor's engine. "I saw your mom."

"Mom's good." Kellan shrugged. "She just dropped off a beef roast."

Evan gave a curt nod of his head. He waited for Kellan to tell him the reason for stopping him, but he knew it had nothing to do with his mom bringing a roast.

"She met Kylee and mentioned she looked worn out. I'm gonna go check on her."

Evan chuckled. "Okay. Hey, can you bring me something to eat when you come back?"

"You're not coming in to eat?"

"Naw, I really want to get this field finished today. Just bring me a sandwich okay? And a pop,"

"Dr. Pepper?" Kellan asked.

"Yes."

"Can do, I'll take the truck since you won't need it. See you in awhile."

Evan waved to Kellan as he drove off.

Chapter Ten

After Kellan's mom left, Kylee felt rested and decided to face her enemy…the vacuum cleaner. She really wasn't in the mood to vacuum, but she wanted to clean up the particles of dirt beneath her bare feet. In the evenings when Kellan came home he was always good about taking his boots off by the back door. She appreciated it and remembered him saying on the first day they met how he didn't like mud on the carpets. Kylee knew it was her shoes that tracked the dirt further into the house. She thought about asking them to remove their boots before coming in but didn't have the heart to ask since they'd be putting them on again within a short time. She didn't want to be the reason for taking their time away from working in the fields. Besides, she wasn't quite sure she wanted to smell their stinky sweaty feet. She made a sour face.

Plus, Kellan would probably give her a smart ass answer along the lines of; this is why he hired a housekeeper. This thought brought a smile, and she laughed as she plugged the cord into the outlet then turned on the power button. Kellan had asked her to stay off the stairs today with the vacuum cleaner while he was gone. A few days ago she would've felt he was being a bit overprotective but today his need to keep her safe made her feel wonderfully warm. She, too, didn't want to take any chances of falling again.

The vacuum hummed loud before making an odd high pitch screeching sound like nails on a chalkboard as it abruptly stopped working.

"What? You've got to be kidding me!" Kylee shouted. Just to make sure it didn't work she turned the power button off and on again repeating the process three times before her temper exploded. She gave the vacuum cleaner a frustrated kick with her foot.

"You, stupid piece of shit," Kylee cursed the machine as though it was human and it could understand her. She didn't even have the chance to vacuum anything with it before it died. Oh, how she hated this thing!

Kellan heard her cussing all the way from the kitchen when he walked into the house. Worried about her he hurried in and stopped abruptly when he saw her kicking and cursing the vacuum cleaner. Leaning one shoulder against the door jamb he suppressed the roaring laughter that threatened to erupt. His blood level raised a few degrees when she bent over giving him a good view of her cute ass sticking up in the air, staring at him. Playful thoughts stumbled through his mind teasing his other head. With her hands on her hips she stood up pushing the machine with her foot grumbling, "Stupid thing."

Gosh, she was the cutest, funniest, mad woman he had ever seen in his whole life as her ponytail bounced on the back of her head. A sexy spark of desire shot through him. *Oh, I am hot for her! I want her! I need to touch her!* His long strides swiftly carried him to her. In a matter of seconds his hands were on her hips touching her and pulling her against him. Kylee leaped and gasped at the surprise embrace, but it took only a short second for her to recognize it was Kellan who had her.

"Shhh, it's me, Sweet Girl," he whispered in her ear and felt her relax. However, the memory of her bottom in the air clouded his thoughts as he envisioned her naked waiting for him to slide into her. He instantly was hard. He wondered if she'd object if he carried her upstairs for an afternoon of love making. He groaned achingly.

"I like it when you touch me," Kylee whispered seductively. His sparking touch ignited a fire between them. She yearned for his passion and wanted him so much! Thinking about their naked bodies touching made her vagina wet.

"I like touching you." Kellan squeezed her hips affectionately as she melted against him.

Trapped in his electrifying hold Kylee had no where to go, but she didn't want to be anywhere else. His hands were hot, strong and possessive. It made her feel like a desired gift. He rubbed her hips with the palms of his hands moving them freely over her body. Reaching his hands inside her shirt, he pulled the bra off her bountiful breasts. His fingers stroked her nipples turning them hard. Then he removed her shirt. Peering over her shoulder he could see her perky nipples, and his erection grew bigger. Moving his hands over her waist he unfastened her jeans sliding them along with her underwear down to the floor. She stepped out of them, and he kicked them away. An intense heat engulfed them. He caressed her inner thigh before slipping one finger upward checking if she was ready for him. She was.

"I'm hot for you, Sweet Girl," Kellan hummed.

"Tell me how," she whispered provocatively.

"What if I show you?" Kellan's voice rang seductively as he nibbled her ear.
He firmly pulled her backside against his jeans. "Feel that?"

"No." She teased and rested her cheek on the side of his face running her fingers through his hair. The movement of her fingers sent shivers down his spine. Next he slid his jeans down then pulled her back against his briefs where there was less material between them. "Do you feel that, City Girl?"

This time she licked her lips sensually as she smiled whispering, "No."

"Sweet Girl, I know you're teasing." He smiled playfully as he slid his briefs all the way off kicking his clothes over to where hers lay. Fiercely he tugged her back against his front side.

"Feel that?" He laughed wickedly knowing she couldn't deny feeling his hard erection now that they were naked.

"Yes." She breathed excitedly. Her hands gripped his hair. She needed him, wanted him and was impatient to feel him inside her heated sexual pool.

"Oh, baby," he said in fascination as he kissed her neck.

Kylee bent her head back begging him to take her, and Kellan didn't think he had ever heard anything as desirable as her invitation. He accepted her invitation by swiftly entering her and quickly lost control as his need to possess her was far too great. He slid fast and hard in and out of her quickening his pace when she pleaded for more. He loved feeling her pool of seduction surround him as her delighted cries had him plunging deeper. Her body shivered, and she shouted out his name as he reared his head back, clenched his teeth and shouted out her name as their orgasms erupted together.

"Oh, baby." Kellan carried her over to the couch and they lay there satiated cradled in a warm loving hug. "Sweet City Girl,"

"Mmm," was all Kylee managed to get out. She was relaxed and didn't want to move. From where they lay she could see the vacuum cleaner on the floor.

"You need a new vacuum cleaner." She yawned.

"Hmm," Kellan hummed. "I guess we'll have to go get one later."

"When?" Kylee asked nonchalantly.

"We'll go today just as soon as I get my energy back," Kellan answered.

Kylee laughed. "I know the feeling." Then she said bitterly, "You know that stupid vacuum cleaner has bad timing."

"How so?"

"It could've quit working before I tripped on the damn cord."

"I agree. That damn thing," he grumbled and kissed her shoulder. He was inhaling her sweet scent of sex and was getting turned on again. Just as he thought to roll her over and make her beg for him again Evan's face popped into his mind and remembered that he was waiting on a sandwich. Kellan groaned. He rolled over Kylee to stand up. "Shit."

"What?" Kylee asked him, sad that he moved away from her.

"Evan's waiting on a sandwich."

Guilt immediately entered her face thinking he was waiting outside. She sat up hastily covering herself with a throw pillow. She completely forgot about the time and the fact that Evan would be coming in to eat. "Oh! My gosh! Where is he?"

Kellan laughed at her feeble attempt to cover her naked body with the small pillow. He handed her clothes to her, and she slipped them on.

"He's out in the field. He's not coming in today because he wanted to finish up the field we're working in, but he asked me to bring him a sandwich and a pop."

"Pop? Oh you mean a soda. It's strange how you guys around here call soda a pop."

"Yeah, it's short for soda pop."

"I know." Kylee nodded. "Just strange that's all."

"How about we head into town for a vacuum cleaner?" Kellan suggested.

"Wonderful idea." Kylee beamed.

"While you are getting ready I'll deliver a sandwich to Evan then be back to pick you up."

Kylee gave him an odd look but said okay. As she marched up the stairs to her room she didn't understand Kellan's plan at all. Why would he deliver the sandwich to Evan and then come back for her? Why not just wait for her? She dressed in shorts and a pink shirt, ran a brush through her hair then slipped on some sandals. She hoped the sandals would be okay to wear and that they wouldn't have any car trouble but just in case she grabbed a pair of socks and sneakers to take with her. Running over the cat had taught her a lesson in how you never know when you're going to have car trouble. Satisfied with her mirrored reflection except for the bruise on her face she headed downstairs. She breezed into the kitchen just as Kellan was zipping the lunch tote closed.

"I'm ready to go," she announced.

He had his back turned to her, and he jumped in surprise. He hadn't expected her to come back so quickly. Kylee laughed because she startled him.

"Wow, I can't believe I scared you," Kylee noted.

"Me neither." Kellan gave her an incredible look and made the mistake of saying, "You're already to go?"

"What's wrong?" she asked misunderstanding his look. "You don't think I look good enough to go into town?" Kylee asked crestfallen thinking she looked awful. With a self-conscious feeling her hand touched the bruise on her face.

He saw her touch the bruise and wished he could take back the words that had her doubting how she looked. This wasn't what he meant. He recouped quickly by complimenting her with, "No, Sweet Girl, you are a breath of fresh air."

"Then what's wrong?"

"I have sisters and they take a long time to freshen up. It didn't take you anytime at all." Kellan bent to give her a quick kiss on the lips then kissed her bruise. "You look fabulous!"

Kylee giggled, "Thanks."

"Have I told you how much I love hearing you laugh?" He gave her a warm smile making her heart beat quickly.

"That's why you said you'd deliver Evan's sandwich then come back for me," Kylee said as it dawned on her. "I didn't understand that part."

"Yes. I just need to grab Evan a –"

"Pop," Kylee finished his sentence in a giggle. Kellan laughed, too.

"I still can't believe I scared you," Kylee said between laughs opening the refrigerator door to pull out Evan's favorite soda pop and tossed it to Kellan.

"Careful now. If you don't stop laughing I'll strip you of your clothes and spank that bare ass of yours." His smile was teasing, but his eyes were dangerously dark filled with a carnal hunger.

Kylee slowly fluttered her eyelashes daring him to make due of his playful threat. Playfully she swept her eyes over his body casting them downward to his crotch where her gaze lingered. She wet her lips with her tongue before bringing her eyes back to his. He was glued to the floor after her hot fluttered gaze swept over him. A vivid heat poured out of her and spilled onto him, and he felt prey to her spidery seduction. He was tangled and powerless in her web of desire. All he could do was stand there and let himself be seduced. Her eyes spiraled down his body again, and she licked her lips lusciously fully aware of how uncomfortable he was in his jeans.

If Kellan could've moved he would have stripped off their clothes and taken her right there. No other woman has ever been able to stir his sexual senses with one hot look as Kylee was doing right now. His heart beat wildly against his chest while his pulse raced out of control through his veins. A breath of air caught in his throat when her eyes blazed a blue fire. Passionate flames burned between them again and there was only one way to extinguish the fire.

"If you keep looking at me that way you're going to see how serious I am," Kellan whispered huskily giving her the opportunity to move away. Instead she stepped closer into his space. He'd never wanted sex so soon again after just having it, but he wanted her again and now! His hands slid into her jeans feeling her velvety skin, and he roughly clutched her against him. Touching her was electrifying! He kissed the curve of her neck and felt her body shiver. The subtle play of sex turned into a drug of passion. He captured her open eager mouth with his lips, and their breathing became one.

"I want you," Kellan hissed.

"Have me, Kellan."

And he did. In record time he had them out of their clothes. He hoisted her up on the counter kissing her breasts. She inhaled sharply over the sexual sensations gliding through her. Kellan felt her body twisting, and he knew she was close to an orgasm. Wanting to feel her hot release showering him he stopped suckling her breasts and lifted her into his arms. He leaned back against the counter then positioned her body so that her vagina sank down onto his penis. Her arms and legs wrapped around his body. Their two bodies connected into a rhythmic pattern. As she came down he met her with a penetrating thrust. Cries of ecstasy escaped her when he dug his fingers into the soft flesh of her bottom. A joyful shivering wave washed over her, but Kellan wasn't done with her yet.

Feeling her hot liquid trickle over him had a potent affect on him. He backed her up against the wall plowing into her with an intense need of satisfaction not only for him; but for her, too.

She let him lift her higher and higher until she couldn't hold on any longer. His satisfying grunts reached her ears as she felt his release shoot into her. A proud smile curved her lips knowing she had satisfied him as much as he had her. She didn't know sex was this wonderful until now, and she wasn't sure she'd ever find a more perfect mate. Exhausted, she collapsed in his arms. Kellan leaned in holding her, breathing heavily, letting the wall hold them up.

"My legs are weak," she mumbled.

"I've got you, Sweet Girl," Kellan reassured her.

"Evan must be hungry by now," Kylee pointed out.

He chuckled, "He probably is."

Kellan was concerned about Evan's hungry stomach but right now he didn't want to move away from her warmth. All he wanted to do was go upstairs and take a nap together. She had to be tired and to tell the truth he was, too, after them making love twice.

Eventually she found strength in her legs to stand. They dressed in the kitchen, and Kylee surprised Kellan again by not running to find a mirror to check her reflection. She had trusted his word about how great she looked. It made him feel good how she was starting to trust him.

"You're sure you want to spend the money on a new vacuum?" Kylee asked as she followed him out the door. "Remember it might be expensive."

"And I told you its okay. Your safety comes first." Kellan stopped walking and turned around brushing her cheek with his thumb. A heated rush streamed through her with the combination of his touch and words. Quietly, she walked behind him still in awe that he had the ability to just up and buy a new vacuum cleaner whereas she was used to having to budget for one. She was convinced he would change his mind once he found out the price of what she wanted and would make her settle for the cheaper version.

Instead of getting into his dusty old farm truck Kellan steered her in the direction of a garage built next to the house. The garage door opened, and Kylee was fascinated to see a shiny black truck; a newer version of his old dusty one. This one had a higher lift and it was sparkling clean. It was beautiful!

"Wow!" Kylee exclaimed her eyes lit up in pure delight. Kellan took pride in his new toy and it pleased him greatly to see her enthusiasm. It was obvious to him that she loved his truck as much as he did. He watched her gently glide her fingers over its sleek edges.

"This truck is awesome, Kellan! Good thing you keep her in the garage with the doors down so she doesn't get dirty."

"She?" Kellan smiled appreciating the fact how she knew vehicles were sometimes referred to in the female sense.

Kylee rolled her eyes. "Yeah, I know how men like to call their vehicles a "she". It's the only female that doesn't talk back to them."

Kellan laughed out loud pleased that she understood this. He couldn't stop smiling at her. "Well, sometimes they talk back to us."

"She's beautiful." Kylee stated then gasped when she felt Kellan's hands on her waist lifting her up into the truck so she had to look down at him. She was about to protest that she could've climbed up herself but seeing the boyish grin on his handsome face she let him have his way. Plus, she liked feeling the heat surge through her when he touched her.

"Yes she is," Kellan agreed with a proud look. "Now, I've got a beautiful girl to go along with my beautiful truck." He patted her leg affectionately sending sparks through her. It amazed her how there still could be a spark between them after their love making. She was still blushing over his statement when he climbed up into the driver's seat. The truck was a perfect fit for him! Closing the door, he looked like a boy who had just won a prize as he sat there with one arm lazily draped over the steering wheel and the other one shifting the truck into gear. He wore a winning smile because he had a beautiful truck, and his beautiful girl sitting beside him.

"I like the soft leather seats," Kylee said as she sank comfortably into them.

Kellan laughed. "They are heated and cooled."

"Nice!" Kylee exclaimed as she watched him set his iPhone in the console cradle. "Bluetooth?"

Kellan nodded. "Yep,"

"Oh! Sweet!" she cried out. Kellan stilled and felt his erection growing because he recognized the sound as the same pleasurable cry she gave just before she had an orgasm. *Nice! I already heard this twice today.* Kellan glanced her way half expecting to see her body shivering.

"Baby," Kellan said in his deep baritone voice unaware of the affect the tone had on her. Sexual shivers passed through her as she melted further into the truck seat. For a moment all they could do was stare into each other's dark sensuous eyes both surprised by how easily they could be persuaded into having sex again. His mind tormented him with sexual thoughts about them having sex in, on and against this truck. *Damn!*

A horn honking behind him brought him out of his fantasy. Kellan looked up and in his rearview mirror he saw Evan driving the tractor. Kellan slowly backed the truck out of the garage and drove over to Evan.

"K-man! Where the hell is my lunch?!" Evan shouted out.

"Here." Kellan held the lunch bag out the window tossing it up to him.

"It's about time!" Evan said irritated but when he saw Kylee in the truck his eyes changed to speculation. "I'd ask what took you so long but I think I already know the answer." His eyes held a hint of humor.

Kellan ignored his comment saying, "I'm taking Kylee into town to get a new vacuum cleaner."

"Okay. Good luck!" Evan gave him a rascal grin adding, "I won't be here when you get back."

Kylee felt Evan was giving Kellan this information for a reason.

"Okay. Have a good night. See ya tomorrow," Kellan bid farewell to him. Then he turned to Kylee instructing her to buckle up.

"He knows," Kylee said her face turning bright red.

"Yeah, I'm pretty sure he knows." He nodded his head smiling.

"Does it bother you that he knows?" she asked.

"Nope. Does it bother you?" Kellan asked gently.

"Maybe a little," Kylee confessed. "But knowing it doesn't bother you makes it a little easier for me, I guess."

"Ev won't tease you about it. He'll be a gentleman. But honestly, Kylee, what's going on between you and me is just about you and me and no one else."

"What is going on between you and me?" she dared asking.

Kellan had a thoughtful look on his rugged face. He didn't have a good answer for her, least of all one he thought she wanted to hear. For some reason, he didn't feel she would welcome him saying that he might be falling in love with her. He answered with, "We enjoy being together."

Just as he predicted Kylee's pretty face filled with relief satisfied with his answer. This confirmed his suspicion that she, too, was skittish for any more commitment other than enjoying each other. Kellan realized he needed to sit on his feelings for awhile. Just because he felt like he was starting to fall in love with her didn't really mean he was. Maybe he was confusing lust for love since he was becoming aware that he may never have his fill of her. This thought scared him and excited him all at the same time. It was a weird feeling since he'd never wanted a woman before like he wanted Kylee.

Kellan took his time driving on the gravel driveway careful not to spit any stones up with his tires. He readjusted himself in the seat. At the end of the driveway he stopped the truck and turned to look at her. "I'll admit I have some sexual fantasies with you and me in this truck that I intend to indulge in but not right now."

Kylee's eyes were full of delight as she teasingly ran her tongue over her lips.

Kellan groaned deeply. "Stop it." Then he warned. "If you keep doing that I'm going to park the truck right here in the driveway and have sex with you, and I'm not going to care who sees us.

"Okay." She giggled.

"I'm hard just knowing that you are wet," he told her. Kylee started to protest, but he gave her an "I know I'm right" look making her blush. He laughed out loud breaking the sexual tension between them as she laughed, too.

As soon as Kellan steered the truck on the asphalt road he stomped his foot on the gas pedal and the engine roared to life under the hood.

Kylee laughed over the fact that he had a lead foot something they had in common. He drove fast over the hills and around the curves. She was thrilled by the speed and impressed that the truck performed so well. Kylee surprised herself that she trusted Kellan completely knowing he would make sure they arrived safely to their destination. Never before had she trusted anyone wholly as she was beginning to with Kellan.

"Kellan, I love this! Thank you," Kylee said.

"Welcome."

"How long have you had her?" she asked.

"A couple of months."

"You're a good driver."

"Thanks."

They drove in silence the rest of the way. Kylee enjoyed the scenery. Fields surrounded them everywhere with the occasional gentle rolling hills that they flew over and then dipped down into a valley only to drive back up another hill. On top of those hills she could see for miles into the horizon with the view of red barns and silos dotting the countryside. It was beautiful. She paid close attention to where Kellan turned heading into town. On the way, Kellan pointed out the grocery store, the meat market, and gas station. He gave her a tour of the town before he pulled up along the sidewalk on Main Street.

"Where's the store we are going to?" Kylee asked.

"Over there." Kellan pointed across the street to a sign that read, "Hank's".

Kylee followed Kellan across the street watching with envy as he confidently walked, his long legs carrying him gracefully. A car stopped for him and instead of honking its horn, the driver gave a cheerful wave. Kellan tugged on Kylee's hand to hurry her across the street. He had noticed how she kept looking over her shoulder as if she was waiting for someone to run over her.

"Somebody will run you over if you don't hurry up and cross the street," Kellan teased.

"Oh, I hope not," Kylee answered fearfully.

"I hope not, too." Kellan gave her a warm smile that had her insides melting. He added with a laugh, "My ride home would be very lonely."

Kylee punched him lightly on the arm, but she was laughing, too as Kellan pulled her closer to his side.

Chapter Eleven

In the distance a redheaded girl with jade green eyes stopped dead in her tracks. She couldn't believe what she saw. Kellan Taylor in town in the middle of the day, and he had a girl with him? How could this be? Kellan Taylor never left his fields during the day! She should know! She had asked him to meet her for lunch several times, and he had rejected her telling her he had too much work to do in the fields during the day. AND…when she asked to meet him for an evening meal he let her down by saying he worked out in the fields from sunrise to sunset. He was just too tired in the evenings.

Ivy hadn't figured out a way, yet, how to get Kellan to invite her over. She would even bring supper to him. Sure, she could invite herself but a part of her was old fashioned, and she wanted Kellan to ask her. She didn't want to feel like she was the one doing all the work to make a relationship and yet she was the one doing all the work.

She and Kellan both had spent their lives in this same little town. They went to school together and graduated the same year. Growing up in a small town where people knew most everybody was a curse and a blessing. Both their mamas had the same small town mentality; "it's good to know the roots of your future spouse." Most of their classmates started pairing up and getting married. Ivy became aware that she, Kellan, and a few others their age seemed to be the only ones left who didn't have someone special in their lives. This made Ivy start to wonder if she and Kellan were destined to be together. She had already tried to set her sights on Evan but there was something about him that didn't fit with her. He was looking for a nice quiet girl and even though she was quiet he wasn't what Ivy wanted. Then there was Dirk, but he certainly wasn't the man for her since he had set his career as a truck driver. Ivy knew she didn't want the man in her life to be out on the road all the time.

Ivy knew she would make a good farmer's wife. She understood the farmer's obsession with the love of his land and animals since her daddy, bless his soul, had worked as a farmer until his dying day. She wasn't the greatest housekeeper in the world, and she didn't really like cooking, but she knew if it was to win Kellan's heart she'd cook and clean for him if this is what it took. Lately, she had begun her dream of one day marrying Kellan Taylor. She knew her mama would be pleased since she knew the history of Kellan's family.

Wait! What did she just see? Did Kellan just hug the girl?! Was it possible her eyes were playing tricks on her? Yes, it was possible, but she reminded herself that she had good eye sight.

Ivy leaned up against her car door disturbed by what she witnessed. All her dreams of being the future Mrs. Kellan Taylor seemed to be vanishing before her eyes. Who was this girl, where did she come from, and why is she here? She had to find out more about this girl who now was becoming her competition. Ivy pulled out her cell phone and dialed the number of the only person who would know about the girl that was with Kellan; his mother.

Chapter Twelve

Kellan pushed the door open and a bell rang as the two of them walked in, and they noticed no one was there to greet them. It was quiet except for the music that played softly through the speakers. Kylee looked in awe at the different displays of vacuum cleaners. Some were displayed on the shelves, others were hanging on the wall and the rest sat on the floor.

Kylee stepped away from Kellan as she walked over to a row of vacuums. She looked at one where the price was $80.00. Kellan walked up behind her, bent his head down next to her ear, and said, "Sweet Girl. I know that's not the one you want."

His warm breath tickled her from her ear all the way down to her toes. She nodded her head and walked further down the aisle. Kylee smelled the heavy cologne in the aura of the salesman before she saw him.

"Good afternoon!" The salesman greeted them cheerfully. Both of them turned to greet him eyeing that his name tag read, Hank.

Hank, the salesman, extended his hand to the two of them. Kellan's big hand engulfed the salesmen's hand as he shook it. Then Hank turned to Kylee forcing his hand into hers. Kylee clasped his hand but the salesman's hand lingered limply in her hand, and she felt squeamish. She tried to let go, but he continued to hold her hand as his eyes leered quietly at her. She was uncomfortable under his stare as she forcibly withdrew her hand from his and took a small step backwards.

"What can I get for you folks?" Hank asked. He looked first at Kylee, but she had her eyes focused on a vacuum in front of her. Hank looked up at Kellan, well aware of how much shorter he was than the tall man who intimidated him. Hank was surprised to see the young farmer in his store. In fact, Mr. Taylor was the last person he'd ever expect to have in his store.

"Mr. Taylor, isn't it?" Hank inquired.

"Yes," Kellan answered. It was written all over the salesman's face that he was pleased to have customers in his store. "Hank, we need a new vacuum cleaner. If you could show us what you have…"

Kylee stood in silence as she noted the words Kellan used. Instead of saying "I" or that he alone needed the new vacuum he used the words, "we and us". This made her extremely happy.

"Do you have anything in mind?" Hank directed his question to Kylee. He knew better than to ask the tall man anything about a vacuum cleaner. He'd be surprised if the young farmer even knew how to turn one on. Kylee caught the lustful look Hank gave her. She blushed under his scrutinizing eyes. He was making her feel very uncomfortable.

Kylee took a step closer to Kellan and looking up at him she asked, "Are you sure? Anything I pick out?"

"Yes, the vacuum of your choice," Kellan reaffirmed. He stared intently at her wondering why Kylee's face was flushed. Did she like the salesman? The thought made him ill.

Kellan's cell phone rang. Looking at the caller id he saw it was his mom and knew he should answer it. "Excuse me. I need to take this call," Kellan announced with a sigh. He walked away from Hank and Kylee to answer his phone. Kylee heard Kellan answer the phone gruffly. It bothered her that Kellan left her alone with this obnoxious salesman who followed her around the store not giving her any breathing room at all.

"I'll be fine," Kylee finally told Hank kindly hoping he would leave her alone. "I'm familiar with vacuums. If I have any questions I will let you know." She didn't want to be rude, but she didn't want him near her either. She looked over at Kellan trying to guess when he might be done with his phone call. She watched him nod his head with a scowl on his face.

"That is quite all right, Miss. Was there a particular brand you were looking for?"

Hank stepped close to her, and Kylee stepped away putting a vacuum between them.

"Are you looking to install a central vacuum unit?" Hank asked licking his lips as his gaze landed on her breasts, smiling as he asked, "Do you have a price in mind?" Hank's eyes never left her chest.

Kylee was disgusted by his rude behavior. Who did he think he was, and why did he think his behavior was okay? She turned away from him and walked quickly across the store to stand in front of the wall display of the vacuum system she wanted. She prayed the guy wouldn't follow her. Maybe she shouldn't have walked so far away from Kellan. She should've walked towards him but during his phone conversation she had noticed his jaw clench and didn't want to bother him.

"Now this is a nice unit!" Hank's voice sneered close to her ear. Kylee jumped at his unexpected nearness. She felt faint as she took several steps away from him. He hadn't taken the hint at all, she thought horrified, but when she looked at Hank he raised his eyebrows up and down at her. She finally understood he was a lecherous man. He didn't care that he made her uncomfortable.

"Sir, you need to please step away from me," Kylee told him firmly and took two steps away from him. That didn't deter him. He looked at her like he was ready to jump on her.

"You are a pretty little thing," Hank drawled. "You could lose the farmer, and you and me could go in the back room and have ourselves a little fun." He patted his privates with his hand to let her know just what kind of fun they could have.

Kylee stood there in shock, appalled by what he just said. She couldn't believe he just hit on her with Kellan so near, and yet, he was so far away. Fear entered her as she took deep breaths of air trying to keep calm. Again, Kylee moved away from the salesman as quickly as she could careful not to back herself into a corner.

Kellan wanted off this phone conversation he was having with his mom. He was livid mad. For some odd reason Ivy had just seen him in town with Kylee and instead of shouting out a "Hi" to him she called his mom asking questions about Kylee. What Kellan wanted to know was why in the hell was Ivy calling his mom in regards to he and Kylee?

"Ivy called me asking questions about you and Kylee. I told her she was your new housekeeper, but she indicated there might be more between you two. Is this true?" His mom asked him.

"Hell. Why'd she call you instead of talking to me?" Kellan retorted angrily into his mom's ear on the other end of the receiver.

His eyes never left Kylee as he listened to his mom baffle her way out of answering his question. He watched Kylee nod and shake her head while she talked to Hank. His eyes narrowed in on the two as he closely watched Kylee take a step backwards from Hank, and it was obvious to Kellan she was putting distance between the two of them. Seeing this made him happy, and he knew now he had been wrong thinking Kylee's blush was because she liked the sales clerk. He saw Kylee walk across the store and noticed how Hank followed her. He watched Kylee turn and say something to Hank noticing how her body language was firm with the man. Then Hank said something else to her, and Kellan saw the appalled look she gave him as she stepped further away. Kellan sensed trouble. Then he saw Hank swagger up close to Kylee's side brushing his shoulder and hip on her. Kellan's jaw clenched tight his body tensed with a silent rage when he saw the salesman overstep his boundary with Kylee. *What the hell! No one touches my sweet girl but me!* He was ready to pound his fist into the salesman's face, but then he caught a glimpse of Kylee's fearful teary-eyed look. It stopped him from thinking about the salesman because he knew Kylee needed his help.

"Mom, I gotta go," Kellan said abruptly into the phone. He didn't care that he hung up on his Mom in mid-sentence as he rushed to rescue Kylee.

Fists balled at his sides, Kellan walked up silently behind Kylee placing his hand possessively on her back. "Find anything?"

Kylee jumped nervously but smiled happily once she realized it was Kellan standing beside her. Instinctively, she stepped close to Kellan as fast as she could. Kellan felt her soft body sag with relief knowing he was there beside her. He put a protective arm around her pulling her closer into him. He heard her sigh then saw the disappointed look on the salesman's face. Kellan's eyes narrowed angrily at Hank.

"I'll be over here if you need me." Hank cleared his throat walking away. The tall farmer made him nervous and with the look of hate he gave Hank, it was obvious to him the farmer didn't like him standing so close to his girl. Hank hadn't figured it out until now that the girl belonged to the farmer. Now he knew and walked away with a smug smile on his thin lips thinking it really wouldn't have mattered if the farmer had indicated that the girl was his. Hank loved women and this one smelled good, and her breasts were just screaming to be looked at. If the farmer hadn't been there, he would have touched them. So, he offended the woman; he didn't care. He didn't think there was any chance the farmer would buy from him, but he didn't care about that either. His overly priced vacuum cleaner store was a front for what really went on behind closed doors. The sooner the couple left, the better. He had some packages that needed to be delivered and was closing up early today. In fact, these two had interrupted him in the middle of his closing early. He was eager to get back to his other job that made him more money than selling vacuum cleaners ever would. He shuffled his feet slowly on the opposite side of the store hoping they would leave soon.

"Thank you, Kellan." Kylee breathed.

"What's going on?" Kellan asked her quietly.

"For starters he has bad breath."

"Go on," Kellan urged.

"He thinks my eyes are on my chest."

Kellan raised his eyebrows. "They aren't?" Despite her discomfort with the sales clerk she laughed.

"And he's just in my space. I tried to step away, but he kept coming closer," Kylee's voice broke, but she kept it together by clenching her teeth. Then folding her arms across her chest she said in frustration, "He brushed up against me."

"I noticed that," Kellan said sourly. "We can go if you're ready."

"But we need a vacuum," she reminded him.

"Not from this jerk. He's not getting our business," he stated hotly.

"Are you sure?" she asked.

"Yes. Let's go." He ushered her quickly out the door not bothering to say good-bye to Hank.

"Ah! The air is much better out here." Kylee breathed in deeply. "Oh! His cologne was nauseating!"

Despite all that had just happened Kellan laughed watching Kylee dramatically gulp in huge amounts of air. He was enjoying his time with her this afternoon. She was a breath of fresh air. She had humor and made him laugh where no other woman had before. She was strong, and she seemed to keep her spirits up even when things were tough like when she fell on the steps. He learned she was determined not to let her injury knock her down physically and spiritually, and just now having to deal with the jerky salesman her attitude was good and she was ready to go on.

"He said I should get rid of you so he and I could have fun in the back room. Then he touched his privates." Kylee shuddered.

Kellan took her hand in his. "You handled yourself well in there. It's a good thing you told me this last part after we left the store."

"Why is that?"

"Because my fist would've landed in his face if I'd known what he said to you. You might have had to call Evan to bail me out of jail."

Kylee laughed even though she knew what he said was the truth. It made her feel great how he would have defended her.

"Thanks, Kellan."

"Hey, no one touches my sweet girl," Kellan said possessively.

"I'm your girl?" Kylee asked. This sounded like more of a commitment than just the fun comment he made earlier.

"Yes, Sweet Girl," Kellan confirmed then added, "At least for now. Listen I should have said this earlier when you asked me, but I didn't think you were ready to hear exactly how I was feeling. However, seeing the sales guy do that to you today made me furious! I know you're not ready for any kind of commitment in your life, and I'm not going to ask you for it, but as long as you're with me, you're my girl. Don't think about packing up in the middle of the night and running away, either. Got it?"

Oddly enough, Kylee liked hearing him say she was his. She smiled up at him. "I got it."

As they made their way back to his truck Kylee asked, "Now what are we going to do about a vacuum?"

Kellan rubbed his chin thoughtfully with his fingers. "Hmm, I'll think of something." He liked the way she used the word "we" as though she had accepted his declaration of her being his girl. This made his heart flip all kinds of crazy!

"Looks like you might already have an idea," Kylee said watching him ponder.

"Maybe," Kellan said, helping her get up into the truck. His hand lingered on her leg as he looked up with apologetic eyes. "I'm sorry that didn't turn out the way we had hoped."

Kylee felt self conscious and looked down at him. "Kellan, I'm so glad you were there."

"Me too, baby," he said softly. "I thought about walking down to the hardware store but then my phone rang, and I answered it staying in the store with you."

"Hell!" he said angrily.

Kylee stared at his angry face. For the first time in her life she wasn't fearful of his display of anger since it wasn't directed at her. She knew why he was mad, and he had every right to be!

"I am so glad I didn't leave you in there by yourself!" Kellan cried in anguish. She could see his thoughts had taken an awful turn by his horrified expression. Her heart went out to this man who cared deeply for her. His concern made her dizzy, and she was glad to be sitting. She didn't think she'd ever find someone who cared for her the way Kellan did. However, in the back of her mind she still questioned how deep his feelings were for her. She was his girl for now but how long will it last? When her work was complete on the house she'd be leaving. Certainly the feelings he had for her wouldn't last past this job. It could be the feelings he had for her was more on the side of lust than love.

"It's okay. Nothing happened." Kylee reminded him, stroking the back of his hand with her fingers.

"But if something had...I never would've forgiven myself for leaving you in there all alone." Kellan spoke regretfully.

"Good thing you got the phone call." Kylee pointed out hoping to distract him from his wallowing. It did but not entirely in the way she had hoped.

"Oh. Yeah," Kellan replied dryly withdrawing his hand from her leg closing the truck door. Watching him through the windshield she saw him scowl.

"Who was on the phone?" Kylee asked when he hopped into the truck.

"My mom," Kellan answered steering the truck into traffic. Traffic was heavier than usual since the factory was changing shifts. He was thankful he didn't work in a factory job punching a time card. He loved being a farmer and being able to make his own hours. Although most of the time he was in the fields from sun up to sun down. He loved planting the seeds, maintaining them all the way through to harvesting time. Sometimes after harvesting he'd help his friend, Dirk, transport his crops by driving one of the semi trucks. Being away from the fields and coming into town this afternoon with Kylee was a rare thing. Hardly ever did he leave the fields during the day which is exactly what Ivy Weaver pointed out to his mom. *Why in the hell did Ivy call my mom and not me?*

"Is your mom okay?" Kylee asked, unsure of how to take his silent frown.

Kellan pursed his lips together before answering, "She's good."

"So why are you frowning?"

Out of the corner of his eye he glanced at her. The corner of her pretty pink lips sagged down the same as his. Kellan sighed deeply, not sure of how much he wanted to tell her. After a moment he said, "My mom can be a busy body sometimes. She gets caught up in the gossip around town. I try to be careful what I tell her about my personal life."

"Ah," Kylee said and thought how hard it must be for Kellan to be careful about what he told his mom so that he didn't become a target of gossip. *Oh no! Did I inadvertently say something I shouldn't have said to his mom?* She turned around hastily in her seat facing him. "Oh! Kellan, did I say something to your mom that I shouldn't have?!" Kylee cried out.

He gave her a strange look. "No you didn't. In fact, you did great with my mom. I could tell you left her speechless." A proud smile spread across his face.

"Okay. Good." Kylee sighed with relief. "Then what is it about the phone call that has you all bent out of shape?"

"It's someone you don't know," he answered flippantly.

"Duh, of course it's someone I don't know since you and Evan, and now your mom are the only people I know in town," she retorted. He was being secretive about the phone conversation. *Who wouldn't he want me to know about? Oh...*

"Was it about an old girlfriend of yours?" Kylee picked.

"No," his reply was filled with a bitter annoyance. *Ivy was never my girlfriend.*

His forehead creased in frustration. He should tell her, but he didn't. Clasping her hand in his he replied, "Kylee, I just don't want to talk about it right now. Okay?"

"Okay." She wished he was comfortable to talk with her about his problem, but she couldn't force the issue. She'd have to wait until he was ready.

"I'm sorry," he apologized and received an astonished glance.

"Why are you apologizing?"

"For not being able to tell you why I'm upset about the phone call."

"Don't worry about it," she replied casually.

"I am." He sighed heavily.

"Don't be." She gave a quick shake of her head. "When you're ready to talk you'll talk." She gave him a genuine smile and squeezed his hand.

Kellan's heart burst happily with her understanding and the warmth of her smile melted his heart. *I know what I'm feeling is love not lust.*

They settled into a comfortable silence. Kylee stared out the window at nothing in particular. They were following another pick up truck. At first she didn't see anything out of the ordinary but then her eyes focused on the trailer hitch as her mind processed what she was looking at.

"Oh! My! Gosh!" Kylee hissed loudly and disgust was all over her face.

"What?!" Kellan was taken aback by sudden outburst.

"What are those ugly things hanging from the truck in front of us?!" Kylee exclaimed pointing to the truck's tailgate. Her pretty face had a horrid look.

"Oh. Those are called truck nuts or truck balls," he answered her rolling with laughter.

"Yuck." She grimaced.

"Don't like em'?" He snickered.

Kylee shook her head vigorously. "No! I think they're vulgar, nasty, and offensive."

He tipped his head back bellowing with laughter.

"Why do they have them?" She wondered out loud.

"To be macho," Kellan sputtered out between laughs.

"Humph,"

"What?" Kellan asked watching her arms fold across her chest.

She shook her finger at him as she voiced her opinion, "I think they are trying to compensate for what they don't have. They are ball envy."

"Ball envy?" Kellan erupted with another deep laugh.

"Yes." Kylee nodded emphatically. "On a personal level they are small themselves so they need to compensate by hanging bigger ones on their trucks." She pointed her index finger in the air.

"Put that finger away before you poke an eye out with it," Kellan scolded her.

She sheepishly put her finger down not realizing how worked up she had gotten.

"Sorry. It's just ugly."

"I wouldn't share the thought about having to compensate with anyone who has them," Kellan warned her.

"Okay." She smiled.

"There is a guy in town who hangs them on his truck, but he walks around town saying these are the only balls his wife lets him have."

Kylee laughed uproariously.

"Some people might think they are art," he pointed out.

"Puh-lease! Art, my ass,"

Kellan had a thoughtful look then declared, "Baby, your ass could be art. The way it fits just right in those tight jeans you wear. That's art in itself!" He winked enjoying the way she blushed profusely.

"Well, art or not, I still don't like them," she stated.

"And you don't have to," he reminded her.

"I'm glad you don't have them," Kylee complimented him.

"Yeah, I just don't think I feel the need to compensate," Kellan said nonchalantly waving his hand in the air then he rested his hand on her leg squeezing it. "Wouldn't you agree?"

Kellan tossed her a playful grin teasing her with his eyes. She answered him by tipping her head back as a melodious laugh escaped her mouth, and this was the only answer he needed. Kellan grinned as he laughed along with her. Oh how he loved hearing her laugh and thought he could live to be a hundred years old, and he still wouldn't ever get tired of hearing her wonderful laugh. This thought had an odd sensation running through him. As he pulled the truck into the driveway he glanced at the front porch. He had a future image of Kylee and him sitting in rocking chairs on the front porch holding hands while watching their grandchildren play in the front yard. Even with her hair gray he saw how beautiful she was. *Whoa! Kylee and I haven't even made plans for next week and here I'm already seeing us with grandkids.* He chided himself over these thoughts. *There are a lot of other things that need to happen before we have grandchildren. My grandpa used to say "Don't put the cart before the horse!"*

Kellan realized he hadn't ever had any kind of future thoughts about a woman before and for the first time in his life this thought wasn't unsettling. Before she came along he never wanted to think about being tied down with one person. Now since Kylee had entered his life he wasn't sure he ever wanted her to leave. Somehow a future without her didn't fit. What was it about this woman that had him all turned upside down?

"Kellan," her voice broke into his thoughts. Slowly he turned his head her way.

"You were a million miles away," she mentioned.

He gave her with a blank stare. "Yeah, I guess I was. Sorry." He turned to get out of the truck, but Kylee grabbed his arm. He paused, feeling the fire from her touch singe through his veins. How could one touch from her ignite such an inferno deep within him? He knew she shared the same burning feeling when he touched her by the way she responded to his glances, his touch, and his kisses. It was like a spring snow melting on a warm sunny day. *Will it always be like this or will our fire burn out over time? No, I don't think it will. Not after the image I just had of us growing old together. I believe it will always be this way. I might be in love with her.*

She interrupted his thoughts by asking, "What are you thinking about?"

"Sweet things, Sweet Girl," he answered casually.

"Since you call me your Sweet Girl I must be on your mind," she mused with a sweet smile. Her comment made him snicker.

"You're right." He tossed her a cunning smile.

She fluttered her eyelashes lavishly accentuating her luxurious eyes. His heart rocketed as he remembered the fantasy he had earlier. His midnight eyes dazzled with desire, and she suspected his mind was full of sinful dreams.

"What are you thinking?" she asked quietly.

He chortled saying nothing, but his eyes gave way to his unruly thoughts.

"Are we having sex?" her fingers tightened on his arm.

"Yesss," he hissed wanting her nails digging into his back while locked together in a hot tangled mess. This one fantasy was causing him all sorts of discomfort. "One day, City Girl."

"Today..." she corrected moving her fingers up his arm gripping his biceps.

Surprised, he sucked in a sharp breath of air his mind processing her words. Kylee didn't know she had this kind of power to ignite a man's passion. Triumphant feelings twisted through her and this time she wanted to take charge. *I wonder if he will let me.*

He caught the coyness in her eyes. *Damn, she is sexy!*

His scorching gaze traveled over her while sparks shot out of her and a storming fire raged over them. Her eyes rested on his tantalizing mouth. Wordlessly, he parted his lips and invited her to kiss him. She leaned forward capturing his mouth, lips and tongue in a searing kiss. Happy sensations danced in her belly spiraling downward. Her whole body was burning, and he was the only one who could cool it. Kylee's brain was no longer in charge; her libido had taken over. With a hasty confidence she removed her clothes and climbed over the console into his lap, removing his clothes, too. She straddled him slowly easing herself down.

He inhaled deeply when she sat on his full length. He clamped his hands on her hips keeping her still. His penetrating gaze reached into the depths of her soul where he could see how much she wanted him; as much as he wanted her. He saw and felt her longing, and her quiet plea to have him.

"Take me, Sweet Girl," he whispered fiercely.

She glided up his tip then glided back down again, repeating this process multiple times. Each time his sounds of satisfaction sent exciting shivers rippling through her. She loved being able to give him so much pleasure. In the end, his jagged breaths and gratifying groans was her undoing but feeling her hot liquid raining on him was his. He clamped his hands on her waist holding onto her tightly as he crumbled under the burning embers of their passion. She collapsed her elated body into his, and he wrapped his arms around her lovingly. They stayed this way until their breathing returned to normal.

His lips nuzzled the smooth skin on her neck while his fingers swirled lightly on her back. "That was..." he paused searching for the right word. "Spectacular!"

"I hope it lived up to your fantasy."

"Even better, Sweet Girl."

Kellan gathered her in his arms and carried her inside up to her room. He laid her down on the bed kissing her softly on the mouth. "I'll go get the rest of your clothes."

When he came back he didn't expect to find her sleeping. His first thought was to wake her up but when he heard her cute snore he didn't have the heart to do so. He positioned her head to rest on the pillow then covered her up with the blankets. He gently sat down on the bed smoothing her hair. His heart hammered heavy in his chest knowing there wasn't anything as beautiful in this world as her.

Kylee had become very dear to him in the short time he had known her. He was intrigued with her since the first day they met. She was a brave woman asking a stranger for help with a stray cat. She was witty and made him laugh keeping up with the humor he dished out. Then when she got hurt it rattled him a lot. Remembering her seemingly lifeless body lying on the floor had chilled him to the bone.

So much has happened between them since her accident. It felt like one big rollercoaster ride. A lot of ups and downs, and he hoped the two of them could stay on the track. Kylee was like no other woman he's ever known. She was the best lover he's ever had. *Lover...* He mulled this word over in his mind and as he did he knew in his heart that she was more than a lover. *I love her and I hope one day she'll be able to love me, too.*

Chapter Thirteen

"Thank you," Ivy automatically responded while walking through the door held open for her.

"Ivy. Hi," a man's voice greeted. She glanced up to see Dr. Chase giving her a bright smile. It made her heart skip a beat. He looked her straight in the eye asking, "How are you?"

Most people didn't notice her, but he was and has. She'd seen him around town, such as: across the street, in a restaurant, and other various places. Sometimes she would catch him glancing at her. He never spoke to her, and she was surprised he knew her name. She thought about giving him a truthful answer but at the last minute decided he really didn't care. Instead, she gave him the same answer she said to everybody.

"I'm good," she mumbled and started forward again, but his next question stopped her.

"If you're good then why do you have sad eyes?" He was pleased when she spun around facing him with an astonished look. He could tell no one ever challenged her answer before. It irritated him that she tried to lie. He hated being lied to. She stared up at him and wasn't intimidated by his height like she was with other men. The handsome doctor had a kind nature. His blonde hair ruffled in the breeze and needed straightening. She was about to reach her hand out to do it but caught herself before acting on the impulse.

Chase caught her hesitant look, knew her thoughts were of him, and wondered what she was thinking. He couldn't help smiling despite the fact that his heart ached seeing the sad look on her pretty face. He wished he could take away her sadness.

Ivy enjoyed the way his smile reached his brown eyes that still gazed into hers. She was envious of his easy going manner acting as though nothing could dampen his spirits. She wished for just a little of his confidence. His comment about her sad eyes had her at a complete loss for words. No one had ever questioned her answer before.

"Uh...er...thanks for noticing," she said flustered. Thinking their conversation was over she turned away and started walking off.

Caught off guard Chase watched her walk away. He hadn't expected her to agree with him, in fact, he had expected her to argue about having sad eyes. He was disappointed she didn't because he wasn't ready for their brief encounter to be over with. On a whim, Chase jogged to catch up with her.

"Ivy, wait."

She was shocked when the doctor caught up to her.

"You're welcome," Chase said, his steps falling in beside hers. "Anything you want to talk about? I'm a good listener."

Silently, she walked across the street to the park with Chase following her. She was reeling over the fact how he had talked to her, knew her name, and now continued walking with her. She was a bit flabbergasted and didn't have any direction on where she was going. She stopped at the water fountain since it always instilled a peaceful feeling. With her arms folded across her chest she turned to look at Chase.

"Dr. Chase," Ivy began, but he held his hand up stopping her.

"Please Ivy, call me Chase. No doctor in front of it."

"Okay. Chase," she began again but stopped when he closed his eyes with a contented sigh.

"My name sounds wonderful when you say it," Chase said as a refreshing feeling washed over him. When he opened his eyes she was giving him a strange look, but she had a seldom seen smile on her face. He took her smile as a good sign. He sat down on the edge of the water fountain.

"Come sit with me, Ivy," he invited softly.

With a slight hesitation, she sat down keeping a friendly distance between them. His heart was beating loudly against his chest, and he hoped she couldn't hear it, fearing she would run away if she could. He had been watching Ivy from a quiet distance and noticed when asked how she was doing, she always carefully responded with "I'm good" or "I'm okay." The truth being, she wasn't because he always saw sadness in her eyes. Today wasn't any different from any other day except for one detail. He finally summoned up the courage to speak to her. So far, he was thrilled with the results. Her questioning eyes silently stayed on him.

"Ivy, you have pretty green eyes," he told her and wasn't surprised when she gave him a doubting look.

"So why did you ask how I am as though you care?" she asked and was taken a back when his face registered shock.

"I do care, Ivy," he spoke gently, his eyes tender with care. Her eyes filled with disbelief and a breath of air caught in her throat.

"Nobody ever does," she whispered. "But you're a doctor, so is that why?"

He scooted closer. She could smell his spicy scent, and her heart pounded hard in her chest. She swallowed nervously since this was the closest she's ever been to a man.

"But with you, it's more than a job. I like you, Ivy," he carefully said smelling her rose scent. Tenderly, he ran his fingers over her clasped hands that lay in her lap. He scanned her green eyes for a sign showing him she believed what he said. Then there it was! Her eyes changed from sadness to a hint of hope. He breathed a sigh of relief because she finally believed him. If she hadn't, he wasn't quite sure what else he could have done to convince her, other than kiss her, but she was too skittish for a kiss. She was innocent and pure. A need to protect and cherish her grabbed a hold of him.

A swirly feeling tingled inside her when he touched her with his hand, his eyes, and his words. She couldn't believe he just admitted how he liked her more than he would a patient and even though she was filled with a hope that he could really like her she still was hesitant.

Chase saw Ivy pinching her arm. "Why did you just pinch yourself?"

"To make sure I'm not dreaming," she answered shyly.

"Well, if I'm dreaming I don't want to wake up." He laughed and for the first time ever he made her laugh, too! He never had seen anything prettier! A pleasant sensation tugged at his heart. Suddenly, he wanted to be the only man in her life to put the happy sparkle in her eyes.

"Thanks for making me feel better."

"You're welcome." He smiled cheerfully. He was very pleased with himself for finally having the nerve to talk to her because her beautiful smile was all worth it. For the rest of the day he walked around with a goofy grin holding on tightly to the memory of her finally smiling…for him and him alone!

Chapter Fourteen

Chase pulled his truck into the parking lot reading the sign in the window, Rick's Veterinarian Clinic. His feet just about danced to the door, and he was whistling when he walked inside. Making eye contact with the receptionist a joyous smile appeared on his face. When she returned a sunny smile Chase knew he had become addicted to the warming effect her smile had on him. This was the main reason he stopped in here.

"Good morning, Chase," she greeted him. The way her green eyes sparkled like gems he knew this greeting was different from the one she gave everybody else.

"Morning, Ivy. How are you today?" Chase walked over to the desk where she was petting a multi-colored cat. The cat seemed to be enjoying the attention for its eyes were closed and it was purring. He reached his hand to pet the cat, too, and was careful not to touch her hand in the process. Being this close to Ivy was causing his heart to beat faster. The cat pushed its head into Chase's hand obviously wanting more of his touch. Chase obliged by scratching behind the cat's ears. The cat purred louder causing Ivy to break out in a small laugh.

"She likes you," Ivy said with a pretty smile revealing the dimple on the left side of her cheek. *So do I.* She wanted to add this but was still too shy to say it. Her heart skipped a beat with Chase this close to her. Since the day they walked to the park Chase started coming into the veterinarian's office where she worked. He never stayed long, but he did stay long enough causing her heart to beat wildly. When he asked how she was she gave him honest answers and it felt good having someone listen to her even if she wasn't having a happy day. She couldn't believe how happy she was after his visits. Their hands collided as they both scratched the same ear on the cat.

Chase wrapped his strong hand over her delicate one while his brown eyes gazed into hers. He saw a hopeful fire sparking in her emerald eyes confirming that she liked him a lot. A fierce need for her surged through him, but he wanted all of her: body, mind and heart.

Ivy's heart beat quickened. She liked his touch and apparently so did the cat because it purred loudly. He had touched the back of her hand in the park, but with him holding all of her hand in his, this was much different. It stirred sensual feelings inside her that she'd never experienced with anyone else. As he leaned his elbows on the counter his face was the same height as hers. It was a lot easier to look into his cocoa eyes making her feel as though she was melting into him. Smelling his cinnamon scent she'd never smelled anything so scrumptious before.

Now she yearned to taste his lips and wished they were anywhere but here where she might have leaned into him for a kiss.

Chase remained by the counter breathing in her sweet honeysuckle perfume. He wondered if her small pouty lips would taste like honey. He wished he could whisk her away from here to a private place to enjoy the taste of her sweetness. This wasn't the place to experience their first kiss. They would be too easily interrupted. At the right time he wanted to show her how he really felt. He wanted to tell her she was the reason he stayed awake most nights wishing to hold her. What was happening here today was a good beginning.

Maybe one day he'd get up enough nerve to ask her out for lunch or go see a movie. He'd come close a few times in the past but just as he was about to ask her another guy caught her longing eye, and he lost his confidence. He had watched Ivy from a distance long enough to know that she had her eye on Kellan Taylor. For the life of him he couldn't understand what Ivy saw in the man! Many times he has watched her watching Kellan with a longing in her pretty green eyes. Sometimes she ran across the street haphazardly just to talk to the man. Chase knew Kellan wanted nothing to do with her, and he wished Ivy could see this, too. He also wished Kellan would see how Ivy was hoping for more from him, but the farmer was dense and had no idea. If he did he would have been able to extinguish Ivy's flames of hope. Chase wondered if Ivy knew about Kylee, the woman who seemed to be capturing Kellan's heart. If she did, maybe he'd finally have his chance with Ivy.

He glanced down at his watch and saw he was due for his next appointment. He stood up towering over her but even though he was taller than she was, Chase knew without a doubt she would fit perfectly in his embrace.

"Well, it's time for me to go." Chase announced.

Ivy thought she heard reluctance in his voice but then thought maybe it was wishful thinking on her part.

"Have a good day, Chase," Ivy wished him merrily. Then she added cheerfully, "It was good to see you."

Chase paused in the doorway as he looked back at her with a delightful grin. Her farewell words triggered a yearning deep inside him, and his blood ran hot as he felt her honesty. His brown eyes delicately roamed her face then he flashed a charming smile her way that left her breathless before he turned around again exiting the clinic.

As Chase drove away from the clinic his heart was heavy. He was glad he stopped by to see Ivy and then again he wasn't since the visit shook him up. He realized this was the first time he had been this close to Ivy; closer than the day at the park.

He couldn't help it she was like a magnet to him. The time was coming soon where he would need to reveal his true feelings for her since it was getting harder to be around her and not be able to kiss her the way he wanted to.

A few days later Chase stopped by the veterinarian's office again just to see Ivy. It was early in the morning before the clinic was officially open, and Rick hadn't made it into the office. He had two coffee cups in his hands as he knocked on the office door. Ivy greeted him with a surprised but delightful smile.

"What are you doing here so early?" She beamed at him as she opened the door.

"I thought maybe you could use a cup of coffee." He handed her the extra coffee cup and breathed a sigh of relief when her face lit up.

"Oh! Gosh! This is perfect! Thank you, Chase!" she gushed. "I haven't had a chance to make any coffee."

His chest tightened seeing how excited she was at the simple gesture. He was even more pleased about his spontaneous decision to bring her coffee this morning. It was well worth getting the chance to see her but even better by how thankful she was. Then she did the most unexpected thing. She hugged him hard, wrapping her arms around his waist in a long hug. Chase set his coffee on the counter then returned her hug but wasn't prepared to feel the strong emotions rapidly running through him. It was that feel good feeling that filled him with love. He knew Ivy was unique as another wave of wanting her washed over him. For a moment it was just the two of them feeling each other's heartbeat of emotions.

"Is this the same cat you had out the other day?" He noticed the cat sitting on the counter. She nodded and stepped out of his arms.

"The cat seems to like you, and you her, yes?" he asked.

"Yes. She purrs when she sees me, and I feel so bad at night when I have to put her back in the cage. It's like she's looking at me with her sad eyes and I can feel her asking me why I don't take her home." Ivy said sadly.

"Why don't you take her home with you? I'm sure Rick would let you have her." Chase said nonchalantly, but she was shaking her head no.

"Why not?" His eyes were genuinely curious.

"My mom is allergic to cats."

"You live with her then?"

"Yes." Ivy answered bashfully. She was embarrassed at having to admit this to him. Chase was a man who had seen the world outside of the small town she lived in. What could he possibly ever want from a small town girl like her who still lived with her mom?

"Ivy, have you ever lived on your own?" Chase asked making conversation.

"No," she gave a big sigh bowing her head looking at the floor thinking how pathetic she sounded.

"Why do you act like this is something to be ashamed of?" he questioned.

She lifted her head and looked him with despair in her green eyes. She tipped her head to one side as she said, "I must seem boring to you with all your traveling experience."

Chase's eyebrows scrunched together as he made a sour face. "All of my traveling experience? Ivy, where have I traveled to?"

She pursed her lips together trying to decide if she had offended him by the face he made. Deciding it didn't really matter if she had, she forged on with her answer. "For one, you're not from around here. So I'm basing your travel experience on from wherever it is you came from."

Chase threw his head back and let out a laugh that exploded from deep within him. She smiled ruefully watching him grab a hold of his gut because he was laughing so hard.

"Am I right?" Ivy said with a huff because he was laughing at her.

"Yes but only about one thing," he said.

"And that is?" she asked impatiently arching her eyebrow.

"I traveled some before coming here, but…" Chase trailed off. His brown eyes focused on her green cat eyes. Her stance was a defensive one, and she looked like she was ready to pounce on him if he said the wrong thing. A humorous smile twitched at his lips, but he didn't dare give her the wrong impression that he was laughing at her when in reality it was just the opposite. He wanted her even more than before. The fact that she thought she was boring brought sadness to his heart.

"But?" Ivy asked him in an irritated voice.

"But I don't think you are boring," Chase said in a matter-of-fact tone.

"So you have traveled a lot in your life," Ivy said pointedly.

"Yes, but only because—." Chase trailed off when he heard Rick coming in through the door.

"Morning," Rick greeted them as he kept walking to the back room quickly. He couldn't help the all knowing smile spread wide across his face as he closed the door behind him giving them privacy. It was clear to Rick that Dr. Chase had his sights set on his receptionist and from what he could see the feeling was mutual.

Chase glanced at his watch then declared in a resigned voice, "It's time for me to go, honey." He stroked her cheek with his finger. "I have a busy schedule coming up, but I want you to remember that I'll be thinking of you."

"Wait," Ivy called just as he was about to exit. He turned to look at her. "You didn't finish your sentence."

"You're right, I didn't." Chase sent her a teasing wink as he ducked out the door.

Ivy nodded watching him go. She touched her cheek with delighted feelings churning inside her where his finger had been. She all but danced through her day as Chase's words of he didn't think she was boring kept replaying in her mind, and he called her honey. She couldn't wait until she saw him again.

Chase drove off with another heavy heart. He had an unusually busy schedule coming up, and he knew he wasn't going to see Ivy as much as he had been. He was already missing her! It saddened him how Ivy perceived herself as boring. Oh, she was far from boring! She could be a complex woman and this might scare away most men but not him. Ivy needed a strong man to rely on and love her unconditionally. *I'm the man for her! All she has to do is trust her heart and when she does I know she'll love me forever!* He thought about the many nights he lay awake praying that one day she would choose to love him. He smiled thinking his long awaited day was getting closer.

Two days went by, and Ivy hadn't seen Chase. In the afternoon, on the third day of not seeing him she had an unexpected delivery. One dozen long stemmed yellow roses arrived from the flower shop in town with a note that read: *Ivy, I'm thinking about you.*

She blushed profusely when the flowers arrived. The customers in the lobby gaped from her to the flowers, and she could see the flabbergasted looks on their faces. Rick teased her about them with an all knowing smile of who they were from even though Chase hadn't signed his name. She, too, knew they were from Chase and it warmed her heart.

The next morning Ivy saw Chase in town when she was coming out of the post office. Their eyes met from across the street, and he waved to her. Her heartbeat quickened, and she returned the wave with a smile before he disappeared into a store. She was disappointed that he hadn't crossed the street to talk to her or motion for her to come over. In the next few days this became a habit when he would see her from a distance. Ivy remembered Chase saying he had a busy schedule coming up and at the time she didn't understand exactly how busy he was going to be. She had become used to him dropping by the clinic but a week had passed, and he hadn't stopped by.

Monday morning when she was walking out to her car Chase pulled up next to her in his truck. Ivy's heart skipped a beat while she tossed him a shy smile. He got out of his truck opening his arms to her saying, "C'mere."

Ivy ran into his arms. Once there, she realized just how much she really had missed him.

"Ivy, I've missed you. I'm cursing my work load. I'm running late, but I just had to see you!" Chase said this while wrapping his strong arms around her liking the way her hands rubbed his back.

The next days dragged on slowly. Ivy's smile was friendly on the outside, but she was dying inside. The hug she and Chase shared days ago had worn off, and she was left with an uneasy feeling. She hadn't even seen Chase in town, not his vehicle driving by, or across the street. No where. It was almost as if he had disappeared into thin air! This did nothing for her sense of stability. She started thinking maybe Chase had changed his mind in wanting to be with her and now was avoiding her as he knew her schedule, where she would be, and what time.

Later in the week, Chase stepped out onto the sidewalk with a few of the hospital's board members. He had just finished having a business meeting with them and was ready to say good-bye but some of the board members were forcing him to make small chit-chat, something he wasn't in the mood for. His thoughts were on Ivy and the fact that he hadn't been able to see for a very long time. He squinted bringing his hand up to his forehead to shield his eyes from the sun and saw Ivy across the street. His heart stopped seeing her beauty, and he stopped listening to the conversation around him. He raised his hand to wave to her. She waved back with a hesitant smile. His chest squeezed tight as he sensed something wasn't quite right. Ignoring the board members he jogged across the street over to her.

"Ivy, what's wrong?" Chase asked in concern.

Ivy stared up at him in shock. How did he even know there was something wrong when she herself wasn't quite sure of what to make of all the feelings that were tossing around inside of her? She shrugged glancing down to the ground. She was feeling insecure because she hadn't seen him for days, and she feared that he didn't want anything more to do with her. However, seeing him today took away some of the anxiety but not all of it. She was slightly embarrassed how he had sensed this in her. She tried to throw him off by saying, "A friend of my mom's died, and she's taking it hard."

His eyes roamed her face then he shook his head slowly, "No, that's not it."

He took her hand leading her away from the middle of the street. "Ivy, don't lie to me. I can see in your eyes that something's wrong."

"It's silly, Chase, really. It's good to see you." She gave a small laugh hoping to steer him away from her foolishness but no such luck.

"It's good to see you too, Ivy. It feels like forever since I last held you." Chase held her face in his hands then watched as her shoulders drooped in relief. That was it! He saw the worry drain out of her. His heart danced with joy, and his chest tightened with a happy feeling knowing that she had missed him, too.

"Ah, honey that's it isn't it?" Chase placed his index finger under her chin lifting it so he could gaze into her beautiful green eyes.

"Isn't it?" he asked again. Ivy nodded. Her eyes misted then one by one emotional tears rolled down her cheeks as the truth tumbled out of her.

"I missed seeing you, Chase, and I was worried that you were avoiding me and didn't want to see me anymore." She sniffed.

"Ah, honey. I hate not being able to see you. It feels like my schedule has exploded and has me running in all sorts of directions. Ivy! I have really missed seeing you and holding you." Chase stroked her cheek with his finger. "Honey, I wish I could stay longer but I've got another appointment I need to get to."

He pulled her into his arms with a fierce need not caring who saw them and hoped Ivy didn't mind. As she melted into him he knew she didn't mind the public display of affection. For a moment, it was just the two of them as the rest of the world faded away.

"Okay." Ivy nodded understanding why he had to go, but she didn't want him to leave.

"Ivy, have you received the flowers?" Chase asked thinking that if she had she wouldn't have been so insecure about his feelings.

"Yes, the yellow roses," Ivy answered. "They were beautiful, thank you."

"Good," Chase said, but he didn't dare sadden her further by telling her she should have received more. He would need to check with the florist and find out why the other bouquets hadn't been delivered. He was reluctant to leave. Disappointment was written all over her face and it broke his heart. An idea struck him, and he didn't know why he didn't think of it before.

"Ivy, have supper with me tonight at six-thirty. Can you meet me at the café?" He gave her a big smile when she agreed. Before they parted Chase lifted her hand to his lips kissing it tenderly.

"I'll see you at six-thirty, Ivy."

"See you then," Ivy said cheerfully and was amazed at how much happier she was the rest of the day. The rest of the day crept slowly. Finally, it was time to say good-night to the stray cat that got hit by a car. She felt a special bond with this cat and named her, Lucy.

At six o'clock Ivy got in her car and drove downtown to the café. She was early but wanted to sit on the bench outside the diner and wait for Chase. She was apprehensive about going inside alone. She knew she'd be at the top of the gossip chain if she went in looking like she was waiting for someone. This way if for some reason Chase didn't show up she could be heartbroken in private. Its not that she believed he would stand her up intentionally, but she had an uncanny feeling about the evening.

Ivy was right about that uneasy feeling. At seven o'clock there was no sign of Chase. Caught up with shock and grief she felt hopeless. At eight o'clock she knew he wasn't coming. She had given him the benefit of the doubt that maybe he had gotten waylaid on an appointment. An hour and half later than the time they were supposed to meet, Ivy knew he stood her up! She walked to her car with a heavy heart and drove home. Several scenarios rolled around in her mind of what could have happened, but the simple fact is she was greatly disappointed. She held herself together until she got home and crawled into bed. She finally allowed the tears to stream down her face. She was disgusted by how she had let hope persuade her into thinking he might really care for her. Sleep finally came but when morning arrived she woke up feeling horrible as last night's details surfaced.

While she dressed thoughts tumbled in her mind. *He told me he missed me…after I said I missed him. Then he told me that he REALLY missed me…why would he say this if he hadn't? Why did he lead me on? Some men like to lead women on, but I really thought my heart was telling me he wasn't like this. I thought he was more kind hearted. I am so naïve about men! Chase deceived me. How could I be so stupid?!*

She felt ill.

What if there was another explanation? He did say he had a busy schedule and had to go. What if there had been a medical emergency? We never exchanged cell phone numbers so he couldn't contact me.

When Ivy stepped into the kitchen she saw her mother sitting at the table with her head in her hands crying. Ivy rushed to her side. "Mama, what's wrong?"

"Pearl's in the hospital. She had a stroke."

Ivy comforted her with a hug. Another friend of her mother's had died a few days ago and now her other dear friend had a stroke. "Mama, how can I help?"

Her mother sighed. "Can you drive me to the hospital? I just feel I need to sit by her side. I was supposed to go today to get blueberries to make pies for the bake sale at church, but I won't be able to do this. I'll have to call the church and let them know I won't be making the pies."

"Mama, I'll take you to the hospital then drive over to Paula's fresh market in Junction City to get the blueberries. Then I'll come back and pick you up at the hospital," Ivy suggested.

"Oh, Ivy, are you sure? I know it's your day off, and you probably have other things planned."

"No mama. It's okay. Let me do this for you," she insisted.

Her mother nodded then sadly walked out to Ivy's car.

Ivy followed her then stopped abruptly as she saw a bouquet of flowers on her windshield.

"What on earth are those?" her mother said.

Ivy picked up the bouquet of flowers. She had mixed feelings about them. There was a note inside that read: *I'm Sorry*

Ivy gently put the flowers in the backseat with her purse. She knew the flowers were meant to bring a smile but they didn't. In fact, it dredged up angry feelings. *What exactly was he sorry for? Sorry for leading me on? Sorry for making plans with me? Sorry for standing me up on our date? No, it wasn't a date it was just two people meeting for a meal.* She plastered a fake smile on her face and got in the car.

"I wonder who the flowers were supposed to be for," her mother mentioned. Ivy said nothing but it hurt that even her own mother didn't think the flowers could have been for her. She said nothing as her mother continued about the stupid flowers suspecting that maybe they were supposed to be for Ms. Elsie's girl who was a pretty young girl who gets a lot of attention from the boys.

Ivy gritted her teeth in frustration. Never before was she so happy to see the hospital!

"We're here," Ivy announced pulling up to the front door. Her mother got out of the car. "Mama, I'll be back to get you in a couple hours. Are you sure you'll be okay?"

"Yes, Ivy. I have my crocheting with me." Her mother held up her crochet bag for Ivy to see. "Drive safe."

Ivy watched her mom walk wearily through the front door before driving away.

Chapter Fifteen

Kellan was standing by the kitchen sink looking out the window sipping coffee from his cup. Today he was taking Kylee over to Junction City to buy a new vacuum cleaner. Their last shopping trip for a vacuum cleaner felt like a lifetime ago but in reality it had only been a week. It was a long week filled with a lot of early mornings and late evenings leaving him exhausted every night. He was snoring as soon as his head hit the pillow. He walked around the house observing all of the hard work Kylee had been doing this past week, too. He was very much impressed.

The main floor was completely re-done from corner to corner, top to bottom. The second floor was done except for one bedroom, and all that was left to do in this room was painting the walls and cleaning the wood floor. Right now it looked like Kylee was going to meet the deadline. As happy as he was with this, it also struck sadness in him knowing that with Kylee being done with the job, it meant she'd be leaving. A tight feeling clutched his chest because he didn't want to think about her leaving. The stubborn side of him pushed the horrible thought out of his mind. He would have to come up with a way to keep her here someway, somehow. He didn't know how yet but was confident he would think of something. Maybe she would agree to stay as his permanent housekeeper. He knew he certainly wouldn't be able to find someone as great as Kylee to keep the house clean or love the house as much as she did. This was one of the reasons she was unique in her work. She poured her heart and soul into this house loving it as though it was hers. Kellan surmised this could be the way she was with the rest of her jobs and it's why she had come highly recommended.

Kellan hadn't ever remembered a time when this house shined bright without all the dust and grime that had settled in over the years. His mom hadn't been as good of a housekeeper as his grandma had been. Back in the day, each spring his grandma would wash the rugs and hang them on the clothesline freshening them after a harsh winter. She'd roll them up for the next winter season. During the summer months the hardwood floor would be exposed and it was cooler without the rugs on the floor. Stories had it that once the rugs came up his grandparents hosted dance parties. It was a lot easier to dance on the hardwood floor than the carpets as with the warmer weather people were able to spill outside onto the lawn. As Kellan's parents moved into the house they had carpet permanently installed, covering up the hardwood floor. This was a lot less work for his mom to maintain, especially with a dusty gravel driveway near the house.

Kellan loved this house! It was the only house he had ever lived in except for the short time he was away at college learning about the new generation of farming.

Kylee was making a serious change in this house. It sparkled and shined. He was lucky to have her, and his heart filled with pride over her hard work. He could feel his grandma's happiness shining down from heaven.

They were taking the day off because of all their hard work. There hadn't been too many days in Kellan's past where he had allowed himself to take a day off, but this was one of them. Secretly, he was looking forward to spending the quality time with Kylee. He was missing her. They hadn't had any time together since the day things got heated up between them in the dining room, the kitchen, and in his truck. He had a big grin just thinking about that memorable day.

Kellan smelled her flowery scent before he saw her. She breezed in looking refreshing like a cool drink of something sweet, and he knew all too well how good she tasted. She was breathtakingly beautiful! The light pink shirt accentuated her round breasts and the blue jeans she wore fit perfectly around her butt making him remember the last time he held it in his hands here in the kitchen. He felt a slow burning sensation ignite inside him. Lost in her beauty, he walked her way as her sunshine smile warmed him. The sky blue eyes staring at him were filled with the hope of a kiss. Kellan said nothing as he gently cupped the sides of her face with his hands while his midnight eyes grazed over her lovely face. The bruises had faded and the freckles had appeared spreading across her nose and cheeks. *She's beautiful!*

He bent his head down brushing his lips on hers in a long kiss. Oh, how he had missed her soft lips melting into his. He felt her hands on the back of his head pulling him closer. The kiss deepened as Kellan pushed his tongue inside her mouth sending enjoyable sensations tingling through them.

"Scrumptious." Kellan breathed heavily leaning his forehead against hers.

"Good morning," Kylee greeted her pink lips curved into a cheerful smile.

"Are you ready to go?" Kellan asked.

"I am."

She was a little apprehensive about being alone in Kellan's truck since the last time they had steamy sex in it. Also, she was nervous about how the conversation would flow between them. She reminded herself that there was a radio to listen to if the silence got too awkward.

"I've brought the truck around to the front door," he informed her. "I've also got coffee in two travel mugs for us."

"Thank you," Kylee said breathlessly. Her heart skipped a beat over Kellan's thoughtfulness. "So you're going to allow coffee in your truck?"

Kellan shrugged, "Well, if you spill anything in my truck you'll need to clean it, and I've seen the way you clean so it's a pretty safe bet you'll clean it well." He laughed good-naturedly.

She slugged his arm and he playfully swatted her bottom when she passed him. She squealed as she shuffled quickly out the door, down the few steps, and out to Kellan's beautiful truck. She opened the door and was about to hop in when she felt herself being lifted up off the ground.

"Kellan! I can get in myself!" she shrieked.

Kellan laughed wickedly in her ear then teased her with, "I like it when you scream out my name."

Her face flamed as she threw him a look. He let out a deep growl of laughter closing the passenger door. She saw him laughing as he walked around the front of the truck and when he got in he was still laughing.

He patted her knee affectionately as he said, "I love this."

She gave him a quizzical look. "Love what?"

"This." He waved one hand freely in the air. "It's our first day off together, and I like not having guilty feelings about not being in the fields today. We've worked hard and deserve a day off."

Kylee nodded. "We've definitely worked hard. I've been so tired at the end of the day I haven't had energy left for much of anything." She sent him an apologetic, shy look blushing, and he understood what she was saying.

"Me, too, Sweet Girl, I've been the same way. Once my head hits the pillow I am snoring like a pig."

Kylee laughed. "So we deserve a nice relaxing day off. You know in the past, I've never allowed myself to take the time to unwind, but I never thought about feeling guilty for it."

Kellan took a deep breath, and he explained about his guilty feelings. "Growing up my dad worked all day in the fields, fed the pigs, and milked the cows. If you wanted to spend any quality time with my dad you joined him in the barn. He'd be in to eat everyday at noon and then he'd take a nap for an hour before heading back out to the fields. The cows always came first because they were on a daily schedule of being milked every morning and night at a set time."

He glanced at her, amused that she was engrossed with what he was telling her.

"Wow! Talk about being tied down!" Kylee exclaimed. "A farmer's wife could get very jealous of her husband's cows."

Kellan laughed rolling his eyes at her. "My mom was glad when she finally convinced my dad to sell the farm and move into town. They do a lot more traveling than they ever used to do now that they don't have any cows to milk."

He had a thoughtful look on his face as he continued, "Don't get me wrong, my dad is great and provided well for us, and I wouldn't trade anything in the world for growing up on a farm. I love being a farmer and working in the fields, but I knew that farming the way my dad and grandpa did wasn't what I wanted. I want to be able to get away from the fields a little more than what my dad did. The years I was away learning about modern day farming gave me a taste of this, and I knew I didn't want to be tied down to the farm so much. I like what I've got now. Working the fields is what I love to do and even though I've got my busy seasons I've still got room to play like—."

"Today," Kylee finished his sentence.

"Exactly like today." Kellan gave her a lustrous smile. He liked the way she had really listened to him when he had spoken of his thoughts. Soon they reached the city limits of Junction City. Kellan realized it was the fastest trip to Junction City he'd ever taken. His grandma's words of 'how time flies when you're having fun' echoed in his brain. He really never quite grasped that saying until today. He was having fun with Kylee as time ceased to exist when he was with her.

To Kylee's relief, the flow of their conversation made the trip go by fast. It felt like they had just pulled out of his driveway not ten minutes ago and now Kellan steered the truck into a parking lot in front of a brown brick building. Painted on the door was red lettering that read, Vacuum Cleaners Sales and Service. When they walked in there was a woman sitting at the counter. She stood giving them each a warm friendly smile extending her hand greeting them and asked how she could help them.

After shaking hands Kylee noticed how the sales woman sighed deeply batting her eyelashes at Kellan. Her hand lingered longer than necessary in his, but Kylee did notice how Kellan didn't return the sales woman's flirting advances. However, this didn't stop the apprehensive feelings running through Kylee even when Kellan placed his hand on her back guiding her to the vacuum cleaners displayed on the wall.

"We need a new vacuum cleaner. Can you show us what you have?" Kellan questioned the sales woman, his hand still on Kylee's back.

"Yes. Please follow me." The sales woman gave them a thorough tour of the store. She showed them all the cleaners they had starting with the lower price to the highest price. Kylee had to admit that despite the sales woman's flirtatious attempts with Kellan the woman knew her products. The woman's sales pitch included looking at both of them, which was good. However, when the sales woman thought Kylee wasn't looking, she tried very hard to catch Kellan's gaze. Every time Kylee glanced up to see if she caught Kellan's eyes, Kylee was happy to see Kellan's eyes on her. He winked at her often making her heart jump wildly. Kylee was thankful the sales woman hadn't tried to touch Kellan the way Hank had with her. Kylee wasn't convinced she would be able to keep her jealous emotions at bay the way Kellan had. The sales woman walked away from them.

"Do you see anything you like?" he asked her.

"Besides you, yes," Kylee answered. Kellan chuckled but caught her frown while her eyes scanned the price tag on a vacuum cleaner.

"Remember, I told you price is no concern," he reminded her thinking she was concerned over the expense.

"No, that's not it. Have you noticed how the prices are much lower here than they are at Hank's?" she pointed out.

"No, I didn't pay attention. How much of a difference?"

"A lot. Almost twice the price at Hank's than here. How is that sleaze ball staying in business?" she questioned with irritation. "Your mayor should run him out of town."

Kellan looked thoughtful. "That's interesting."

"Here's the one I want." Kylee pointed to the vacuum she wanted.

Kellan carried the vacuum cleaner box of her choice to the cash register. He handed the sales woman his credit card. The woman had a lollipop in her mouth and was twirling her tongue around it as she took his card. This disturbed Kylee, yet she couldn't blame the woman for trying. Kellan was smoking hot! He was dressed in clean blue jeans that accented his firm butt and the white t-shirt showed off his muscular upper body. The thought of running her hand over his chest feeling the hard muscles beneath her fingers spiked a feverish temperature of desire racing through her before it settled low in her belly. His tantalizing mouth was an invitation to every woman who wanted to be the one to soften those hard lips. What they didn't know is that he already had a woman who could melt those lips into sweet sugar. Kylee thought about where Kellan's hard loving lips have touched her body; on her mouth, neck, stomach and…she inhaled sharply while exhilarating shivers shot down her spine before she exhaled an erotic sigh.

As Kellan waited impatiently for the sales woman to finish scanning his credit card, he heard Kylee gasp behind him. He whipped his head around looking at her suspiciously. This sigh normally happened during sex just before she's going to-- *wait…what? No! She's not having sexual thoughts about me right here in the store, is she?* He looked intensely into her eyes and saw the flush creeping into her face.

"Well, I'll be damned," he mumbled under his breath, grinning. The confirmation of her sexual thoughts sent a heated rush charging through him.

He tore his eyes away from Kylee for a moment as the sales woman handed him his card. As he was withdrawing his hand from the sales woman, she caught his hand firmly. Caught off guard his hand jerked causing the card to fall on the floor. The sales woman gave Kellan an alluring smile thinking it was her touch that sent his card falling. Kylee also thought this was the case. Kellan gave a frustrated groan as he bent down to pick up the card feeling the sales woman's eyes on his butt the whole time. As he stood up he caught Kylee's 'deer in the headlights' look, and he instantly knew she had misconstrued his flustered state of mind. She was thinking it was because of the sales woman's hand on his.

Oh, shit! This isn't good!

Kylee caught Kellan's 'oh shit' look. Devastation sank into her. She was convinced he liked the sales woman flirting with him and was probably wishing she wasn't here. The jealousy was clear on her face before she turned her back on him, but not before he saw the hurt look on her beautiful face. He picked up the box and followed her out the door hearing the sales woman's voice trailing behind them.

"Thank you for your business today, Mr. Taylor. Please let us know if you aren't happy with your purchase. We have a 100% guarantee." The sales woman enjoyed his backside as he left the store.

"Damn it," he grumbled putting the new vacuum cleaner in the back seat. He slammed the door in frustration. *Why does Kylee believe the sales woman and not me? Ugh, I'm not interested in the sales woman, but how am I going to convince her of this? She won't even look at me!*

Kylee was already buckled into her seat and purposely turned her head away looking intently out her window when he hopped into the driver's seat. He cursed silently. He was irritated by how quickly Kylee's jealousy spiked causing her to jump to the wrong conclusions about him and the sales woman. Yet, he knew her being jealous was a good sign that she really liked him a lot…probably more than she was willing to admit to herself.

"Kylee, you are jumping to conclusions about what you think happened back there in the store," Kellan began. "You've got in all wrong."

"Oh, I don't think so," she said heatedly.

"Yes, you do." Kellan tried again but Kylee cut in by mimicking the sales girl's high pitched voice. "We have a 100% guarantee."

He gave her an exasperated look. "She says this to all her customers."

"I'm sure she does," Kylee said dryly with a roll of her eyes. "Except that she wanted you Kellan right between her legs. She flirted with you the whole time we were in there, and you just ate it up. Maybe you'd like to eat her up," Kylee accused him viciously.

Kylee noticed Kellan's clenched jaw. She suspected that she might be going too far with her words but couldn't stop. The words kept tumbling out of her with so much emotion behind them! She was mad, jealous, and hurt by how Kellan had been so flustered with the sales woman's flirting that she couldn't see straight.

"Do you want to go back and let her give you some of the 100% guaranteed loving she offered you?"

"Are you even listening to yourself? You are way off base on this one!" Kellan shouted loudly. His voice echoed in the truck, and his face was hard as stone.

"I can find something to do while you have your fun with her, if that's what you want," Kylee said bitterly as though he hadn't even spoken.

He gave her an unbelievable look. In the past, yes he would have welcomed the sales woman's flirting. He probably would have asked her out on a date or depending on how loose she was he might've had sex with her in the back room. But today he didn't give a rat's ass about the woman. It was Kylee, and her wonderful sexy sigh that had him all twisted around.

"That's not what I want!" he shouted in exasperation.

"I know you were attracted to her," Kylee said in a hurt voice.

"Bullshit!" Kellan ground out. He opened his mouth to speak but decided not to. He was so mad at her right now he didn't want to say anything he'd regret. He pulled the truck into the city park, turned the engine off, and silently stared out the window. She peeked at him, and anger was clearly written all over his face. He glanced back with pure frustration in his eyes before getting out. He slammed the door so hard it shook the truck.

Kylee sat for a moment before it dawned on her how she wasn't frightened by his anger. This puzzled her because previously she would have been afraid. Her craziness had angered him but even in her jealous rage she had trusted him not to physically harm her. It was a crazy jealousy that had her overreacting. With a great feeling of regret she couldn't figure out why she had acted the way she did. Each of Kellan's steps took him farther away from her and had her heart feeling empty.

How can I blame him for walking away? I'm wrong and owe him an apology. Why did my jealousy take over and steer me in the wrong direction in the affairs of my heart? My heart...it's the only answer I have for behaving like a wild woman! My anger is really geared towards the sales woman who had the audacity to steal my man. My man...that's it! She laughed mulling over the fact that she considered Kellan to be her man. A possessive feeling consumed her as she thought about the sales woman boldly twirling her tongue around the lollipop, and Kylee was fuming again!

She'd never experienced jealous feelings for a man before. It felt good and crazy all at the same time. Now she understood why she acted so badly, but it still wasn't a good excuse. She needed to apologize to Kellan, and it had to be now, but she couldn't wait for him to come back to her. She needed to make the first move on this one. How quickly their fun morning had turned badly, and it was all because of her jealous feelings.

Kylee paused as she recognized for the first time in a long time this was her apology to make and hers only. She was good at apologizing for other people but now this apology was of her own doing. *Oh boy! It was a doozie!* Strangely, enough she was okay with it. In fact, it made her happy and this had her laughing at her own lessons in love today.

Kellan was sitting with his legs stretched out in front of him on a big rock surrounded by water. It looked as though the rock had been made just for him; his own rock island. Kylee saw the stepping stones that led to the rock. She decided to stay on the shore because it didn't look like there was enough room for her. Plus, knowing how angry Kellan was he might just throw her into the water. It would be deserved, but she didn't want to tempt fate and end up riding home in wet clothes.

Kylee took a deep breath and called out to him, "Kellan!"

He didn't turn around or even acknowledge he had heard her, but she knew he did. She pursed her lips together then called out, "I'm sorry for the way I reacted."

His only movement was to cross one leg over the other.

"Kellan, I'm sorry for how I reacted. I was jealous of the sales woman, and I know now I had no need to be. I reacted badly. I'm sorry. I shouldn't have said those things to you," she apologized sincerely.

He nodded but kept his back to her. Kellan did feel her sincerity and it was good to hear her admit her jealousy, but he wasn't ready to let it go just yet. "Like which things?"

"How you were attracted to her," Kylee said rolling her eyes at the way he was making her work hard for this apology.

"What else?"

"That you wanted to sleep with her," she answered with regret.

Kellan quickly got to his feet and faced her. "Yeah, like I wanted to sleep with her. That was ridiculous!"

Kylee gave a shake of her head shrugging her shoulders.

Kellan tilted his head narrowing his eyes. There in her bluest of eyes he saw the jealousy lingering, and he knew she didn't quite believe how ridiculous her accusation was.

"Are you still feeling jealous of the girl?" Kellan asked. He watched her head nod up and down slowly. Her eyes raged silently, unsure of how to react to the remaining possessive feelings. Unable to stop himself Kellan smiled and tossed his head back laughing. She threw him a killing look not understanding what was so funny.

"Sweet Girl, women are going to flirt with me but you can't overreact like this." Kellan stood on the rock with his hands on his hips.

"I'm sorry, Kellan. I don't know what got into me," Kylee cried out in anguish. Her eyes pleaded with his when she said, "Please don't be mad at me anymore."

It was then that Kellan realized she truly wasn't quite aware of the extent of her emulous feelings.

"It was jealousy, Kylee. It got into you."

Kylee shrugged her shoulders. "Fine! Then I was jealous."

"Kylee, why were you jealous?"

"I-I don't know why."

"Oh, Kylee, you do know why."

Kylee stared at him. Yes, she did know, and he was going to make her say it. She turned her back to him. When she turned around again to look at him she jumped because he was standing a few feet away from her. She didn't even hear him leave the rock.

"Why, Kylee?"

She let out an exasperated sigh before saying, "Because I have feelings for you."

"That's right, Kylee. You have feelings for me. Say it again."

"I have feelings for you, Kellan," she said affirmative.

He took her hands in his. "Kylee, I have feelings for you, too. I told you this once before and this morning I told you that I love being with you, but you didn't believe one damn word I said."

"I-I," she stuttered. "Just because you love being with me doesn't mean you love me."

"It's a start. I've never even wanted to be around a woman before as much as I'm around you," Kellan admitted. "Crazy City Girl, you are mine and mine only. But, I'll tell you this I can't stop women from flirting with me but what I can tell you is I won't encourage it. Like today, I didn't encourage her advances."

"But you got flustered," Kylee mentioned. She let go of his hands stepping away from him.

"When?" Kellan asked her with a hint of a smile.

"When she touched your hand you dropped your credit card and then when you stood up you looked so flustered…" Kylee accused remembering the scene.

Kellan took a step closer. "And, what happened right before all that?"

Kylee shook her head not understanding what he was asking.

"I turned to look at you, and you were blushing like a schoolgirl, right?" Kellan took another small step closer.

She nodded, but her eyes questioned him.

"Do you remember what you did that made me turn to look at you?" He watched her face fill with recognition as a crimson flush rose from her neck up.

"Oh," she whispered.

Kellan nodded in satisfaction. "Yes."

"I sighed," she said.

"Yeah, Sweet Girl, you did." He stepped closer into her space but didn't touch her. His voice was sultry when he spoke, "That sexy sigh you have when you're getting ready to come for me."

"Yeah, I remember now. That's why you were flustered?"

"Yes!" Kellan towered over her. He was having a hard time not touching her and only God knew how much he wanted to, but he was determined for her to make the first move. "You and you alone had me flustered. There isn't anyone else in this world that can turn me on like you can."

Everything about him at this moment was passionate. His eyes, voice, words, and the way he stood over her. She noticed how careful he was not to touch her, but she sensed he wanted nothing more than her touch on him.

"Who were you thinking about in the store?" he asked passionately.

"You,"

"What about?"

"Me touching you,"

"Where, baby?"

"Here." She displayed her hands on his chest gripping the lean muscle then she hastily removed his shirt so that she could touch his bare skin.

Kellan let out a guttural groan at her electrifying touch. "Oh, Sweet Girl, I was instantly aroused when I heard you sigh."

"You were?" Kylee asked in surprise.

"Yes. Don't you know by now how much you turn me on?" To prove it Kellan pulled her to him grinding his groin against her pelvis. She was shocked to feel him as hard as the rock he had been sitting on. She gave him a triumphant look knowing the kind of affect she really did have on him.

"I'm this hard for you and only you, Sweet City Girl. Your eyes, your voice, your smell turns me on! No other woman has had such an effect on me before."

"I'm sorry for the words I said to you, but I'm not sorry for hating the woman for flirting with you," Kylee pouted angrily. "She had no right to flirt with you especially with that damn lollipop in her mouth!"

"Oh, baby, I was thinking about you the whole time with the lollipop except your mouth was somewhere else on me," he said truthfully.

Kylee gave a sultry laugh. He wound his arms around her back lifting her up. He pinned her body between the tree and his stroking her cheek lovingly with his fingers. She threaded her hand through his hair pulling his face close giving him a fierce apologetic kiss. "And, I was thinking about all the places on my body you have kissed."

Kellan groaned again. He was touched by her honest response as he whispered, "Oh, baby."

He tightened his hold bringing his mouth down hard onto hers dipping his tongue eagerly inside her warm wet mouth, deepening the kiss as if he'd never tasted her before. She sighed melting into him. He was becoming her whole being. No man had ever touched her so physically and emotionally the way Kellan did. His hands snaked their way under her shirt and bra feeling her breasts. He played with them until her nipples hardened then he lowered his mouth sucking on them. With his hands free he unfastened her jeans tickling her lower belly with his fingers. His mouth left her breasts exposing her nipples to the cool air, but he quickly covered them with his torso liking how they felt against his bare chest. His mouth embraced her lips again as his one hand ducked inside her jeans going past her underwear slipping his fingers inside her vagina finding it moist.

"Sigh for me, baby," Kellan demanded as he fiddled his fingers inside finding the one spot that threw her into a wild frenzy making her come quickly. She sighed making him hard.

"Come for me again, baby," he requested in a low husky voice. He devoured the velvety side of her neck with a lusting appetite. He hadn't tasted her for days. His fingers continued sweeping her internally. His storm of kisses sent never ending shivers down her spine followed by her beloved sigh. With a resounding cry she let herself be carried away on the river of ecstasy. He captured her screams in his mouth and let her body cascade over the waterfall of fulfillment and chuted into his embrace. She was weak in his arms as he refastened her jeans changing their positions so he sat on the ground, leaning his back against the tree with her in his lap. Kylee lay limp in his arms unable to move feeling completely satiated.

"You're mine Sweet City Girl. You're mine and I'm not interested in anyone else," Kellan said softly.

"You didn't get satisfied." Kylee yawned closing her eyes.

"You satisfied me other ways." He stroked the hair out of her face enjoying the quiet around them while she napped. She had satisfied him when she had admitted her feelings for him. He was delighted by her honest answer. For the first time in his life he was content to sit here and not have to be in a hurry to be somewhere else. He was happy holding the woman he loved knowing she, too had feelings for him. There was hope for the two of them after all! There was a good chance he quite possibly could be the happiest man on earth today.

"Kellan,"

"Hmm?"

"I trust you," Kylee whispered softly. An emotional ball grabbed his heart and squeezed it tight when he heard these three little words that had a big effect on him. He inhaled deeply then choked on a quiet sob. He would cherish these treasured words forever. Now he definitely knew he was the happiest man on earth.

Chapter Sixteen

After they left the park they stopped at the hardware store to pick up bags of organic fertilizer for his friend, Charlie's landscape business.

"Can we stop at Walmart before heading back home?" she asked.

Kellan reluctantly agreed. She smiled at his answer and it lit her whole face. He didn't think he ever saw anything so beautiful as her sapphire eyes. They reminded him of the sparkling blue lake water he enjoyed jumping into when he was a boy. She was refreshingly beautiful. He couldn't wait to be home with her but for now he was stuck in a store, his least favorite place to be. Once inside the store Kellan grabbed a shopping cart. "Lead the way."

Kylee was amused by the way he followed her around the store. His eyes piqued with interest when she stood undecidedly in front of the nail polish shelf.

"Try this one." Kellan handed her a bottle that was hot pink.

Kylee's eyes danced delightfully over the color. A musical laugh escaped her as she expressed enthusiastically how much she liked it.

"It'll look good on you," Kellan said in his low baritone voice bringing a low boil to the bottom of her belly. He gingerly placed it in the shopping cart.

Kylee thought they did well together and there was only one brief awkward moment she had with Kellan when she needed feminine products. When she blushed and stammered profusely about him being in the aisle with her, Kellan gently reminded her that he had sisters, so he was used to this aisle as he had to endure shopping with them many times.

"I think I'm ready to go," Kylee said.

"Are you sure? I don't think we bought everything in the store, yet." Kellan laughed as he teased her.

She rolled her eyes. "Ha-ha."

The two of them stood in the check out line waiting for their turn. He noticed her shifting her weight restlessly from one leg to the other.

"What's wrong?"

"I have to use the restroom. It seems the lines are always slower than usual when you need to go," she grumbled.

"There's a bathroom over there next to the hair salon. Go ahead. I'll pay and meet you with the cart just outside the bathroom door."

"I can't let you pay for all of this," Kylee protested.

"Sure you can," Kellan argued but then he looked at her prideful look and sighed in defeat. "Okay. You can pay me back if you want to. Now go pee." He urged her on.

Reluctantly she went but only because her bladder seemed to be bursting at the seams.

Kylee was washing her hands when she thought about Kellan having to put her tampons with the rest of her purchases on the counter. She laughed quietly over this. She stuck her hands under the automatic dryer as it echoed loudly in the bathroom. She hated their noise. Because of the noise she couldn't hear anything around her including the footsteps beside her until it was too late, and she felt herself being pushed sideways. Kylee shrieked! Frantically she tried to grab the wall in front of her, but there wasn't anything for her to hold onto. She slid face first down the wall onto the dirty floor. When she tried to get up Kylee felt something heavy pressing into her shoulder blade forcing her to stay on the ground. Then she heard a female's voice hiss above her. "You are a slut! Stay away from him. He's mine!"

The pressure eased off of her, and she heard the bathroom door closing behind that person. In shock, Kylee stayed on the ground dazed and confused over what had just happened. The words "stay away from him" and "he's mine" echoed in her mind. She winced in pain as she pushed herself into a sitting position.

"Ma'am, are you okay?" A woman rushed to her side kneeling in front of her. She wore a blue smock and had a name tag on. It registered in Kylee's mind that this woman was an employee.

"Ma'am, did you fall?"

Kylee shook her head in confusion. "No, I was attacked."

"Oh no! Stay right here. I need to get my manager. You'll need to fill out an incident report." The employee stood and was gone before Kylee had a chance to protest that she was okay. She didn't want to fill out any form. She was embarrassed and just wanted to find Kellan and go home.

When Kellan had paid for the purchases he pushed the shopping cart over to the restrooms sitting down on a bench. He stretched out his long legs, folded his arms across his chest, closed his eyes, and leaned back on the bench. Then simultaneously he felt the weight of someone falling on his legs and heard a grunted cry. "Ooof!"

Opening his eyes he saw a girl picking herself up off the floor. Quickly, he bent down to help her up, but she was already standing.

"I'm sorry, Miss. Are you okay?" Kellan asked.

The girl bobbed her head up and down but wouldn't look at him obviously embarrassed. Or so he thought. The girl wore dark sunglasses so he couldn't see her eyes. However, he did notice the long strands of red hair hanging out of the straw hat she wore, and she smelled like apples. This scent was familiar, but he didn't know how.

"I'm fine, thank you," the girl mumbled, quickly walking away. Kellan watched her go feeling there was something oddly familiar about the girl. Shaking his head he couldn't place her. He wished Kylee would come out soon. He was itching to get home. He watched as an employee ran out of the bathroom running straight for a woman who looked to be a manager. The two women looked back towards the restroom, and his chest tightened…Kylee. Something was wrong he could feel it. He walked swiftly over to the women's restroom. Opening the door he immediately saw Kylee crouching on the floor. "Kylee!"

Instantly he was by her side helping her up. Bracing her against the wall his hands roamed her body checking for signs of pain as he asked, "Are you hurt?" His face filled with anguish and a panicked worry. She remembered seeing this look on the day she fell down the stairs.

Kylee squeezed her hands on his arms. "I hit my head on the floor, but I think I'm okay."

Kellan let out a low growl as his hands gently touched the top of her head. "How many fingers am I holding up?"

"I hope it's two," Kylee answered.

Kellan nodded, but was worried, "How many now?"

"Four."

"How many now?"

"One,"

"Okay. Do you see double?"

"Kellan, no, I'm okay!"

"Because seeing two of me would be okay, you know."

She snickered.

"Kylee, what happened?"

Anger flashed across her face. "I was attacked! Somebody pushed me to the floor when I was drying my hands under the blower!"

"What?!" He shouted loudly. Two employees walked in and they weren't sure what to think about the tall intimidating man shouting at the customer who just got attacked.

"Get away from her!" The employee who had found Kylee warned Kellan.

Both of them knew she had misinterpreted Kellan's outburst. In unison they spoke, "We're together."

The two employees sighed with relief since they didn't know how they would've defended the girl and themselves against the tall man towering over all three of them.

"She was attacked!" Kellan's voice thundered, echoing in the bathroom.

"Yes sir. This is what I'm told. We need to have her fill out an incident report." The woman dressed in a white buttoned blouse with tan slacks had a lanyard badge around her neck. In hopes to calm the big man she extended her right hand saying, "I'm Marcy, the manager on duty. If you could follow me to the security office and we'll get the report filled out fairly quickly." It was said with authority. She was used to people trying to bully her. Kylee thought she was handling Kellan's temper very well.

"Where is the office?" Kellan asked in an edgy voice.

"It's by customer service," Marcy informed him, her hands clasped in front of her. "Follow me, please."

"Are you okay to walk?" Kellan asked Kylee. She silently nodded taking Kellan's hand, and they followed the store manager.

Kellan anxiously paced in the small security office while Kylee filled out a form. "I'm going to go load the groceries into the truck. I'll be back for you. Stay put and don't go anywhere." With a stern look he shook his index finger at her.

Kylee nodded and just about shoved him out the door. His pacing was driving her crazy! She knew he had good reason to be frantic but the pacing wasn't making her feel any better. Kylee had just finished filling out the long form when he came back. He was still edgy. He looked over the form before letting her turn it in. She watched his jaw tense while he read it. When he was finished his eyes slid to hers with a helpless look that made her heart crumble. She hated seeing the worry etched in his face.

"Thank you both. I'm truly sorry this happened," Marcy apologized. Her face also had concern strewn across it. "We'll have our security team view the cameras for leads on who attacked you."

"Thank you," they answered in unison each of them shaking the manager's hand. Although, they all knew it would be a long shot that they would find anyone. He didn't think they would find any leads since the restrooms didn't have cameras.

Kellan picked Kylee up in his arms. She protested, "I can walk!"

"No way! I'm not taking the chance of someone running you over in the parking lot," he stated. Kylee looked for a sign that he might be teasing, but his face was firmly set.

"Oh! You're serious." Kylee frowned.

"Yes."

"Ma'am, you left one line blank where it asks if your attacker said anything to you," Marcy stated.

In his arms Kellan felt Kylee tense. He watched her scrunch her eyes together as though she was trying to remember something but then she gave her head a quick shake saying, "I don't remember."

Kellan's eyes narrowed. He didn't believe her when she told the manager she didn't remember anything, but he didn't question her. He was ready to go home.

"Well, if you remember anything you forgot to mention about your attack please let us know," Marcy said handing Kellan her business card with her name, title and phone number on it.

"Thank you," Kellan thanked her again then left. Kylee was embarrassed that he carried her. People were looking at them with strange looks, but Kellan didn't seem to mind.

"People are looking at us weirdly," she said to him.

"I don't care about them I only care about you."

Once they reached the edge of town Kellan pressed his foot down on the accelerator and the truck picked up speed. He was anxious to be home safe and sound away from the city. He swung his gaze over to her. She felt his piercing eyes and looked up from the grocery receipt she was reading.

"What?" She asked.

"You can tell me now what your attacker said to you." Kellan demanded.

Her jaw dropped slightly in amazement. "How did you know?"

He took a deep breath of air. "I know you."

Kylee threw him a 'yeah right' look.

Kellan smirked before saying, "When you're caught off guard your body automatically tenses. If you're afraid you tense up, then yell, then cry. If you tell a lie you scrunch your eyes together as though you're trying to think of an answer that will sound good. When you're happy you laugh and the smiles spread for miles across your face. You mutter to yourself when you think no one else is around. And the one I really like about you is when you let out that sexy sigh I know you're wet for me." Kellan winked. Kylee gaped feeling the blush creep into her face on that last one. *Okay, so he knows a lot about me.*

"It was a female, and she attacked me when I was drying my hands under those loud blow dryers. It was perfect timing because no one could hear me screaming."

Kellan gave a curt nod of his head. He had to agree since he hadn't heard her scream either and it frustrated him so much he accelerated the speed on the gas pedal while she continued.

"She pushed me down on the floor. Ick! That floor is so dirty. Who knows how many germs are on me! When I was on my belly she put her foot on my back keeping me there so I couldn't get up then I heard her say, "You are a slut. Stay away from him, he's mine."

Kellan was speechless and confused. Why would anyone say this to Kylee? He frowned remembering the girl who had tripped over his legs a few minutes before the store employee came out of the bathroom.

"What is it?" She asked noticing the recognition crossing his face.

He gave her a silent look. He didn't want to tell her but since she trusted him he had to give her the same courtesy. So he did. He told her about the girl with red hair, the dark sunglasses and smelling like apples who had tripped over his legs.

"That's strange." She made a sour face. "Any thoughts?"

Kellan shook his head. "Sounds like a jealous woman."

"Yeah, I know. A jealous ex-girlfriend of yours?"

"I doubt it," Kellan answered.

"Who were you dating before I came along?"

Kellan shook his head again. "No one, that's just it there hasn't been anyone special in my life until you,"

His words made her heart beat faster. "I'm special?"

"Very." Kellan caressed his thumb over the smooth skin on her hand as it swirled crazy sensations inside her.

"Maybe you have a crazy ex-lover who is jealous?" Kylee suggested.

Kellan threw his head back roaring with laughter. "Oh, the list is long on that one. It would be hard to narrow it down."

Despite the serious situation, Kylee was laughing with Kellan. It was exactly what she needed to take away the worried stress.

"So you think it has to do with me?" Kellan asked.

"Yes. Someone wants me to stay away from you because apparently you are theirs. Or they think you are theirs."

"That's the scary part. They think I'm theirs, and I'm not," Kellan said sullenly. Then he suggested, "You don't think it was someone who mistook you for someone else?"

Kylee shrugged. "That's possible. I never thought about that."

"I'm not trying to take this lightly, but if we were in our hometown and it happened there I'd feel it was targeted for me and you. Junction City is bigger and you could've easily been mistaken for someone else," he stated.

"That makes a lot more sense." Kylee breathed a little easier.

Kellan nodded. "A helluva lot more sense." Kylee yawned.

"Why don't you close your eyes and get some rest," he suggested.

She rested her head on the back of the seat falling fast asleep. Kellan smiled thinking she definitely would need her rest later on this evening for what he had in mind. He held her hand while she rested letting his thoughts linger back to her attack. His mind sorted through the girls he had visited in the past for sex only. He truly didn't believe in his heart that any of them would be jealous enough to attack Kylee. Besides, it had been awhile since he'd been with them and they didn't live in Junction City. He really felt Kylee might have been mistaken for someone else, but he didn't want to completely dismiss the other idea in case it was someone trying to hurt her. Why would someone want to deliberately hurt her? If somewhere there was a girl out there who thought Kellan belonged to her who on earth could it be?

Chapter Seventeen

Ivy had picked up the blueberries for her mother and wanted to make one more stop to Walmart before heading home. She was having the worst day ever and just when she thought things couldn't get any worse she caught sight of Kellan and Kylee walking side by side in one of the aisles. *No! How could this be?!* This was twice now she had seen Kellan away from his precious fields on a good weather day with this woman! And not once did he ever leave the fields to have lunch with her; not even for an hour.

In the last week her thoughts had been little of Kellan and a lot of Chase. However, seeing Kellan in town with ***that woman,*** Kylee, was triggering an awful mixture of jealousy and hatred within her. It didn't matter to Ivy how she was the one responsible for her own destiny. She blamed Kylee for everything that was going wrong in her life.

If Kylee hadn't come to town then Kellan never would have turned away from me but then I never would have noticed Chase. Of course, he had to get my hopes up so he could humiliate me into thinking he actually cared about me.

Pain consumed Ivy. Looking around the store there were couples everywhere! Anxiety and anger rippled through her; suffocating her.

When she was younger Ivy had thought about leaving her hometown many times to see what the world was like beyond the city limit sign. She liked living in the same small town she grew up in but there was always a small part of her bursting to get out. Now each day she stayed she felt herself getting stale and less adventurous. Plus, the thought of leaving by herself made her feel very lonely. Ivy had started to accept that this was probably the place she would live for the rest of her life as an old maid. Gone were her visions of getting married and having children. Growing old together with her husband and surrounded by grandchildren in her old age was now a fantasy.

Like most girls she had dreamed of a handsome fairy tale prince to come and save her from the clutches of the evil queen. She had dubbed her hometown as the evil queen. However, as she grew up and days of fairy tales passed, Ivy knew there wasn't ever going to be a prince to come rescue her. If she wanted something in life she alone had to make it happen. She was the driver of her own car. And with that in mind, she unfortunately had set her sights on a man who moved way too slow for her and now she saw him moving farther away from her and into the arms of another woman.

Ivy should have listened to her instincts the first day she saw Kellan and the girl together because there was something amiss about the whole thing. She knew Kellan well enough that field work didn't stop for just anybody. She shouldn't have trusted Mrs. Taylor's nonchalant answer about the two of them having a work relationship only. Ivy suspected that Mrs. Taylor might not know what was going on with her son and his new housekeeper. If Mrs. Taylor had seen them today in the store she'd clearly see there was something more between the two than just working together. This was definitely not Kellan's normal schedule.

Since when did Kellan get a girl housekeeper? Rumor had it that he had hired a guy to come help him with the house repairs. Gosh, if she'd known he wanted a girl housekeeper she would've never taken the job opening at the veterinarian clinic and instead offered her services to Kellan. However, if she had done this she never would have fallen in love with the injured cat Rick had brought in one day. Someone had run over it with their car. Ivy assumed the driver had left the cat for dead on the side of the road. Her heart went out to the poor helpless animal, and she cursed the people who had done it. A powerful jealous rage seized Ivy, and her heart twisted in pain knowing how Kellan was falling for this girl and Chase had led her on. Crazy as it sounded, it was all Kylee's fault for her broken heart!

Ivy followed the two around the store at a safe distance so she wouldn't be seen. Her heart broke watching Kellan follow Kylee, and she wished Kellan was following her. *Why does he want Kylee?* She hated how they smiled at each other, laughed together, and he even picked out a nail polish color for her! She despised how comfortable they were with each other especially when Kellan tucked a loose strand of hair behind her ear. Ivy detested the soft way Kylee gazed into Kellan's eyes. Kellan's gestures were so simple, yet Ivy knew this was an odd thing for Kellan to do. After watching Kellan all these years he didn't touch women the way he did with Kylee. Just trying to say Kylee's name it got stuck in her throat. The blood drained from her face, and she was rooted to the spot she stood in. She took in deep breaths of air while the room spun around her. She grabbed a hold of the shopping cart to keep from falling as she bent to her knees. Composing herself she stood up scanning the store for the couple.

Hurt sprang deep inside Ivy again. Pure hatred for Kylee raced through her veins. The woman was ruining her life! Ivy spotted them standing in the check out lane. Then she saw Kylee go into the women's bathroom. Ivy abandoned her shopping cart and followed Kylee into the bathroom. Ivy no longer had control of herself as she let her emotions take over. She pretended to be waiting for an open stall.

Ivy watched Kylee wash her hands then move to the automatic dryers. It was just the two of them in the bathroom. Before Ivy knew what she was doing, her arms shot forward pushing Kylee with all her strength knocking her sideways. She could see Kylee losing her balance so Ivy pushed her again. This time Kylee frantically tried to grab a hold of the smooth wall to keep from falling but it was no use. She fell to the floor!

Ivy stifled a laugh. Once Kylee was on the floor, Ivy jumped at the chance to keep the girl pinned to the floor by placing her foot on Kylee's back and told her to stay away from Kellan. Ivy didn't actually say Kellan's name, but she just somehow knew Kylee would understand that she was talking about Kellan.

Ivy felt powerful standing over the helpless girl. One way to get rid of Kylee would be to break the bones in her back, paralyzing her. But, as Ivy was coming out of her cloud of hatred she realized what she was thinking and doing. She shocked herself back to reality. Deep down Ivy knew she didn't really want to hurt the girl.

"Oh no!" Ivy gasped in sheer agony over what she was doing and retreated.

Bewildered by her own actions, Ivy fled the bathroom quickly. Tears of shame filled her eyes, and she wasn't watching where she was going. She couldn't believe it when she tripped over Kellan's legs! She was so thankful she had worn her dark sunglasses and hat so he wouldn't have noticed her. She came too close to being caught and knew Kellan would have put two and two together if he had recognized her but thankfully he hadn't.

Ivy left the store in a hurry and didn't bother going back for the groceries she had left in her cart. Regret and shame washed over her. Frantically, she searched for the keys in her purse then stuck them in the car ignition and drove away from Walmart and Junction City as fast as she could. She panicked all the way home hoping the police hadn't been called, and now she worried and prayed she wouldn't be spotted on any camera surveillance.

Guilt filled her while she cried hard not liking herself one bit. This was so unlike her! She didn't even recognize her image in the mirror. She didn't think she'd ever be able to forgive herself for what she just did. With Chase out of the picture she had to get Kylee away from Kellan or for sure she would end up alone for the rest of her life but physical violence wasn't the solution. Every mile away from Junction City was one more mile closer to home. By the time she reached the city limits of her hometown she felt a little better but still very disappointed in herself. Time would tell if Kylee heeded her warning. Ivy decided to write Kylee a letter warning her to stay away from Kellan. In a week's time if Kylee hadn't left town, she might have to mail it to her.

It was a long sorrowful day for Chase. He couldn't find Ivy at all. He drove past her house, but her car wasn't out front. He went to see her at work only to discover it was her day off. If only he had been able to have supper with her the night before he would have found out about her day off. However, certain things that were beyond his control had taken place causing him to miss their date. He felt horrible when it happened, yet he had no way of contacting her.

If he had been able to see her last night surely she would have mentioned her day off. His appointments were light today and they could have arranged to do something fun. He might've gone on a picnic with her. He sensed she would love this, and he knew a perfect spot. It was off the beaten path on a quiet hill with a great view of the rolling hills and valleys surrounding the area. It was a great place to have good conversation and get to know her better. Chase wanted to know all there was about Ivy. She tugged at his heart, and he was beginning to think this was why his road led him here to this town. Chase let out a frustrated sigh wondering where she could have gone. He ducked his head down as he headed toward the pharmacy.

Ivy received a text from her mother letting her know someone had driven her home. She glanced at her reflection in the rearview mirror. The red hair had to go! She now blamed her evil actions today on the red hair. She drove to the pharmacy to purchase a box of hair coloring. She couldn't make up her mind about which color to choose so she bought several. She paid for them at the register then walked out the door looking down at the ground avoiding eye contact. She wasn't in the mood to talk to anyone nor did she want to see their pretend smiles. With her head tucked down she wasn't watching where she was going. Her shoulder bumped into something hard throwing her off balance, and she fell to the ground.

"Ouch!" Ivy cried out in pain rubbing her left shoulder.

"Ivy! I'm so sorry! I wasn't paying attention. Oh, honey, are you all right? Are you hurt?" Chase apologized repeatedly as he lifted her up off the ground. He couldn't believe his good fortune of literally running into her after thinking about her all day.

With a bewildered look Ivy stared at Chase with devastation written all over her face. *Damn it!* She quickly jerked away from him.

"Don't honey me! I don't want your help!" Ivy hissed angrily. "Of all people to run into it had to be you, Chase. I hate you! Stay away from me!"

Chase let her rant on but his heart was breaking. He wanted to touch her but knew he couldn't since it would only make matters worse. He wanted to explain what happened, but he knew she wouldn't listen. All he could do was let her go, watch her get into her car, and drive away in anger. Her tires screeched as she exited the parking lot. He hated how she was so upset and hoped she arrived safely to her destination. Tears stung his eyes and he cast them downward to avoid other people's attention. Looking down he saw Ivy's shopping bag on the ground. Picking it up he carried it to his truck wondering how long he should wait to talk to her.

When Ivy got home from the pharmacy she realized she had left her shopping bag on the ground. She drove back to retrieve it but it wasn't there. Instead of going inside to see if anyone had brought it in Ivy just came home. She had one box of hair color in her cabinet so she used that one. It wasn't any of the colors she had picked out in the store, but it certainly got rid of the red hair. Looking at her reflection in the mirror she glanced at the dark brown color. *Well, this is close to my original color. Maybe I should stop being the girl with the rainbow of hair colors. Let the gossip chain talk about someone else for awhile. Besides, it's getting to be expensive and tiresome. And while I'm at it maybe I should try changing my way of thinking.*

She heard her mom's feet shuffling down the hallway then stop in the doorway of the bathroom. "Thank you, Ivy, for picking up the blueberries. There will be a lot of people at church who will be very happy that I'm able to make these pies."

"You're welcome," Ivy replied softly hating the reminder of what she had done. "Mama, who brought you home from the hospital?"

"Pearl's doctor."

"Who is that?" Ivy asked.

"The good looking younger doctor who is newer to town but no one seems to know much about him. I think his name is Chandler? No, that's not it, Chance, Chris…"

"Chase?" Ivy cut in.

"Yes, that's it. Chase," her mother said.

"Chase is Pearl's doctor?" Ivy asked in a small squeaky voice. "Why did he drive you home?"

"Yes. The good doctor came by to check on her. He told me Pearl was sleeping, and it would be awhile before she woke up so if I wanted to come back later I could. I told him how my daughter was coming by later to pick me up, and that's when he offered to give me a lift home. I knew how much it would help you out, so I let the good doctor bring me home.

Where ever he's from he has good manners. He's a quiet fellow, but he had this sad way about him."

"Sad?" Ivy asked curiously.

"Yes, I think he cares very deeply for his patients."

"Chase is Pearl's doctor?" Ivy said this more to herself still disbelieving what her mother had told her.

"Yes. I already told you that," her mama snapped. "He was the one who brought her into the hospital the night of her stroke. He had been out to visit her, and I guess he saw all the signs of a stroke and called the ambulance. Then he followed the ambulance all the way to the hospital and stayed most of the night with her from what the nurses have said. All those nurses at the hospital have nothing but good caring words to say about Dr. Chase."

Ivy stared at her reflection in the mirror. *Oh no! Chase did have an emergency, and he didn't stand me up! I jumped to the wrong conclusion! Could he really care about me? He did call me honey when we ran into each other. Maybe I should've tried to find him before I left town to find out why he didn't show up for our date. If I had I wouldn't have done what I did to Kylee. I wish I hadn't done it. How can I ever ask Chase to forgive me for hurting another human being? He's a doctor who stands for peace and is against violence. Will he ever forgive me for my act of violence?*

"Oh, damn," Ivy muttered furious again with herself. She really messed up. Maybe this was the universe's way of telling her it was never meant to be between her and Chase. Sadly, she watched as most of her hope washed away down the drain along with the color red that had been in her hair. Maybe it was time she boldly took a step outside her comfort zone leaving this place she called home.

She needed to take good turns in her life as she started over. Focusing on the person she needed to be from the driver's seat of her life.

Chapter Eighteen

Kylee heard screaming and felt her body falling fast to the ground. She was in the store bathroom again with her face being pushed down to the cold hard floor, only this time she tried to fight back. Rolling over she felt the hard wall on her back. Using her elbows she pushed herself away then heard Kellan's voice calling for her. Freeing herself, she sat up her eyes open as she stared into the darkness. She was confused. *Where am I?* She raised her hand to her forehead and felt sweat on it. *I'm in bed but not my bed. Kellan's bed but where is he?* Scared she yelled out his name.

"Kylee, I'm right here. Shhh, don't be afraid," Kellan said. "Oh, Sweet Girl, you were having a bad dream."

Kylee twisted around her eyes glancing in the direction of his voice. She saw his silhouette in the dark walking over to her. He sat down next to her touching her shoulder.

"I was dreaming about the attack today." Kylee sobbed pushing away from him when he tried to pull her closer. She got out of the bed and started pacing and shouting in anger, "I can't believe I let myself get attacked! I am so mad at myself!"

Kellan watched in a helpless silence. He knew she was scared about what had happened. She had been so calm and tired on the drive home but now the reality of it seemed to finally hit her. He had been waiting for her to crack. If she hadn't been so exhausted or if she had been awake when they got home she might have lost her composure earlier.

"I-I..." Kylee stopped standing still in the middle of the room. "Kellan!"

"What?" He whispered.

"There was nothing I could do. The push came out of nowhere," she cried helplessly dragging her shoulders down.

"I know, baby. There was nothing I could do either, and it scared me."

"Kellan?"

"What?"

"Can you just hold me?" She begged between sobs.

"Oh, honey. C'mere." He gathered her up lovingly into his arms and held her tight stroking her back lovingly. She melted into his warmth, her hands on his chest, and she wept. He cradled her and spoke soothing words in a hushed voice, "Sweet Girl, I've got you. You're safe." Then he added, "You're always safe in my arms."

Tears sprang into Kellan's eyes thinking about today. It had been a rollercoaster of a day but one he wouldn't take back for anything in the world. They had started out happy on the way to the city then she got jealous of the sales girl when they were buying the vacuum cleaner. He smiled over the memory of making up in the park.

Kellan couldn't believe how fun shopping had been with Kylee. Shopping wasn't his thing, and he avoided it as much as possible. He was blessed to have been born the only son into a family where he was surrounded by females. His mom bought a lot of his groceries and brought him home cooked food that would last for days. His sisters loved to help him out, too, by bringing their baked goods or picking up items at the store for him. He rarely went into a store other than the hardware store, feed store, or other farming related stores. The women in his family loved to spoil and take care of him. In return, for payback, he did have the swimming pool that everyone enjoyed using. He felt it was a win-win for everybody.

Kylee had fallen asleep in the truck on the ride home, and he carried her up to his bed. He didn't think twice about bringing her to his room. It felt so natural and now with her bad dream he was glad he had. Holding her also felt very natural. Seeing her on the floor in the bathroom today scared him to no end. It was the second time his heart had lurched to his belly at seeing her hurt. His heart poured out to the sweetest girl he had ever known, and he hoped her attack had been one of mistaken identity. He felt a fierce protective feeling consume him. She was his for now, and he knew in his loving heart it was only a matter of time before she became his forever.

Her crying had stopped, and she rested quietly in his arms. He felt her warm breath on his bare chest, and her breathing became a rhythmic pattern. A slow smile spread across his face as he watched her sleep. Cradling her, he leaned back on the bed bringing her with him, snuggling her close. He was perfectly happy being here comforting and loving her. Kellan knew that from now on she would be sleeping in his bed every night. He should just clear out a drawer and make room in the closet for her clothes.

The sound of thunder rumbled and vibrated through the house waking Kylee. It was a frightening sound. She snuggled closer to the warmth of Kellan hugging her body. It was good being back in his arms and bed again. She had missed these endearing moments during the past few days when he had been pushing hard to get work done in the fields and had been coming home late. She was happy he was here now cuddling her close. Kylee remembered how he had comforted her after the bad dream letting her cry. Tears welled in her eyes thinking about how gentle and caring he had been. He had stroked her back while whispering kind words telling her she was always safe in his arms. He didn't tease her nor was he angry at her for crying. He simply held her and loved her. *Does he love me? I don't think it's possible. He cares for me and he wants me in his bed, but I don't think he loves me. Still...what if he does end up loving me, then what? Would I stay? Can I love him in return? Yes, I think I could but the thought of us loving forever seems too much to hope for. For now I am happy sleeping beside him and waking up next to him.*

She was close in completing the semi-remodeling of the rooms. With a sad thought her work here would be done, but until the day came and she had to leave, she would round up as many cherished times together as she could. She would take these memories with her carrying them in her heart forever.

Kellan stirred and pulled her tighter to him. She gasped feeling his arousal against her backside.

"Are you awake?" Kylee whispered.

In answer to her question, Kellan grumbled burying his lips into the crook of her neck placing soft kisses up and down it. The kisses turned into a tender need then a desired want as he opened his mouth wider nipping at the nape of her neck grazing his teeth along the way sending sexual sensations through her. She was instantly aroused. He kissed her bare shoulder where her night shirt was held by a thin strap.

"Let's take this off." Kellan skimmed the night shirt over her head exposing her bare back. He ran his hand lovingly over her smooth skin. He turned her over. Kissing her neck savagely he trailed hungry kisses down to her succulent breasts. Heartily, he took one breast in his mouth sucking it, rolling his tongue and scraping his teeth gently over the feathery nipple turning it hard. His fingers played on her peaked nipple while he took her other breast in his mouth giving it the same loving attention. He groaned as though he couldn't get enough of her. Kylee's body squirmed beneath him while her delighted screams were filled with the utmost of pleasure she has ever experienced. Wanton shivers along with those wonderful sexy sighs he liked to hear rolled out of her multiple times.

Kellan pushed her breasts together so her nipples were side by side as he flicked his tongue back and forth putting them in his mouth at the same time. Kylee cried out his name as her body shivered out another orgasm but Kellan didn't stop his sweet torment on her. She inhaled sharply when he flicked her nipples with his thumbs making her come. Covering her mouth with his he captured her orgasmic cries. She met his kisses with urgency pulling his mouth onto hers needing to feel his tongue entwined with hers. She was exhilarated by the way he had fiercely just made love to her breasts, but she wanted more and saw in his black fiery eyes that he wasn't done.

Kellan's appetite was strong, and he was aching to be inside her. What started out in hopes to be a slow love making process quickly turned into a fiery need to feel the pleasure they gave each other. Her eyes burned with fire. He positioned himself between her legs entering her swiftly. All plans to take it slow had gone out the window as soon as he felt one drop of her warm wet liquid. She was so wet that Kellan slid into her fast and hard slamming himself deep inside her all the way into her inner core. She arched her hips taking him all in. He pushed deeper inside her, hell bent on pleasing her.

A gift of hope is what he strived to give her at this moment as she held on to him tightly, her fingernails digging into his skin. He hoped to wipe away her painful memories of the past. He wanted this union between them to be the turning of a new page in their book. He hoped she could see him in her future because he could see her in his. Kellan wanted her more than a lover in his bed. He wanted her forever. He wanted to marry her, have children with her and grow old together. The fantasy he had of them sitting in rocking chairs on the front porch holding hands was something he wanted with Kylee more than anything else in the whole world. If he could have this, he knew he wouldn't ever need another gift for the rest of his life. She would be his special gift, forever.

His name came out of her mouth like a sweet song as she arose higher over the mountain's peak as she climaxed letting the wings of hope gently carry her through the clouds of love bringing her down into the arms of the man whose gift was love. He released her name in a sweet ardored whisper across his lips. He saw her descend lovingly into his arms, and he embraced her, their bodies clinging to each other.

Kellan gave a depleted grunt mumbling out of breath, "Sweee-t-Grrl."

Kylee lightly ran her fingertips across his sweaty back loving the fact how he was still inside her. She wrapped her long legs around him when he attempted to exit her. "No. Don't go," she whispered, and he stayed. She began to move her hips slowly against him and much to her delight she felt him get hard again.

"Kylee, don't start something you can't finish," he warned her.

"Oh, I can finish. The question is can you keep up?" She met his warning look with a devilish grin, and he was hard again. He pumped into her as she raised her hips matching his hard thrusts into her. She wanted him moving inside her as much as he wanted to be there. Unable to hold back he released first. She groaned wickedly in his ear as he collapsed again on top of her. After his breathing returned to normal it was then Kellan remembered he had finished first and left her hanging.

"I'm sorry." He looked at her apologetically.

"Hmm, I guess I was the one who couldn't keep up." Kylee laughed over the teasing comment she had made to him earlier.

"Ah, Sweet Girl." Kellan tucked a strand of hair behind her ear. "I promise I'll make it up to you." His eyes were sheepish with guilt. "But, I need to rest first."

"I'll hold you to that promise." Kylee started to scoot off the bed.

"Where're you going?" Kellan asked.

"I'm hungry."

"Me, too." Kellan tugged on her arm. "But we're not going anywhere for awhile. It's raining and there's no need to rush getting out to the fields today."

"Oh. Okay," Kylee said as she rolled back to him. They stayed in bed the rest of the morning. Once Kellan got his energy back he definitely kept his promise to her by making her come again, this time he waited until she was completely finished before letting his own self come inside her.

"I'm really hungry now," Kylee told him. Kellan left her side long enough to fix lunch. He brought it upstairs, and they had a picnic lunch on his bed and had each other for dessert. It rained all day and the two of them shared a magical day of sex, sharing stories about themselves and growing up, naps, holding each other and loving each other physically and emotionally. Exhausted by the day they fell asleep side by side sleeping peacefully through the night.

The next morning Kellan locked his lips over Kylee's in a voluptuous kiss. When the kiss ended he said, "Good morning."

"Good morning," Kylee said breathlessly. Slowly she got off the bed and walked into his bathroom. When she came out Kellan was wearing a pair of blue jeans and nothing else. Kylee thought he looked very sexy standing there with his bare chest, bare feet and disheveled hair. Her insides fluttered at the sight of him. She walked over placing her hands on his magnificent wall of chest. In the beginning it was hard for her to accept the magnetic pull Kellan had over her. Now she accepted it along with the intense electrifying power she experienced when she touched his ribbon of muscles. He sparked many intense feelings of heat making her feel so alive that it was hard not to want to be around him.

Kellan's heart thumped wildly watching her confidently walk towards him. She was naked head to toe, and he thought he hadn't ever seen anything so beautiful in his life. He hissed sensually when she touched him. He loved her electrifying touch because it made him feel so alive. He held her hands on his chest and kissed her tenderly. Then he brought her hands down to her sides causing her breasts to rub against his chest.

"Baby, you are so sexy," Kellan groaned and heard her tummy grumble. "And apparently very hungry." Reluctantly he let go of her.

"I'll make you breakfast, Sweet Girl," Kellan announced.

"I didn't know you knew how to cook."

"Eggs," he answered.

"Awesome. I like eggs."

"Scrambled, is this okay?" Kellan asked.

"The best kind there is." Kylee laughed.

"I knew there was a reason why I loved you," Kellan spoke with ease as he headed down the stairs. Kylee stood rooted to the floor. *What? Was he being serious or joking about why he loved me? He had to be joking since we had been laughing about eggs. Well, I'll have to ask him about it when I go downstairs.*

The early light of dawn was appearing in the eastern sky when she entered the kitchen. Kellan saw Kylee shiver in the cold morning air. "Kylee, go get dressed in long sleeves while I get breakfast started."

"Okay." Kylee ran up the stairs leading into her bedroom. She opened up the dresser pulling out a pair of sweatpants and a t-shirt. Closing the drawer she heard an odd sound over by the bed. She stood quietly trying to recognize the sound. It was a muffled splat sound along with a drip. Following the sound she walked over to the bed where it was a lot louder. Kylee looked up at the ceiling just in time to see a drop of water land with the muffled splat on the mattress. She placed her hand on the mattress where the water landed revealing a large wet spot. Water touched her feet, and she gasped in horror when she saw the pool of water that had formed behind the bed. Then her eyes followed another spot in the ceiling. This one was dripping faster than the one above the bed.

"Kellan!" She yelled as she hastily hurried down the steps. "The roof is leaking in my bedroom. I need some buckets and a mop."

"What?!" He asked incredibly. "In the basement you'll find both." He ran up the stairs to her bedroom while she ran down to the basement for the buckets.

"Ah shit," Kellan muttered a string of curses as she entered with the mop and buckets. She began sopping up the water, and he helped by emptying the water and placed bigger buckets under the leaks.

"You'll need to move out of this room. You can't stay in here even after we clean it up. It won't be safe. Not only could the roof collapse but there could be mold growing in there, for all I know. Who knows how long the leak has been forming?"

Kylee was silent as she began loading clothes in her arms.

"Load me up, too." Kellan held his arms out for her to place clothes in them. Smiling, she accepted his help.

"Where am I moving to?" She asked.

"Upstairs. I've got just the place." He winked and thought this couldn't have worked out more perfectly had he planned it. With a smug smile he said, "Take it right upstairs to my room."

"What?"

"Yes my room. I'll clear out a drawer, and there's plenty of room in my closet for hanging your clothes."

Kylee's jaw dropped unable to believe what he was saying. Did he already have this planned? "Are you sure?"

"Yes," Kellan said in a matter-of-fact voice. "I've missed having you in my bed. After being together all day yesterday…Yes, Kylee! I want you in my bed every night from now on!" He touched her face with his hand. "Say yes."

"Yes to sleeping with you in your bed." Kylee beamed.

"Well, I plan on doing more than sleeping in it, but I'm pretty sure you won't mind that part, either."

For the next hour they moved all of Kylee's things out of the room she was occupying into her new room with Kellan. Evan arrived with donuts and an older version of himself in tow; his Dad. Kylee learned Evan's dad was a part-time handyman and a semi retired farmer. Evan helped his Dad work on the roof making the necessary repairs while she and Kellan ate the donuts.

"It was nice of Evan to come over and help his Dad with the repairs," Kylee commented between the bites of her chocolate donut.

"Yeah, Evan's great. He's always ready to help a friend. This is the way he was brought up. As you can see his Dad is the same." Kellan smiled.

"You've got chocolate on your face, Sweet Girl." With his thumb he rubbed the chocolate off her face just as Evan and his dad came in through the back door. Kellan knew both men saw him wipe her cheek, but he didn't care. He had nothing to hide from them and trusted neither Evan, or his dad would say anything to anyone.

"That's a mess, Man!" Evan said.

"Thanks for coming over so quickly!" Kellan shook hands with Evan's Dad.

"No problem. I fixed it to the best of my ability. If it rains again it won't flood the inside of the house, but you need to get a professional roofer over here to fix the shingles properly. Otherwise by winter you'll have a bigger mess than you do now." Evan's Dad said firmly.

"I'll do it, thanks. Do you recommend anyone?" Kellan asked.

"Yeah, Baker's oldest boy does a great job for a fair price."

"Cool, I'll give him a call."

"I'm gonna run my Dad home then I'll be back," Evan told Kellan.

"Okay, you can help me install a new mailbox when you get back," Kellan said.

"What's wrong with the one right now?" Evan asked innocently.

Kellan pursed his lips together not wanting to answer Evan's question because he was going to surprise Kylee. The new mailbox was going to have two doors on it. One door for the mailman to reach from the road and another door for Kylee to reach from the yard, and she wouldn't need to be in the road to retrieve the mail. One day he noticed how a car had whizzed past her on the road while she was getting the mail. It disturbed him knowing that if the car had lost control it could've hit Kylee killing her. Never before had he ever thought about how dangerous it was to retrieve his mail until he saw the car driving too fast past her. The thought of her not being in his life hardened his features.

In irritation he said, "It's time for a new one that's all."

"Kylee!" Kellan called her name a couple of times as he walked up the stairs. He was being careful not to scare her.

"In here!" Kylee called out from the bedroom. This was the only room she had left to finish. He found her standing with her back to the doorway over by the dresser. Scanning the room he could see she had worked hard on the floors today. His breath caught in his throat at all of her hard work. With the bedroom window open he could smell the scent of the flowering blossoms floating through the screen. A breeze scurried through the window and ruffled the hair around her shoulders. Mesmerized by it all Kellan moved his feet over to where she stood and wrapped his arms around her backside. "This room looks great. Did you know this used to be my room?"

"Does that mean I'll find dirty magazines hidden under the mattress?" She teased.

"You might."

She had heard him walk into the room but was surprised when his long arms came around her, but she loved it. She sagged into him sighing happily and rested her arms on his clasped hands.

"I've got something to show you," he told her. "C'mon." Taking her hand he led her down the stairs, through the front door and out to the mailbox. She gave him a quizzical look.

"A new mailbox to help keep you safe," Kellan declared. "Let me show you how it works." He opened the two doors on the box. "You put the letter in through the back door and put the flag up. When the mailman comes by he takes it from the front door. Then he puts the flag down and places the new mail inside. Whenever you come out to get the mail you don't even have to go into the road. You'll be able to stand here behind the mail box. This is a lot safer for you." He placed his hand on her cheek tenderly.

Amazement blossomed on her face. He was something else! It warmed her heart that he did this to help keep her safe. Unexpectedly, she threw her arms around his neck and kissed him on the mouth. Kellan grunted in surprise, and Evan laughed from behind.

"Thank you, Kellan! I love it! And you, too, Evan."

"Do I get a kiss, too?" Evan asked turning his cheek to her. Laughing Kylee innocently stepped forward to kiss his cheek, but Kellan quickly pulled her back.

"Not a chance, my friend," Kellan warned. "Find your own girl to kiss."

"Are you afraid she'll want me instead of you after one kiss?" Evan wiped the sweat off his brow with the back of his hand.

"Yeah right," Kellan scoffed.

At the speed of lightning Evan leaned into Kylee giving her a quick kiss on the lips surprising both Kylee and Kellan. Evan stepped back laughing at Kellan's look of disbelief. He was enjoying the way he goaded Kellan by kissing his girl.

"What the--! Son of a ---!" Kellan stammered trying to collect his wits over what had just happened. He should've known better and shouldn't have underestimated his friend's teasing.

"I'm just getting you back for all those other times." Evan whistled through his teeth. "Remember Janie, Shirley, Lucy, the twins--."

"Run, my friend!" Kellan narrowed his eyes vengefully onto Evan as he lunged towards him. Evan sidestepped from Kellan then took off across the front yard whooping like a little boy who just got away with stealing candy from the jar. Kellan chased Evan around the yard as though they were young boys again. Finally Kellan gave up making his way back to an amused Kylee.

"What's so funny?" Kellan asked her, smiling.

"The two of you running around like boys. I'm sure you had lots of fun growing up together."

Kellan smiled ruefully. "Lots of fun memories with that guy."

"Are you really mad at Evan?" Kylee asked in concern.

"Depends," Kellan answered vaguely.

"On what?"

"Did you like the kiss?" He asked. She made a grimacing face. "That's what I like to see."

"I like your kisses much better." Kylee smiled.

"That's what I like to hear." He stood in front of her. Cupping her face between his hands, he tilted her head up as he crushed his lips possessively onto hers staking his claim. She was his and no one else's. He was kissing her in the middle of the front yard where anyone could see them, but he didn't care!

"Okay! I got your message loud and clear. Kylee is off limits. No more kissing her!" Evan called out to them. "Are we working in the fields today or what?"

Kellan looked up at the sky. The sun was shining through the clouds with traces of blue sky. "I've got a fence that needs mending. Do you want to help with it?"

"I'm your man," Evan announced.

"Great. While you guys are working I've got some cleaning and organizing to do upstairs," Kylee informed him.

"We aren't working too late today. Tonight we're going over to Charlie's to deliver the fertilizer and hang out," Kellan told her.

"Oh. Ok. Let me know when you leave," Kylee said and started walking across the yard. She was confused in her feelings about Kellan going over to his friend's house and not inviting her. This upset her as the negative Nellie's entered her mind. She was good enough to share his bed but not good enough to be introduced to his friends? She was well aware of feeling hurt. She heard him calling her name, but she ignored him and slammed the front door shut. The writing was on the wall for her; Kellan wasn't ready to introduce her to his friends or he just wanted a sexual relationship. She needed to confront him on his intentions about their relationship.

"Kylee, wait!" Kellan called out to her. She had misunderstood him when he said "we're going over to Charlie's". He meant she'd be going, not Evan.

"She's upset, you know," Evan pointed out.

"I do know. She misunderstood when I said we." Kellan sighed in frustration.

"Well, in her defense you were a little confusing," Evan reiterated. "First you said you and I weren't working long today and then…"

"I got it!" Kellan snapped holding up his hand to stop him from speaking. "I'll be right back."

Kellan started to run after Kylee but stopped when he heard a horn blasting behind him as a vehicle turned into the driveway. He turned to see his other sister's car barreling up the driveway with his nieces and nephews waving their arms out the window excitedly shouting his name.

"Looks like Linda's back from vacation." Evan laughed.

"I guess so." He was happy to see the family, yet annoyed he wasn't able to smooth things over with Kylee right away. He jogged over to his sister's car greeting everyone with hugs.

"How was your vacation?" Kellan asked everybody and they all answered enthusiastically with "Awesome!"

"I see you guys are ready to go swimming." Kellan noted their swimsuits, towels, and goggles.

"Yeah!" The kids screamed.

Chapter Nineteen

Kellan left his sister out by the pool with the kids, but she followed him inside. "Linda, you can't leave the kids unattended by the pool," he told her.

"They are having a snack and have strict orders not to go in until I come back out. Plus, Evan's out there with them."

"He's not here to babysit," Kellan lectured.

"Duh, I know that." Linda made a sour face.

"So when did you get back?"

"Yesterday,"

"Where's Dave?" Kellan asked. He was surprised that his sister was here today after arriving home the day before. Normally she didn't grace his presence until about three days later. He could see this small talk was driving her insane by the way she chewed on her bottom lip.

"He's helping his Dad," Linda answered her brother wondering why he was so chatty today. Silence rolled between them.

"So, how's your new housekeeper working out?" Linda asked him trying to be nonchalant about it. "Kyle's his name right?"

Kellan held back a smile. *Aha! Now I know why she's here. She is chomping at the bit to know more about my male housekeeper.* He grunted a chuckle. *I bet this bugged her while she was on vacation. She probably drove my brother-in-law crazy with all her wondering questions. Poor guy!*

"Have you talked to Mom since you've been home?" He asked.

Linda shook her head. "No, but I left her a voice mail letting her know we're home."

Kellan thought this was interesting. His mom was waiting for Linda to find out about Kylee on her own. He watched Linda's face but nothing registered on it tipping him off that she had played a prank on him. He was gonna love seeing her face when she found out the truth.

"Why do you ask? Did something happen with the housekeeper? Did he show up? Did you fire him already? What?" Linda questioned him. Just then Evan came in.

"Evan have you met Kyle?" Linda directed her gaze to him.

Evan had an insane look on his face. Laughter was erupting inside him, and he fought for control trying not to let it out. "Ah, I'll be outside with the kids. Let me know when you're ready, K-man."

Linda gave an odd look to Evan's retreating back. "So did you fire him?"

"I haven't fired anyone." Kellan said.

"Well, can I meet him then?" Linda asked in an exasperated voice.

"Meet who?" Kellan teased.

"The new housekeeper," Linda said in frustration.

"I guess if you want to." Kellan shrugged his shoulders. Just then as if on cue, he couldn't have planned it any better, Kylee floated through the doorway completely unaware of anyone being here. She stopped dead in her tracks and gave a startled yelp. Kylee stared at the woman in the kitchen. She was tall slender with long blonde hair and blue eyes. She was a female version of Kellan. Kylee realized this was Kellan's sister, but she wasn't prepared for how much they looked alike. Kylee also suspected this was the sister who had written the message incorrectly about Kyle vs. Kylee.

Kellan cleared his throat. "This is Linda, my pain in the ass sister. She's back from vacation."

Kylee gave Kellan a knowing smile understanding this definitely was the sister who had written her name down wrong.

Linda took Kellan's ill introduction of her well. "Ha-ha. That's what you think but once people get to know me they find out that you're really the pain in the ass." Linda tossed this back with a conniving grin.

She then directed her gaze at Kylee, but Kylee spoke first, "I've met your mom, and the two of you look a lot like her."

"Oh, you've met my mom?" Linda asked astonished. She hadn't been gone for very long. How had Kellan met a girl and already introduced her to their mom? Linda was shocked because she didn't think her brother would ever find anyone desperate enough to like him.

"Have you met our other sister?" Linda asked.

"I haven't." Kylee shook her head. Kellan was thoroughly enjoying the show in front of him. He knew his sister was under the impression of Kylee being his girlfriend and not his housekeeper. He couldn't wait to see the look on Linda's face when she found out.

"So, it's not really any of my business..." Linda began.

"You're right it's not your business," Kellan piped in, but Linda continued ignoring Kellan. "But this seems kind of sudden."

Kellan watched while Kylee pursed her lips together holding back a laugh. He could see Kylee was enjoying this as much as he was, and he fell in love all over again.

"Oh, have you met Kyle the male housekeeper?" Linda rambled on. "Wait. I didn't catch your name."

Kylee took a step forward extending her hand to Linda introducing herself, "I'm Kyle."

A stupefied look crossed Linda's face as the words Kylee spoke soaked in. Her jaw dropped but no sound came out.

"What?" She squeaked when she finally found her voice.

Kellan let out a deep gut wrenching laugh. Kylee gave Linda a bright smile.

"Your name is Kyle?" Linda asked in a hoarse whisper.

"Kylee. It's spelled, K-Y-L-E-E. When you took the message you forgot to add the last E."

"Oh, my gosh!" Linda exclaimed her face stricken with shock. "I'm so sorry!" Linda apologized while Kellan continued laughing. The look on her face was priceless. He now wished he could have recorded it and won some money with funny home videos.

"I had no idea. I'm really sorry. The phone was full of static," Linda apologized again while punching Kellan in the arm hard. "Jackass,"

This made him laugh harder.

"It's okay. It happens a lot," Kylee told her. "You can imagine how many surprised faces I get."

A huge smile spread across Linda's face as she pictured her brother's bewildered look. "Surprised the hell out of you, didn't it?" This thought had Linda laughing. "Well, it's nice to meet you Kylee-e." Linda prolonged the E in Kylee's name. "Well, I better get outside with the kids. I'm sure Evan is tired of babysitting."

The way Kylee led Linda into thinking she was a girlfriend had Linda thinking she was the perfect girl for her brother who loved to prank people. Of course, Linda did, too, and many, many, many times the two of them pranked each other, although they were always better as partners in crime. Linda wondered if anything would evolve between Kellan and his housekeeper. She kind of hoped so. This was the first woman Linda could see as a good match for her brother.

Kellan made sure Linda had left the house before he sought out Kylee. He found her upstairs scrubbing the floor. He whistled his arrival so he wouldn't scare her.

"Oh man! That was hilarious! Did you see her jaw drop to the floor?" Kellan replayed what had happened with his sister.

Kylee stood up stretching her arms in the air. "That was funny!"

Kellan walked into her space and when Kylee brought her hands down she had no where else to put them except around his neck. "Sweet Girl, you did great! Thanks for playing along." To show his appreciation he kissed her long and deep.

"You're welcome," Kylee said when the kiss ended. "It was fun and funny."

Kellan laughed again. "I'm going to pay for that one, but gosh, it was worth it. Hey, I want to clear something up with you."

"Okay, what?"

"Earlier when I said we are going to Charlie's tonight. I wasn't talking about Evan and me. I was talking about us."

"Oh, you were?" A happy smile danced across her face. She pressed her cheek against his chest. Her arms tightened around him, and he embraced her melding their bodies.

"Yes." Kellan inhaled her sultry fragrance. "I could hold you like this forever."

"I'd let you," Kylee confessed then sighed sadly. "But we can't."

"Not now, but tonight plan on it." Kellan kissed the top of her forehead before walking out of the room.

Kylee was in a much better mood while she worked scrubbing the years of dirt away from the hardwood floor in the old bedroom. She looked forward to being with Kellan this evening and meeting his friends. She was relieved how he had intended for her to go with him from the very beginning. Then with a nervous thought she wondered what should she wear?

Chapter Twenty

Ivy carried the pies her mother had baked. She set them down on the table then rubbed her left shoulder. She had injured it when she ran into Chase at the pharmacy thinking now she should have let him look at her shoulder. It had been bothering her as she tried not to use her arm too much and was successful until today when she was carrying the pies. Wincing she turned around coming face to face with Chase.

"Ivy, let me look at your shoulder," Chase said quietly, yet sternly. Ivy nodded and let him lead her out to his truck. He lifted her up onto the tailgate of his truck carefully examining her shoulder with a confident ease. Ivy felt a tingling sensation surge through her when his hands were on her.

"It's not broken but bruised. You need to put ice on it to keep the swelling down." Chase dug into his cooler that was in the bed of his truck, pulling out an ice pack and placing it on her shoulder.

"I wish you would have let me look at it when it happened," Chase scolded.

"I was mad," Ivy reminded him, glancing quickly into his smoldering eyes then looked away shyly.

Chase sighed, "I know."

He wanted to ask if she still was mad but since she let him examine her shoulder he suspected that maybe she wasn't as mad as she was.

"Thanks for driving my mama home from the hospital." Ivy's eyes swept past his, but she saw him nod his head.

"I didn't know she was your mama until we got closer to your house," Chase commented.

This time Ivy nodded as they co-existed awkwardly beside each other. She sat on his tailgate fearful of jumping down without his assistance. She could ask him to help her, but she wasn't quite ready to leave. His cinnamon scent wafted over her. It calmed her.

Chase thought he had Ivy right where he wanted her; sitting on his truck's tailgate too nervous to get down. He kept the ice pack on her shoulder enjoying her picturesque beauty. Nervously, she swung her legs from the tailgate looking everywhere carefully avoiding his eyes. Her hands fidgeted in her lap as she bit her lower lip. Removing the ice pack he moved his other hand up to her mouth gently pulling her lip away from her teeth. He wanted nothing more than to kiss those lips. Ivy moved her eyes to his and saw the longing he had for her. In a trance, Chase parted Ivy's swinging legs standing between them he pulled her closer. He spoke her name quietly, but his voice was commanding, and his eyes demanding. He took her fidgeting hands into his steady hold.

"Ivy. I'm so sorry for missing our date the other night. I had an emergency with a patient," Chase said with sincere regret.

"With Pearl," Ivy said.

Chase nodded solemnly, "Yes." He gripped her hands tight. "She was my last appointment for the day. When I showed up at her house I could see the signs of the stroke and called for an ambulance. I followed the ambulance to the hospital but by the time I got there her stroke had worsened. I needed to stay and help her to the best of my ability. Ivy, I would have called or sent you a message, but I didn't have your phone number."

She knew he was telling the truth. "I believe you Chase. I'm sorry for yelling at you outside the pharmacy."

Chase shook his head. "I guess in a way I deserved it. When I left the hospital it was late, but I went to the café just in case you were still there. You weren't, and I didn't blame you."

"I waited outside on the bench for a long time," she said teary-eyed.

"Oh, honey, I'm so sorry." His rich brown eyes were full of regret and sorrow.

"I went by your house but the lights were off. Even though I wanted to wake you, I didn't feel I had the right. Instead, I left the flowers I had for you on your windshield."

"They were pretty." Ivy sniffed tears falling from her eyes. She would have wiped them away but he still held her hands in his so she was left with her tears sliding down her cheeks.

"Ah, honey." Chase placed his warm lips on her eyelids and cheeks kissing away the tears. Following the tears that slid down her face, he brushed his mouth tenderly over her salty lips giving her a slow sweet ardent kiss. The kiss was powerful, and she could feel the sincerity of his heart pouring into her.

Ivy was smiling brightly, and her emerald eyes sparkled when he stepped back. He caught a glimpse of her hair. On impulse, he lifted a strand of the darker color rubbing it between his fingers with a fascination in his cocoa eyes. Ivy's breath caught in her throat as she remembered the reason why she had changed the color. Chase caught the hint of sorrow in her eyes and interpreted it as she thought he didn't like the color, which wasn't the case at all. He loved it! Her look was softer versus the raging fiery red. He knew she was spunky and this would never change no matter what color her hair was. He gave her a wink and a pleasing smile as he simply said, "I like it."

It thrilled her that he liked her new hair color and it showed on her pretty face. "It's the original color."

"It's a good color for you," Chase complimented, and his heart leaped when she gave him a radiant smile. "Ivy, can you stay and talk with me?"

She nodded her head yes flashing him a warm smile, and Chase's heart echoed loudly in his ears. He eased himself up on the tailgate next to her. He dazzled her with stories about his life, and she was amazed at how easily their conversation flowed from one subject to the next. It didn't matter what they talked about Chase was a good storyteller as well as a good listener. He listened to her stories with an intense interest. She felt his sincerity in everything she told him.

Here I am sitting with Chase on the tailgate of his truck, in the middle of the church's bake sale, and I think I might be falling in love with him. How weird is this? There are several reasons why I shouldn't fall in love with him, but I'm not going to think about that today. Tomorrow will be soon enough.

With the deep caring way he was looking into her eyes she wanted to cherish this moment and carry it with her for the rest of her life.

Chapter Twenty-One

Kylee was surprised when she discovered Charlie was a girl. She should've suspected something when Kellan was careful about not using "he or she" when talking about Charlie. Kylee covered her surprise but pinched Kellan, and he begrudgingly admitted he might have forgotten to mention Charlie was a girl.

"My name is Charlotte, but all my friends call me Charlie," she explained with a welcoming smile. Kylee instantly liked her. "C'mon, I'll show you around."

Charlie showed her around the landscaping business with Kellan following them. Charlie found this amusing. There was something different about Kellan. It was the way he stayed near Kylee even when Charlie introduced her to the other girls. Charlie speculated there was definitely something going on between the two of them. Silently, she watched Kylee talk with Kellan in a soft tone before she gave him a reassuringly nod. He squeezed her hand, his eyes lingering on hers for a moment before he walked away.

Kellan watched Kylee join Charlie and the other girls sitting in lawn chairs sipping on margaritas. Charlie was well known for her homemade margaritas. A lot of people teased her that if the landscaping business didn't turn out she could open up her own margarita bar. They said people would be lined up out the door for them. Kellan's heart jostled seeing how easy Kylee fit in with his group of friends especially the women who seemed to welcome her with ease. In fact, she seemed to be fitting into his life like the perfect puzzle piece that had been missing all this time. For reasons he couldn't explain he was A-okay with this.

"Hey, K-man how're ya doing?" A familiar voice called out to him. Kellan looked over to see his good friend, Dirk.

"Dirk!" Kellan exclaimed. He slung his arm around Dirk's shoulder giving him a half hug. "It's good to see you!"

Kellan rolled a big log over to Dirk and sat down on it. It had been cut for firewood but for now it would be a good place to sit.

"When did you get back?" Kellan asked.

"Day before yesterday," Dirk smiled. "I heard some interesting gossip about you."

"I bet you have. Is it about my male housekeeper?" Kellan frowned. Although after his sister's visit, he guessed most people would get wind of the mix up.

"So what's the deal?" Dirk never believed much about the gossip around town until he heard the facts.

"Well." Kellan paused. "According to the message Linda took it was Kyle that was coming to be my new housekeeper, but much to my surprise Kylee showed up."

"Ah-ha." Dirk gave his friend a wicked grin. "That's gotta be interesting."

Kellan gave Dirk a quirky smile. "It is. Never a dull moment."

Dirk laughed but really wasn't sure what Kellan meant by the comment.

"There she is sitting next to Charlie." Kellan pointed Kylee out to Dirk. Dirk whistled through his teeth at the blonde hair girl laughing with the other women.

"She's a looker," Dirk said as he took a swig of his beer hiding his grin behind the bottle. He watched Kellan's eyes narrow at him with a possessive look.

"Don't tell me you haven't noticed," Dirk taunted.

"I think you need to keep your eyes off her," Kellan suggested with a warning voice and a petulant stare.

Dirk cackled as he shook his head. "Now don't go gettin' all crotchety on me."

Kellan smirked. "Crotchety?"

Dirk nodded. "Yep, like an old maid. Besides, I'm not interested in a woman who's already taken."

"What?" Kellan asked suspiciously.

"Yep, you're a lucky guy Kellan because she's only got eyes for you." Dirk laughed at Kellan's blank look. "She keeps looking over here at you with a sexy little smile on her face."

Kellan looked sharply at Dirk who laughed at him. "Man, you've got it bad."

Kellan opened his mouth about to protest but then snapped it shut. This was Dirk he was talking to. Dirk was one of his best buddies along with Evan. He trusted these two men with his life. They were his brothers even though they weren't blood related.

"You're right." Kellan smiled.

"I'm happy for you man." Dirk slapped him on the shoulder. "Just don't have the wedding without me," he teased.

Kellan laughed rolling his eyes. "Married? Aren't you jumping the gun a little?"

"We'll see." Dirk shrugged.

"Did Callie come back with you?"

"Yeah, but I had problems with my rig and had to drop it off so it could be worked on. She'll need to take me back so I can pick it up."

"Aw, that sucks." Kellan made a sour face. "Did she come with you tonight?"

Dirk shook his head. "I think she has a boyfriend, but she won't confirm anything with me. She's being very evasive about it. Have you heard anything through the grapevine?"

Kellan shook his head no. "Pretty much when you guys are out on the road no one talks about you. It's like you're out of sight out of mind, lucky you." Kellan elbowed Dirk in the side.

Dirk threw his head back laughing. "You love this town and everything that goes with it including the gossip."

Kellan laughed along because he knew Dirk was right. He did love living in this small country town he grew up in. He had spent his whole life here except for the time he was in college. He only spent time away to get an agricultural education. Then he came back home to apply the technology he had learned to farming the fields. Technology had come so far since he was a boy helping his dad on the farm.

Kellan was one of the few prosperous farmers in the county. In the beginning, he had to borrow from his family so he could buy the acres he needed to fill his vision. The first years were focused on paying back the money he borrowed from his parents and uncle. Then he began making a profit. From living in a farming community all his life Kellan was well aware of the ups and downs that farm life had to offer. At times he surprised himself of his decision to be a farmer, and other times he just felt it was in his blood and there was no other choice for him but farming. Knowing the ups and downs of the seasons Kellan had learned to invest his money. Over the years he had invested what he could in real estate, the stock market, opened a retirement account and several other types of savings accounts. Most of his investments had suited him well over the years allowing him to be able to have saved enough money to fix up his house. Kellan was third generation of Taylor farmers and proud of it.

"Hey, what do you know about Hank's in town?" Kellan threw out to Dirk.

"Hank, the vacuum cleaner salesman?" Dirk asked with a frown on his face.

"Yeah, him." Kellan nodded.

"Not much. Why do you ask?" Dirk gave Kellan an odd look. Kellan explained to Dirk in detail about Hank hitting on Kylee, and his suspicions of what might have happened if he had left her alone with him. Kellan's body shuddered, and his face scowled at the memory.

"Be happy that you stayed, Kellan," Dirk spoke softly to his shaken friend. He hadn't ever seen Kellan so worried over a woman before, not even his sisters.

"Plus his prices are very high for this small town. I'm not sure how he stays in business," Kellan told Dirk about the store over in Junction City where they ended up buying the vacuum and the prices were a lot lower.

"That's interesting," Dirk mumbled. "I'll do some checking and let you know what I find out."

Kellan nodded. "That'd be great. Something just doesn't feel right."

Dirk shook his head and groaned a drawn out, "Oh, I hate it when you say that."

Silence fell between the two men as they both knew nothing good would come out of Kellan's ill feeling. Kellan broke the silence by telling Dirk about the attack on Kylee in the public restroom and what her attacker said to her.

"That's strange," Dirk commented with a sour face.

"Yeah, tell me about it," Kellan added dryly.

From across the yard where Kylee sat she saw the scowled look appear on Kellan's rugged face. It made him look intimidating. Her mind wandered back to the first time she met Kellan and how she had been afraid of his height and the confidence flowing from him. It took her awhile to get used to his stern looks but once she got past all this she loved what she found. He was a man with a soft touch, a gentle heart, a passionate lover, and cared for her personal safety. He was a man she trusted and who had wiped away all the bad things she had endured in previous relationships. He is a man she could love for the rest of her life. She knew now that the worry on his face was because of her, and she wondered what he and his friend were talking about.

Sensing a lull in the conversation with the women, Kylee got up from her chair, grabbed three more bottles of beer then walked over to Kellan and the man. Kellan sensed Kylee's presence before he saw her and unbeknownst to him a smile automatically appeared on his face. He swung his arm out catching her from behind guiding her close to his side. Graciously, she moved to stand next to him giving him a warm smile handing him the beer she brought. Kylee then handed Dirk the third beer.

Dirk flashed a sexy smile her way as he often did to the female gender. "Woman who brings me a beer without me having to ask is a diamond in the rough, my friend."

Kylee gave Kellan's friend a smile as she extended her right hand. "Hi, I'm Kylee."

Kellan frowned as he took the beer bottle out of her hands, twisted the cap off before handing the bottle back to her. He hoped Dirk's charming ways didn't sway Kylee away from him. "Kylee, this is Dirk Maslund."

"Maslund. As in Maslund Trucking?" Kylee asked him as she placed her hand on the back of Kellan's neck rubbing his skin lightly with her fingers. She was reassuring Kellan how he had nothing to worry about and that she was still his. The gesture didn't go unnoticed by either of the two men. A sly smile crossed Dirk's handsome face as Kellan relaxed feeling her communication loud and clear. She leaned her body closer to Kellan.

"The one and only," Dirk confirmed.

"I've seen your trucks out on the road," Kylee commented. "You get around."

Kellan cackled wickedly. "You can say that again."

Kylee caught Kellan's sexual innuendo on her last sentence. "I didn't mean it that way!" She defended herself. Both men now snorted with laughter.

"But it's the truth," Kellan said laughing.

Instead of denying what Kellan said Dirk did just the opposite as he wore a proud smile on his face as though he had just received an Olympic Gold Medal. The three of them sat in conversation for awhile Kylee learning things about Dirk and his life out on the road and she loved hearing stories about Kellan growing up. Dirk had a lot of them.

Kellan saw Ivy appear, and he was instantly irritated remembering the day she had called his mom inquiring about him being in town. He still wanted to know why so he decided to confront Ivy about it. Feeling comfortable about Kylee talking with Dirk and Evan, Kellan excused himself for a moment.

Ivy looked around the crowd of people that had gathered at Charlie's tonight. Somebody had handed her a margarita and out of kindness she accepted it, but she knew she would hardly drink any of it since she was driving. Feeling eyes on her Ivy turned her head slightly to the left to see Chase smiling at her. Her stomach somersaulted then their eyes met and Ivy lost her breath for a second. Chase's warm smile washed over her like the sunshine. She was intrigued by the way her body reacted to his smiles. Smiling shyly at Chase she started walking over to him but was stopped by Kellan Taylor.

Chase saw Ivy walk out the back door. Her beauty took his breath away. She wore a lavender sundress baring her tan shoulders. He felt a jolt in his gut when their eyes and smiles met from across the yard. His heart thumped loudly when she couldn't take her eyes off of him. He thought time stood still while Ivy slowly walked towards him. Then time did stand still for Chase when Kellan Taylor stepped in front of Ivy.

Chase watched the scene between the two unfold with an odd emotion. First, he saw disappointment flicker across Ivy's face. Second, was the shock on her face when she saw Kellan. Third, an understanding gaze was on her face that turned to defeat, fear and guilt. He was at a complete loss after witnessing this run of emotions in Ivy. He wasn't quite sure what to think of it all. Then he saw Ivy wince in pain when Kellan grabbed her sore arm hard as she tried to step around him. Chase couldn't stand to see her in pain, and he quickly walked over to them.

"Ivy," Kellan spoke with authority. "We need to talk."

Ivy looked up at Kellan in surprise. He was the last person she expected to see standing in front of her and for the first time ever in her life she didn't want to see or talk to him. She didn't appreciate the way he demanded that they talk. Ivy questioned why she never saw how demanding Kellan could be. His brooding eyes did nothing for her. Her heart didn't skip a beat nor did his presence bring a smile to her face instead it brought a frown. Now he stood in the way of her and Chase. Chase. He was the one she was destined to be with, and he was the one she was destined to lose. A feeling of despair crept into her. She gave a frustrated sigh as she quickly tried to step around Kellan. This confused Kellan since she had never avoided him in the past. In fact, he was the one usually trying to dodge her.

"No, you're going to talk to me." Kellan grabbed her sore arm as she walked away. He was aggravated with her, and his fingers dug hard into the flesh on her arm as she tried to pull away from him.

"Let me go!" Ivy said sternly, but she was wincing.

"Kellan, you're hurting her. Let go," Ivy heard Chase's quiet commanding voice behind them. Kellan instantly let go apologizing for hurting her.

"I need to talk to you about the other day in town," Kellan said irritated.

Ivy's body went rigid, and her face turned pale with guilt. Her fingers fidgeted on the plastic cup she was holding. Chase's heart raced with fear over the sudden tension in Ivy.

Kellan saw her guilty look. "Yeah, you know exactly what I'm talking about."

"I'm sorry, Kellan. I have no idea what came over me," Ivy started apologizing quickly. "If I'da known—"

"—if you would have known that I'd be pissed off about it, you wouldn't have done it? Is that it?" Kellan interrupted her. "Why on earth did you call my mom asking her why I was in town? So what if I was?"

Ivy snapped her mouth shut the minute Kellan interrupted, but she gaped at him in awe as he continued asking her questions about the first day she saw him and Kylee in town together. He wasn't even talking about their trip to Junction City. He had no clue what she had done to Kylee. Relief flooded through her, and she began to relax a little but then she caught Chase's speculative eyes on her. She knew he was reading her body language very well, perhaps a little too well. Ivy stood quietly with her head bowed taking Kellan's wrath of words.

"Sorry? Is all you have to say?" Kellan gave her an incredible look.

"Yes."

"Why didn't you just call me?" Kellan asked. Those words struck Ivy hard and Chase couldn't help the smile spreading across his face as he watched Ivy strike back at Kellan.

"You're kidding with that question, right?" Ivy raised her head up confidently then matched Kellan's piercing stare, her emerald eyes flashing wildly. Ivy sent Kellan a daft look letting him see how she felt about him. Kellan looked stunned giving her a confusing stare. This was so unlike the girl who had been chasing him for the past year; who had been nothing but passive until tonight. She now stood in front of him with aggressive eyes.

"As if you'd answer your phone once you checked your caller id and saw that it was me..." Ivy accused Kellan haughtily, pushing past him as she stormed away leaving him speechless.

Kellan watched her disappear into the crowd of guests, but her accusatory words tumbled around in his mind. With a resigned sigh Kellan knew she was right. He never would have answered his phone if he knew it was her calling. He knew Ivy wanted more than a plutonic relationship with him, but he never felt this way about her. He had tried his best to let her down easy not wanting to hurt her feelings. Hell, he even tried to point her in the direction of Evan, but that didn't work out so well. After a few dates they parted mutual ways. Neither of them wanted the other. Kellan chuckled softly noting how Chase had come to her rescue tonight. Then he saw Chase follow Ivy which had Kellan guessing that the doctor might be interested in her. If he was, Kellan silently wished him luck. Kellan shook his head as he walked back to Dirk, Evan and Kylee.

"Why are you frowning?" Dirk asked Kellan.

"I think Chase might like Ivy," Kellan answered.

"And, that's a bad thing, why? It gets her off our backs," Dirk commented then watched Kylee frown feeling as though he had just let the cat out of the bag.

"She likes you guys?" Kylee asked with a keen interest.

Kellan sighed heavily throwing Dirk an annoyed look. "Yes. She's tried hard to get us to make her our girlfriend."

"You and Evan more than me." Dirk smiled, laughing wickedly. "She doesn't like my career choice, lucky for me."

"I think she's more Evan's speed," Kellan tossed out.

"No, she's not," Evan defended himself. "She's too high spirited for me. I think she's on the verge of being irrational. Besides, she likes you more, Kellan."

"Well, I'm not interested in her, and I've made this clear," Kellan spoke sternly. Kylee could tell Kellan didn't want to talk about this Ivy, girl anymore, but she couldn't help wondering more about her. She wanted to ask more questions about Ivy but the conversation between the three men changed over to Dirk's trucking business. She quietly listened to them talk. Finally Kellan asked her if she was ready to leave, and she cheerfully smiled saying, "Yes."

An all-knowing smile spread across Dirk's face as he was amazed by the happy change in his friend's eyes full of love for the woman sitting next to him. Dirk watched Kylee and Kellan leave hand in hand. With a tinge of jealousy he couldn't help wondering if he'd ever find a girl to love. The career he chose for himself made it hard to meet women, well, decent ones. There were a lot of women out on the road happy to indulge him for a few hours. But it was harder to meet a faithful woman who wanted to get married and have kids. Good women didn't just fall from the sky! Dirk laughed. Only time would tell if he was destined to fall in love, but for now he was happy with the way his life was. There was no need to disrupt things.

Chase sauntered off to find Ivy, but his heart weighed heavy with what he just witnessed. He was confused by Ivy's quick apologies to Kellan then she abruptly stopped apologizing when she realized Kellan was talking about something completely different. Her frozen face had become relieved. Whatever Kellan thought Ivy had done apparently wasn't the same thing as what Ivy thought Kellan should be confronting her about. It was clear to him that Ivy and Kellan weren't on the same page. Watching her fidgeting hands, seeing the remorseful guilt in her eyes, Chase's heart sank to the pit of his stomach knowing Ivy had done something bad and was hiding it from Kellan. He knew it was only a matter of time before Kellan found out. Depending on what it was, Chase wasn't convinced Kellan would be forgiving.

Chapter Twenty-Two

"Ivy, wait up!" Chase called out as she was getting in her car. He could see she had been crying and hated it.

"Chase, you need to leave me alone." Ivy turned around when she heard Chase.

"I can't leave you alone. I like you too much. I'm sorry, honey, but you're stuck with me," he declared and reached out the palm of his hand capturing her chin. "Don't run from me. Run away from everybody else but never me."

"Oh, Chase." Ivy gazed deeply into his brown eyes. "I hated how Kellan demanded that I talk with him. Any other day before I met you I would have loved for him to give me the time of day but…"

"Go on." Chase urged her by squeezing her chin lightly. Her skin was delicately smooth.

"Not anymore. He frightened me, he hurt me, and then he just made me mad," Ivy spatted. Chase gently rubbed her sore arm where Kellan had grabbed it. "Thank you for coming over by me."

"Nobody hurts my girl," Chase said with a fierce conviction.

"I'm your girl, Chase?" Ivy asked in surprise, but her eyes told him she wanted this more than anything else in the world.

"More than you know, Ivy. I've traveled this world looking for you. The day I saw you a peaceful feeling came over me, and I knew this was why God led me to this town. It was to find you." Chase placed his hand on her heart then picked up her hand placing it over his heart.

He closed his eyes while a relaxing smile covered his face then recalled, "I was coming out of the café carrying my morning coffee. It was a cloudy day, in fact, I remember thinking it could rain any second, and I had forgotten my umbrella. I looked across the street, and my heart stopped beating. I saw this attractive girl with hair the color of tree bark looking back across the street my way." Chase opened his eyes. "It was you Ivy. The wind blew through your hair as you tucked a strand of it behind your ear. I saw a hopeful sparkle in your green eyes. I couldn't move. You took my breath away."

Ivy stood quietly listening to Chase's first memory of her. His delightful words stirred her heart. "The jeans and sweater you wore fit nicely showing off all of your wonderful curves as this dress does tonight." Chase stepped closer moving his hand from her chin to cheek. "Breathtaking."

"What was I looking at?" Ivy asked because this wasn't her first memory of Chase. She had a funny feeling it wasn't what she was looking at but whom.

Chase's smile turned grim. "You were looking at Kellan. He was standing right behind me."

Ivy nodded. "Yep, that sounds like me." Then in a sad voice she said, "I do remember seeing Kellan. I waved at him, but he was talking on his cell phone and didn't see me."

Chase couldn't hold his frustration back any longer. When he spoke his voice was bitter, "No, Ivy, he did see you. He just chose to ignore you hoping you'd go away."

"What?" Ivy asked in disbelief.

Chase sighed heavily knowing the truth was going to hurt her, but he had to say it. "When I saw you waving at Kellan he turned his back on you. I said to him, 'Hey man, the girl across the street is waving to you.' He looked at me and said, "I know. I'm hoping she'll leave me alone if I ignore her."

Ivy's jaw dropped wide open leaving her speechless as the truth punched her in the stomach. She was feeling hurt, humiliated and angry, yet it all made sense to her along with all the other times she saw him talking on his cell phone, obviously ignoring her then, too. "Why didn't he just tell me that he didn't like me? Instead of letting me look like a fool all over town chasing him. Ugh, he's such a…" Ivy trailed off her fists balled angrily at her sides.

"He's a jerk!" Chase finished.

"You're being kind," Ivy said touching her hand softly on his clenched jaw.

"Yes," Chase replied curtly giving her a tight smile.

"Thanks for being honest with me, Chase." She glided her hand off his jaw, down his neck and rested it on his shoulder.

"You handled yourself well with Kellan tonight. You walked away leaving him speechless." Chase chuckled. "You should have seen his stupefied look. It was priceless!"

"I have been stupid all this time chasing Kellan, and I don't even know why. He doesn't stir my senses the way you do."

"Oh?" Chase asked interested in the last part. "I stir your senses?"

"You make my heart dance," Ivy confessed. Her coy smile caught his heart filling it with joy by this new revelation of how he made her feel.

"Your touch is gentle, yet strong. Your smile warms me like a blanket against the cold weather. You give me all your attention when I talk to you, making me feel important. Your voice and scent calms me. Your arms around me make me feel safe." Ivy rested her hands on Chase's sides pulling him very close to her.

"I think I might be falling in love with you," Ivy said.

Chase's insides felt all topsy turvy hearing her confess the feelings of love she had for him. He had finally captured her heart!

"Honey," Chase whispered deeply placing his hands firmly around her. "I have already fallen in love with you."

Ivy thought she might cry with happiness because he admitted to already loving her. An overwhelming joyful love for this man consumed her. Closing her eyes tightly she accepted the strong emotions that rose inside her. She needed and wanted Chase emotionally and physically. The way he protectively held her and the possessive look in his eyes excited her. It let her know he wanted her. This made her feel desirable while uninhibited sensations sashayed through her. She ran her hands up Chase's sides and over his broad shoulders bringing her hands down across his wide chest. She opened the top buttons on his shirt and boldly slid her hands inside. Her fingers lightly grazed his skin outlining the ripples of muscle on his upper body. An intense electrifying feeling shot through her when she did this.

Chase inhaled deeply when she softly raked her fingers through his chest hair. The rest of the buttons popped open as Ivy trailed her fingers downward stopping at the waistline of his jeans. She laid the palms of her hands on his exposed skin gliding them over his tanned torso from front to back. Feeling his taut muscles gave her an exhilarating feeling. He gave a low growl as his hands gripped her waist. Her touch was magnificently intimate. Lifting his hands, he cupped her face. His fiery eyes blazed passionately into hers silently sending her a message that he was going to kiss her. She tilted her head back inviting him to drink from her lips. Slowly, Chase lowered his mouth pausing for a second, teasing her in anticipation of the kiss before encasing his lips around hers. Moving his mouth seductively he savored her sweet succulent flavor. The kiss they had on his tailgate was nothing compared to this one. Her soft mellow lips that hadn't ever been kissed until now were his.

Chase's lips absorbed hers deepening the kiss, and she moved her mouth with his. Much to his delight, Ivy slipped her tongue inside his mouth first, and he accepted her playful invitation. Their tongues teased, twirled and rolled around discovering the other's exquisite taste. Chase was intoxicated with her. Her summery breath aroused a fierce need within him. He needed to protect her and make her his while he branded her with urgent kisses. A fierce possession came over him, and he wanted her to be his forever.

Chase knew he'd crave her flavor from now until his last dying breath. He wanted more. His hand wound into her hair, pulling her head backwards, tilting her chin up giving him good access to her mouth. He kissed her hard and hungrily as her ragged breath blended with his. He separated her lips with his tongue indulging on her refined honey taste. It was as though he was dining at a fancy restaurant and she was a rare delicacy, one he would cherish forever.

"Ivy. You're intoxicating," Chase whispered nibbling on her neck with gentle loving kisses.

"Chase," Ivy whispered seductively. She captured his mouth with a hungry force pushing her tongue deep inside his mouth wanting more of his spicy rich taste. Before Chase came along she'd never experienced the pleasure of a man's passion. Now that she had, a yearning ache had developed. She didn't want his kisses to end nor the wonderful feelings he was stirring deep within. Chase had awakened the sexual desires that had lie dormant inside her for so many years. A fire burned deep in her something she'd never felt before for any man; not even Kellan.

At the mention of Kellan suddenly she had ill thoughts. Sadly, she remembered why she couldn't be with Chase. A sickening feeling swept over her. *Everything I'm experiencing with Chase feels like it's a day late and a dollar short and it's all my fault! How could I have messed up my life so badly that when I finally found a man who loves me, and I love him...it just isn't meant to be because of the unforgivable things I've done!*

Chase felt her hands pushing against his chest. Fearful he had hurt her with his hunger he stopped kissing her. He saw her pained expression. "Honey, did I hurt you? I'm sorry I lost myself in you." He gently pulled her into his arms where he felt at peace and knew she felt safe. "You mean the world to me, Ivy."

His words calmed her but wrapped in his tight hug he suffocated her with his loving emotions. She knew her own heart was pouring love into him and this was why he held her dearly. What she did to Kylee nagged her, and she couldn't lead Chase on like this. She couldn't give him false hope.

"Chase. It's too late for us." Ivy wept in his arms.

At first Chase thought she was referring to the time of day as he answered, "I'll make sure you get home at a decent hour."

He felt her head shake against his chest then felt the wetness from her tears soaking into his shirt. His heart constricted. He lifted her head to look at her. The palm of his hand was on her cheek, and her body betrayed her by the words she spoke as she turned her head into his loving hand. "Ivy, talk to me. What is it, honey that has you in turmoil?"

"No, Chase. I've done something terrible, unforgivable."

"Ivy, nothing is unforgivable. You can tell me." His cocoa eyes gazed deep into her emeralds. She sighed because he had this way of melting her heart, mind, and soul. She wanted to tell him, wished she could, but she knew he would hate her. She could live with Kellan hating her but not Chase. Never Chase. Ivy shook her head silently, but Chase could see the heartache etched in her face. He felt the same heartache, but he didn't understand the reason for it and wished she'd tell him.

"Ivy, whatever it is we can work it out together. Trust me," Chase begged. "I love you, Ivy. This will never change."

"It will change. You'll hate me forever, and I can't live with the thought of you hating me." Ivy wept sad tears.

"You'd rather live with a broken heart, is that it?" Chase asked, but his tone was angry. Then he was outraged when she nodded her head. He didn't understand why she couldn't trust in his love for her to tell him what was bothering her. This broke his heart because if she did trust him she'd know that he would love her no matter what.

"Yes. I'm sorry, Chase. You need to forget about me." Ivy pushed him hard on his chest making him stand away from her while the tears fell from her eyes.

"Please don't push me away, Ivy," Chase pleaded one more time as she got into her car.

"I have to, Chase. It's for your own good. You're a doctor and you are peace," Ivy said before closing the car door and locking it so he couldn't open it. The confusing, devastating look on Chase's loving face was more than she could bear. Her heart crumbled to pieces while her foot stomped on the gas, and her tires screeched on the blacktop road. Ivy didn't know what else to do. She loved Chase with all her heart but it would be devastating if he ever found out what she did to another human being. He was a doctor who believed in life, and she had acted out in jealousy and anger to hurt somebody. No, he wouldn't ever forgive her for it.

What did she mean when she said I'm peace? Chase watched her drive off, his heart twisting in pain. *We just shared the sweetest, lovingest moment I've ever had with a woman. She left me here confused, devastated and with a broken heart. What in the hell happened tonight? This was one of the best and worst nights of my life! How could this have happened the same night? Ivy told me to forget about her, but I can't. She is the woman for me and I will get her back! I'm not giving up on her! Ivy is my everything, my love, my heart!*

Days later Chase's devastated face still haunted Ivy's memories. A part of her wanted to believe that maybe Chase would forgive her. The guilt about what she'd done started to gnaw on her insides. She started making plans to leave her small hometown since it was getting unbearable to see him around town. He looked awful, and his happy go lucky attitude was gone. His smile was sad when he met people on the street, and her heart broke because it was her fault he was miserable. She watched him by staying in the shadows careful not to let him see her but somehow he sensed she was there because his eyes always searched for her.

His sadness had her thinking she might have been wrong to push him away. He truly looked like a guy who had just gotten his heart broken. Maybe she was wrong thinking his love for her wasn't strong enough to forgive her, but she felt it was too late for her to have a second chance. Her mind was made up, and she was leaving town for good. However, before she left Ivy decided to set Chase's grief of a broken heart free by confessing to him what she did. This way his feelings of heartache could be shifted to feelings of hatred for her. She hoped by doing this it would help her feel a little less guilty. Yes, this would be her reconciliation, her cross to bear to take all the pain and guilt with her. Setting his heart free of heartache was definitely something she could do for the man she loved. It would make leaving much easier. She should have left town a long time ago. If she had, less people would have gotten hurt, including her.

Chapter Twenty-Three

"Why so quiet?" Kellan questioned Kylee on the drive home.

"What were you and Ivy talking about?" Kylee asked hoping he would give her an honest answer. He didn't speak right away, and she saw his thoughtful expression.

"Do you remember the day we went to Hank's?" Kellan started turning the truck off the main road onto a dirt road where he drove slower. He shifted the gears into four wheel drive making it a lot easier to drive through the mud bogs. They were surrounded by fields on both sides of the dirt road. Kellan steered the truck through a thick grove of trees before it opened up to a big grassy field. Then he parked the truck in the middle of the field.

"How could I forget that creepy man, ugh?" Kylee shuddered.

"Remember the phone call I got?" Kellan asked then continued when she nodded her head yes.

"It was her calling you?"

"No, it was my mom, but Ivy had called her asking why I was in town and who you were?"

"Why did she care?" Kylee wondered out loud.

Kellan shrugged. "I have no idea other than small town gossip, but it bothered me a lot that she didn't call me. I felt she was being sneaky. So tonight I asked her why."

"What'd she say?"

"She apologized saying she didn't know what had gotten into her," Kellan answered.

"What'd she say about why she didn't call you?"

Kellan gave a derisive laugh shaking his head. "That I wouldn't have answered the phone if I knew it was her, and she's right. So in a way I guess I deserved to be on the gossip chain."

Kylee laughed holding onto his arms when he swung her down to the ground from the seat of his truck. "You know. In a roundabout way, Ivy calling your mom actually saved me."

"How so?" Kellan inquired. His hand lingered on her backside rubbing it lovingly as he reached behind the seat pulling out a blanket. He led her over to the back of the truck and lifted the handle on the tailgate lowering it so they could sit on it. He spread out the blanket then lifted Kylee up setting her on it. She swung her feet from the tailgate. Kellan hopped up next to her as the early night sky turned from a blue-violet to a dark cerulean color and sparkling diamonds appeared one by one.

"You had thought about walking down to the hardware store leaving me alone in the vacuum cleaner store. Then your mom called so you stayed. Just think if Ivy hadn't called your mom, your mom wouldn't have called you, and you would've left the store leaving me with ---"

"Okay, okay, quiet." Kellan placed his fingers over her mouth so she couldn't finish the rest of the sentence. "I can't bear to think about what would have happened to you if I had left the store. I get your point it's a good thing she called my mom." Kellan set his mouth on hers in a sensuous kiss.

"How exactly did you make it clear to Ivy that you weren't interested in her?" Kylee asked when their mouths parted.

Kellan's mind was fuzzy from the kiss as he answered shaking his head, "I told her I couldn't meet her for lunch."

He was done talking about Ivy, but Kylee wondered how he could possibly think he had been clear to the girl.

"Kellan," she began her voice doubtful as her mind was suddenly struck with a disturbing question. *Is it possible that Ivy is the one who attacked me in Junction City?* She was about to voice her concern, but Kellan's next words had her head spinning.

"Please no more talking about her. She means nothing to me. You're the one I love, Kylee, not her."

"You love me?" Kylee was surprised.

"Yes, I do, for awhile now." Kellan's kisses became persuasive making her forget about everything around her except for him and his loving words.

"Kellan, I…"

"Kylee, don't panic," Kellan interrupted her with another long kiss. "You don't need to say anything. I know you love me, but you're not ready to say the words. I'm all right with this, but I wanted you to know how I truly feel right here." Kellan trapped her hand between his heart and hand.

"Kellan," Kylee whispered his name fiercely. She tilted her head back looking up at the starry sky. "I'm not sure I deserve you."

"Bullshit. You deserve me more than you know. Your past is the past. I know you've been hurt but that's behind you. You're strong for leaving the abusive relationship. So strong, and I'm proud of you for it. I've never wanted a woman as much as I want you."

Kylee looked at him in awe as he continued.

"You have a kind heart like the day you came walking up my driveway carrying the cat in your arms, your beautiful face full of concern for the poor thing. You intrigued me. Then you were brave climbing up on the tractor with a strange man, but you kept your cool trusting me. If you had read my thoughts, you would've never gone down the road with me." Kellan gave her a naughty smile.

"But you did, and I thought you had spunk. You also can take my teasing and dish it back to me. I like how we can make each other laugh, and you've got a quick mind. I liked it when we teamed up together playing the prank on my sister. That was priceless!" Kellan tucked a loose strand of hair behind her ear that had fallen into her face.

"Kylee," Kellan spoke in a sharp husky tone. It had her gazing longingly into his piercing blue eyes. "You are the most beautiful woman I have ever met…inside and out." He caressed her cheek with his thumb. "I'm crazy about you," he declared passionately.

Quiet tears of happiness fell from her eyes. She tried to blink them away but it was no use. Her heart leaped with great joy as Kellan expressed his true feelings for her. She felt the same way about him but there was a big emotional lump caught in her throat that wasn't allowing her to speak. Kellan gave her delicate kisses on her eyelids, the top of her nose, and her cheeks kissing away the tears that had fallen onto her lovely face. She breathed slowly feeling the love of his kisses. His breath was warm causing her body to respond feverishly. She wanted him now more than ever before. Kylee breathed his scent and let him pull her closer crushing her body against his.

"It took bravery to leave him, and I'm so glad you did because you followed your heart and found your way to me, my sweet strong girl. My life is better with you in it." Kellan lifted her chin with his fingers forcing her to look him in the eye. Her eyes glistened in the moonlight.

"Kylee, I need you," he whispered fiercely, his voice raw with emotion. "I need you more than I have ever needed anyone in my life. I want you more than anything I've ever wanted in my life. I want you in my bed at night sleeping next to me. I want to hold you in my arms comforting you from your nightmares, and make love to you whenever we want. I want to kiss you good night and kiss you good morning. Stay with me, my beautiful brave sweet girl that I love."

Kylee caressed his rough cheek with the back of her hand. "Oh, Kellan, I've never felt like this for anyone else the way I do for you. My heart pitter patters every time I'm near you or think about you. One look from you and my blood boils. When you touch me my insides melt but it's hard for me to say the words you want to hear but—"

"No. You've already told me what I need to hear." Kellan gazed deeply into her eyes. Kylee saw the subtle change in him noting the sobriety of his emotional feelings ringing in him. She could feel the intensity of his raw feelings stirring deep within him and saw the love in his dark eyes. It affected her beyond words.

"I see your love for me in your eyes every time you look at me, and I feel it when we make love. You're all I need." His deep abiding love was clearly visible to her. The palm of his hand touched her cheek while his eyes caressed the rest of her lovingly.

"You're all I need, Kellan," she whispered.

"Show me, baby," his voice rustled.

Kylee pulled Kellan's head towards her taking the lead in kissing him. She placed her mouth possessively over his letting him feel how much she belonged there. Her tongue extended into his mouth circling around his in a captivating kiss that had him plummeting into the depths of her love. He felt her whole body lean into him, and he was more than happy to hold her. In her eyes he could see the craving desire of passion burning rapidly through her. Her loving taste lingered on the buds of his mouth. She murmured a moan as he kissed her neck vigorously.

Kellan discarded her shirt and bra and knew he was going to find her breasts taut with excitement. His mouth melted on them enjoying the hardness of her nipples. His tongue flicked the buds giving her exquisite pleasurable shivers shooting throughout her body. She arched her back pushing her breasts into his face. He let out a hungry groan as he tenderly took one breast into his mouth and then the other sucking on them. His tongue ran over the nipples giving her extra pleasure, and he felt the sensations gripping her. He quickly discarded the rest of their clothes and pulled her naked body onto his; laying them both on the blanket.

Kylee's fingers kneaded the strong muscles on his chest then she bent her head placing delicate kisses over his torso making her way down his thighs kissing his already hard penis. She took him in her mouth giving him fulfilling enjoyment. He groaned gruffly, and he lifted her back to his mouth for a searing kiss. His fingers were insistent on her nipples pinching them hard while he kissed her in a deep prolonged kiss. Her body shivered out an orgasm. Knowing how wet she was he felt his erection growing bigger, and he was ready to bury himself deep inside her, filling her with his love; needing to consummate his declaration of love to her.

"Kylee," Kellan whispered with an impatient hunger brewing in his eyes. He rolled her over onto her back as he positioned himself between her legs but paused for a moment fascinated by the way the moonlight shone on her naked body.

"Beautiful," Kellan praised. He wanted to cherish this moment a little longer to take his time loving her but once he dropped his mouth on her luscious lips he felt weak. In his attempt to savor her taste on his hard lips he lost the battle when she slipped her tongue inside his mouth wrapping him up in her wonderful taste. He was spiraling out of control as his need to have her consumed him. Outside her opening he felt the warmth of her liquid dripping onto him. Instead of entering her slowly, his impatience took over. He slid fast and hard into her and didn't let up his urgent pursuit until he completely showed his love for her.

"Ah. You feel good," he cried out breathlessly.

Kylee accepted all of him by arching her body to meet each of his deep thrusts as they moved in a perfect rhythm together. She wrapped her legs around his thighs, and he lifted both of them into the heightened passions of their love. Kylee felt free as she soared higher and higher letting herself be carried away. She clung to him as her body quivered beneath him enjoying the wonderful sensations fluttering through her. She cried out his name, digging her nails into his back accepting his love as he released himself into her. Kellan threw his head back and clenched his jaw as her name swept ardently across his lips.

Under the enchanted night sky filled with sparkling stars and moonlight, they shared the most intimate moments when they came together as one. Sharing in the afterglow of their love making, they lay lovingly in each other's arms on the soft blanket in the bed of his truck.

Kellan's mellow intense look showed his love when his eyes poured into the depths of her soul. It was this enchanted moment that made Kylee realize there could be unending nights of making love together. Suddenly she wanted this more than anything in the world! She, too, wanted to share his bed and wanted him to be the last person she saw at night and the first one to see in the mornings. She loved how close she felt with him; not only with his body but with his mind and heart, too. She felt safe and knew no harm could come to her as long as she was with him. This man could make her laugh, hold her when she cried, chase away her demons, and still love her. For the first time in her life she thought she could truly be happy and it all had to do with Kellan. She knew now what she was feeling was love, but even as she opened her mouth to tell him 'I love you' still no words came out. She was speechless when it came to saying these words. All she could do was show her emotion as the tears dropped.

"Kylee, why are you crying? Did I hurt you?" He asked concerned.

"No." She shook her head. "These are tears of happiness."

"Okay." He pulled her tighter. "I'll accept these kinds of tears."

"Kellan,"

"What?"

"I'm happy with you." She nuzzled her face against his neck and felt him take in a deep breath, "Me too."

"Will you hold me and keep me safe?" She wound her arms around his waist.

"Always, my, sweet girl," he snuggled his body next to hers and rested his chin on her head whispering, "I love you."

In answer to him loving her she hugged him harder. Even though she hadn't verbally said the words Kellan could feel her love seeping into him. Her telling him she was happy and asking him to hold her was all he needed.

Chapter Twenty-Four

The days turned into nights and they fell into a routine that happily suited them. Due to the recent rainy days, the crops were growing quite nicely. Kylee had to admit she liked the rainy days because Kellan stayed home and they spent quality time together. When it wasn't raining, Kellan was busy in the fields while she put the finishing touches on the house in anticipation of the Historical Homes Tour. She was feeling sad with the nearing of this event because it would mark the end of her job here with Kellan. She wasn't sure what the future held for them. She knew Kellan loved her with all his heart, and she returned his love even though she still wasn't able to say the actual words. For some reason the words seemed to be stuck in her throat. Even though they talked about futuristic things together there hadn't been any substantial commitment from him assuring her of how much he wanted her to stay forever.

She wondered if he was waiting to hear her say the words I love you. She thought in desperation *what if I can never say the words he is longing to hear?* She knew in her heart that her tender eyes, gentle caresses and loving kisses wasn't going to be enough for him forever, yet so far it had been. Oddly, this was enough for Kellan. Kylee's heart expanded with love and often she wanted to weep because he didn't demand the words from her and felt she didn't deserve his understanding.

Kellan was full of compliments about the way she had made the house come alive again with a positive energy. Each night he delicately held her sore hands caressing them tenderly and thanking her for all the hard work, dedication and love she had contributed to making the house come alive again with her magical touches. He also made sure to tell her how much he loved her. Her eyes misted with tears, and he knew this was her way of saying, "I love you."

With Kellan home most nights they spent time together walking on his property before the light of day faded into darkness. Kylee discovered that what he said to her on the first day, "as far as your city eyes can see, I own", wasn't as far from the truth as she had first thought. She hadn't been impressed then but now she was by how much of the farming business he had built for himself. He told her how he had borrowed money from family, invested what he could while paying off his debts, and working hard through it all. He confided that even though his debts were paid, he now saved every penny he could as he still continued to work hard.

On the warmer evenings they swam in the pool, curled up on the couch together watching a baseball game, sat on the front porch swing and talking about anything and everything: childhood memories, wishes for the future and discovered other things they had in common while watching the sun sink into the horizon before heading to bed. Kylee slept beside Kellan in his bed every night since all of her clothes had been moved into his room.

Kellan had become quite comfortable with their daily routine working as a team. He hoped Kylee felt the same way. In fact, his plans were to make things permanent with her once the Historical Homes Tour was done. He knew Kylee loved him every time her sky blue eyes met his, and he knew he loved her by the way his heart beat wildly in his chest every time he saw her, smelled her, or sensed her presence. Kellan loved her more than anything in this world. He never imagined himself being so much in love with one person as he was with Kylee. He envisioned once more the two of them sitting on the front porch watching their children and grandchildren growing up. He wanted her today, tomorrow, and forever. Yes, Kellan wanted Kylee to be by his side for the rest of his life.

Kylee looked up at Kellan's peculiar smile. "Why are you smiling like that?"

Kellan pulled her closer as they walked outside. "I'm happy, Sweet Girl."

"I am too. I don't want it to end." She snuggled into him.

"Who says it has to end?" He tossed out feeling Kylee shrug her shoulder.

"I hope it doesn't," she mumbled then turned her head to the end of the driveway as they watched a beat up old brown pick up truck turn into the driveway. She felt encouraged by Kellan's words asking why their happy had to end and hoped he would ask her to stay here after the home tour, but she didn't want to get her hopes up too much in case something went wrong. She tried not to think about the bad luck of the past. The bad luck always seemed to come when things were going good in her life. She forced herself to think about positive thoughts.

It was hard to focus on good things when the handyman, Kellan hired to fix the leaky roof pulled into the driveway in a brown battered truck. Kylee noticed the truck nuts hanging from the hitch. Even before the man got out of the truck Kylee already had a negative feeling. She had her eyes cast downward when she heard the truck door creak open. Then she saw black leather cowboy boots step onto the gravel. Her gaze lifted as the man got out of the truck and swaggered over to them with an odd confidence. The man was dressed in black jeans and a black short sleeve shirt making Kylee think this was odd clothes for a roofer to wear in the hot sun. The handyman was a lot shorter than his customer and had to raise his head to look up at Kellan, but Kylee guessed this happened a lot in the shorter man's life. His body was burly, and she had a hard time distinguishing if his body was made up of muscle or body fat. His face was pudgy, and he had a red beard matching the red hair on his head. He had beady black eyes that swept over Kylee's body making her skin crawl.

The handyman introduced himself as Leroy. That was it, no last name, just Leroy. Kellan introduced himself then introduced Kylee. Kylee made brief eye contact with Leroy shaking his limp noodle of a handshake making her squeamish. She quietly followed the men around to the back of the house where the damaged roof was. Kellan pointed up to the part on the roof where it needed fixing. With his back turned Kellan missed the handyman's lecherous eyes skimming over Kylee's body lingering briefly on her breasts before giving her a quick interested smile. Then he stepped forward giving his attention to Kellan. Leroy's daring move had her feeling disgusted. She frowned at the handyman's back as Kellan instructed Leroy about the roof. Feeling Leroy's black eyes on her, she knew Leroy wasn't listening to Kellan. *Why is he not listening to Kellan?*

Kylee took a step closer to Kellan not trusting the man with the fire red hair. He reminded her of a leprechaun searching for his pot of gold. However, she couldn't help feeling that Leroy thought her to be his treasured gold by the way his gaze ran over her body. She made the mistake of catching Leroy's eyes. He suavely licked his lips winking at her; instantly she felt sick. Feeling queasy, she gripped Kellan's hand wishing for a way to tell him how uncomfortable Leroy made her.

She quietly followed the men as they continued walking around the rest of the house. Out of the corner of her eye she watched Leroy's eyes glance over the house with an odd, thoughtful look. It made her feel squeamish again. Kellan grabbed Kylee's hand insisting she walk with them placing her between him and Leroy. She quickly stepped around Kellan walking on his other side away from Leroy. Leroy agreed to begin repairs on the shingles right away promising it wouldn't take long to repair. The two men shook hands for the estimate on repairing the shingles.

Kylee wished she could ask Kellan to stay near the house. However, after all the rain this past week she knew he needed to be in the fields. She also knew the roof needed repairing and sending the handyman away wasn't an option because he was the only repair man available. The other roofer in town Kellan had hired suddenly got sick and was on bed rest. Her only comforting thought was she would be inside working, and Leroy would be outside. Kellan and Evan would be back in a few hours for the noon meal. Kellan kissed her good-bye wishing her to have a good morning.

"I got spoiled these last few days. I'm going to miss you," Kylee pouted.

Kellan groaned, "Me, too, Sweet Girl," he kissed her again, "Noon needs to come soon."

Kylee flashed him a bright smile and headed into the house for her morning chores. She was already looking forward to the noon meal. She stuck to her routine of collecting the mail from the mailbox once she heard the mailman's horn as he drove off. Then as twelve o'clock neared she looked forward to seeing Kellan. Laughing out loud to herself she realized how accustomed she got to Kellan being home with her and how much she liked spending time with him.

"Hey, Sweet Girl," Kellan's voice spoke to her as he came in through the back door making sure he didn't sneak up on her. She turned around seeing his loving face coming in through the door. Her smile was warm and welcoming. He stepped forward and she stepped into his outstretched arms.

"I missed you, Kellan," she sighed.

"I longed all morning to do this," he whispered brushing his lips at the nape of her neck. She turned her head kissing his cheek.

"Kellan," Kylee sighed happily her arms going around his waist in a big hug. He smelled of sweat along with the smell of freshly cut grass. His farmer's working man smell was comforting. "I wish we could go upstairs for awhile."

Kellan groaned as he nibbled on her ear. "Don't tempt me."

Their embrace was broken from the commotion coming through the back door.

Evan's voice called out, "Kylee, do you have an ice pack?"

Kylee grabbed one and met Evan with a concerned look. "What happened?"

"It's not me, it's Leroy. He bashed his hand with the hammer," Evan explained then stepped aside revealing a hunched over Leroy sitting on the vestibule floor.

"Bashed his hand with the hammer…" Kylee mumbled but it struck an odd chord in her mind. She knew accidents happened but for an experienced roofer to hammer his whole hand just didn't seem quite right…maybe a finger or thumb but the whole hand?

Kylee handed the ice pack to Evan who tossed it to Leroy. Leroy managed to fumble the ice pack with his good hand and it skidded across the floor near Kylee. She picked it up feeling Leroy's eyes on her the whole time. She walked over and handed the ice pack back to him. Glancing down she noticed his venomous eyes but didn't see his hand snaking out to grab her wrist until it was too late. He yanked her hard down towards him. She lost her balance and knew this is what Leroy wanted by the way he chuckled viciously in her ear.

She heard him inhale deeply then grunted, "You smell good." He said this for her ears only. With her free hand she quickly pushed herself off and away from him. She rushed straight into Evan losing her balance, but he gripped her arm steadying her and saw the disgust on her face. Evan saw her cringe as Leroy thanked her in a loud, obnoxious voice. She fled from the room as Kellan entered sensing he had missed something important. Kylee let the back door slam shut while Kellan's eyes questioned Evan who threw him a baffled look.

Kylee was silently fuming by the time the men came into the kitchen and much to her dismay Leroy followed them in. Leroy winked, licked his lips, and ogled her the whole time with his sinister black eyes.

"Kylee, Leroy's joining us for dinner," Kellan informed her. He stepped over to the cabinet retrieving another plate missing the disappointment on her face.

Kylee thought about faking sickness so she wouldn't have to sit at the same table with Leroy but then decided she shouldn't let him scare her away. This was her time with Kellan. Surely, he wouldn't be so bold and do anything in front of the men at the dinner table, but she should've known better. They all sat at the table, said grace then dug in. Kylee ate in silence listening to the conversation around her. Leroy chomped on his food and talked with his mouthful, much to her distaste. *He's rude and has no table manners!*

At first she did a good job ignoring him but towards the end of the meal she was tired of him staring at her as though she was dessert. She gave him a disgusted look. As crazy as it sounded she felt Leroy had somehow planned all of this. She hated how he kept his tongue lolled out of his mouth when he grinned or winked at her being sure to do this only when Kellan and Evan had their eyes averted from him.

Kellan didn't fail to notice Kylee's tension and her lack of conversation; only talking when spoken to. He didn't miss the pleased grin on Leroy's face every time Kylee squirmed uncomfortably in her seat.

Evan caught Leroy winking at Kylee who abruptly excused herself from the table. He was in awe over the man's outright flirting, and he wondered how Kellan didn't seem aware of Leroy's actions. Then Evan caught Kellan's simmering hot eyes and knew he was well aware of the effect Leroy was having on Kylee.

"Mr. Taylor, thank you for the meal. It was very good," Leroy thanked Kellan standing up from the table soon after Kylee had excused herself. Kellan also stood.

"I'd like to thank the woman personally for such a fine meal, if you don't mind," Leroy announced taking steps towards the door where Kylee exited. Kellan quickly stepped in front of Leroy stopping him.

"I do mind," Kellan said with a stern, threatening tone matched by his steely blue-black eyes. His broad chest stood like a stone wall in front of Leroy as his body language sent a slow warning to the handyman not to go beyond him or face the consequences.

Leroy heard Evan's chair scrape the floor behind him and understood the aire around him. If he dared to fight the man in front of him he would also have to fight the man behind him. Leroy knew he didn't have a fighting chance with either one of the men. He backed off deciding he'd get another chance with the woman. Leroy raised his hands slowly saying, "Hey, sorry man. Just thought—"

"You thought wrong. It'll be best if you get back to work," Kellan snarled.

Leroy turned around and gave one quick glance to Evan who looked just as fierce.

Leroy climbed back up the ladder with a sinking feeling of how he really had misjudged these country boys. He thought they weren't paying attention when he had flirted with Mr. Taylor's woman, but he had been wrong. His flirting might have gotten him fired and this wasn't going to sit well with his boss. The reason he had been sent there in the first place didn't have anything to do with fixing the leak in the roof. Well, if he got fired, so be it. He'd just have to implement plan b.

"That sonofa --." Evan swore after Leroy left the house. "Are you gonna let that asshole keep on working out there?"

"Damn it, I don't have a choice," Kellan snapped. "There isn't anyone left in town who can fix the roof before the tour of homes. I had Baker's boy lined up to do the work, but he got sick of all of sudden. Food poisoning they think. I am between a rock and a hard place, damn it. What do you suggest I do?"

Evan nodded. "I know, man. It's just that he's…" Evan trailed off as Kylee breezed back into the kitchen with a bitter look.

"Kylee," Kellan said her name trying to judge the anger in her. Kylee flashed her eyes bright at Kellan. "What's going on?"

Kylee clenched her teeth as she let go of what she was feeling. "Kellan, I know we need him to fix the roof, but I don't like him. He was making passes at me behind your back this morning when we met him, but I ignored him. Then he grabbed my hand today with the ice pack pulling me down to him and he said I smelled good." She shuddered, her face twisted with disgust.

Kellan was appalled by what she just told him. He had no idea but this explained her hurry to leave the room earlier.

"Oh, Sweet Girl," he pulled her into his arms. "I'm sorry. I had no idea about this morning, but I did at dinner today. I could see you were uncomfortable and didn't know why until I saw his satisfied smile when he thought I wasn't looking."

Kylee felt Kellan's tension.

"And, then the bastard wanted to go and thank you for the meal, but he had other ideas on his mind. I'm sure of it! He's gotta go!" Kellan declared.

"No, Kellan. He's all we've got," Kylee argued. "If we don't get the roof repaired the house won't be done for the tour."

"Kylee, Shhh. We'll figure something out, but you can't be alone here in the house with that man around. I do not trust him! He's leaving!" Kellan stated. Kylee opened her mouth, but Kellan placed his fingers kindly over her lips. "No, Kylee. You're safety is the utmost importance to me."

Kylee nodded understanding and loving him for it. She eagerly flung herself into his arms in a wild hug as she said breathlessly, "Thank you, Kellan. I love you."

Kylee felt her heart bursting at the seams with love unable to hold it in any longer. She just said what she felt as the words spilled out of her pouring deep from within her heart. She pressed her body lovingly into Kellan's having no idea how wonderful he felt inside hearing her say she loved him. Her love crept into his veins filling his whole inner being.

Kellan hadn't thought he needed to hear her say the words she loved him but now that she had, he was even more exhilarated by her love than before. He was wrapped up in a fierce rollercoaster of emotions as he buried his head into her shoulder inhaling her loving scent, hugging her tight. She meant the world to him!

"Kylee, I love you, too, my sweet girl." He stroked her head affectionately with his hand wondering if he could ever love her more than he did today.

"Kylee, lock the door behind me. I'm going with Evan to escort Leroy off the property, but I don't want him to try to get inside in the process," Kellan said after awhile of them holding each other. "Then I'm sending Evan home and coming back inside to make love to you for the rest of the day," he promised cupping her face between his muscular hands. He lowered his unyielding lips onto her open mouth wrapping her up in a velvety smooth kiss leaving her ragged and tingling all over.

Kellan and Evan walked around to the back of the house where they expected to find Leroy working. Instead, they found him gone along with his tools. Together the two men walked around to the front of the house to the driveway and found his truck was gone, too. Kellan felt somewhat relieved.

"Do you think he's gone for good?" Evan asked.

Kellan shook his head. "Gosh, I hope so. I'm gonna stick around here this afternoon just in case he chooses to come back."

Evan nodded. "Okay. I'm gonna call it a day, too."

"Thanks, Ev. I'll see you tomorrow." Kellan whistled a happy tune as he walked up to his bedroom where he knew Kylee was waiting for him. He slid into bed with her.

"Kylee," his voice was husky with emotion. His enamored eyes danced across her enjoying her beauty and his handsome face held a playful smile. "I'm going to make love to my beautiful gorgeous sweet girl who told me that she loves me. Say it again."

"I love you, Kellan," Kylee declared as her blue eyes danced with love.

Kellan's mouth sought hers in a demanding kiss. True to his word the rest of the day they made exquisite love, treasuring the newfound spoken words of love that they declared repeatedly to each other verbally and physically as the hours of the day turned into night.

"Keep the doors locked this afternoon while I'm gone, and keep Jake inside with you. He'll protect you, won't you Boy?" Kellan rubbed Jake's ears. Jake whined his response and nudged Kylee's hand with his wet nose. Kylee laughed petting his head.

"He likes you." Kellan rubbed his nose with hers then rested his forehead on her temple. "I think he's got good taste."

Kylee laughed making him feel better about leaving her this afternoon.

"Do you think Leroy will show up?" Kylee asked concerned. Kellan had hung around the house this morning as a precaution in case Leroy had decided to come back today.

"I don't think so, but I don't want to take any chances," Kellan said.

"I understand your concern, but it's not fair that I have to feel like a prisoner." Kylee pouted.

"If I lock the door and don't hear you knocking how will you get in?" Kylee asked.

Kellan smirked at her as he answered, "Through a window, since I've done it before."

Kylee laughed out loud remembering her first night here when she had accidentally locked him out. He drew her into his arms and his lips locked over hers in a deep fortified kiss. This had Kylee weak in the knees and wishing he could have kissed her longer.

Kellan groaned fervently, "Kylee," he clamped his hand on her cheek affectionately and repeated, "Keep Jake inside with you."

She nodded, locked the door then checked all the other doors making sure they were locked, too. With the doors locked she felt safer to run the vacuum cleaner. Later in the afternoon, Kylee heard Jake growling in the next room and headed that way. Jake was standing at the front door; a low guttural growl coming from his throat. Kylee not only heard but saw the front door knob jiggle in an effort to open from the other side. Kylee's first thought was maybe it was Kellan trying to get in, but her instincts told her otherwise. Jake wouldn't be growling if it was his master trying to get in, instead he'd have a happy whine versus this low threatening growl.

The door knob made an even louder noise of the intruder. Jake jumped up on his hind legs and his huge front paws pounded on the glass window ferociously barking at the person on the other side of the door trying to get in. The curtain on the window of the door swayed open. Kylee gasped in fear when she saw Leroy on the other side of the door. She flattened her back against the wall and prayed to God he didn't see her. She was deeply in shock! Leroy was trying to get into the house! Almost as if he knew she was by herself, but how? Had he been watching the house all day? Why did he wait so long after Kellan left? And, oh what would she have done if she hadn't locked the doors? Why was he here at the house and trying to get in? She knew he meant to do her harm, but she didn't know why? He was the one who walked off the job, although Kellan was going to fire him anyway.

Kylee really appreciated Kellan's persistence to keep his dog in the house with her today. She felt it was Jake's barking and jumping up on the door that kept the intruder outside instead of kicking down the door to get to her. Jake stopped barking and came to sit with her on the couch. She petted his head speaking to him in hushed tones thanking him. He whined nudging her hand with his wet nose as if he was saying "you're welcome." She smiled warmly at Jake realizing she and the dog just had a bonding moment.

Kylee knew she needed to tell Kellan about what happened. She picked up the phone to call him but then didn't. By the way Jake was quietly sitting next to her she knew Leroy had left so there wasn't any reason to have Kellan come home. She almost typed out the words in a text message about what happened but knew Kellan wouldn't react well at the typed message. She decided to tell him in person when he got home.

She made sandwiches for supper and fell asleep on the couch waiting for Kellan to come home. The next thing she knew she was being lifted up by warm, strong arms. Smelling his sweet, sweaty scent she opened her sleepy eyes.

"Sorry I'm late." Kellan kissed her lightly and carried her effortlessly upstairs. He looked worn out. Kylee caressed the side of his face. She traced her index finger around his tired eyes, down over the bridge of his nose then ran her finger across his lips.

"Kellan, you're so tired." She rubbed her thumb across his mouth. He caught her hand in his bringing it to his mouth kissing it lovingly.

"So are you."

"Lay with me, Kellan," she invited in a tired voice. He obliged as he lay on his back on top of the blankets next to her. She rolled her body into his, stretching one arm across his torso while her other arm lay next to his side. Everything she meant to say to him about the day fell from her mind as she breathed in his scent, calming her, and she fell back asleep.

The next morning Kylee told Kellan she was going into town to run errands and stop at the grocery store. As Kylee put the truck into drive her parked car caught her eye. She spun the old farm truck's tires in the gravel thinking she never dreamed in a million years she'd like driving a truck as much as she did. She even started thinking about trading her car in for a truck or maybe a Jeep. She could visualize Kellan rolling in laughter over the idea of his city girl wanting to trade her car in for a truck. Kylee focused on the list of things she needed to pick up and which stores to go to first. Her mind wandered to the last 24 hours and dread set in as she remembered she completely forgot to tell Kellan about Leroy trying to get in the front door yesterday. She couldn't believe she had forgotten to tell him! He was going to be pissed when he found out! She needed to tell him tonight.

Kylee decided to make the supermarket her last stop. With her list in hand and purse swung over her shoulder, she hopped out of the truck then strolled into the store grabbing a shopping cart on her way in. She was glad she left the store as her last stop. She had too many groceries to pick up, and her cart was filled by the time she got to the check out lane. Glancing at her watch she saw it had taken her much longer than she had originally anticipated it would. She'd never make it back in time for lunch, so she sent Kellan a text letting him know she was still in town and wouldn't make it home by noon.

His text was immediate with, **no worries. See you later. Drive safe.** His concern for her to drive safe warmed her heart. Loading her bagged groceries back into her cart she was only half paying attention to the customer behind her conversing with the cashier.

"You're leaving town? For good; not ever coming back?" Kylee heard the cashier say in shock.

"Yes. It's time for me to see what's out there in the world besides this town." Kylee heard the customer say. Just as Kylee set the last bag in the shopping cart she heard the cashier say, "Ivy, just be careful out there. Come back and visit us when you can."

Kylee looked up seeing the woman for the first time. So this was Ivy. She hadn't ever seen the girl up close before, only from a distance at Charlie's party and it was dark. The girl had shoulder length dark brown hair verging on black with green cat like eyes, and she was shorter than Kylee. Somehow, Ivy didn't fit the description that Kylee had conjured up in her mind. She wasn't quite sure what she expected her to look like; but not this. She had imagined her to be confident with a face full of makeup but this wasn't the case. Ivy was almost on the plainer side of life with a quiet manner; almost an air of innocence about her. Kylee was surprised Evan hadn't fallen for Ivy because she seemed to be perfect for him.

"Ivy," Kylee heard herself say out loud as the girl slowly turned her head. Ivy gave her a solemn nod of recognition. Kylee had an uneasy feeling about the way Ivy recognized who she was even though they hadn't ever been formally introduced. *Small towns, I guess.*

"It's nice to meet you." Kylee held out her hand to Ivy who shook her hand with hesitancy but yet it was a firm handshake.

"Nice to meet you," Ivy said slowly swallowing nervously with a caught off guard look in her eyes. She was at a loss for words, but her mind raced *if Kylee knew it was me who had pushed her in the bathroom then I don't think she'd be so cordial with her greeting.*

Kylee thought Ivy looked nervous to be around her, striking her oddly, but then she remembered the girl was leaving town. *Maybe she's nervous about leaving town.* The two women walked out the door together and as fate would have it they were parked next to each other.

"Did I hear you say you are leaving town?" Kylee asked Ivy.

"Yes," Ivy answered quietly, agonizing over the fact that she had to make small talk with this woman. She tried to push her guilty feelings aside.

"For a vacation?" Kylee asked. *Why am I so chatty with this girl? After hearing the guys talk about Ivy she seems much different than the girl they were talking about. Her eyes are beautiful and piercing green, sort of reminding me of a cautious cat. Sort of like the cat I ran over. I wonder if the cat found a loving home.*

"Not on a vacation. Um…moving away from here," Ivy stammered.

"Where are you moving to?" Kylee asked non-chalantly.

Ivy shrugged her shoulders. "I'm not sure yet. I haven't quite decided. It's just time for me to see what else is out there."

"Well, I wish you the best of luck on your journey, and I hope you find whatever it is that you're looking for," Kylee said sincerely, but she saw a longing for something in Ivy's eyes. Was it hope?

"Thank you." An odd soft feeling overcame Ivy making her think that Kylee may not be so bad after all. If things had been different, no Ivy corrected herself, if she had been different and given Kylee a chance there could've been a good possibility she and Kylee might have been friends. Ivy sat in her car watching Kylee drive off in the old truck no longer wishing it was her driving home to Kellan, in fact, Kellan no longer lived in her head. Ivy's only memories were now of Chase, and she wished it was her driving home to see him. As she drove home she cried for what could've been.

Chase saw Ivy drive by him in her car. He also saw her tears and was concerned over the fact of how she was driving and crying, not a good combination. He couldn't help feeling a little happy about her tears because that meant she still had feelings for him. Chase made up his mind right then and there that he needed to fight for Ivy against herself. He couldn't let her go. His love for her was too deep, and he needed to show her how much he loved her. He had to find a way for her to tell him what was bothering her and what the reason was for her pushing him away. He turned his truck around and followed her home. Outside in her driveway Ivy closed her car door leaning her back against the car as Chase approached her with a determined look on his face. Her heart raced like an Indy car was in her chest. He still looked devastatingly handsome. She wished with all her heart that she could be with him forever. His lips were firmly pressed together, and Ivy wished she could kiss them feeling his love like she did the night at Charlie's before she pushed him away.

"I know you still have feelings for me, Ivy. Your tear stained face says it all."

Chase remembered the way her lips parted the night they kissed in the dark, and he wanted nothing more than to kiss away her fears and doubts. If he thought this would work then he would plaster endless kisses all over her.

"Answer me this," Chase demanded but was interrupted by Ivy's mother's voice calling out to her from the front door.

"I'll be inside in a minute, Mama!" Ivy called back then focused on the proud man standing in front of her. "What Chase?"

"Did you kill somebody?" He asked her.

"No." Ivy gave him a ridiculous look. "No, I didn't kill anybody but—"

"Hush," Chase said angrily. He was relieved to know she hadn't killed anyone. Although, he didn't think this was the case but the way she acted he thought he better ask. He was still mad at her.

"Okay, then. Ivy, you need to know that I love you with all my heart, and I'm not going to let you go. You're going to tell me exactly what you did and then we're going to find a way to fix it, together," Chase promised her. When she opened her mouth to protest he silenced her with a deep sensuous kiss. It touched her heart sending sparks flying through her.

"Go inside. Your mama's worried. We're talking soon." Chase steered her towards the front door watching her go inside. As he drove off he realized he had blatantly kissed her outside in front of her house where all her neighbors could see, and Chase really hoped Ivy didn't mind him showing the world how he felt about her.

Chapter Twenty-Five

By the time Kylee got back to the farm she was tired and cranky from her shopping trip. Quickly, she unpacked the truck putting away her purchases then sprawled out on the sofa waiting for Kellan to come in from another late night in the fields. Next thing she knew it was dark outside when she rolled over and saw Kellan in his jeans. Was he dressing for the day or undressing for the night? She was sleepy and didn't know what time it was. Kellan sat down on the edge of the bed placing a delicate kiss on her forehead. "Morning, Beautiful,"

In response, she mumbled a sleepy "morning". She slid her arms around his neck pulling him closer. He let her pull him down. He caressed his lips zealously on her mouth anxious to taste her. She met his kiss with the same urgency. It had been awhile since she felt his hard wanton lips or his pressing tongue. She understood why he needed to work late, but she missed him all the same. *Why is he leaving so early this morning?* "Wait, did you say morning?"

"Evan's tractor is stuck in the mud. I'll have to winch him out," Kellan answered her unasked question as if reading her mind.

"Be careful," Kylee wished him. "Will you be coming back this morning or staying out 'til noon?"

"We'll just stay out 'til noon," Kellan informed her.

"Which field?"

"Over on County S. Roll back over and get some sleep." He kissed her passionately before leaving her side. He covered her up with the blanket then smoothed her cheek with the back of his hand. Then quietly and reluctantly he left. More than anything in the world he wanted to stay in bed this morning to make love with her; feel, touch, and hold her. Since the rain stopped he'd been working nonstop in the fields making up for the time they lost on the rainy days, but Kellan was missing Kylee something fierce. If Evan hadn't needed his help he would still be in bed with his beautiful sweet girl. Kellan climbed up in his tow truck, revved the engine then headed out to help Evan.

Kylee was unable to sleep after Kellan left so she got up, showered, dressed for the day then made her way down to the kitchen. She threw biscuits and sausage patties in the oven then fried some eggs. When the oven timer went off she layered the egg, sausage and a slice of cheese between the biscuits making sausage egg biscuits to feed an army. She wrapped them in tinfoil then put them into a basket. After she poured coffee into a thermal carafe she placed it into the basket before heading out the door and called, "Jake, come."

After the incident the other day she now kept Jake close to her. Kylee climbed in the old farm truck she was used to driving. The sun was just starting to show in the eastern sky. She made a couple of turns on different roads remembering how to get out to the field where Kellan was. Then she saw them. She turned the truck into the field bouncing and laughing in the seat as she drove the truck over all the bumps and dips on the dirt path.

"Who is this crazy person?" One man commented then the other piped in with.

"This idiot is driving too fast. Stupid fellow has no idea what you could drive over popping a tire."

Kellan heard the men talking but didn't bother to stand up or look to see what they were talking about. He was crouched on his hands and knees covered in mud busy working on unfastening the winch off Evan's tractor. By the time he got here Evan's dad was here with a couple of his buddies but it was Kellan who had done the grunt work of wading into the mud hooking up the winches. Kellan trusting Evan's dad put him in the tow truck easing his son out of the mud while Kellan adjusted the straps. Kellan wasn't sure how exactly the other older men had been helpful. Oh, they sure had their opinions of how to do it but in the end it was Kellan and Evan's teamwork that got the tractor out of the mud.

On any other day Kellan might have found some kind of humor with the two opinionated older men seeing himself and Evan in thirty years doing the same thing but this morning wasn't one of those days. He was tired, hungry and covered head to toe in stinky mud and thinking about Kylee. His loins ached while thinking about her.

Now these two gentlemen were ridiculing the driver heading their way commenting negatively about the headlights flashing in their eyes. Knowing that this new driver irritated the men put a small smile on his tired face. Kellan sat back on his knees catching his breath. What he wouldn't give for a cup of coffee right about now.

"Thanks, Kellan!" Evan called out from up in the tractor.

Kellan waved his hand up. "Any time, man,"

The truck stopped quickly as a cloud of dust billowed around them. The two older men coughed in the dust. Kellan then heard a familiar feminine laugh floating in the air as he heard Evan say, "Isn't that Kylee?"

"What?" Evan's words didn't quite register on Kellan's tired brain but as he looked around the tow truck he saw Kylee laughing in a carefree manner with her ponytail bopping behind her head as she got out of the truck and made her way to the passenger side. He liked the way her blue jeans wrapped snugly around her bottom causing an even harder ache in his loins. He watched her carry a big basket as she made her way over to him with a bright cheerful smile.

Kellan's heart swelled with pride when he saw her. He laughed out loud remembering the men's comment about the crazy driver only to discover it was his girl who had irritated the men. He loved it!

"I brought breakfast!" Kylee announced.

Evan's dad took the basket out of her arms and placed it on the tailgate of his truck. Thanking Evan's dad, she waved to Evan keeping eyes on Kellan as she continued walking towards him.

"Dang fool hardy woman driver." One of the older men said but Kellan cut in sharply, "Watch it!"

"A dang fool hardy woman who brought you breakfast!" Kylee snapped at the two men tossing them a saucy smile. The two older men's mouths hung open for they were speechless and not used to a female snapping back at them. Kellan's lips twitched upwards as he burst out laughing.

"And here I thought you were home sleeping," Kellan drawled.

"I couldn't sleep after you left so I got up and decided to bring you breakfast," Kylee admitted with bashful eyes at the mere suggestion to the men of how they were sleeping together. *What if Kellan didn't want anyone to know?*

"I'm sorry," Kylee apologized in a quiet voice that only Kellan heard.

"For what?" he asked.

"Indicating we might be together,"

"But we are together," Kellan whispered back.

"You're okay with other people knowing?"

"Yes. Are you?"

"Yes." Kylee smiled brightly then hugged him mud and all.

"Baby, you're covered in mud," Kellan mentioned as he held her. She stepped back laughing at the mud on her. "Here you missed a spot." Kellan smudged some mud on her cheek.

The two older men gaped at the younger couple then one of them spoke up, "Yep! It would make sense this sassy girl belongs to you."

Kellan looked pleased over the comment while wiping the mud off of his hands with a towel that was handed to him. "She sure does."

Kellan folded his hand into hers, winking. "I don't suppose you have any coffee in that basket?"

"I do," Kylee said emphatically. Kellan gave her a long quiet look. The way she said "I do" jarred his emotions. His heartbeat quickened while envisioning Kylee saying these words in her wedding vows promising to love him until death do them part.

"Are you okay?" Kylee asked Kellan unable to read his expression. She tugged on his arm bringing him back to reality. A thin smile appeared on his tired face.

"I'm wonderful, Sweet Girl, and so are you." He pulled her back into his muddy embrace finding it hard to believe this treasured woman was his as she wrapped her arms around him not minding the mud on her.

"Thank you."

"Thank you for what?" Kylee asked.

"For bringing coffee for one, two for breakfast, three for coming into my life, four for being you, five for –"

"Okay! I get it!" Kylee laughed happily holding her hand up to his mouth to make him stop.

"No, five is important," Kellan said in his low gravely voice, the one that made her weak. "Five is for loving me."

"Oh, Kellan," Kylee whispered her face flushing with embarrassment because he said it loud enough for the others to hear. But she didn't mind when he placed his hearty lips on hers in an intense kiss, leaving her breathless. She felt the deep love he had for her in the kiss. She touched her hand to his muddy cheek gazing tenderly into his eyes with love. "I love you, too."

It was well past nine o'clock when Kylee got back to the house. With a bounce in her steps she got started on the day's work. She threw her muddy clothes in the washing machine then stepped into the basement shower instead of running all the way back upstairs. After her shower, she rummaged through the dryer for clean clothes as she mentally put her "things to do" list together. In the kitchen she placed the beef roast in the oven along with sliced potatoes, carrots, and mushrooms cooking them together. *It should be good timing for the meal this afternoon.*

Kylee was in the front room when she heard a horn honking outside. When she looked out the front window she saw a gray car in the driveway with a man waving a big package out of his car window. The delivery man was motioning with his hand for her to come outside to retrieve the package, and she was irritated how he didn't come up to the house with it. Instead he blasted his horn again! With an agitated sigh she walked out the front door to get the box. The delivery man had bushy eyebrows and a thin mouth that sneered at her as she got closer. He shot her an annoyed look and snapped, "It's about time you mosey your way on out here. I was about to leave it on the ground."

"Well, that's not very nice," Kylee spat back giving him a pathetic look as the delivery man shrugged his shoulder giving her an I-don't-care look.

While the delivery man backed the car into the road, he turned his head sideways looking over his left shoulder, and she saw a long white scar on the right hand side of his face. He stomped his foot on the gas pedal causing the car to swerve as it took off down the road. *Boy, he is the rudest delivery man I've ever encountered.* She held up the box feeling how light the package was, curious to know what was inside. Since she was already outside, Kylee walked over to the mailbox retrieving the mail as well. When Kylee got to the front door she turned the handle but it didn't open and it was then she remembered she had forgotten to unlock the front door. Jake barked on the other side of the storm door.

"I don't suppose you could unlock the door for me?" Kylee asked the big dog. "Crap," she grumbled and was mad about how she completely forgot to unlock the door leaving Jake inside. In fact, she didn't even think about. All she was thinking about was the rude delivery guy honking his stupid horn. "Ugh!" She let out a frustrated sigh then said to Jake through the screen, "Be back in a minute."

Kylee circled her way around to the back of the house. Rounding the side of the house, she stopped dead in her tracks when she saw Leroy leaning against his truck near the back door. Her mind raced frantically. *Where on earth did he come from and when did he get here? I didn't hear him pull into the driveway or hear Jake barking. Maybe Jake barked when I was in the shower! Oh, no!*

Fear punched her in the stomach as panic struck her every nerve and dread circled inside her. *Was this a trap? Were Leroy and the delivery man working together? That's why the delivery man insisted I come out to get the mail! It was a ploy to get me out of the house and I am so gullible! I put myself in great danger! He's pretty smart waiting all these days giving me a false sense of security thinking I was safe. Oh, shit!*

Slowly, she reached her hand inside her jeans pocket pulling out her cell phone. Keeping her distance from Leroy but watching him closely, trying to decide what she should do and judge his next move. Leroy had positioned himself close to the back door knowing she would have to walk past him to get inside. She hugged the box to her chest hiding the cell phone from Leroy as she sent Kellan a text that read, **LEROY HELP**

She stood still for a moment. *I have nowhere to go. I could run, but where? Maybe the barn, but I don't think I could outrun him.* Fear, dread, panic with a bit of crazy urged her on. As she walked closer to the door Leroy's eyelids drooped, and she felt his nasty gaze slide over her. He smiled viciously and spit a wad of chew landing near her feet. He laughed uproariously when she gave a disgusted look.

"Well, now darlin'," Leroy drawled. "It looks like it's just me and you. Your strong man isn't here to help you, is he?" He sneered. "I've got my orders to scare you away but I've got something else in mind."

"Scare me away, but why?" Kylee ventured.

Leroy shrugged. "You've been teasing me since the day I got here. I know you want me."

Kylee opened her mouth to deny his accusations, but Leroy stepped forward before she had any time to react he seized her shoulders digging his fingers roughly into her skin. She whimpered in pain dropping the package and the mail listening to it fall to the ground.

"You're hurting me!" Kylee cried out in pain moving her body twisting her way out of his hard grasp. With her arms free, she lifted her hand up with the cell phone in it connecting her fist with Leroy's cheek.

In surprised pain he yelled out rubbing his cheek. He hadn't expected her to fight back. He thought she was going to be an easy target, but he had misjudged her. Angered by this, he lunged for her as she ran in the direction of the barn. He caught her ankle just as she reached the edge of the grass, and she fell hard to the ground. He then yanked her leg pulling her face first through the grass towards him. She dug her fingernails into the grass trying to get a firm hold but it was no use. He was too strong! With Leroy holding her one foot she quickly rolled over onto her back swinging her loose foot into his side. He swayed in pain letting her foot go. Kylee tried to stand, but Leroy aggressively looped his arm under her stomach hauling her up against his hip. Quick thoughts entered her mind, and she tried to think of way to get Leroy into the house where Jake was.

"I'll let you have me if that's what you want but inside the house," Kylee said as a tempting offer. He gave her a surprised look with a delectable smile at the prospect of her going with him willingly. Then his face scowled as if he remembered something.

"Nice try," Leroy sneered. "That big dog is inside. Out here is just fine."

He tightened his hold on her violently shoving her up against his truck pinning her between him and the vehicle. He squeezed her breasts tight in his hands and ground his arousal hard against her. He then squished his lips on hers, but she bit his mouth with her teeth. He shouted in pain and backed his face away as Kylee spit in his face. This riled him! He sliced his hand across her mouth, splitting her lip. She tasted her own blood but this only awakened a new understanding of Kylee's rage and determination of how she wasn't going to be a victim anymore! She was going to fight her way through it or at least die trying.

"You disgust me!" Kylee spit another wad of saliva into his face. She saw his fist coming at her and was able to move her head sideways as his fist connected with the truck and not her. He grunted in pain opening his truck door pushing her backwards onto the bench seat. She swung her arm out, but he blocked her hit. Then he bound her arms on her chest with one hand while his other hand fumbled with unfastening her jeans. She knew his plan was to take her against her will. Her shorts were still on, but his weren't; he was naked from the waist down. She knew once he accomplished getting rid of her undergarments it would be only a matter of seconds before he invaded her. She was even more determined not to let this happen.

"No!" She shrilled and tried to scoot away.

"That's right scream for me, Bitch," Leroy snarled. He grabbed her legs hard pulling her back towards him again. She managed to free her hands and scratched his face, but he caught her hand bringing it down to touch his hard cock. "Feel me, Bitch."

She saw his keys dangling from the ignition and grabbed them, covering them with her fist. In an attempt, to distract him she screamed at the top of her lungs. It worked! Her piercing scream threw him off guard giving her ample time in raising her knee into his body. It stopped his predatory pursuit long enough for her to shoot her arm forward stabbing him in the shoulder with the key.

Leroy yelled out in shock. She watched his face wretch painfully as he arched his body backwards falling out of the truck and onto the ground. Then she heard vicious barking and growling and sat up in time to see Jake pounce on the man. Leroy yelped in pain clutching his leg where Jake had it in his mouth. Startled, she watched as Jake didn't let go of Leroy's leg. She stumbled out of the truck, leaning on the open door for support. Leroy was yelling in pain begging her to get the dog off of him. She let out a hellacious laugh over Leroy's current disposition. She didn't care what he wanted. She hated him, and she was more than okay with the dog tearing him to pieces. However, the thought of having Leroy's body parts scattered all over the yard didn't appeal to her. She commanded, "Release, Jake!"

The dog obeyed but didn't move away from Leroy. Instead, Jake started barking and snarling at the man, baring his teeth, herding him away from Kylee. She was confident Jake would die to defend her, if push came to shove. Exhausted, she gave into the wave of nausea that swept over her and sank into the grass unable to move.

Kylee heard concerned voices surrounding her then she heard sirens in the distance and more voices. Something cold was pressed on her face, and she heard her own voice grumbling against the cold. She became aware of Kellan's soothing voice and heard his worry. When her eyes fluttered open she saw his pained expression.

In an attempt to soothe his distress, she spoke, "I'm okay, Kellan."

He pursed his lips together, looking down at her with a storm raging in his eyes. She tried giving him a reassuring smile but winced in pain remembering Leroy had smacked her across the mouth. Her recalling eyes shadowed an evil look in Kellan. He said nothing but gripped her hand tightly. She didn't make any more attempts to lighten his mood. Instead she squeezed his hand back saying, "I love you."

Tears pricked his eyes, and he spoke on an unsteady breath, "me too."

I can only imagine how he felt when he came home and saw me on the ground. He must have been scared to death! I know that's how I would've been if the roles had been reversed! He looked at her with desperation in his eyes, and she choked back a sob understanding how horrible it must have been for him.

"I didn't know if you were alive or de…" he trailed off not able to say the word *dead*.

"I'm alive," she said.

"My sweet brave girl," he whispered teary-eyed. He was relieved beyond words. Kylee could see and feel that she was the love of his life.

"Help me sit up," Kylee instructed. Reluctantly, he did, but he held her. His hands covered her arms protectively, tightening his hold causing Kylee to wince beneath his touch. Kellan hastily lifted her shirt sleeves revealing the dark bruises on her arms. Kellan let out a strangled cry. "Oh, baby!"

His cry had emotional tears falling from her eyes. Kellan muttered a stream of cuss words that ended with "bastard is going to pay." Cradling her close, she buried her face in his chest while his smell and touch comforted her.

"Where are Evan and Jake?" Kylee asked as Kellan carried her over to the tailgate of his truck. She watched his face pucker into another painful expression when he saw the bruises between her legs. Tenderly, his hand touched the bruises. Standing between her legs, he quietly looked at her as a mixture of diabolical emotions twisted across his face, hardening it. He was at a loss for words, but his body language spoke loud and clear about the physical harm he wanted to do to the man that hurt his woman!

The dark storm brewed in his eyes again. His hands balled into fists at his sides, his jaw tense, and Kylee could feel the agony ripping through him. Knowing that words wouldn't be any kind of consolation to him right now, she just laid her head on his shoulder. Kellan wrapped his arms around her protecting what was his. He rubbed his hand up and down her back. She felt his rigid body melt into hers and soon she felt the safety of his love pour into her.

They stayed wrapped in each other's love as they heard the sirens wailing in the distance getting louder as they got closer to the house. Kellan grimaced thinking the sound of the sirens was bound to bring onlookers to the house.

"Evan is making sure Jake doesn't rip into Leroy before the cops get here," Kellan whispered fiercely.

"Making sure you or Jake doesn't?" Kylee asked.

"Yes," Kellan said in a vengeful tone.

"Where is Leroy?"

Evan poked his head out of the barn just as the police cars rolled into the driveway turning off their sirens but Kellan could still hear Jake barking. Evan walked over to Kylee and Kellan. He heard Kylee's question about Jake so he answered her.

"Jake's got Leroy trapped in the hay loft," Evan answered. Kylee looked over Kellan's shoulder to see the murderous look in Evan's eyes, too. His brotherly love touched her heart.

"I wondered why he didn't leave in his truck when he had the chance," Kellan commented. His eyes turned back to Kylee when she let out a small gasp.

"I have his keys." She held out her fisted hand. Slowly, he uncurled her fingers seeing how the key was embedded in her hand, leaving a mark. He saw it had blood on the tip of the key and made a comment about it.

"I stabbed him in the shoulder with this when he was on top of me," Kylee said in a far away voice. Kellan cringed imagining how scared she was.

The officer that walked up beside them started writing down Kylee's description of stabbing Leroy. Then he expertly asked her questions about the attack and quickly wrote down her statement then he placed the key in an evidence bag.

"Who did you stab?" Another officer stepped forward with the name Perry on his name tag. He was a burly of a man and looked sternly at her as if he already found her guilty. Kellan didn't like his demeanor but took a deep breath giving the officer the benefit of the doubt since looking like a badass was probably part of his job description, at least he hoped so.

"Leroy. A man I hired to do roof repair on the house. I fired him a few days ago," Kellan answered coolly, but inside he was shaking with rage. Kellan extended his right hand forward to the officer introducing himself.

"I'm Officer Perry. Can you tell me what happened here?"

Kellan relayed his story of where he was and that Kylee was home when she had sent him a text about Leroy being here. Kylee recounted the details the event to Officer Perry and the other policeman. She started with the delivery man honking outside insisting she come out for the package. Then she mentioned how the front door was locked and that she had to go around to the back door. Officer Perry asked her how she planned to get in if the back door was locked, too. Kylee explained she had a key to get into the back door but not the front storm door.

She continued explaining how Leroy was at the back door waiting for her then described word for word Leroy's attack on her and how she fought back. She saw Kellan's proud eyes on her when he learned of her defending herself. Kylee noted the officer's holy crap look when she mentioned Leroy's plan to rape her. Then she told him of Jake's attack on Leroy.

"I thought you said Jake was in the house when you went to get the package," Officer Perry asked again with a quizzical frown.

"He was, oh." Kylee frowned realizing this part of her story didn't make sense.

Officer Perry gave her a scrutinizing look then his eyes shifted to a silent accusation that she wasn't telling the truth. Kylee looked helplessly at Kellan. "He was in the house and outside. I'm not making it up."

Kellan placed his index finger over her lips quieting her. He didn't say anything but in his eyes she saw he believed her and it calmed her. She took a deep steady breath and smiled at him. Whatever happened would happen but knowing Kellan believed her was all that mattered.

"Oh, and the other day he tried to break into the house," Kylee added.

"What!" Kellan was livid hearing this new bit of information. Again his body shook with rage, and his voice rose louder, "He tried getting inside the house!"

Kellan's jaw was tense when Kylee recounted the event. She looked away with sheepish eyes remembering how she forgot to tell Kellan about it. "I'm sorry, I forgot to tell you, but I didn't really have a chance to. By the time you got home it was late, and I was sleeping and then the early mornings," Kylee lamely tried to explain to an angry Kellan. "I'm sorry, I didn't mean to keep it from you it just slipped my mind."

Kellan nodded, "No. I get it. I'm not mad at you. It's him I'm mad at." He stroked her cheek with his hand wanting to take away the fear she had in her eyes.

"How do you know it was Leroy?" Officer Perry asked.

"I saw him through the window."

"But he didn't see you?" The officer asked.

"No, I don't think so," Kylee answered truthfully. Kellan was anxious to be done with the questioning. He wanted nothing more than to take her inside and just hold her in the quiet, but he knew that was a long way off.

A truck pulled up next to them, and when a tall man got out of it Kylee recognized him as the doctor who had examined her when she fell down the stairs.

"Kellan, you called the doctor! Why? I told you he didn't rape me." Kylee was appalled.

Kellan squeezed her hand then said with venom in his voice, "We are going to do this the right way. We are having the son of a bitch arrested for assaulting you."

Kylee tried to protest but the murderous look was back on Kellan's face, and she knew if they didn't go through the right channels to arrest Leroy she stood facing life without Kellan forever because he was going to kill the man for what he did to her. She nodded silently.

"Kellan, can we take her inside for the examination?" Chase asked.

Kellan nodded then without another word to anyone he lifted Kylee into his arms and walked into the house, up the stairs and into his bedroom. Chase followed in silence, but he wore a satisfactory smile on his handsome face as Kellan carried Kylee into his bedroom. He saw the love in their eyes. Lucky man, he thought sadly because the affairs of his own heart were in turmoil. He hoped Kellan knew how wonderful it was to love someone and be loved in return.

Kylee leaned back on the bed and let the doctor do a thorough examination of her body. Kellan stayed with her through it all holding her hand when he could. He hated seeing where Leroy had roughly touched his sweet girl. He had known about her arms, her face and legs but was sickened about the ones on her breasts. It could have been much worse he realized if his dog hadn't been there to protect her. He silently said a prayer of thanks to God blessing him for Jake, and his protective canine instinct. The dog had kept her safe from further harm.

Kellan only left Kylee's side when one of the officers came for him. He followed the officer outside to find Jake sitting on top of Leroy growling ferociously. Leroy lay on his belly in the grass with his hands clasped over the back of his head yelling. "I didn't do anything! I'm innocent! Could somebody please get this dog off of me?"

Kellan stood at a safe distance from Leroy with a look of hate. *Leroy has no idea how lucky he is to have Jake on top of him versus me.*

There's nothing more I'd like to do than bash my fists into the bastard's face sending him into the middle of next week. Instead, he stayed where he was not doing anything to help the man. *Jake on top of the man is definitely a blessing in disguise.*

"Yeah right, you didn't do anything," Evan mocked. "That's why the dog is on top of your naked ass." Evan spit a wad of saliva onto Leroy's back then dug his steel toed boot into Leroy's ribs. Kellan was touched by the brotherly concern Evan had for the both of them.

The officers took pictures of the dog laying on Leroy's back.

"This actually is good proof in knowing he's guilty. Good dog you have here!" Officer Perry stated.

After hearing this statement from the officer, Leroy saw his plan going up in smoke. After the dog had chased him up into the hayloft he had formed a plan to accuse Kylee of attacking and wanting him and that he had to fend her off physically. He was convinced the police officers would have been stupid enough to believe him because he could be quite convincing. However, he hadn't planned on the dog attacking him when he had come down from the hayloft. It was embarrassing!

"Kellan, you need to see the front door," Evan told him with an amused expression. Kellan walked with Evan following the officers to the front door.

"Well, I'll be damned," Kellan said in awe. The front door had been forcefully pushed open just enough for Jake to squeeze through. Kellan sighed with happiness because this now corroborated Kylee's story about how Jake was inside and then he was outside protecting her. Kellan's heart swelled with pride for his amazing dog.

"Damn!" Kellan wiped away the tears that stung his eyes.

An officer was taking pictures of the mail still scattered on the ground. As Kellan had guessed, people started gathering on the side of the road asking what happened. He knew he should call his family before they heard it through the grapevine, but he didn't feel like talking to them so he sent them a brief text message.

Kylee was attacked, but she is fine. The policemen are here and I'll call you when things are settled down.

Then he sent a separate text: **Mom, Kylee's favorite cookies are chocolate chip and peanut butter.** He knew his mom would need something to do to calm her worries and by baking cookies for Kylee, she would feel this was her way of helping.

Chapter Twenty-Six

"I saw Ivy at the grocery store the other day. She's seems like a nice girl," Kylee said while Chase finished his examination with her. Chase smiled and nodded his head.

"I wish I could've gotten to know her better, but I don't think there will be time to do so before she leaves."

Chase whipped his head around quickly giving her a puzzled look. "What do you mean before she leaves?"

"She's leaving town," she informed him wondering how he didn't know the girl was leaving since Kellan had indicated they might be seeing each other.

"Well, I wonder where she's going."

Kylee shook her head. "She didn't even know where she's headed but said she needed to see what else was out there in the world." Shrugging her shoulders she added. "I hope she finds peace."

Chase gripped his medical bag hard in his hands. He stared into space for a moment; his mind racing about Ivy leaving town. She needed to see what else was out in the world? Why would she need to do that? Chase had a feeling that Ivy's decision to leave had everything to do with the bad thing she did. He needed to see her!

Kellan came back in the room as Chase was finishing up. Chase left the two alone descending the stairs with his thoughts on Ivy. Once he was finished up here he was going to go find Ivy and find out the damn truth of what the hell was going on once and for all.

Kellan helped Kylee dress into clean clothes then there was another knock on the door. Officer Perry stuck his head inside the room letting them know that Leroy was in handcuffs and was being put into the police car as they spoke and that Jake's actions had been recorded. Kylee looked quizzically at Kellan in regards to Jake's actions.

"C'mon, I want to show you something." Kellan held out his hand. She took it and followed him downstairs to the front door. He showed her the door where Jake had busted it open enough to squeeze through.

"And this is how he got outside," Kellan said. Her mouth formed a big "O" as her eyes registered fear, sad, and awe. He gave her hand an affectionate squeeze but the pain pierced his heart wishing he could take away the sadness and fear she was feeling. Again all he wanted to do was carry her to a quiet place and just hold her.

"Jake jumped on Leroy pinning him to the ground so he couldn't get up," Kellan told her with pride in his voice.

This brought a small smile to Kylee's pretty face. "Remind me to get him the biggest bone ever!"

"He'll love that!" Kellan grinned.

"Is there anything else you can think of?" Officer Perry asked Kylee.

Kellan was waiting for Kylee to say no but when she glanced up at him she had a worried expression. "What is it, Kylee?"

Kylee spoke about what Leroy said to her about him having orders to chase her away but he had other ideas. They all gave her a peculiar look, but Kylee voiced her concern about how she felt it was a set up.

"Anything you can tell us about the delivery man? Did he have any tattoos, facial marks, did he have any kind of accent, did he—"

"Yes, on the right side of his face he had a long white scar, he had bushy eyebrows, and he was wearing a baseball hat so I couldn't see the color of his hair," Kylee said remembering.

"Good, thank you. This is a great description," Officer Perry thanked.

Evan piped in with, "What about the package you had to go out to get, did you open it?"

Kylee shook her head. Kellan walked into the kitchen then came back with the small stack of mail and a box. The box was addressed to Kylee, but her first name was the only thing written on it; not even a return address or a stamp. There was nothing indicating what delivery company it came from which pointed to the possible conclusion this might have been a set-up. Then a blue envelope caught Kylee's eyes. She reached for it as she saw this one was addressed properly to her. It looked like an envelope an invitation or a thank you note would be sent in. Not thinking anything suspicious about it, Kylee opened the envelope as the policemen opened the box. She pulled out a white piece of paper, unfolded it then gasped in horror! The color drained from her face as she read the words. She held the paper out to Kellan as the tears stung her eyes.

"Kylee, what is it?" Kellan took it from her shaking hands. His jaw clenched tightly, and he scowled as he read the nasty words hand written in black and white. The letter read: **I warned you once to stay away from him. This is your second warning. Leave him now or else...**

Chase stood google-eyed next to Evan watching as the letter was passed around gathering fingerprints. It amazed him at the lack of knowledge people had about preserving evidence. The police could have limited the number of hands touching the letter sweeping it for fingerprints in hopes of finding the person who originally wrote it. With so many people touching it there was no way they would be able to use this as a good source of evidence, because any good defense lawyer would reject it in a trial. Chase didn't touch the letter but was able to read it over Evan's shoulder when he had it in his dusty hands.

The letter was very threatening to Kylee's life. Chase hated what it was doing to her. He admired Kylee and thought she was honest, hard working and highly suited for Kellan. Maybe it was what he liked most about Kylee; the fact she wanted Kellan, which left the door wide open making it easier for Ivy to walk into his own arms. Chase was making notes on his iPad half listening to the conversation around him hoping it wouldn't take too much longer. He was anxious to find Ivy and confront her about leaving town, but he sensed he needed to stay here just to make sure he was no longer needed.

"What does it mean I warned you once?" Officer Perry asked after reading the threatening letter looking at both Kellan and Kylee. Kellan exhaled slowly then explained about Kylee being attacked in the public restroom over in Junction City.

Chase slowly brought his head up worry in his eyes when he heard about Kylee's attack. "Kylee was attacked? You didn't call me," Chase accused Kellan. "How bad was it?"

"It was over in Junction City," Kellan said defensively. "And she's all right."

Chase shook his head bitterly. "Did you have a doctor check her out? Or was it your own conclusion that she was all right. You should have called me when you got home."

"Yes, probably should have. However, it was a long day, and I took your advice from last time. If there had been any signs she wasn't okay I would've taken her to the emergency room and called you." Kellan pacified Chase in the beginning but then in the end he sent him a frustrating glare. Chase didn't back down and sent Kellan his own condescending look.

"Boys," Officer Perry cut in sternly giving them both a threatening glare as he warned them, "I don't want to have to put you both in jail but I will if it comes down to it."

"The store had us fill out an incident report so you can verify our story with them," Kellan continued bringing his attention back to the officers. He managed to completely ignore Chase. Chase sensed things were wrapping up and he was no longer needed. He put his iPad back into his shoulder bag and handed Kylee her prescription for pain medication. Kylee thanked him, shook hands, and he started to leave.

"What day did you say the attack was in Junction City?" Officer Perry asked Kellan.

As he walked through the front door Chase heard Kellan give the date of the attack. Throwing his shoulder bag through the open window into the backseat of his truck his brain absorbed the date of Kylee's attack. Connecting the dots of certain events fear of the truth sank into him. He slowly got into his truck while dreadful thoughts entered his mind.

"Oh. No!" Chase rasped closing his truck door. He was glad no one could see his horrified look, especially Kellan. A horrible feeling dropped to the pit of his stomach as he had a pretty good idea who Kylee's attacker was. Was the same person responsible for Leroy's attack on Kylee today the same person as in Junction City? Oh, he hoped not, but only one person could answer the question, and he was headed there now.

Officer Perry nodded as he wrote in his notepad. "We will need to take the note in as evidence."

Kylee squished her way into his arms as Kellan answered for both of them. "Okay, but I will need a copy of the police report when you're done."

The officer nodded. "I'll let you know when it's complete."

The police officers left as the three of them stood in the silence. Evan cleared his throat with a pained expression. Kellan caught his look and with his eyes he questioned Evan. Kellan gaped at Evan with a hundred things running through his mind. *This confirms Kylee had been the target in the store's bathroom. This also confirms that Leroy was sent to chase Kylee away. But why? What was the man's plan? There are so many horrible scenarios. It was obvious that somebody in this town wants me all to themselves but I have no idea who it is. It's been a long time since I've been serious about anyone. Even the women I've fooled around with weren't interested in a serious relationship. Kylee is being targeted and hurt because of me!*

Guilt seized him as his blood boiled again and it was a wonder that they couldn't see steam coming out of his ears. Kellan roared out a string of cuss words and stormed out of the house enraged. Kylee started to go after him, but Evan stopped her.

"No, Kylee, you have to let him cool down on this one. It's gotta be his way."

"What is his way?" She asked.

Evan paused considering his response. *In the past it would've been a lot of things: getting drunk, starting a bar fight as his fist connected with an angry participant, out to the barn where he kept a punching bag, a good fast run, or sometimes Kellan found a softball game to play in. This was a lot like a bar fight except there was no alcohol involved.*

"Evan." Kylee brought him out of his thoughts. "What is he going to do?"

"Hard to say," Evan said truthfully.

"Are you going with him?" She asked worriedly.

"I'll be there when he needs me," Evan said, but he really had no idea what Kellan was going to do.

"Do you know when that will be?" Kylee snapped at Evan; her eyes held worry. Evan raised both his eyebrows but gave her the benefit of the doubt knowing she was concerned about Kellan. Of course, she had good reason since Evan hadn't ever seen Kellan this wound up before.

"My, aren't you sassy tonight," Evan said dryly.

"I'm sorry," she apologized. "My emotions are getting the best of me."

Evan reached out and patted her hand. "He'll be okay. He just needs a little time to get his emotions in line. He'll be back."

Kylee, not knowing when Kellan would return, headed upstairs to bed taking Jake with her. Evan stayed at the house making sure Kylee stayed safe until Kellan returned home. It was the best way Evan knew how to be there for Kellan. He sure hoped he wouldn't need to go pick up his inebriated friend from a bar. Worse, Kellan could land himself in jail just so he could beat the shit out of Leroy.

Evan thought about how sassy Kylee could be. For the life of him he couldn't figure out why Kellan was attracted to this feature. Evan wanted a woman who didn't give a man so much grief. Yes, this was exactly what he wanted, a nice quiet woman.

Kellan came in later…he was sober…not even one drop of alcohol. He was quiet when he sat down in the chair across from Evan. He looked emotionally drained.

"I thought maybe you'd try to find a way to jail." Evan commented.

Kellan nodded. "I thought about it." He sighed, took a deep breath, looking as though the weight of the world was on his shoulders. "What am I going to do, Ev? She's in danger because of me. How can I keep her safe when I'm the reason she's getting hurt?"

"Kellan," Evan took his own deep breath. "I don't know what the future holds for any of us but what I do know is the answer you're searching for lies only with one person, and she's upstairs sleeping."

Kellan gave a curt nod of his head. "Yeah,"

"Go to her Kellan. She loves you and you her," Evan said. "Not to sound cheesy or anything, but love will find a way."

Kellan tossed Evan a lopsided grin then thanked him for staying.

"No problem. Good night, see ya tomorrow," Evan wished him good night.

Chapter Twenty-Seven

Chase pulled into the parking lot of the vet's clinic relieved to see Ivy's car parked next to Rick's. After leaving Kellan's place and seeing Kylee after her brutal attack, it left Chase rattled, and he hoped to God Ivy wasn't responsible for any of this! Still, he couldn't help the sickening feeling in regards to the date of the attack. Everything that had happened before and after it may have a lot to do with how Ivy has been acting. The night he didn't show up for their date, the turmoil in her eyes, the reason she was pushing him away, and her telling him she had done something horrible all pointed back to the date of the attack.

Maybe there was a simple explanation…maybe it was all coincidence of Ivy just being in the wrong place at the wrong time…and her strange reactions these days were because of something else.

"Ugh!" Chase slapped the steering wheel in frustration. He didn't want to go in and find out the answers to his speculating questions, but he knew he had to. With heavy feet Chase entered the office through the front door expecting to see Ivy standing at the desk, but she wasn't there. The office was empty, but he heard voices coming from the back and headed that way. Chase knocked loudly on the swinging door as he called out, "Anybody home?"

"In here!" Rick called out. Chase found Rick and Ivy in the back room where Rick did surgeries on his animal patients. The room had two examining tables with built in cages that lined up against one whole wall of the clinic. Chase scrunched his nose at the pungent smell of animals in the room and knew he made the right choice to be a people doctor. Chase saw Ivy cleaning the animal cages and walked over by her. When she turned around she wore a pleasant smile.

"Hi." Chase greeted her cordially.

"Hi." Ivy said noticing he seemed edgy. There was a change in him from yesterday when he boldly kissed her in front of all her neighbors. Suddenly she felt uneasy; afraid that he might have changed his mind about wanting to be with her. Her heart beat wildly against her chest, and it wouldn't have surprised her if he could hear it.

"Pull up a seat. You look like you could use a break," Rick commented to him. Chase sighed heavily, nodding his head as he sat down on a wooden stool across from Rick as Ivy continued washing the cages.

"I hear the cops were called out to Kellan's in regards to a brutal attack? What's this all about?" Rick asked Chase.

Chase heard Ivy inhale sharply as he glanced her way with an uneasy look. "Kylee, Kellan's girlfriend was attacked."

"Oh! How terrible! Is she okay?" Rick asked worriedly. He hated to think of such a malicious act going on in his small home town.

Chase nodded slowly. "She's okay. As it turns out Kellan's dog saved her by attacking the man." Chase's face gave way to a small smile over that fact.

"Wow! The dog saved her? How cool is that!" Rick exclaimed. "Animals do amazing things."

Chase listened to Rick babble on about the amazing things animals did but out of the corner of his eye he watched Ivy. She had a scared, distraught look on her pretty face. He noticed she had put the cleaning bottle down and was now holding her favorite calico cat, the one they both had petted the day he was here. He watched her hands fidget along the cat's back stroking its ears.

Ivy was well aware of Chase's stern eyes on her. The mention of someone attacking Kylee today brought back the bad memories of her attack on the girl. It was something she couldn't stop thinking about. She hoped once she was far away from this town her memories of the incident would fade away. She couldn't help wonder why Chase was being distant with her right now. At first she thought maybe it was because Rick was in the room, but she didn't think that was it, especially after he kissed her yesterday in public. Something wasn't right.

Rick said, "Take the cat for instance. Kylee was the one who saved it."

Ivy's head rose up sharply when she heard Rick say Kylee was the one who saved the cat she was holding in her arms. *No way, it couldn't be! There was no way Kylee saved this cat otherwise it would mean...that Kylee was a good person...* Ivy took in a deep rapid breath.

"Did you say Kylee saved this cat?" Ivy squeaked.

Chase swung his gaze over to Ivy seeing her shocked look of disbelief. The color had drained from her face. She carefully set the cat down on the table in front of them and steadied herself with both hands by gripping the edge of the table.

Chase watched in agony as Ivy inhaled huge amounts of air deep into her lungs and sweat beaded on her forehead after she heard how Kylee had saved the cat.

Rick answered, "Yessiree, she walked about a mile down the road to Kellan's place carrying the cat. Kellan said she was pretty worried about it and hoped it would live."

"She did? She was?" Ivy gasped in utter shock upon hearing this bit of news about Kylee. Ivy felt strangely horrible as a comprehension of what she'd done came over her. *How could I have been so wrong?*

Anyone who cared this much about a dying cat didn't deserve the treatment I have given her!

"Yep." Rick nodded his head in a matter of fact manner as he turned around to put his veterinarian tools away in a drawer. He wasn't aware of what was going on with Ivy, but Chase was since he hadn't taken his eyes off of her.

Panic rose in Ivy while the guilt of her harsh actions against Kylee churned in her stomach. Ivy was having a hard time facing the truth about how wrong she'd been about Kylee. Knowing how the woman cared enough to carry the cat she fell in love with for a long distance instead of letting it die on the side of the road…well, any ill feelings Ivy had for Kylee instantly melted away. Ivy was ashamed of what she had done. She could feel the walls closing in around her and felt beads of sweat on her forehead, and her mouth went dry as though she had just swallowed a cotton ball. Ivy sucked in another deep breath of air, but it didn't help. She needed fresh air!

Fleeing from the room, Ivy heard Chase calling her name, but she didn't stop. She couldn't face Chase right now! Honestly, she wasn't sure if she ever could look at him again! *I'm leaving town right now! My car is already packed and I'll call my mom on the road.* She grabbed her car keys and purse as she ran out of the building.

Chase ran after her, but she had a good lead on him. He saw her from across the parking lot fumbling with her car keys trying to unlock the door. Seeing how upset she was as the tears streamed down her face he couldn't let her drive in this condition, not this time. He had let her drive away upset too many times, and her luck was running out. He had seen his fair share of motor vehicle accidents when people got behind the wheel of a car when they were emotionally upset, and he didn't want Ivy to end up as a statistic. No matter what she had done, Chase loved her and didn't want to see her hurt.

Ivy paused when she felt Chase's warm hand on her shoulder. He didn't need to speak for her to know it was Chase. "Chase, I can't talk to you right now."

"I can't let you drive," Chase spoke with authority. "You're too emotional."

"I need to go." Ivy sobbed in a whisper.

Without thinking, Chase boldly picked her up from behind. She yelped in surprise, but he didn't set her down until she was sitting in the passenger seat of his truck. He fastened the seatbelt around her then locked the door as he closed it. Still caught in surprise, Ivy sat dumbfounded over Chase's speedy action to hold her captive in his truck.

Yet, she made no attempt to get out as she let him drive away with her. This assertive side of his was thrilling as it heated her insides.

Chase patted her knee affectionately with his hand while tears streamed down her lovely face. His heart was breaking for her. The tears kept coming and Ivy just let them fall while the guilt gnawed viciously inside her. Coming through the open windows the fresh air felt good while Chase drove fast down the country road. She took in deep breaths of the air and wondered where he was taking her. Maybe she should just tell him to take her to the police station so she could confess what she did.

"You should've just let me drive my own car, Chase," Ivy said to him noticing he had turned onto a dirt road.

"I couldn't let you drive when you're so emotional. You could've had an accident."

Ivy shrugged. "I might have wrapped myself around a telephone pole. Believe me when I say no one would have missed me."

Chase gaped at her. "Ivy. I would miss you."

A new batch of tears threatened to spill hearing his kind words. He was being so nice to her but the guilt tumbled wildly in her stomach.

Ivy shook her head. "No. You're wrong. Pull over I'm going to be sick!"

He stopped the truck on the deserted dirt road and had barely put it into park when she jumped out and squatted in the grass to vomit. Chase knelt next to her holding her long hair away from her face and rubbed her back while she continued vomiting. Ivy was touched by his display of kindness. No one had ever done this for her before. She wasn't even sure Kellan would do this for her. Ivy sat back on her knees crying. Chase left her side and Ivy wondered if he was going to leave her here. She would have been okay with this since she wasn't feeling like she deserved anything nice right now. She was really beating herself up for the horrible thing she did to Kylee and for what? Because for the longest time she had fabricated in her mind that she and Kellan were meant to be together and she lashed out in jealousy when things didn't go her way. She was pitiful and she had acted like a…like a…L-U-N-A-T-I-C! *I am so ashamed of my behavior!*

Chase handed her a paper towel and a bottle of water. "You're vomiting like a pregnant woman."

"Well, I'm not!" Ivy retorted. She stood up quickly, walking back to the truck she took a stick of gum from her pocket and put it in her mouth. Chase followed her. He bent over to pick a white wildflower and gave it to her. She accepted it but looked at him with quiet interest. She didn't understand why Chase was being nice to her now when he had been so distant at the clinic.

"Yeah, I know." He tossed her a taunting smile.

"How do you know?" Ivy asked in a guarded tone, but her eyes accused him wrongly. Then she said with a hurting tone. "You think I'm not pretty enough to be in a compromising position of becoming pregnant?"

He let out a ridiculous laugh causing her to glare at him with wounded eyes. She tilted her head back not realizing how her pouty lips lifted towards him. He wanted those lips on his. Swiftly, he grabbed her by the waist pinning her between him and the truck. Still irritated with him thinking he was laughing at her, she twisted in his arms, but in doing this Chase got a tighter hold and curved her body closer in line with his. His face was inches from hers, and she could feel his warm breath. She had no where to go except to be in his arms. Ivy was annoyed with letting herself get caught in his arms, yet this was exactly where she wanted to be, and his cinnamon scent was arousing her.

Chase was only aroused with her being this close. Breathing in her flowery scent, his only thought was how much he wanted her, but he needed to stay strong. One kiss with her, and he feared he would lose himself making love to her right here then in six weeks her vomiting would definitely be because of her being pregnant. Her breathing was labored, her beating heart vibrated against him, and her eyes raged with desire. Chase knew Ivy wanted him, but he needed and wanted only one thing from her; her declaration of love for him.

Rubbing his thumb over her sulking lips, his cocoa eyes seductively caressed her emerald eyes. When he spoke his voice was rich with a confident alluring tone rendering her speechless. "Ivy, my pretty girl, I know you're not pregnant because I haven't made love to you, yet."

Ivy melted helplessly in his arms. All her mental and physical strength drained out of her. Chase felt her weaken in his arms and a satisfactory smile reached across his lips. He loved her with all his heart, and he hoped she would trust his love to tell him the truth.

"Ivy. Tell me what's going on," Chase whispered as she lay limp in his arms. In a hazy daze she nodded her head slowly. She knew it was time to tell him the truth. Not only did he need to know, but she needed him to know.

"Ivy. Are you the one who attacked Kylee in Junction City?" He asked. Tears pierced her eyes as he asked what she had done. She nodded her head slowly hoping he didn't move his arms away from her because if he did she'd fall like a ragdoll to the ground.

"Oh, honey," he said in sorrow. Wiping her tears, he swung her up in his arms hugging her tight then he dropped the tailgate on his truck and sat her on it. "Tell me everything."

"I was feeling a sense of loss that day," Ivy began between sniffles while the tears continued. He handed her his handkerchief.

"The night before is when I didn't show up for our date?" Chase asked with despair in his eyes. When she nodded he pinched his finger and thumb on the bridge of his nose squeezing his eyes shut in agony reliving the disappointment. "I kick myself for not knocking on your door that night. I should've called you to explain. I should've been on your doorstep early the next morning begging for your forgiveness. It's my fault," he said in anguish.

"No, Chase. This isn't your fault, it's mine. I'm the one who did it, not you." Ivy stroked her fingers along his arm. "I blamed Kylee for everything sad that was going on in my life."

"Honey, why?" Chase asked. "She's got nothing compared to you."

"Well, at the time she had Kellan when I thought he and I were destined to be together. You know how for the longest time I only had eyes for Kellan."

He nodded his head sadly. "Yes."

Ivy continued, "Then Kylee came along changing that destiny, which turned out to be okay because we started talking. I really like you, Chase. I didn't know how much until you started hanging out more at the clinic."

Chase enclosed his hand over her hand that was rubbing his arm. It was turning on one specific muscle in his body that he couldn't give in to, not until he knew the truth.

"But, when you didn't show up for our date I was down on my luck. I had convinced myself it was all Kylee's fault for my disappointed feelings. If she had never come along I wouldn't have found my way to you only to be heart broken. She was the reason I couldn't have Kellan and now she was the reason my heart ached for you."

Chase understood Ivy's reasoning and was probably the only one in this world who did. However, he didn't condone her physical violence, but he loved her.

"Chase, I'm not sure what came over me that day. I was eaten up by a jealous, hated rage burning inside me." Ivy shuddered remembering the horrible feelings.

"I didn't even recognize myself, and I didn't like what I did," Ivy whispered miserably. "I wish now I hadn't seen them the first time or this second time."

"There was another time you saw them?" Chase inquired. Ivy nodded. Sensing there was more to it, than him missing their date, he hopped up on the tailgate next to her. "Okay, Pretty Girl. Tell me everything starting with the first time you saw them together." His eyes quietly searched hers asking for the truth.

Ivy took a deep shaky breath, "Okay."

She knew if she was going to have any peace at all in her life she needed to confess her sin and what better person for the job than Chase, the man she loved with all her heart. Sensing her hesitancy, he slid her over to him, cuddling her to his side, resting his chin on the top of her head. Ivy felt a warm tingly feeling fill her. There was something about the way he nestled her against him as though it was the most natural place for her to be. She felt safe and love tugged at her heart allowing her to trust and be honest with him.

"One day I saw them in town together. They went into Hank's Vacuum Cleaner store. I suppose they were looking for a vacuum cleaner." Ivy frowned.

Chase said, "Ah, yes. That would make sense."

"Why does it make sense?" Ivy's eyes questioned him.

He shrugged saying, "Doctor-patient confidentiality."

She folded her arms over her chest then turning her head the other way she indignantly said, "Fine, I won't tell you the rest of the story."

Chase laughed. "Okay, I trust that what I tell you will go no further than this tailgate." He felt the nod of her head and knew in his heart she wouldn't tell anybody so he explained to her about his visit to Kellan's house after Kylee had tripped on the vacuum hose and fell down the stairs.

"That's awful!" Ivy exclaimed.

Chase pushed her away from him for a moment giving her a 'yeah right' look. He didn't believe her. "Are you sure about that?"

Ivy gave him a forlorn look. "Okay, in the beginning, you're right. I would have loved hearing about Kylee falling on the stairs. But after learning today she was the one who saved the cat I have doubts about my original thoughts."

She had somehow turned into a person she hardly recognized and felt lost and confused about her misguided, jealous rage. Chase pulled her back next to him pleased with her honest answer.

"Go on you saw them at Hank's." He guided her back to the story.

"Well, I thought it was odd because Kellan Taylor doesn't leave the fields during the day! He's up at sunrise working in the fields until sunset everyday unless it's raining taking an hour off for lunch and even then he won't come into town for a lunch break, believe me I've tried."

"I'm sorry he hurt you, honey. But a man who isn't willing to take one hour out of his busy day for you isn't worth the tears," Chase reproved.

"I know this now, and I was chasing the wrong guy." Ivy rubbed her hand on his leg. "You took me by surprise on the day you officially talked to me. You asked me why I had sad eyes when I said I was good." She giggled. "No one ever challenged me before. And then there was another day when you ran across the street to check on me. It felt good knowing somebody cared about me."

"You can't lie to me, Ivy. I see you the way others don't." He placed his hand on top of hers stopping her from rubbing his leg. He knew she had no idea the sexual effect her hand on his thigh was having on him. He loved her innocence.

"So I wanted to know how this girl got Kellan Taylor out of the fields on a beautiful sunny afternoon and who was she? I'd never seen her before. So I called up his mom to find out details. Well, his mom led me to believe Kylee was his new housekeeper and it was a working relationship, but I didn't quite believe her. She didn't see them laughing or him helping her in and out of the truck. There was something odd about them having just a work relationship," Ivy said hotly.

"Ah, this is what Kellan confronted you about at Charlie's."

"Yes, he wanted to know why I called his mom instead of him," Ivy confirmed. "Obviously, Kellan's mom is unaware of their growing relationship. This surprises me because Kellan's mom always knows what's going on around town."

"Then when I saw them in Junction City at the Walmart, I discovered they most definitely were in more than an employer-employee relationship. They touched each other affectionately, laughed, and gazed into each other's eyes dreamily. Ugh! It was hard for me to watch since my own heart was breaking. I was disgusted! Kellan was supposed to be mine but then I had you and then I didn't have you. Since I didn't have you, Chase, then Kylee had to go so I could have Kellan back." Ivy sniffed back a fresh set of tears.

Chase's heart crumbled over Ivy's confession. She had such little faith in herself.

Ivy took a deep breath of air. "I saw my opportunity when Kylee went into the ladies room. When I followed her in I really had no idea what I was going to say to her but then when I saw her no words came and instead my hands extended out pushing her back against the wall. The push caught her by surprise knocking her balance off then I used it against her by pushing her again only this time she fell to the ground, and she hit her head. Then I said for her to stay away from him or else."

Chase winced. He hated seeing head injuries and as a doctor he had seen many and knew that sometimes they could be fatal even when the person thought they were okay. Ivy had no idea how lucky she was that Kylee was okay and hadn't been hurt worse by the head injury. Ivy caught his pained look when she turned her eyes up at him. "I know it was bad. I felt horrible the minute I did it. I pulled my hood up over my head and ran out of the bathroom as fast as I could only to trip over Kellan's long legs. Gosh, that was embarrassing."

"He didn't recognize you, I guess?" Chase hedged.

"No. I kept my face hidden, and I didn't say anything to him as I quickly got up practically running away from him," Ivy declared. "Although, I thought this is what he was talking about at Charlie's party."

"Yeah, I wondered about the tension in your body at the time."

"You saw my tension? Do you think anybody else did?" Ivy panicked.

"No, honey, people don't notice you the way I do." Chase rubbed his hand on her arm fully aware of how Ivy's breathing quickened.

He had a relieved look on his face. "I'm glad Kellan didn't recognize you otherwise he would have put two and two together." Chase didn't mention the fearful thought he had thinking there was a good chance Kellan could still figure it out. Instead, he mentioned, "Obviously your threat didn't work."

"Obviously," Ivy rolled her eyes.

"What then?" Chase asked.

"Then I ran into you at the pharmacy, literally ran into you," Ivy reminded him.

"After the pharmacy I went home got rid of the red color in my hair then found out how wrong I was when my Mama told me about you being Pearl's doctor. I was devastated knowing how bad I messed things up for us." Ivy's face was apologetic. "I saw you at the bake sale, saw you at Charlie's party and you know the rest from there," Ivy finished.

Chase gave her a skeptical look. "That's all of it?"

Ivy nodded her head. "I'm truly sorry for everything. I wish I could take it all back, but I can't."

"Isn't there something else you left out?" Chase questioned her sarcastically, wishing she hadn't stopped telling him the truth about the letter. In his heart, he knew without a doubt she had written it.

Ivy didn't understand his sarcasm. *Maybe, he found out I'm leaving town.* She shrugged. "Yes, there's something else. I'm leaving town, Chase. But, before I left I was going to find you and tell you the truth so I could free your broken heart."

"Free my broken heart?" He gave her a ridiculous look.

"Yes. What I've done is something I will have to live with for the rest of my life. This is why I didn't, couldn't tell you. I couldn't live here with you hating me. But, since I'm leaving and now you know the truth of my violent act your heart can stop mourning for me and start hating me."

Staring at her with a loss for words he saw that she truly believed he could hate her. Of course, most people would hate her for this, but not him. He loved her too much! Even though she hadn't said the words he knew in her crazy ways she loved him, too. However, he was still pained by the thought of how she hadn't told him about Leroy and the letter.

"Ivy," Chase spoke in a frustrated tone. "What about Leroy and the letter?"

Her eyes questioned his. She opened her mouth to speak but no words came out making him believe she was lying to him even when she asked, "Who? What?"

Chase gave her an incredible look. "Leroy? You know the guy Kellan hired to fix the shingles on his house. What did you tell him to do to Kylee?"

Ivy gave him a bewildered look. "I have no idea who or what you are talking about."

Chase looked devastated as his heart crumbled because she had decided to stop being honest with him. He hastily jumped down off the tailgate saying in an exasperated voice, "Damn it, Ivy! If you're going to stop being honest with me then we're done!"

"What? Wait!" Ivy cried out frantically. She quickly scrambled to her knees her eyes pleading with Chase. "Tell me what you are talking about. Chase, I am telling you the truth! I do not know this Leroy guy you are talking about!"

"Bull!" His eyes were fuming as he reached out for her, but she rapidly stepped back further into the bed of his truck where he couldn't reach her. She knew Chase could easily climb up to get her but for now she delayed having his angry hands on her even though despite his fury Ivy knew he'd still be gentle with her. Her pulse quickened thinking about his strong hands pulling her close like he did before. Instinctively, she wet her lips with her tongue.

Chase watched as her green cat eyes flashed fear when he reached for her. He hadn't meant to scare her and was sorry for it. He was so sure she was lying about Leroy except her eyes pleaded with his begging him to believe her. Maybe he had jumped to the wrong conclusion about her denial in knowing Leroy. He wanted to believe her and didn't really understand why he didn't. He chuckled and gave her credit for leaping into the middle of the truck bed where he couldn't get her. If he wanted to get her out, he would, but he didn't want to scare her again. Watching her tongue run across her vibrant lips had sensations stirring deep within him.

"Ivy."

She looked at the grim expression on his handsome face. "I'm telling you the truth, Chase." Tears welled up in her eyes again. "If you want to leave me for what I did to Kylee I won't hold it against you. I will understand the decision, but for you to walk away from me because you think I'm not telling the truth that I won't stand for!"

Chase watched her stomp her foot when she finished telling him what she won't accept. He started taking steps away from the truck then turned around staring at her his hands on his hips letting the wind ruffle his blonde hair. My how he loved the crazy woman standing in the back of his truck bed fighting for his love.

"I know what I've done to Kylee was bad, Chase, but please believe me when I tell you I'm now sorry! After finding out today Kylee was the one who saved the cat I knew right then and there how wrong I've been about her and wrong about Kellan."

"You're the one I should have been asking to lunch, you're the one I should've been setting my sights on. I remember you holding doors open for me then flashing me that happy go lucky smile of yours. My heart skips a beat every time I see you, and I get tongue-tied a lot when I'm around you. I'm sorry, Chase. Please don't leave me," Ivy begged, pleaded and then she cried out to him the words he longed to hear. "I love you, Chase. I love you. Please don't leave me."

Chase looked at her in awe as she confessed her feelings to him. This was what he needed to hear and what he wanted to hear from her…that she loved him! Seeing her crying for him melted his heart. He walked back to her holding out his hands.

"I love you, Ivy. Come here and let me hold you," Chase whispered choking back an emotional lump lodged in his throat. Her sight was pitiful with tears streaming down her pretty face over her freckled nose to her cute mouth. He drew in a quick breath of air as her hand closed in his. His chest squeezed tight as the beat of his heart echoed loudly in his ears. Emotions rained down on him as he was consumed by an overwhelming feeling to comfort her, to hold her, to protect, to cherish and to love this woman who wrapped her arms tight around him. He felt her melt into him accepting his strength.

"Ivy, I have dreamed of you saying you love me," Chase confessed huskily.

In answer to him she hugged him tighter. He took out his handkerchief wiping her tears away with it. Ivy had never felt loved as she did now with Chase. She knew he wasn't going to leave her, ever.

"You're not going to leave me," Ivy said and it was more of a statement than a question.

"No, honey, I'm not. You're stuck with me." Chase stroked her hair with his hand lovingly.

Ivy wept in his arms. "Chase, I love you. Don't ever let me go."

"Even as you were pushing me away, I couldn't let go of you. Never my pretty girl will I ever let you go."

Chapter Twenty-Eight

"Chase. Who is this Leroy guy?" Ivy asked him quietly.

Still holding her tight Chase answered, "Some guy Kellan hired to replace a few shingles on the roof of his house. He fired him, but he came back today and attacked Kylee, almost raping her."

"That is terrible, Chase. I mean it."

Chase smoothed the hair off her face. "Come to find out he originally had been sent there to harm Kylee." Then Chase sighed heavily as he slightly backed away from her but kept his hands on her arms. "Ivy, of all days to send the letter I wish it wasn't today."

"I don't understand."

"Leroy told Kylee that he was ordered to get her, but he was going to have his way with her first. With the attack on her in Junction City along with the letter the police suspect it's all one person."

"I can see how this looks," she said slowly. "Oh, Chase. Once the police figure out I'm the person responsible for Kylee's attack in Junction City they are going to think I'm responsible for Leroy, too. Oh!" She panicked realizing how bad this all looked.

"And the letter," Chase finished.

"What letter are you talking about?" Ivy let out a frustrating sigh.

"The letter you sent to Kylee that read, `I warned you once to stay away from him.  This is your second warning.  Leave him now or else…`"

Ivy slowly absorbed the words of the letter in question. Fear sliced through her as she knew the source of the letter, it was hers, but how was it possible?

"Chase." She looked at him with fear.

"You do know about the letter," Chase implicated.

"Yes, but I didn't send it." She gripped his arms hard. He knew she was telling the truth as he watched the color drain from her face and heard her taking in quick panicked breaths.

"Shhh," Chase whispered smoothing the sides of her face with his hands. "Take a deep breath in slowly then exhale slowly." He inhaled and exhaled with her. "Good." He encouraged her. "Do it again."

Ivy obeyed and Chase had her repeat this process until she was calmer.

"Ivy, I believe you." Chase looked her square in the eye holding her steady in his outstretched arms. She nodded while her body began to tremble realizing how awful this looked for her.

"Oh, Chase! I'm going to go to jail," Ivy wailed. "It's just a matter of time before the police figure it out it was me, except I didn't mail the letter."

"Ivy, it's going to be okay. Shhh," Chase touched her face when he saw the panic rise in her again.

"What did you do with the letter?" He asked her.

"I threw it away in the trash can in my bedroom." Ivy gasped. "Oh. No. Chase, I asked my mom to mail some letters that were on my desk in my room, and she must have seen the letter in the trash can and mailed it!" She collapsed her head in her hands shaking it back and forth in misery quietly understanding how everything looked, especially now with the jealousy letter.

Chase shook his head knowing how bad this looked for Ivy. The physical attack alone would send her to jail. As long as she didn't confess to the letter a good lawyer could probably get it tossed out since Chase was witness to all the fingerprints that had touched the letter as it was passed around. "I wonder who hired Leroy," Chase muttered out loud.

"What?"

"Sorry, I was just thinking out loud." Chase shrugged. "Let's go for a drive."

Chase drove down the dirt road until they came to a small white house, and he turned into the driveway. He got out, went to the other side, and opening the door he held out his hand for her. Hand in hand they walked to the porch where a rocking chair sat opposite the porch swing. Sitting down on the porch swing she gave him a shy smile and was delighted when he sat next to her. She took in a deep, relaxing breath of fresh air. Exhaling, she looked up at the clear blue cloudless sky. The house sat on the ridge overlooking the town below in the valley. The grassy meadow before them was covered with yellow wildflowers. Ivy thought it was breathtaking.

Chase put his arm around her while the other hand lay casually on her leg, and she placed her hand over his. "Chase, are you going to turn me into the police?"

"No," he answered in an affirming tone.

"Why?"

"I love you," Chase said tenderly kissing the back of her hand.

"Oh, Chase. I'm so glad you found me." She stroked his cheek lovingly with her fingers.

"Me, too, you are the prettiest girl this side of the Mississippi River." Chase declared his heart overflowing with love. Placing his hand behind her head he drew her face closer to his where only a whispered breath stood between them. He heard her breath catch just before he placed his mouth on hers. Taking his time with their kiss he reveled in the smooth soft texture of her lips covering his. Overjoyed by the way she widened her mouth his tongue tangoed seductively with hers. They were lost in each other's delightful taste and when the kiss ended they each savored the other one's flavor on their own lips.

Resting her head on his shoulder she teased, "You've seen prettier girls on the other side of the Mississippi River?"

"I don't know. I haven't been on the other side," Chase confessed laughing. She laughed with a carefree feeling something she hadn't experienced in a long time.

"Oh my," she gasped between laughs. "I haven't laughed like this in a long time."

"I hope you'll laugh more with me. You are so pretty when you laugh. Your eyes sparkle," Chase noted. As a way of saying thank you she smiled cheerfully.

Chase glanced at his watch saying, "We should go."

"Go to the other side of the Mississippi River?" Ivy laughed.

Chase gave her a tender smile matching the carefree sparkle in her eyes. "Would you go with me to the other side of the Mississippi?"

"Yes."

"You're magnificent," Chase said in awe. When he woke up this morning he hadn't envisioned he and Ivy making future plans together. Heck, there were a lot of things he hadn't anticipated on happening today. "I'd like this more than anything in the world," Chase softly said noting her misty eyes of joy.

"Me, too," Ivy agreed then asked half-heartedly, "When can we go?"

"I'm serious, Ivy. I want to take you with me when I go. Since you were already planning on leaving I was hoping we could leave together, but first we need to go back to Rick's."

"Oh yeah, to get my car," Ivy guessed with a hint of sadness. She wasn't ready to leave Chase but knew she had to.

"Well, there's that, but I was thinking about something else."

"Like what?" She asked.

"I'm taking the cat home today." Chase announced with a twinkle in his eye.

"My cat," Ivy's voice squeaked.

"No, I was thinking it could be our cat." He squeezed her hand gently with a quiet promise of a future between them hanging in the air. Her heart fluttered excitedly gazing into his serious face. She wanted to be with Chase more than anything in the world!

"Oh, Chase. You are serious. You do want to be with me!" Ivy said in fascination.

"Yes!" Chase laughed. "Why do you not believe me, Pretty Girl? How many times do I need to kiss you, hold you or say I love you before you believe me?"

"Well, I don't know." She shrugged. "How long do you have?"

"I have forever," he told her with an amusing smile.

"You're like a dream come true, Chase. A dream I thought I'd never have."

"Well, wake up, Ivy, because I'm real. Do I need to pinch you to remind you that it's real?" He teased her reminding her of that day in the park.

Ivy exclaimed, "No, I believe you! This is real!"

He cupped his hand under her chin giving her a long steady look of pure love. Her heart flipped while a certain degree of heat sizzled through her. Her body trembled under his penetrating loving gaze pouring into her. Gently rubbing his cheek her eyes radiated with the love she had for him. His chest tightened seeing her happy that she finally believed his love for her.

"What about me going to jail?" Ivy asked.

"You're not going to jail."

"How do you know?" She challenged.

Chase placed his hand on his heart. "It's something I feel." He ran his hands up her arms, her shoulders, her neck, then held her face between his strong hands. "We'll find a way to get through this."

We! Ivy never thought she'd find happiness in such a short word that had a huge smile spreading across her face. She felt the weight of the world being lifted off her shoulders. "Chase, I like the sound of we."

"Pretty Girl, we're in this together, you and me. If only I had made my feelings known to you long before now you might not be in this mess." He sighed guiltily rubbing her cheeks with his thumbs. "Kiss me again, my pretty girl."

Ivy leaned forward happy to indulge him. She ran her fingers through his hair as his mouth set on hers again in a deep alluring kiss. Crazy as the whole situation was Ivy never felt happier. It seemed so natural to be with him, and she believed him when he said they were in it together.

"Let's go, honey. We've got a lot of things to do before we leave town." Chase grabbed her hand leading her to his truck then helped her up into it. The happy go lucky smile was back on his handsome face where it belonged, and Ivy was delighted knowing it was because of her. Her knight in shining armor had arrived, and despite the ugly situation they were facing, one thing certain was that Ivy did trust Chase when he said together they would get through it. She trusted and loved him wholeheartedly! In her heart she knew he was the man she had been waiting for all her life as she was the one he had been searching for all his life. For the first time in her life, Ivy truly felt blessed!

"Chase, you are my knight in shining armor." Ivy laughed.

"Yeah," Chase patted his truck's dashboard. "I'll whisk you away in my old Chevrolet. My horse is a 350 powered engine."

Ivy laughed. Chase didn't think there was anything more beautiful in this world than Ivy at this moment. She had the most carefree glitter of happy on her pretty face. His heart filled with an amazing love for her. A love he knew would last forever.

Chapter Twenty-Nine

Kellan sat in the chair next to the bed watching Kylee sleep. She was the most beautiful woman he'd ever met. She was spunky, sassy, fun loving, gentle, kind hearted…the list was endless. He could go on for days. He had been proud of her for the way she fought to defend herself against Leroy and had been so relieved to find out she hadn't been raped. She was sweet, his sweet girl who didn't deserve the sour part of life. She meant everything to him, but what happened to her today knocked him down. Tears of relief fell from his eyes. He wanted nothing more than to crawl in bed beside her, but for some reason he held himself back. He couldn't help feeling responsible for all the bad she's endured since meeting him because of some woman's jealousy to be with him. He couldn't figure out who it was. A big lump caught in his throat as he watched her move restlessly between the sheets. She whimpered in her sleep while mumbling the word no. Then her voice rang out loudly, "No! No, no, no…."

He inhaled a deep breath when she sat straight up in bed her arms frantically searching for something. Kylee woke up to cold surrounding her. She spoke Kellan's name in a panicked voice then wept.

"Right here my sweet girl," Kellan whispered slowly rising from the chair to sit next to her on the bed.

"Hold me, Kellan," Kylee sobbed.

He gathered her up in his arms holding her dearly. Here is what he longed for earlier today to find a quiet place to hold her.

"I was stupid to run out on you earlier this evening. I should have been holding you making all your worries and fears vanish. I'm so sorry." He clung to her as she clung to him. "You're the only thing that matters to me, Kylee."

Kellan held her, cherished her, touched her head, and rubbed her back while she cried away all her fear and sadness from the attack today. He knew this was the only way to comfort her and realized she, too, was comforting him.

"Kylee, I love you. I love you with all of my heart and I need you."

She pushed her body more into his. "I love you Kellan."

"I was so proud of the way you fought back today," he said in a hushed tone.

"I decided I wasn't going to be a victim anymore."

"Kylee, I could've died when I read your text that Leroy was here. I couldn't get here fast enough. Then I saw you…" Kellan's voice cracked with heavy emotion as he took an unsteady deep breath, "on the ground…" Tears blurred his vision. "I think you scared the death out of me, Sweet Girl."

"Why did you leave tonight?" She asked.

"I was scared, angry, frustrated, lots of things," he admitted. "I felt responsible for Leroy."

"Why?"

"I hired him, and I wasn't able to keep you safe," he said in exasperation. This admittance was his undoing as the tears fell from his eyes. Kylee felt a teardrop on her hand. Without words she reached up wiping his tears away. In a loving silence they rested their heads on each other's shoulder.

"Kellan, you're not responsible for Leroy's actions or anyone else's," Kylee spoke quietly. Seeing him like this, his helpless feeling of not being able to keep her safe melted her heart.

"But, it's my fault you're getting hurt. Someone is determined to keep you away from me," Kellan cried out in anguish.

Kylee gave a low guttural laugh. "Kellan, someone may be determined to keep us apart, but I'm determined to keep us together. How about you? Are you in to keep us together?"

He pushed her down gently on the bed with a pleasing smile. "Yes, I'm in for keeping us together."

Carefully, he ran his fingers over her split lip. Tenderly, he placed a soft kiss on her lips knowing how it hurt. Then he lifted the camisole over her head delicately running his hands over the bruises on her breasts. His jaw tensed as anger flickered briefly in his eyes before kissing them softly. Kylee sighed, happy having him kiss her, but Kellan abruptly pulled back.

"Did it hurt?" He asked his face full of concern.

"No." Kylee breathed. "Touch me again."

He sent shivers up and down her spine when he kissed her belly. She felt his pause at her opening. "Touch me Kellan."

He didn't touch or kiss her vagina. Instead he pulled his body up next to hers draping one arm over her mid section and rested his head on her shoulder.

"I just want to lie next to you like this," he said.

"I want you to touch me and make love to me," she insisted.

"Please just let me hold you," Kellan pleaded. Quietly she snuggled into his embrace. He whispered words of love in ear. "Sweet Girl, you're mine."

"I am?"

"Yes," Kellan confirmed. "Mine all mine."

"Show me, Kellan. Show me with your love how I'm yours." She felt so safe in his arms and any other time she would have wanted to stay wrapped in his loving embrace but right now she needed something more from him. She needed his gift of love to erase the bad memories of Leroy's attack.

Suddenly, Kellan realized what Kylee needed. Without words her body spoke to him, and he understood how she needed to feel the warmth of his love burn inside her. Little did he know he, too, needed this; it was the only way they were going to be able to move forward to forgive what happened. He kissed her silky hair and brushed away the tears on her cheek with his fingers.

This tender touch tingled all the way to her toes, and she needed to feel him touch her, everywhere. She extended her hand behind his neck bringing his mouth closer to hers. Gently she covered her bruised lips over his mouth giving him a slow arduous kiss. It pained her to do so, but she didn't care because she needed to feel him and the excited sensations that ran through her body. Kellan became lost in the kiss and soon he was opening his mouth wider to her hungry kisses. His tongue darted deep inside hers unable to get his fill of her delicious taste.

"Baby," he whispered huskily. "I love you so much."

He rolled her onto his chest as she flattened her body on him, and he felt her aroused breasts against his skin. Her action caused a ripple of excitement searing through him as he rolled her over onto her back. Carefully, he ran his hand over the bruises on her body then tenderly he kissed the bruises as if trying to kiss the hurt away. His hands glided over her inner thighs before he splayed his fingers over her sex when she begged him to touch her.

His touch triggered an urgent need to have him inside her. She let out an impatient groan and before Kellan knew what was happening she had tossed one leg over his hoisting herself on top of him. He saw the frenzied need in her eyes as he helped position her body to accept him. She took him in one long thrust and moved her hips with his setting a fast pace. She never felt more alive and free than she did with Kellan at this moment. She needed this, needed him so much!

Arching her back, she felt him deep inside her and it felt great! She needed his love, the one gift he could give her for the rest of her life. With her climatic cry Kellan poured his love into her, and hers onto him. She collapsed on his chest happy to be close to him.

Kellan hugged his arms around her and they laid together as their breathing returned to normal. Her long hair tickled his chest but he didn't care. She was beautiful!

"I love you, Kellan. I wish we could stay like this forever," she wished.

"I love you with all my heart, Sweet Girl. I never thought I could love another person as much as I do you." Kellan rolled Kylee over onto her side keeping her in his warm embrace. His blue eyes danced zealously. "I can't let you go."

"Good." She giggled. "I don't want you to let go of me."

"Marry me," Kellan proposed touching the side of her face with a shaky palm. "I was going to wait until after the tour of homes to ask you but today I saw how precious life can be. I don't want another day to go by without you knowing how much I love you and want you in my life. Kylee, my sweet girl, will you marry me?"

In fascination, Kylee stared into his eyes. This was the last thing she expected him to say! But there it was in his blue-black eyes…her future with him! She loved him more than anything in the world, and tears of happiness stung her eyes. This is where she wanted to be for the rest of her life…here with Kellan in his arms and in his heart. She had finally found where she was meant to be…in his life; their life.

"I only have one condition," Kylee said with her eyes dancing happily.

"That is?"

"That it's forever!"

Kellan arched his eyebrows, his prankish eyes twinkled as he chuckled in a mocking voice, "I don't know forever is a long time."

She giggled and lightly pinched his arm.

Laughing he let out a playful resigning sigh. "Well, if you insist. I can do forever."

"I'm worth it."

"Yes, you are," he agreed gently cupping her cheek in the palm of his hand.

"Then the answer is yes," she spoke softly.

"Yes, you'll marry me?" He asked.

Excitedly, she nodded her head up and down. Her eyes danced happily as she choked on the tears lodged in her throat and answered in a confirming whisper, "Yes!"

Chapter Thirty

The leaky roof had been fixed, and the finishing touches on the interior had been completed. Hand in hand, Kellan and Kylee proudly showed off the house. It warmed her heart when he presented it as "our" house. Kylee liked the way "our house" sounded. She had fallen in love with it through all the hard work. Each room had been cleaned, a coat of fresh paint applied, and the hardwood floors stripped to the original look. The result was homey and bright. It was perfect for their new life!

Kellan could almost feel his grandma peeking through the clouds of heaven smiling down on them because of all their hard work of restoring it. He was proud of how Kylee poured her heart and soul into the work of making his house into their home. People toured and were very impressed by the restoration. They congratulated them on their engagement; news traveled fast in a small town.

It was late afternoon when they finally were able to change out of their dress clothes from hosting the tour and into casual wear before they headed into town for the fireworks display which was the last event for the Historical Homes Tour Festival.

"Can't we just skip the fireworks? I'd rather spend the evening here with you doing whatever." Kellan kissed her neck in hopes of persuading her into staying home.

"I want to go and then come home and do whatever." Kylee waved her hand when she said to do whatever but winked her eye at him knowing what he had in mind. "Besides, your mom was pretty insistent on us going. We're supposed to meet your parents at the front gate at six."

Kellan rolled his eyes adding dryly, "I'm sure she was. I think she wants to show off her future daughter-in-law."

"Well, she is something to look at, I hear." Kylee giggled then shrieked when Kellan picked her up pinning her between him and the mattress. She didn't protest as he quickly aroused her with his hot urgent kisses and playful tongue caresses. They made love and were late meeting his parents.

Kellan and Kylee cuddled on a park bench waiting for the fireworks to start. Most of the town was there, and Kellan had to admit it felt good to have the woman he loved sitting next to him. His mom hadn't been happy that they had been late, but she still had plenty of time to introduce Kylee, her future daughter-in-law, to her friends.

"Everybody keeps walking by us with those apple pie turnovers. They look delicious! Do you want me to go get us some?" Kylee offered.

Kellan's eyes danced naughtily over her body then he whispered in her ear, "Naw, baby. There's only one pie I want from you."

Kylee giggled loudly as Kellan's sister, Linda, came up behind them asking, "What's so funny?"

"Pie," they answered in unison laughing together.

Linda gave them a strange look as she rolled her eyes. "The two of you are more perfect together than I thought."

"Thanks," they replied.

"Did you see mom?" Linda asked.

"Yes," Kellan answered.

"She was mad when you were late," Linda ventured watching her brother shrug.

"It won't matter how late we are when we start giving her grandkids." Kellan laughed.

"So true," Linda laughed, too. "See you later. Enjoy the fireworks."

"Thanks," they replied and watched Linda walk away.

"Babies, huh?" Kylee asked liking the idea of them having children.

"Yeah," Kellan said slyly. "My babies' momma is very pretty."

Kylee laughed remembering this was his answer to her question about how many kids he wanted. "Lucky for me my babies' daddy is very handsome."

Kellan tipped his head back laughing deeply. *I love this woman so much!*

His eyes darted over the crowd looking for Evan or Dirk, but his gaze caught Chase and Ivy sitting together on a blanket in the grass.

"What are you staring at?" Kylee poked him in the ribs, and he pointed out Chase and Ivy.

"Oh. They look happy," Kylee commented. "I guess she decided not to leave town."

"Leave town?" Kellan inquired.

She told him about the day she saw Ivy in the grocery store.

"Interesting," he mumbled.

"Chase and Ivy look like they are in love," Kylee mentioned.

"Do you think that's what we look like?" Kellan asked gazing deeply into her beautiful sky blue eyes.

She returned his loving gaze saying, "I hope so."

"I love you," they said together then both laughed happily.

Kylee sighed leaning into Kellan. "I'm happy, Kellan."

"Sweet Girl, me too," he said looking back at Chase and Ivy.

In the distance he watched as Ivy awkwardly stood up from a kneeling position stumbling and put her hands out in front of her to keep from falling. It was this split second Kellan had a feeling of déjà vu. *I've seen her stand and stumble like this before but where?* Suddenly he remembered where! He let out a shocking gasp as a shudder ran through him. He withdrew his arm from Kylee as he sat forward leaning his elbows on his knees.

"Aw, shit," he muttered in an agony of anger. "This can't be happening! It can't be true!" He looked at Kylee in horror and moaned, "Oh, baby!"

"What is it?" She cried her face filling with concern and worry.

"I think I know who attacked you at Walmart," Kellan whispered in anguish. He stood and started pacing.

"Damn it! I knew when she tripped over me there was something familiar, but I pushed it out of mind but now…" Kellan exclaimed in a hushed voice. He gave Kylee one long horrified look before clenching his fists at his sides.

"Kellan, tell me who." She held her arm out to him. He grabbed it and she led him away from the crowd. She was relieved when he followed her.

"I think it was Ivy," he told her angrily as he paced.

She frowned and didn't know anything about the girl with the sad eyes she had met in the grocery store the other day, but she trusted Kellan.

Kellan gave a strangled cry when he saw Chase and Ivy in the parking lot and he started their way. Kylee hurried along behind him.

Chase helped Ivy limp next to him. After she stumbled she complained of her ankle hurting, and he suspected she might have twisted it. He suggested she stay on the blanket while he went to get bandages from his medical bag, but she insisted on coming with him. Secretly, he didn't mind if she came along because he was having a hard time being away from her. Out of the corner of his eye Chase saw Kellan heading their way with a hardened face. He heaved a heavy sigh then muttered to Ivy with a warning in his eyes. "A storm's coming."

Ivy looked up into the cloudless sky as she felt Chase squeeze her hand lovingly then heard Kellan's hard voice, "Ivy! I need to talk to you!"

Ivy tensed as she turned her head to the side seeing Kellan's steely eyes raging down on her. She couldn't help the tears clouding her vision and was unsure of what to do or say. Chase stepped in front of her feeling the need to shield her from Kellan's fury. Ivy sensed Kellan knew it was her who tripped over his legs in Junction City. From the distraught look on her face Kellan sensed Ivy knew exactly why he was here.

Kellan wanted to push Chase away from Ivy, but the doctor's protective stance told him that he would be in for a fight. Kellan saw himself in Chase knowing if roles were reversed and Chase was coming after Kylee this is how he would be ready to fight and protect the woman he loved.

Ivy clenched Chase's hand feeling secure and blessed he was here with her because he loved her with all his heart. He was a man who adopted a cat for her, wanted to know everything about her, wanted to take care of her, and make her happy for the rest of her life. She had a chance for a wonderful future with Chase and there was no way Kellan was going to ruin it for her! She was determined to keep their promised future! Chase's love empowered her. Ivy felt relieved that the truth was finally going to come out.

"Ivy! What the hell?!" Kellan took a threatening step towards her inhaling her scent. "Apples," he declared with a stern look. He pointed his index finger into her face inches away from her nose but much to Kellan's surprise Ivy sat still. "You were the one who tripped over my legs that day in Junction City!" Kellan accused her. "And, don't tell me you weren't there. I know it was you. I smelled your apple fragrance, and I smell it today, too. It was you, Ivy!" He yelled.

"Yes, I did trip over your feet," Ivy said calmly leaving Kellan bewildered that she admitted the truth to tripping over his feet. Then Ivy swung her gaze to Kylee who was standing behind Kellan and shocked them both by admitting another truth.

"Kylee, I was the one who pushed you down in the bathroom. I am so sorry! I wish I could take it all back, but I can't. My intention was to quietly watch you but instead my jealousy took over, and I pushed you to the floor and said mean things to you." Tears dripped from Ivy's sorrowful eyes.

"The guilt of what I did has been eating me up. Again, I am so sorry!" Ivy cried out her apology.

"Why, Ivy? Why did you do it?" Kylee asked her as Kellan stared speechless over Ivy's blatant confession.

"I blamed you for my broken heart," Ivy said sheepishly.

"Ivy, tell her why you blamed her," Chase encouraged.

"You see I had been chasing Kellan for awhile hoping he'd see me as more than a friend," Ivy began. "Then you came along, and Kellan liked you instead of me, which was okay because Chase came into my life. But the night before we were in Junction City, Chase and I had a misunderstanding. My heart was breaking, and I blamed you for it."

Kylee's expression was baffled.

"I'm sorry, Kellan, and I'm sorry, Kylee. It was wrong of me to hurt both of you," she apologized remorsefully.

In a way Kylee felt sorry for the girl. She just wanted somebody to love her. Kylee knew Kellan had made mistakes with Ivy by not being honest about how he felt about her. It still didn't make it right for Ivy to physically attack her, yet she felt the girl's apology was honest.

"Well, you still need to face the music, Ivy, about attacking Kylee. It was wrong and it's unforgivable!" Kellan shouted.

Ivy inhaled sharply upon hearing his brutal honesty that he wanted her to go to jail. The part of it being unforgivable angered her, and she tossed Kellan Chase's very words to her, "Nothing is unforgivable!"

Chase's face gave way to a small proud smile.

Kellan threw her a crazy look. "Come again?"

"Well, some day you might forgive me, but I'm not going to sit around waiting for that day to come," Ivy said. "What I am going to do is learn how to forgive myself and ask God to forgive me."

"Good luck with that, but I guess you'll have time to do this when you are sitting in jail," Kellan threatened.

Ivy inhaled a slow deep breath. "You think I'm going to jail?"

Kellan narrowed his eyes at her. "Yes." His accusing eyes swung over to Chase. "How long have you known?"

Chase shook his head knowing what Kellan was thinking. "I didn't know anything when you called me the day Leroy attacked Kylee."

Kellan swung his vicious eyes back to Ivy. "Were you in cahoots with Leroy? Did you hire him to scare Kylee?"

"NO!" Ivy said heatedly. "I know how it must look, but I had nothing to do with that monster! I swear to you nothing at all! I don't even know him!"

Kellan stared at her in silence watching the disgust and distaste run across her face, and he believed she was telling the truth. However, he wasn't going to admit it. He paced because he was so furious. "What about the letter, Ivy?"

"As far as the letter is concerned there's no way to prove Ivy is connected to it." Chase chimed in giving Ivy a sharp look telling her not to say anything.

"The words say it all," Kellan argued.

Chase shrugged. "Maybe, but I was there when Kylee opened the envelope. Too many people touched the letter as it was being passed around. Hell, I bet my dead grandmother's fingerprints could be on it," Chase argued his point with a small laugh. "A good lawyer could definitely get that piece of evidence thrown out of court."

Kellan's face stormed with anger. "Well, I have heard Ivy's confession, and I plan on going to the police with it."

Kellan took a menacing step towards Ivy, but she held her piercing eyes with Kellan's looking him square in the eye not letting him see her fear over his threat of going to the police. He was livid inside and didn't appreciate the way Ivy stood her ground with him.

Kylee placed her hand on Kellan's arm tugging him back gently. "Ivy, do you still hate me?"

Ivy said kindly looking Kylee directly in the eye. "No."

"Why?" Kylee boldly asked then watched as a small smile appeared on Ivy's face as she answered, "I fell in love with this cat at work. It had been run over by a car, and I found out you're the one who walked a long way carrying it hoping it could be saved. I knew then that you are a caring and loving person. Most people love dogs and would do anything to save them but not many people do this for cats. You did so I knew I was wrong about you. You are a special person! Kellan's lucky to have you. I hope he knows it."

Kylee waved her hand "bye" silently walking behind Kellan. She brushed away the tears in her eyes as she was moved by Ivy's heartfelt answer. Kellan felt Kylee's hand on his arm. He closed his hand over hers pulling her up to walk next to him. "Kellan, can we go home?"

Kellan nodded and let her lead him to the truck. Kylee drove home as Kellan sat quietly in the passenger seat. She knew he was stunned by the news he just found out and wondered how long he would brood. He brooded in silence all the way home and even now he was quiet in a deep thought as they sat on the front porch enjoying the warm summer night watching the stars and moon appear in the night sky listening to the crickets sing their night song.

"Kylee, what do you think about Ivy's confession?" Kellan asked her.

"I think she's telling the truth. I saw remorse in her eyes when she apologized. She's in love with the cat I rescued, and she loves Chase with all her heart. She is telling the truth about not knowing Leroy, and I know she is sorry for hurting me."

"Do you forgive her?" Kellan asked.

Kylee raised up her eyebrows. "Sure, I guess. I will accept her apology, and I really don't want to see her go to jail."

"Why?"

"Look, Kellan. I saw how Chase and Ivy looked at each other. They are in love and for some odd reason I think that's all she's been wanting is for someone to love her. She's a lot like the cat. The cat needed someone to love it, and it found Ivy. I believe I was supposed to save the cat. That cat is a symbol of saving for Ivy and me."

"Explain."

"I saved the cat and met you. You saved me in more ways than you'll ever know. The cat saved Ivy. Chase and Ivy found each other. I know it might sound crazy but this is what I truly believe," Kylee stated.

Kellan pulled her onto his lap and into his arms. "It is crazy, but I love you, Kylee, my sweet, sweet girl."

"I love you, Kellan."

Their lips met each other's in a resounding kiss.

"Are you going to go to the police?" Kylee asked.

Kellan shook his head with a resigned sigh. "No. I guess not. It is our word against Ivy's. Even if the police could trace the letter back to Ivy, Chase is right. There are too many fingerprints on the letter for it to be a good piece of evidence. And, really as far as Ivy tripping over my feet, other than her confession to attacking you, it only proves how she was in the store the same time as us, and there's no crime in that.

Kellan swung his arm around Kylee's shoulders. "I think the police have a bigger case to work on and that is trying to find out who Leroy was working for. There's something ominous going on around here, and it's threatening the safety of the people in our town."

"I think we should find Ivy tomorrow morning first thing and let her know what we decided," Kylee suggested and Kellan agreed.

Chapter Thirty-One

Chase wrapped his arm around Ivy's waist loving the way she fit beside him. She rolled into him leaning against him for support. Through his bedroom window she could see the sun setting and knew the night sky would be upon them. Chase looked down at her with pride. "Ivy, I'm so proud of the way you handled yourself with Kellan."

"Chase, this might be our last night together." Her eyes sadly looked into his.

"Fiddle faddle. Things have a way of working themselves out."

"Sometimes I think I don't deserve you," she quietly confessed.

"Yes, you do," he said. "You only had to find the right man for you."

"I'm pretty sure Kellan drove straight to the police station telling them what I confessed," Ivy stated.

"Maybe he did, but maybe he didn't." Chase positioned Ivy so he could look in her eyes. "Ivy, really what is there to prove? If the police were able to prove that you were the one who wrote the letter don't you think they would have came to talk to you by now or made an attempt to arrest you? And, you tripping over Kellan's legs, well, that doesn't really prove anything other than you were at the store the same time as he and Kylee."

"My confession does," she pointed out.

"Hmm, you confessed to me, Kellan, and Kylee," he pointed out to her. Then he shrugged smiling mischievously. "I'm not sure I remember you confessing anything. I think I was too drunk to remember."

She gave him a sour face. "You weren't even drinking."

"No, my pretty girl I was drunk on you." He leaned his face closer then he gave her a long intoxicating kiss.

"Hmm, if I live to be one hundred years old I will never grow tired of kissing you," Chase proclaimed.

Ivy laughed then brought his mouth back to hers for another long arousing kiss that made her insides leap joyfully. They were wrapped in each other's arms sprawled out on his bed enjoying the afterglow of their lovemaking. Chase had made their first time making love the most exhilarating experience she ever had. He pleased her in ways she hadn't ever thought possible to love another person as she knew that from his loving cries she, too, had pleasured him. Echoes of the fireworks show in town accompanied their love making.

"It feels like we're in a movie where fireworks go off as we make love. It's almost as if our first love making created the fireworks." Ivy giggled.

He laughed happily. "Tonight they are ours, my pretty girl."

"Chase, I just want to stay in your arms." She squirmed closer.

"Hmm, Ivy, honey. I love you," he whispered in her ear snuggling her tightly. Then he said, "Ivy, we'll be leaving town soon."

She gave him a cheerful smile. "Okay, honey. Where are we going?"

He looked thoughtful. "How about we find our way across the Mississippi River?" She laughed. "Okay, I'm happy to go anywhere with you, but just know I'm the prettiest girl on the other side of the Mississippi, too."

"Without a doubt!"

Chapter Thirty-Two

The next morning news broke out around town about Leroy being found dead in his jail cell. He had hanged himself! However, the coroner's examination proved Leroy had been strangled to death. His murderer had made it look like he had committed suicide. The only visitor Leroy had was Hank, from Hank's Vacuum Cleaner and Sales. Judging from the time of death the conclusion was he died approximately the same time Hank was there. A newly hired police officer on duty that night never returned to work and the Chief of Police suspects the officer might have been working with Hank to insure Leroy was killed without any disturbances.

However, by the time the police arrived to question Hank, he had already left town. Upon further investigation at Hank's business, the police found evidence connecting Hank with drugs and human trafficking. There were pictures of women who had been abducted hanging on his office wall. The FBI had been called in as this was already a federal case they were working on.

Everything about Hank's store now made more sense to Kellan. It explained the high prices the man had on his products in this small town. Selling vacuum cleaners had only been a front for what was really going on behind his closed doors. The FBI had taken over the case, and they didn't think Hank would be back. The local law enforcement rested easier and slid back into their laid back routine but in the back of Kellan's mind he feared Hank would return to finish his plans of abducting Kylee. He kept his worries to himself praying the FBI knew what they were doing. He really hoped Hank had other plans and would never return to this town again.

The information about Hank and Leroy working together verified that Ivy was telling the truth, and she had nothing to do with Leroy. The only thing she was guilty of was attacking Kylee in the bathroom along with the warning letter she had written.

However, the letter had been forgotten and the police tied Kylee's store attack with Leroy and Hank. Besides, the only people who knew the truth about Ivy's confession could be counted on two hands and they weren't going to say anything since Kylee had forgiven Ivy. Ivy was free to start living her life with Chase.

Chase had received a medical grant to pursue his career of being a concierge doctor. He purchased a Class A motor coach with a trailer that would serve as his medical office. Ivy was joining and assisting him as they started their life together traveling the United States. Chase's medical skills will be available to those who might not be able to afford the high quality of a doctor and those whose jobs require traveling. Chase and Ivy felt this was their way to pay back the universe for blessing them in so many ways. The greatest blessing being each other!

* * * * * * * * * * * * * * * * *

"It's been two weeks! Where are the girls you promised me, Abel?" Hank shouted into the phone.

"They are coming! I've had some staffing issues."

"No more excuses! Frank is chomping at the bit! One more week or else," Hank threatened the man on the other end of the phone. He sure hoped Abel would come through because the man was resourceful when it came to finding pretty girls. Hank needed Abel and didn't want to have to get rid of him like he had to with Leroy.

Chapter Thirty-Three

    A smile covered Kellan's face as he stood on the church altar dressed in his tuxedo waiting for Kylee to appear in her wedding gown. He had been ecstatic when Kylee had agreed to a shorter engagement if it meant having a longer marriage with him. A mad rush of excitement broke loose when his family found out how soon after the Historical Homes Tour they planned to be married; two weekends later.
    Kellan realized Dirk was itching to get back on the road. However, he was happy when Dirk agreed to join Evan as duo Best Men for him. He let out a delighted sigh when Kylee appeared as the congregation stood all heads turning to look at the beautiful bride. Seeing her in the wedding dress was well worth the wait!
    Kellan's breath caught in his throat as she made her way down the aisle resembling a billowing angel of white. The dress exposed her bare shoulders and dipped elegantly low to her breasts. The dress fit her perfectly and it swirled around her legs while she sashayed closer to him. He thought she was perfect in every way!
    As Kylee took her last step down the aisle she stood in front of him. Kellan held his hands out, and she clasped hers into them. She caught the devilish grin on her soon to be husband's handsome face. Looking lovingly into his dark seductive eyes it made her insides burn with a passion.
    Kellan brought his face closer whispering softly for her ears only, "I love you, my sweet city girl. You've got me on fire."
    Kylee tossed her head back as a merry laugh escaped from her. When she looked back at Kellan he was chuckling as he winked at her. She held his eyes for a moment before she whispered back, "I'm not a liar when I say me, too."
    A broad smile spread across his face as he knew this was the girl he was meant to spend forever with. He squeezed her hand, and she squeezed his. The vows were said and finally the best part of the whole wedding finally came for Kellan when he heard the Pastor say, "You may now kiss your bride". However, Kellan's lips were making contact on his wife's mouth before the Pastor spoke the word kiss.
    Kellan couldn't wait to get to their honeymoon destination but knew he needed to wait. There was cake to cut, the first dance, throwing the bride's bouquet along with a bunch of wedding rituals he had to live through first.
    Hours later the newlyweds were happily alone. Their bodies were entwined while they lay together in the afterglow of their first time making

love as a married couple. Their honeymoon destination was close to home. They stayed in a private cabin on huge woodland acres in a hidden cove on Green Lake. It was secluded and a wonderful picturesque place. They agreed not to let Kellan's family know where they were going, otherwise they wouldn't have ended up being alone for very long.

"Sweet Girl, I love you even more that you didn't want a tropical paradise vacation," Kellan teased. He planted hungry kisses over her abdomen while his hands caressed her breasts until they stood erect knowing this wasn't the only thing erect in the bed.

Kylee gave a pleasurable sigh at the sensations shooting through her. "Maybe another time but today all I wanted was my husband naked in bed as fast as I could get you here."

She reached out laying her palm flat on his manhood. He was strong in her hand and it delighted her to no end how she turned him on. She was the reason for his hard erection. He would soon be deep inside her consummating their marriage again as husband and wife. It was a vow she carried within her heart and knew he felt the same.

She remembered her walk down the aisle trying to go slowly for the sake of the guests to see her wedding gown, but all she wanted to do was run into Kellan's arms. The sight of him in his tuxedo took her breath away. He was handsome, but her thoughts were on his perfect muscled body beneath the tuxedo. During the ceremony, through their desired eyes, a secretive thought revealed itself between them; they couldn't wait to feel their unclothed bodies intertwined as they made love for the first time as husband and wife.

With the ceremony behind them Kylee was excited to start their married life together. If someone had told her a year ago what her future held she never would have believed it.

"I love you, Kellan," Kylee whispered tenderly. "You're my gift."

"City Girl," he whispered lovingly. "You're mine, too. My sweet angel gift,"

"Forever," they declared softly.

Kellan entered her with a desired need knowing his wife would accept the urgent rhythmic pace he set for them. She was just as hungry for him as he was for her. She wrapped her arms around his neck holding tightly as her husband carried them higher and higher into the clouds of love. A heavenly cloud scattered drops of love around them. Husband and wife's two souls joined as one, uniting their bonds of love into a tighter hold than ever before.

Kylee held her husband and Kellan held his wife in a mutual soft unspoken language of love. With their fingers interlocked they faced each other. Kellan held his sweet wife who meant the world to him. He pulled her closer knowing deep in his heart he would cherish her, protect her, and nurture her in sickness and good health. He would thank the good Lord for all of their days and knew he would love her until his dying day. Looking deeply into her eyes, he saw that she felt the same as him and an inner peace settled between them as they held each other in love.

Dear Readers,

I hope you enjoyed Kellan and Kylee's story as much as I did writing them. They are my first published characters and will forever hold a special place in my heart.

Thank you for choosing to read my book. If you liked this book please leave me a happy review on amazon.com and tell your friends about it.

The next book in the series is, Dirk's Angel of Destiny. Look for it on Amazon.com

        Enjoy the Journey!
        Jeni

Made in the USA
Monee, IL
27 January 2021